**"Elves," Mr. Silver repeated.
Efluviel's stomach turned. "What, to eat?"**

Miss Gold sniggered. "Bless the child," she said. "No, not to eat. Mordak's—" Her lip curled. "*Enlightened*. He's even got this sign hanging on the wall opposite his desk. *Elves; they're not just for breakfast any more*."

"Mordak's been thinking long and hard about a new direction for Evil," Mr. Silver said, and she noticed that his voice had got harder, less flippant. "He wants a leaner, more flexible, more responsive kind of Evil, one that's not stuck in the old going-nowhere rut of the past. He wants to make Evil relevant to now, to the now generation. He reckons it's time to jettison all the worn-out attitudes, all the stuff that really puts people off. He believes it's time to redesign Evil from the ground up, to face the challenges and opportunities of a diverse, rapidly-changing society."

"He's thinking of calling it," said Miss Gold, "New Evil."
Efluviel frowned. "Good name," she conceded.

The Good, The Bad and The Smug

By Tom Holt

Expecting Someone Taller
Who's Afraid of Beowulf?
Flying Dutch
Ye Gods!
Overtime
Here Comes the Sun
Grailblazers
Faust Among Equals
Odds and Gods
Djinn Rummy
My Hero
Paint Your Dragon
Open Sesame
Wish You Were Here
Only Human
Snow White and the Seven Samurai
Valhalla
Nothing But Blue Skies
Falling Sideways
Little People
The Portable Door
In Your Dreams
Earth, Air, Fire and Custard
You Don't Have to Be Evil to Work Here, But It Helps
Someone Like Me
Barking
The Better Mousetrap
May Contain Traces of Magic
Blonde Bombshell
Life, Liberty and the Pursuit of Sausages
Doughnut
When It's A Jar
The Outsorcerer's Apprentice
The Good, the Bad and the Smug

Dead Funny: Omnibus 1
Mightier Than the Sword: Omnibus 2
The Divine Comedies: Omnibus 3
For Two Nights Only: Omnibus 4
Tall Stories: Omnibus 5
Saints and Sinners: Omnibus 6
Fishy Wishes: Omnibus 7

The Walled Orchard
Alexander at the World's End
Olympiad
A Song for Nero
Meadowland

I, Margaret

Lucia Triumphant
Lucia in Wartime

The Good, The Bad
and
The Smug

Tom Holt

www.orbitbooks.net

Copyright © 2015 by One Reluctant Lemming Company Ltd
Excerpt from *The Outsorcerer's Apprentice* copyright © 2014 by One Reluctant Lemming Company Ltd
Excerpt from *Monster* copyright © 2009 by A. Lee Martinez

"Santa Claus Is Coming to Town" by John Frederick Coots and Haven Gillespie copyright © 1934 (Renewed 1962) EMI FEIST CATALOG INC.

Orbit
Hachette Book Group
1290 Avenue of the Americas
New York, NY 10104
www.orbitbooks.net

Printed in the United States of America

RRD-C

First U.S. edition: July 2015

Published in Great Britain and in the U.S. by Orbit in 2015

10 9 8 7 6 5 4 3 2 1

Orbit is an imprint of Hachette Book Group.
The Orbit name and logo are trademarks of Little, Brown Book Group Limited.

The Hachette Speakers Bureau provides a wide range of authors for speaking events. To find out more, go to www.hachettespeakersbureau.com or call (866) 376-6591.

The publisher is not responsible for websites (or their content) that are not owned by the publisher.

Library of Congress Control Number: 2015937808

ISBN: 978-0-316-36881-0

The good guys are good and their hats are white as snow. The bad guys are bad and wear black hats, or spiked helmets, or hoods, or crowns or turbans – it's all a matter of fashion, as we'll hear in due course, from someone who ought to know. Meanwhile the list has been made and checked twice; so which are you?

Quite.

The annual Academy of Darkness awards ceremony, colloquially known as the Wickeds, is without doubt the high point of the year for the Evil community. You can bet your life (or, if you're a member of the Academy, somebody else's) that everyone who's anyone in the higher echelons of the Great Darkness will be there. Malign sorcerers leave their towers, crazed priests abandon their reeking altars, barbarian warlords park their hordes on the wide plains that encircle the hallowed venue, the Undead plaster themselves all over with barrier cream; the civil services of all the Five Kingdoms grind to a temporary halt as their chamberlains, viziers and Grand Logothetes exchange their flowing black robes for straw hats and colourful floral-pattern shirts and set off down the road towards the Bronze Mountain. Under that awe-inspiring peak lie the Caverns of Argo, hewn from the black volcanic rock, where the ceremony has been held for the last four Ages. It's a time for wild parties and frenetic networking as the nominees hustle for precious last-minute support, while the necromancers are fully occupied raising eligible voters (once an Academy member, always a member) from their long-neglected graves.

The goblins will be there, of course. For as long as anyone can remember, they've set up their temporary HQ in the Old Sewer, from which they sally forth by night to schmooze the unwary. They never win anything, it goes without saying. The last goblin to be recognised by the Academy was Gork VII back in the Second Age, who won a minor gong for something technical to do with fortifications. The really prestigious awards – worst villain, worst henchman, most diabolical plan – have always eluded them and, although nobody can tell you precisely why, it's universally accepted as part of the Way Things Are. Maybe it's their collective unfortunate manner, or the rough and ready nature of the hospitality provided at their receptions; perhaps it's true that nobody, no matter how evil they may be, actually likes goblins. But still they attend, regular as clockwork each Samhain Eve, fur combed, claws trimmed, tusks polished till they gleam, their faces wearing their customary look of hope tempered with realism. One thing nobody in the evil biz has ever tried to deny; goblins are good losers.

Maybe not for much longer. On the evening of the ceremony, as the crowds gathered to watch the worst and darkest arrive at the cavern mouth, there was a new and disconcerting buzz going around among the people-who-really-know, a new name on everybody's lips. In the ten short years since he snatched the Iron Sceptre from the stiffening hand of his predecessor, King Mordak had been rewriting a lot of the tired old preconceptions about goblins. A whole new way of doing evil, was what they were saying. It wasn't just Mordak's arbitrary and bewildering social reforms – universal free healthcare at rusty spike of delivery, for crying out loud – though those were intriguing enough to baffle even the shrewdest observers, frantically speculating about the twisted motives that underlay such a bizarre agenda. It was the goblin himself who'd caught the public imagination. Mordak had *it*; the indefinable blend of glamour, prestige, menace and charm that go to make a genuinely world-class villain. There were even a few voices whispering in the wilderness that if (perish the thought, naturally) the time came to choose a new Dark Lord, one of the hats in the ring might just possibly be the Iron Crown of Groth; and, once the shock had worn off, there was a steadily growing chorus of voices muttering *well, actually* ... Accordingly, when the gates of the Sewer ground back on their creaking hinges and Mordak made his appearance, wearing the Iron Crown and his trademark floor-length mantle woven from the nose hair of his slaughtered enemies, there was a distinct murmur of excitement and even a few faint cheers.

Mordak wasn't in the best of moods. He'd known before setting off to come here that he stood no chance for worst villain (the Great Dragon had that one sewn up, no question about it) or most diabolical, because the fix was definitely in, Lord Snarl's people had been hustling everything that moved for the last six months, everybody knew it was all bought and paid for well in advance by the big money, and even if it wasn't, it was just a popularity contest and nothing to do with real talent or ability, and besides, who really cared less about the opinions of the bunch of brown-nosed, totally-out-of-touch time-servers who made up the Academy, and honestly, if they ever did decide to land him with one of those ridiculous cheap pot-metal paperweights he'd only stick it in the outside toilet, because having something like that on your mantelpiece was as good as a public confession that you'd irretrievably sold out and no longer had enough professional integrity to stuff a small acorn. Really, he couldn't care less, and the only thing bothering him was the thought that he'd wasted a month getting here and a week hanging around being nice to people he couldn't stand the sight of when he could have been back home getting on with some useful work, and now he had to go and spend a very long evening pretending to be interested while a lot of poseurs who'd never done a day's actual harm in their worthless lives strutted up and down making interminable speeches, not that he'd have minded if the food had been worth eating and he stood a hope in hell of being able to catch a waiter's eye without having to gouge it out of its socket with his thumbnail first. A couple of wraiths he knew vaguely waved to him and he smiled feebly back, then trudged up the red carpet and into the overheated, fume-filled cavern.

He wasn't in the least surprised to discover that the Undead had snagged all the best seats, as usual, so he and his party found a dark corner as far away from the band as he could get and picked up the menu. Nothing had changed there, either – every year he wrote to the committee asking them to provide a humanitarian option, and every year it was the same; you could have cow, or you could have sheep, and if you didn't fancy either of those, you'd be better off bringing sandwiches. He opted for the cow, with fried potatoes and a glass of milk.

As he picked tentatively at his food, he couldn't help noticing that people were glancing at him when they thought he wasn't looking, then quickly turning away. Curious. True, like any goblin he wasn't a sight for the faint-hearted, but practically everybody there had known him for years, so it couldn't be that. He checked to see if his fly was done up and his claws hadn't burst through the toes of his boots, then shrugged and went back to gnawing his cow. Maybe this year he wouldn't stay for all the speeches. He could pretend he'd had an urgent message from home, sneak back to the Sewer and read a book. It was a tantalising idea, and he dismissed it, because that was exactly what they'd want him to do, and he was damned if he'd let a bunch of humanoids sideline the official representative of Goblinkind at a major occasion. A careless waiter got a bit too close; out shot a nine-fingered paw, and secured the wretched man by the lapel.

"Can I get bones with this?"

The waiter looked at him. "Bones."

"Mphm. Well?"

"Certainly, sir. Bear with me, I'll be right back."

Like hell he would. Far away on the top table, the MC was pinging his glass with a spoon. Mordak yawned. Talk about boring. You wouldn't do it to an Elf.

Ten minutes later, as the MC announced with apparent regret that unfortunately the Great Dragon couldn't be here tonight, the waiter came back. He was carrying a silver tray, heaped high with hocks, femurs and tibias. "Your bones, sir."

Next to him, Duke Ozok let out a soft, low moan. He'd been gnawing his own claws, poor fellow, for a desperately needed calcium hit. "Um," Mordak managed to say. "Yes, right, very good. Thank you."

"My pleasure, sir."

It was to the eternal credit of his companions that they didn't all start grabbing at once. "Crunch quietly, for pity's sake," Mordak hissed. "We don't want to give 'em an excuse to have us thrown out."

The MC was reading out the nominations for Most Diabolical Plot. "What do you reckon, Chief?" Ozok muttered, his mouth full of needle-sharp splinters. "Snarl, or the zombie bloke?"

"Snarl," Mordak predicted, accurately as it turned out. "Well," he added, as the winner waddled up to the podium, "that's that for another year. What say we cut it short and head for the bar?"

"Want to hear his speech," replied Ag of the Black Chasm. "I like the speeches."

The awful thing was that Ag was telling the truth. "Fine," Mordak sighed, "we'll stay. Any of those knuckles left?"

The speeches dragged on, as speeches at such events do. Mordak ground a dry-roasted shin to powder between his back molars and let his mind wander. The local government reforms he was trying to push through Pandemonium – the whole concept of local government had come as a shock to the goblin nation, whose idea of just powers derived from the consent of the governed was still firmly anchored to free collective bargaining with spiked clubs. Not that there was anything inherently wrong with the old ways, at that. Take the legal system, for example. Only six months ago, he'd sent observers to compile a report on how the Elves did civil litigation (Elvish lawyers were renowned through the Middle Realms for their skill and learning), and the observers had come back with a strong recommendation to stick with traditional trial by combat for commercial and property disputes; compared with the Elvish system, they said, it was quicker, cheaper, fairer and infinitely less traumatic for the participants—

The speeches were finally over, but the MC was back on his feet again. It was time, he said, to announce a special one-off award, to honour someone who'd done more for the Dark principle they all loved than anyone else living or Undead; someone universally respected by his peers, an industry legend, who represented the very worst of the Bad. Put your claws together, ladies and gentlemen, for the winner of the award for Outstanding Lifetime Achievement in Evil: *King Mordak*.

The thing about a loud noise, such as a thousand well-fed

guests all cheering at once at the top of their voices, in a high-roofed cavern is that the sound can't get out. Instead, it bounces from wall to wall like a tennis ball, setting the menisci of the wine-glasses quivering and causing fine plumes of black dust to fall from the ceiling. Suddenly blinded by inexplicable tears, Mordak lurched to his feet and tottered helplessly between the tables towards the podium. He turned towards the sea of smiling faces, opened his mouth and found he couldn't speak. The MC thoughtfully handed him a jewel-encrusted skull of water; he took a long swig and held up a trembling paw for silence.

"I'm sorry," he mumbled. "I really don't know what to say."

But he said it anyway. Thank you, he said, dear friends, he said, you have no idea how much this means to me; and so on and so forth. It was all the usual stuff and, by the strange alchemy of the awards ceremony acceptance speech, he meant every word of it. First of all he thanked the Dark Lord, then various high-ranking goblins, the Academy, all the sorcerers he could think of who hadn't been actively rude to him in the last six months, then anyone else he could think of at all; he spoke for seven impassioned minutes about the plight of the giant spiders of Doomwood, whose habitat was daily encroached upon by heartless human charcoal-burners; he reprised highlights (and some lowlights) of his recent speech to Pandemonium about declining productivity in the tin mines of Br'zg; he thanked a dozen or so minor functionaries in the Goblin Arts & Tourism Executive he'd neglected to mention earlier; then he dried up comprehensively, stood panic-stricken and open-mouthed for fifteen seconds in complete silence, grabbed the handsome malachite statuette from the MC's hand and fled back to his seat, glowing like a furnace.

"And it's not really selling out," said Grorg, for the seventeenth time, as the goblins trotted wearily through the pitch darkness of the tunnels. "Not *really*. I mean, yes, you said over and over again that all this awards stuff is just a load of Elf-poo and anyone who's demoralised enough to accept one is basically just admitting he's turned his back on everything Evil really stands for, but—"

Grorg seemed to have run out of words. "But?" Mordak said.

"Well."

"Yes?"

The tunnels they were following lay under the Beige Mountains, the cloud-capped rocky spine of the Middle Realms. Nobody now remembers who built the network, or how long ago; a thousand miles of low, echoing passages, all the way from the Bronze Mountain in the south to Goblinhome in the far north. Goblins routinely run fifty miles a day in the tunnels.

"Well," Grorg repeated. "We all knew you didn't mean it."

"Didn't I, now?"

"Well, no, obviously, or you wouldn't have accepted the gong. Stands to reason. If you'd really meant it, you'd have told that bloke, stuff your stupid award, you'd have said, stuff it right up. But you didn't, did you?"

"No."

"There you go, then," Grorg said cheerfully. "You can't have meant it, then. All that bumf about the Academy being a bunch of self-serving tossers. And all that other stuff you said about the Great Darkness losing its way and standing at a crossroads and giving Evil back to the people and so on and so forth. That was all just because you were pissy about never winning anything."

"Ah," Mordak said. "That explains that, then."

"Course it does," Grorg said happily. "And now that

they've finally given you one, after all these years, not a proper one, of course, more like a whatchercallit, consolation prize, kind of like an award for being around the longest without ever getting an award—"

"You know, I hadn't quite seen it in that light."

"Really? Anyway," Grorg went on, "now you've finally got one, at last, that'll be the end of that and we won't have to listen to you bitching all the time. Not," he added generously, "that we minded. Your loyal subjects, and all that. You want to bitch all the time, you go ahead, we're right behind you, all the way."

"Thank you," Mordak said. "I appreciate that."

"It'll just be nice to think you won't be doing it any more," Grorg continued, "because, well, we're with you right up to the hilt, one hundred and twenty per cent, King Mordak right or wrong, but it really was starting to get on our tits, you know?"

"I can imagine."

"Course you can," said Grorg. "Get on anybody's tits, that would. But you won't be doing it any more, so no worries. That's how I see it, anyway."

Ten days of this, so far. Another ten days to go. Mordak gritted his fangs and started to run a little faster.

The thing was, Grorg and Ozok and all the rest of them were quite right, in their refreshingly forthright way; they usually were, which was only to be expected, because they were *goblins*. Important not to lose sight of that fact – and it was so easily done, now that he was spending an increasing amount of his time with humans, dwarves, even (he shuddered instinctively) Elves. Around the longer-tongued species it was hard sometimes to remember exactly why a goblin was the best possible thing to be. When you're constantly in the company of sentients who treat your entire nation as a kind of dangerous joke, you tend to get nudged back on to the defensive, and you overlook the simple fact that it's the crudity, the boorishness, the violence, the total lack of refinement and yes, the cannibalism that have made Goblinkind what it is today. Only, of course, we don't call those things that. We call them *integrity*.

Well, Mordak, I do, anyhow. Grorg and Ozok would say, *being a goblin*, than which there is no higher accolade. It was also the term they used to describe freedom, wisdom, Evil and the pursuit of happiness. And if goblins pursue happiness like wolves pulling down a wounded antelope, why the hell not? It happens to be a singularly elusive and treacherous prey.

"No, what surprised me," Grorg went on, "was, they still gave you the gong, even though you're doing all this bleeding-heart-liberal stuff. I mean, I'd have thought that would've scuppered your chances good and proper. But there you go."

"I don't know," Mordak said. "Maybe they take the view that a healthy, well-fed, well-educated, deeply aspirational goblin army with decent boots on its feet and the knowledge that the fruits of victory will be fairly distributed is likely to kill a whole lot more Elves than a starving, dysentery-ridden rabble."

"Anything's possible," Grorg conceded. "And you just don't know what goes on inside their heads, do you?"

Not for want of intrusive enquiry. "Quite," Mordak said. "Maybe it's part of some kind of elaborate leg-pull, and they're just taking the piss."

"Now there," Grorg said sagely, "I think you might be on to something."

It goes without saying that bleeding-heart liberal is practically a term of abuse among goblins, who like their offal cooked all the way through. Maybe Grorg was right. It was the sort of thing the Academy might think was screamingly funny, given that he'd never exactly made a secret of his opinions about awards in general and theirs in particular. On balance, though, he was inclined to doubt it. They took themselves too seriously for that. Time, he decided, to change the subject and talk about something else. Fortunately, among goblins, subject-changing is quite straightforward.

"Grorg."

"Yes, Boss?"

"If you mention the Academy one more time before we get home, or my award or awards in general or anything like that, I'm going to rip your ears off. All right?"

"Sure thing, Boss."

"Thank you."

"No worries, Boss." Pause. "Boss?"

"Yes?"

"Are we nearly there yet?"

Ten more days. "We're getting there, Grorg. We're getting there."

The South Cudworth and District Particle Physics Club had started off, sixteen years ago, with three men and four-fifths of a 1968 Norton Commando. The idea was that George and Mike, two retired engineers, and Norman, a retired college lecturer, would restore the bike in the shed behind Norman's bungalow as a way of passing the long, long days of summer. The bike was still in bits in Norman's shed, because for all their skill and ingenuity, not to mention that of Norman's friends and the friends of their friends, from the Helsingfors Institute of Technology to University of Zhangzhou, some things simply aren't meant to be.

Along the way, however, as they tried more and more ingenious ways to solve the problem of the tappet adjuster lock nuts and the main crankshaft lower shell bearings, they found they'd stumbled upon other lines of enquiry, mostly involving the fabric of the universe and the nature of space/time, that might not be directly relevant to the job in hand but which were at least marginally easier to solve. The South Cudworth group discovered dark matter at least eighteen months before the boys at the Lux project – there was a great big gob of it gumming up the air intake, which was why the bike tended to tick over for twenty seconds and then cut out – and it was in the process of finding out where the crank case oil leak came from that Norman first encountered the elusive Higgs boson. Naturally, the shed behind the bungalow soon became a bit on the cosy side for work of this nature, so it was fortunate, to say the least, that Norman happened to win the Euromillions jackpot six weeks running, making it possible for the Club to buy the disused quarry five miles down the road and fit it out with all the latest gear.

The Club's latest experiment was arguably its most ambitious yet. It was also uncharacteristically low-tech.

"With a floured rolling-pin," Norman read out, peering at the laptop screen through his thumb-thick lenses, "roll the dough out thinly until about one centimetre thick." He blinked. "What's a floured rolling-pin?" he asked.

The others looked at him. "A rolling-pin with flour on it?" someone suggested.

Norman's eyes were starting to glaze over. "Why would anybody put flour on a rolling-pin?" he said. "It doesn't make sense."

There was a long silence. Then Maurice, until about ten years ago the assistant director of MIT, said, "Do you think it could possibly be some kind of rudimentary parting agent?" Derek slapped his knees with the palms of his hands. "You know what, I think he's right. So the pastry sticks to the flour and not the pin—"

"That's actually rather clever," said Clive, who'd been something rather grand in the European Space Program. "I think they did something quite similar with the Teflon coating on the thrust intake manifolds on the GX-760."

"Splendid," Norman said. Then he stopped and looked round. "Have we got any flour?" he said.

It was mostly Derek's fault that the Club had branched out into multiverse theory in the first place. Derek (recently retired Skelmersdale professor of semiconductor physics at Imperial College, London) had approached the bike problem from a radically different angle. In an infinite multiverse, he argued, new alternate realities are created with every bifurcation of the sequence of events. Thus, when the bike picked up its first little niggling rattle back in '71, there was, so to speak, a fork in the road; in one reality, the bike started making pinkle-pinkle noises when the engine manifold exceeded a certain temperature, in the other it carried on working perfectly. And so on; each new deterioration giving rise to a further delta of alternative universes, until the number of realities that were identical in every way except for the health of the Norton's gearbox exceeded the calculating capacity of conventional mathematics. But in one alternative, one single solitary universe among the teeming billions of offshoots, the bike had never gone wrong at all. In that continuum, it was still as good as it had been the day it rolled through the factory gates at Andover. Now then (said Derek), if only there was a way in which they could access that universe, go there, find that pristinely unbuggered bike and bring it back across the interdimensional void to this reality; well, there we'd be, job done. A bit of a sledgehammer to crack a nut, admittedly; however, bearing in mind how much effort and resources the Club had put in to doing it the more orthodox way, and how little progress they had to show for it, maybe it was worth a shot, at that.

"Preheat a deep-fat fryer filled with sunflower oil to 180 degrees," Norman recited, provoking a sharp intake of breath from the back of the lab. "Well? What?"

Clive had that look on his face. "We're not going to try using that thing again, are we? Not after the last time."

"Nonsense." In his professional life, Norman had set opposing proton beams to collide at energy levels of 1.12 microjoules per nucleon. Even so, he looked a little thoughtful.

"This time, I've read the instructions," he pointed out. "It'll be perfectly safe."

"We ought to get someone in to do all this," said George, nervously fingering his calorimeter. "There's a woman in the village who does cakes for special occasions, you know, weddings and funerals and things. I'm sure if we asked her—"

Norman didn't seem to have heard him; but then, he had only been ten miles away when the Very Very Large Hadron Collider went sky-high, so that was only to be expected. "When golden brown," he went on, "remove doughnuts from oil with a slotted spoon." He took off his glasses and rubbed the bridge of his nose. "A spoon, presumably, with slots in."

Clive sighed. "Why's it all got to be so *complicated*?"

"I think it's amazing," said Maurice. "To think that there's stuff like this going on every day in houses all over the country. Mostly, as I understand," he added, "performed by women."

"Miracle we're all still here, really," muttered Derek. The others looked at him, and he shrugged. "Yes, all right, but we had this woman lab assistant once, and you know what she did? She only tried to calibrate the electrostatic collimator with a Schmidt-Nagant reverse parallax oscilloscope. Honestly, we didn't know where to look."

"For the icing—" Norman shook his head. "Well, we don't need to bother with any of *that*, thank goodness." He turned away from the screen and beamed at the others. "I believe we can manage it, don't you?"

They knew him well enough to recognise a rhetorical question when they heard one. "I think I missed a bit," said George. "What came after *take twenty-five grams of caster sugar*?"

After a while, the Club's initial apprehensions gradually wore off and they began to work together as a team, particularly after Derek took over from Clive as Principal Stirring

Officer. There was an understandably anxious moment as the partly formed doughnut modules were lowered into the hot oil – Maurice, who was doing the countdown, turned away and couldn't bear to look – but Norman's cool head and steady hand with the fire extinguisher saw them through, and once the alarms had been switched off and the extractor fans had whisked away the worst of the smoke—

It had all been Derek's idea; but if Norman hadn't worked with Pieter van Goyen and Theo Bernstein on the Very Very Large Hadron Collider (before it blew up) he'd never have come across van Goyen's theory of the Induced Causality Loop, which the great man was developing shortly before he mysteriously disappeared. When Bernstein subsequently moved a decimal point the wrong way and reduced half a minor Alp to gravel by accidentally blowing up the VVLHC, Norman remembered some of his late-night conference-bar conversations with van Goyen and started thinking deeply about accidents, coincidences and the reckless deviousness of truly brilliant physicists; before long he was convinced that van Goyen had been behind the VVLHC disaster, and that it was somehow a part of his secret and presumably incomplete research. Reconstructing that research, with only the conversations to go on, wouldn't be easy. The same went for putting back together the contents of the shoe-box that contained the component parts of the bike's carburettor, and of the two tasks, Norman opted for the one that might just possibly prove feasible. The result – in his cups, van Goyen had babbled about something he called the YouSpace device; Norman didn't care for the name particularly, but he couldn't be bothered to think of anything else, so the YouSpace device it became. The transdimensional portal activation unit was vast, and the third biggest computer ever assembled was only one of its many systems. The portal itself, the actual thing you used as a gateway to get from one alternate universe to another, just by looking into it and making a wish – well, he'd trusted van Goyen this far and he hadn't been disappointed, and he distinctly remembered the old fool saying, the portal itself is nothing more complex than an ordinary, everyday—

"It's ready," Clive said.

With shaking hands and a pair of white plastic tongs, Norman lifted a single shining doughnut out of the roiling fat and gazed at it for a moment, rather as Columbus must have done when he first set eyes on the New World and wondered how he was going to break it to King Ferdinand that he'd been completely wrong about a short-cut to India. It was such a small and simple thing, nothing more than a circle of fried batter surrounding an empty space. Was it really possible that—?

"Look out, boys," Maurice said. "Norman's having a Boromir moment."

Norman didn't actually get the reference, but the tone of voice was eloquent enough. "I was just looking," he said.

"Well, don't," Derek said firmly. "Remember how it's supposed to work. You could end up anywhere."

Or everywhere, Norman thought. The doughnut was definitely looking at him. *Hello, sailor*, it seemed to be saying. "Rubbish," Norman said. "The machine isn't turned on." He looked up. "Is it?"

Clive swivelled round to look. "Oops," he said, and reached for a switch. "No," he said.

For a split second, Norman's blood turned to ice. Slowly and carefully, as though defusing a bomb, he laid the doughnut down on the workbench and took a long step back.

There was an awkward silence. Over the last six months they'd discussed every conceivable aspect of the YouSpace project except one; namely, who was going to try it out. For some reason, they'd never got around to talking about that.

"Well," Clive said, nudging Norman in the small of his back. "Go on, then."

Norman scowled horribly at him. "I'm not—"

"Yes, you are. You're our leader, isn't that right, lads?"

A resounding declaration of loyalty confirmed that he was. Norman had gone a funny colour. "Now come on," he said reasonably. "Where's your scientific method? We can't just run bull-headed into a manned test programme, we've got to work up to it gradually, in controlled phases. Scientifically," he added hopefully.

"Scientifically?" Derek queried.

"Mphm." Norman nodded firmly. "I was thinking, to start with—"

"Yes?"

"Mice?"

They thought about that, and while they were doing so Norman's heart rate subsided to a modest 120. "We haven't got any—"

"Then let's get some."

An hour or so later, Norman whisked a cloth off a small wire cage to reveal three white mice. Derek frowned. "I don't like this," he said. "It's cruel."

"No it's not," Norman said, "it's a giant leap for mousekind. Clive, get the doughnut."

Norman opened the cage door, and eventually a mouse hopped out and scampered a few paces along the workbench. Maurice threw the switch, and Clive used the tongs to hold the doughnut directly in front of the mouse's nose. It sniffed a couple of times and started to nibble it.

"It doesn't work," George said.

"We don't know that," Derek replied fiercely. "In fact, it couldn't have worked with a mouse anyway. The user's got to make a conscious choice, or the transponder array's got nothing to go on." He shrugged. "Probably he's quite happy where he is."

The mouse made another determined effort to get at the doughnut. Clive lifted it out of its reach. "Fine," he said. "So it's got to be one of us, then."

It was at this point that Norman felt the heavy hand of destiny on his shoulder. Jumbled quotations about boldly going and far, far better things bounced around inside his head, making it hard for him to think straight; there was also a vague mental image of a statue, in bronze, outside the entrance to the science block at his old university – someone had put a traffic cone on top of its head, so presumably it was Rag Week, but that didn't seem to matter. "All right," he said quietly. "I'll do it."

"Good lad," Clive said briskly. "Um, what is it he's actually got to do, anybody?"

"Just look through the hole in the middle," Derek said. "And make a wish."

Norman closed his eyes and tried to clear his head. The bike, he told himself, focus on the bike. A perfect, concourse-ready '68 Commando, its chrome gleaming, its engine softly purring until a quick flick of the wrist sets the tiger roaring. Then he shifted his mental camera angle to take in the number plate. "I'm ready," he announced, eyes still screwed tight shut. "I'm going now. I may be gone for some—"

"Norman."

Clive's voice, a bit edgy. "What?"

"I think you'd better look at this."

"Yes, in a minute, I'm not quite—"

"*Norman.*"

Norman opened his eyes and made a soft, faint whimpering noise. Standing on the workbench, looking round with wild, hunted eyes at the startled faces surrounding it, was a—

Thing. Bipedal, vaguely humanoid, with a huge head, long arms, short bow legs, possibly four feet six but hard to tell because of the way it crouched; tusks like a pig, claws like a big cat, little round red eyes, snout like a pig, bristles. In one hand it held a small round oxhide shield, in the other a sort of overgrown machete. It didn't smell very nice, either.

"Norman," Derek whispered, "you *plonker*. What the hell were you thinking about?"

3

Ever since she was a little girl, growing up under the tall canopy of the forest glades of Snorien, Efluviel had known she was going to be a journalist. Partly it was because she'd always loved writing; partly because she knew that the Realms were teeming with stories waiting to be told, great truths buried under leaf-drifts of obscurity or stuffed away in the hollow trees of convenience and lies. Mostly, though, it was because eighty-seven per cent of the Elvish nation were employed full-time in the newspaper business, and nearly all the remainder dashed off the occasional freelance feature, essay or book review. Her father was the literary editor of *Elitism Today*, her mother the chief political correspondent of *Supercilious!* The idea that their little girl might grow up to be something else – a local government officer, say, or a lobbyist or a tax inspector – simply hadn't occurred to them.

But that was all right, because Efluviel loved her work, and she was very good at it. Within three months of joining the *Beautiful Golden Face* as a cub reporter, covering the usual uninspiring round of planning appeals and literary lunches, Efluviel had broken her first major story, a gripping account of plagiarism, backbiting and corrupt reviewing practices that implicated some of the biggest names in the Elvish Third

Estate. Immediately promoted to the rank of junior assistant drama critic (the youngest ever, by a margin of some seventy years), she used her unique brand of elegantly allusive snideness to establish herself as one of the leading voices of her generation, and she was already being spoken of as a serious contender for the assistant deputy editorship of *Superior on Sunday* when the blow fell, and all her hopes and dreams came crashing down around her delicately pointed ears like the rafters of a burning house. Mordak the goblin bought the *Beautiful Golden Face*.

To this day, the Elves are at a loss to know how it could possibly have happened. There were, after all, laws about that sort of thing; nobody was quite sure why they weren't applied in Mordak's case, though a series of exposés in *Supercilious!* and *Private Ear* suggested that the acquisition and certain contributions Mordak made to Academician Grorflindel's re-election campaign war-chest might not have been a coincidence. Whatever the truth behind it, the acquisition went through as swiftly and efficiently as an arrow through flesh, and all the Elves could do about it was complain, eloquently and at length, in the pages of their various publications. But not for long. Mordak, it seemed, didn't appreciate having unkind things said about him in his own newspapers. Sudden and unexpected as lightning out of a blue sky, the sequence of events the Elves call the Terror began to unfold.

Editors started to get threatening memos. Stories were deliberately killed. Beautifully written copy was sent back with *People aren't interested in this stuff, write about something else* scrawled across the top in Mordak's distinctively illiterate hand. Respected journalists, particularly those who'd been critical about Mordak or goblins in general, suddenly found themselves arbitrarily reassigned to the gardening pages or Obituaries. On the morning of what was for ever after called

the Day of Weeping, a hundred and twenty-seven arts colum-
nists were herded into a small conference room and viciously
sacked. Loviel, the *Face*'s long-serving editor, retaliated in the
only way he could and went to the union, who immediately
sent Mordak an ultimatum; reinstate the One Hundred and
Twenty-Seven and sign an undertaking not to interfere with
editorial decisions ever again, or the entire staff of the *Face*
would come out on strike. Mordak's reply was swift and
brutal. Go ahead, he said. If you don't want to work for me,
there's plenty of goblins who do.

There were those among the Elves who said that they
shouldn't have surrendered even then. True, by this point
Mordak had also managed to get hold of the *Superior* group,
Sneer and the *Forest Dwellers' Gazette*, so there was nowhere
left for the Displaced to go. The diehards took to the streets
and built a barricade of review copies across the entrance to
Mallorien Square, but Mordak simply ignored them. *Not-
being-a-journalist before dishonour* was a fine battle-cry, but a
million Elves had mortgages and school fees to pay, and if that
wasn't enough, the thought of goblins behind the hallowed
newsdesks of Elvenhome was more than anyone could bear. It
was, people said, the most wicked, evil thing the goblins had
ever done, but they simply had no choice. The strike was
called off, the review copies were dismantled and put back on
TreeBay, and Loviel, after a decent interval, was quietly rein-
stated as the editor of what was henceforth to be called the
Horrible Yellow Face. Thousands of journalists arrived at the
office to find their personal possessions waiting for them in
biscuit-boxes at the front desk. One of them was Efluviel.

It was three months since she'd been fired from the *Face*,
and during that time the only work she'd been able to find
was freelance proofreading. Every morning, an hour before
dawn, she joined the long line of hollow-eyed, desperate Elves
that formed outside the gates of Gloriel Books. You had to be

there early, or you had no chance of getting anything. Some time around about noon, the gates would open and an editorial assistant would wander out with a pitifully short stack of manuscripts; twenty, fifteen, sometimes only five or six. Sometimes it was first come, first served; other days, the assistant would stroll down the line of shabbily dressed hopefuls, the holes in their boots padded out with discarded copyright pages, taking some sort of ghoulish pleasure in the dead faces around her before distributing her meagre bounty, as often as not completely at random. Efluviel hadn't quite sunk to the depths of those who sat all day at the gates holding placards that read *Will Copy-Edit For Food*, but she wasn't far off it. Two Elves she'd been at school with had emigrated to the human cities of the South, while Safariel, who'd once won the Glorfangel Prize for Literary Arrogance, had dropped out of sight completely and had last been heard of working for the Post Office.

Today the queue stretched halfway down the avenue. She took her place at the back of it, pulling her ragged shawl tight around her bony shoulders; as she did so, she noticed two Elves, a man and a woman, sitting at a leaf-strewn table outside the Mallorn Tree café. They were staring at her. She scowled and looked away. It was possible that they recognised her from her brief moment of celebrity, but she doubted it. The moment had been so very brief, after all. She shivered. It was bitter cold and her ear-tips were beginning to throb.

A few minutes later, the two strangers finished their *miruvor* lattes, got up and strolled towards her. She looked away, avoiding eye contact. The woman came closer, deliberately intruding into her space. "Efluviel?" she said.

She looked round. "Do I know you?"

The woman grinned. "I'm Miss Gold and this is Mr Silver. We're your new best friends."

"Go away."

Miss Gold shrugged. "Be like that," she said. "We were only going to buy you a coffee."

"Plenty more where she came from," Mr Silver said. "Come on, we're wasting our time. Probably she doesn't even need the money."

"Hold on," Efluviel said quickly.

"The magic M word," said Mr Silver. "No, sorry, we don't like your attitude. Our apologies for having troubled you."

"Hold *on*," Efluviel repeated. "How do you know my name?"

Miss Gold laughed. "Come and have a coffee and we'll tell you."

Efluviel glanced at the queue. It was very long. "I'll lose my place."

"Oh, there aren't any manuscripts today," said Miss Gold. "In a couple of hours the girl will come out and tell you all to come back tomorrow." She was grinning again. "What have you got to lose?"

Efluviel wanted to hit her, very hard. "Who *are* you?"

"Coffee," Miss Gold said. "Yes or no. You have three seconds."

It was at least six weeks since Efluviel had tasted real coffee; the genuine article, made with freshly ground acorns. An unbearable longing swept over her, like the sea at high tide. "Coffee and an almond slice."

"Sure," said Mr Silver, with a mocking grin. "This way."

A few moments later they were sitting at the table and a waiter was scowling at them over his notepad. There was a menu, handwritten on a little card. "I've changed my mind," Efluviel said, in a voice weak with desire. "I want baklava."

"Three *miruvor* lattes and a slice of baklava," Mr Silver said. The waiter shrugged and wandered away. "Now then," Mr Silver continued. "To business."

"Don't be in such a hurry," drawled Miss Gold. "Let the

poor child have her drink and her cake before you make her storm off in a huff."

Mr Silver shrugged. "You're quite right, of course. We can just sit here and watch the poor people for a while."

"Tell me now," Efluviel said. "What is all this? Who are you?"

"Suit yourself," Miss Gold said. "First things first, though. You're Efluviel, right?"

Efluviel hesitated, then nodded.

"The Efluviel who got fired from the *Face* for writing nasty things about King Mordak."

"Me and about a thousand others, yes."

Mr Silver leaned back in his chair and put his hands behind his head. "I bet you're wondering," he said, "why Mordak bought the *Face* in the first place."

"Because he's evil," Efluviel answered immediately. "Because he's evil and he wanted to strike a deadly blow at the very heart of Elvenhome, and destroy Elvish civilisation as we know it."

Miss Gold nodded. "Partly," she said. "But that's not the whole story."

"It isn't?"

Miss Gold shook her head. Her nose, Efluviel noted with envy, was almost as sharply pointed as her ear-tips. "Rather more to it than that," she said. "You see, the thing about Mordak is, he's really quite bright, for a goblin."

"I'd gathered that," Efluviel said bitterly.

Mr Silver leaned forward and folded his arms on the table. "The main reason he bought the *Face*," he said, "and all the other papers he could lay his grubby claws on, was so as to get Elves."

Efluviel blinked. "What?"

"Elves," Mr Silver repeated.

Efluviel's stomach turned. "What, to eat?"

Miss Gold sniggered. "Bless the child," she said. "No, not to eat. Mordak's—" Her lip curled. "*Enlightened*. He's even got this sign hanging on the wall opposite his desk. *Elves; they're not just for breakfast any more*."

"Mordak's been thinking long and hard about a new direction for Evil," Mr Silver said, and she noticed that his voice had got harder, less flippant. "He wants a leaner, more flexible, more responsive kind of Evil, one that's not stuck in the old going-nowhere rut of the past. He wants to make Evil relevant to now, to the now generation. He reckons it's time to jettison all the worn-out attitudes, all the stuff that really puts people off. He believes it's time to redesign Evil from the ground up, to face the challenges and opportunities of a diverse, rapidly changing society."

"He's thinking of calling it," said Miss Gold, "New Evil."

Efluviel frowned. "Good name," she conceded.

"Quite," said Mr Silver. "And you've got to hand it to him, he's nothing if not a blue-sky thinker. In fact, and don't mention this to a soul, he hasn't completely ruled out the possibility of a coalition with Good."

"A morality of ethical unity, in fact," Miss Gold said. "The best of good and the worst of evil, working together hand in hand for a better tomorrow. Well," she amended, "a tomorrow. Anyway, that's all just background. The thing is, Mordak wants Elves because he realises that we're so much better at running things. You know, admin, efficiency, all that."

"Mordak has the mental clarity to recognise that when it comes to running a bureaucracy, Elves can achieve a degree of blinkered ruthlessness that makes goblins look like teddy-bears." Mr Silver's eyes had started to shine. "Which is why he wants Elves – selected Elves, naturally – working for him, on his team. Which is why," he went on, "he bought the *Face*."

Efluviel blinked. "I'm not sure I follow."

"Really? Oh. Well, it's quite simple." Miss Gold sipped her latte, and went on, "You know how it is. Any Elf with even a vestige of ability naturally goes straight into journalism."

"Well, of course."

"Indeed. Only the dead-beats and no-hopers end up in the civil service, it goes without saying. But Mordak wants Elven bureaucrats. So, he buys up the papers and fires most of the staff." Miss Gold grinned again. "Like I said," she added, "quite smart, for a goblin."

Efluviel's head was starting to hurt. "Is that true?" she said.

"Little Miss Cynical," sighed Mr Silver. "Perfectly true, yes. Which is where Goldie and I come in."

"Please don't call me that," said Miss Gold.

"And you too, if you've got half a brain," Mr Silver continued. "Our job is to headhunt – sorry, unfortunate choice of words – *aggressively recruit* the top one per cent, the brightest and the best." He pointed to the queue opposite. "Out of *that.*"

Efluviel stared at him. "Me."

"Quite," said Miss Gold. "But apparently, Mordak himself has noticed you." From the sleeve of her gown she took a faded newspaper clipping and spread it out on the table.

"Oh."

"Eat your baklava before it gets cold," Mr Silver said, not unkindly. "You remember writing it, I suppose."

The headline read: *Behold the Beast; Mordak buys* Face. "He read that, did he?"

"Oh yes." Mr Silver nodded. "And was impressed by what he saw."

Efluviel's throat was dry, in spite of the latte. "When you say impressed—"

"What caught his attention," Miss Gold said, "was that instead of just spouting rage and fury like everybody else, you'd bothered to dig around and actually come up with a few facts. *True* facts," she added, with a sort of respectful distaste. "Which told him, you aren't like other journalists."

"I didn't know they were true," Efluviel blurted out. "Sorry, what?"

"He *liked* that they were true," Mr Silver said gently. "Well, remember, he's a goblin, they're not like us. They don't give a damn for the purity of classic journalism. They read newspapers to get the news." He shrugged. "What impressed Mordak was the way you'd come up with things that he didn't think anybody would ever find out about. Like the bits about the way Mordakorp doesn't actually pay any tax in Elvenhome. That was supposed to be a secret. But you found out about it."

"And he's *pleased*?"

Miss Gold licked her lips with the tip of her tongue. "That's what's different about Mordak," she said. "He recognises talent, even when it's pointed at him with the safety off. And when he sees it, he wants it, to use against others."

"That's what New Evil's all about, really," Mr Silver said. "Steal good ideas from the enemy and pass them off as your own. Anyway, let's cut to the chase. Mordak would like you to come and work for him." He paused, allowing Efluviel a moment to choke back the reply that came instinctively to her lips. "It's a secure job, with prospects. He pays well. The alternative—" He nodded toward the queue opposite. "Entirely up to you," he said. "Your choice."

Miss Gold yawned. "She hasn't touched her baklava," she said. "It'll be stone cold."

"Maybe she's got the sense to realise that the right decision could mean all the baklava she can eat," Mr Silver said. "Or maybe not. Maybe she's just stupid, like all the others."

Maybe it was pure coincidence that, at that exact moment, the girl came out and told the queue there was no work today.

Efluviel watched the line break up and start to drift away. "What would I have to do?" she said quietly.

Mr Silver allowed himself a brief smirk of victory. Then his face straightened. "Oh, nothing yucky or horrible," he said. "Just research, really."

"Imagine you're on to a really good story," Miss Gold said. "Real sharp-edge investigative journalism."

"Only without the journalism," said Mr Silver. "He wants you to find things out for him. That's all."

"I see," Efluviel said. "Like a spy."

"Absolutely not." Mr Silver shook his head. "Mordak doesn't do espionage. As far as he's concerned, a spy is what you get if you cross a fly with a spider. Besides, why would anybody bother spying on the Elves? All he'd need to do is buy a newspaper."

"Like Mordak," Efluviel said sourly. "Several newspapers."

Mr Silver sighed. "Hostility," he said. "How gauche. Listen, you have my unequivocal undertaking. Mordak will not ask you to spy on your fellow Elves." He leaned back again and steepled his fingers. "He's just not interested enough in us to bother. But he thinks we're useful, for a rigidly limited number of adminstrative functions. Including the gathering of information."

"What sort of information?"

"Ah." Mr Silver didn't look uncomfortable, exactly – he'd probably have needed major surgery before he'd have been capable of it – but a sort of shutter closed behind his eyes. "That's not really any of our business. It's between you and Mordak, if you take the job, which you're entirely free not to do, if you enjoy hunger. Or," he added sweetly, "there's always openings in the Post Office. Like I said before, up to you entirely. Now, perhaps you'd care to make up your mind. Obviously you've got nothing better to do, but we have."

Efluviel looked away and, in doing so, found herself staring straight at the slice of baklava. It spoke to something deep inside her, and she knew what she was going to say. "Here's the deal," she said. "Take it or leave it."

"Ooh," murmured Miss Gold. "Feisty."

"I'll do it."

"Good girl."

"On one condition," Efluviel said, and her heart was beating pit-a-pat. "I'll do this not-quite-spying thing for one year, and then I want my old job back."

Mr Silver narrowed his eyes. "Excuse me?"

"On the *Face*," Efluviel said. "As a reporter. I promise I won't write anything nasty about Mordak," she added quickly, "I'll be as good as gold and not make any trouble. But I want to be a journalist again, it's all I've ever wanted. And if this is what it takes, well—" She shrugged. "How about it?"

Miss Gold and Mr Silver looked at each other, and Efluviel couldn't quite follow the unspoken debate in their eyes. Then Mr Silver smiled at her and said, "Fine. A job on the *Face*."

"Planning appeals," Miss Gold put in. "Arts festivals. Maybe filling in on the sports section."

"Doesn't matter," Efluviel replied, repressing a shudder. "That's my price."

Miss Gold sighed contentedly. "Everyone's got one," she said. "Selling out makes the world go round. Welcome to Team Mordak."

Efluviel waited. The world didn't come to an end. "Do I have to sign anything?"

Mr Silver shook his head. "Best not to have too much down on paper," he said. "Besides, the goblins have a different attitude to contracts and agreements generally. They almost never sue."

"Ah."

"No, they fry instead. The way Mordak sees it, play it straight with him and everything will be fine. Mess him around and he'll have you for breakfast." He paused. "Construe that last remark as you wish. Only please, do be careful to bear in mind that Mordak's a goblin. Enlightened, yes, but a goblin. He likes his employees loyal or lightly steamed on a bed of bruised rocket. No middle ground. He's not a middle ground kind of guy."

Efluviel noticed a strange taste in her mouth, and it wasn't *miruvor* latte. Every instinct she possessed told her to back out now, while she had the chance. But, she decided, she probably didn't have the chance, not any more; not with someone who didn't believe in written agreements or set terms of employment. She had a nasty feeling that she'd effectively signed on the dotted line already, the moment she'd said yes, and any attempt to get out of it would land her in hot water, probably with onions and a stock cube. And anyway, she told herself, I wouldn't change my mind even if I could. A job on the *Face*, for crying out loud. She was going to be a journalist again. For that, was she prepared to do anything, anything at all?

Silly question. "Great," she said. "That's all perfectly fine. So, when do I start?"

"**N**orman," said Clive. "There's a goblin on the work-bench."

Which, when he said it, was entirely true. But not for very long. The goblin looked round at the shock-frozen humans surrounding him, made a sort of vague whimpering noise, and *changed*.

All the members of the South Cudworth and District Particle Physics Club were watching at the time, so what happened wasn't inexplicable for want of professional scientific scrutiny. Of course, as Maurice protested later (volubly, at length, in the saloon bar of the Three Pigeons) it all happened so fast that the human eye wasn't able to take it in. First, the goblin seemed to stretch, then widen, then thicken, then sort of— (At that point, Maurice used unscientific language and howled for more whisky, which the nice lady behind the bar reluctantly provided.)

A fraction of a second later, there was no goblin. His place on the bench had apparently been taken by a short, dumpy, rather gormless-looking young man, with wispy butter-coloured hair getting a bit thin on top, wearing a frock coat, pyjama bottoms and flip-flops. He was still holding the shield and the machete, but now the machete was in his left hand and the shield was in his right.

"Excuse me," he said, with a very faint East Midlands accent, "but is this the Realms of Transcendent Bliss?"

The Club stayed exactly where it was. "Norman," hissed Derek. "Do something."

But Norman didn't seem to have heard him. He was pre-occupied. It's notoriously hard, of course, for someone to know what he really looks like; but Norman had a horrible feeling that the young man standing on the bench bore a striking resemblance to himself, about forty years ago, but with even worse dress sense. As if in a dream, he stared at the stranger and said, "Who are you?"

"Um," the stranger replied. "Only, you see, I was trying to get to the Blessed Realms but I don't actually know what they look like, so I don't know if I'm actually there—" He registered the expressions on the Club's faces, and his shoulders slumped a little. "I'm not, am I?"

"I don't know," said Clive. "You're seven miles from Gainsborough on the A361 if that's any help." He paused, then added, "Are you a goblin?"

"Um." The young man was gazing round the room again, and Norman suddenly realised he was looking for a door. "Stop him," he yelled, but a split second too late. The young man dropped the weapons, flexed his knees, then launched himself off the bench in the direction of the doorway. Clearly he'd overestimated the power of his legs, because he landed on the concrete floor halfway to the door with a terrific crash. George made a distinctly half-hearted attempt at grabbing hold of him, which came nowhere close; then he scrambled to his feet, bolted through the door and slammed it behind him.

The Club stood for a while, listening as the sound of running flip-flops died away down the corridor outside. Then there was dead silence for a while. Then Clive said, "You know what?"

Norman turned and looked at him. "What?"

"I think we may have been going at this entirely the wrong way," Clive said. "Look, instead of all this faffing around, why don't we just replace the entire cylinder head assembly, bang in a new clutch, and have done with it?"

Norman was looking at the bench where the young man had first appeared. There were eight parallel lines scored in the varnish, almost like claw-marks, at the place where whatever-it-was had first appeared. He looked away with an effort and nodded twice. "I think you could be on to something there," he said.

The next day the laboratory was boarded up, some men came to put up a twelve-foot razor-wire fence all round the perimeter, and Clive found a Norton cylinder head and clutch assembly on eBay for only £325 plus shipping. So that was all right.

He ran until he could run no more, then dragged himself into the middle of a dense thorn hedge, closed his eyes, and passed out.

When he came to it was pitch dark, and he found to his horror that he could barely see. For a moment he thought it must be a side-effect of the magic, until he realised that he had human eyes now, and humans have notoriously dreadful night vision. Also pathetic flabby little legs, ridiculously thin skin and absolutely no stamina. He moaned softly, and pulled thorns out of the palms of his hands.

"I am not a human," he told himself. It was vitally important to remind himself of this, because the human body seemed determined to override his memory. "I am *not* a human. I'm a *goblin*."

The ears that heard him say it didn't seem terribly convinced. They were human ears, rounded, hairless, floppy; to begin with, it had felt like they were stuffed with bog-cotton, until he realised that that was as good as human hearing got, and they patently didn't want to listen to what he had to say about his identity. Don't be silly, they seemed to be telling him. Goblin? The very idea.

"I'm a *goblin*," he repeated stubbornly. "My name is Ozork, I was spawned in Number Seven vat in the Consolidated Central Hatchery on the—" He froze. He couldn't even remember his hatchday. Either the magic was stronger than he'd been led to believe, or he'd overdone it badly. That's what you get, he reflected bitterly, for using black market spells bought from a stranger in a tavern. And if this really was the Realms of Transcendent Bliss, you could stick them where the Horrible Yellow Face doesn't shine.

Never mind, he told himself. I don't know where I am, and I appear to have morphed into a human, but at least I'm out of Goblinland. He clung to that thought for a moment, and it gave him strength. Then, using every remaining shred of his mental clarity, he tried to figure out what he could about where he was and what had happened.

A human district, evidently. Furthermore, he was inclined to believe, a district where they didn't get many goblins. The looks on their faces hadn't been the sort he was used to; no hatred, not really very much fear, more a kind of stunned bewilderment, and one of them had said, *Are you a goblin?* in a manner that suggested that he'd never seen one before, didn't believe they existed, still wasn't entirely sure even though he'd seen one. A remote human district, then, proba-bly a very long way away from the Mountains – come to think of it, he hadn't seen them on the skyline while he was running away; he'd never been anywhere where the Mountains didn't dominate the skyline. A very remote human district, then, presumably far out in the east or the west of the Realms; a place where humans built huge stone houses with hard black roads, and wore outlandish clothes, and could look at a goblin without wetting themselves and reaching for the nearest weapon.

At this point it occurred to him that being back in Goblinland wouldn't be such a terrible thing after all.

Which was a pity, because as far as he knew it was strictly a one-way magic. Look through the middle of the peculiar circular bun, said the man in the tavern, and make a wish, and there you'll be. Nothing in the instructions about coming back. Which, at the time, hadn't bothered him in the least, because all he'd wanted was to journey to the Realms of Transcendent Bliss, or at any rate as far from Goblinland as he could get. A good idea at the time, in other words.

All the while, his pitifully inefficient human ears were straining for any sound that might herald the approach of large carnivorous animals. He hadn't heard any yet, but given his new hardware handicap, that didn't mean anything. What he could hear was a low but constant background hum, like the noise of a terrifyingly large swarm of bees. He tried to pin down which direction it was coming from, but as far as he could tell it was coming from all sides – surrounded by millions and millions of bees, he thought, and chances were that the human immune system was as rubbishy as all its other functions; one sting from a bee, he'd probably go down like a felled tree. The magic will change you so that you blend in perfectly with your surroundings, said the man in the pub. At the time, he'd regarded that as a major point in its favour. Idiot.

Even so, he told himself; remember why you did this. You can still remember that, can't you?

Those horrible bees. What sort of bee swarmed in the middle of the night?

The irony was, of course, that it was his dissatisfaction

with goblins and Goblinkind that had driven him to this – dissatisfaction, what a feeble word, but perhaps it was the strongest that this useless human brain could process. Irony, or you could see it as a kind of savage justice. Was that possible? Couldn't you be a better kind of goblin without degenerating into a human? Because that was all he'd wanted; to get away from the crassness, the coarseness, the *stupidity* of his fellow goblins, to a place where he'd be free of all that, free to be himself, to evolve as he knew he could, if only—

Something sharp was sticking into his leg. He shifted a bit, which only made it worse. How could anyone be expected to put up with this hateful, humiliating frailty? Everything hurt; he could barely see, hear or smell, it was liking having a really bad cold, the brain was wired all wrong so that he had to struggle to call up basic words and simple concepts, and this bundle of junk was supposed to be his home and his toolkit as he faced an unknown and inexplicable new world. He dabbed at the corner of his mouth with the back of his hand; no tusks, for crying out loud, how was he supposed to defend himself or crunch up bones? As for his claws, they appeared to have shrunk down into little paper-thin decorations on the ends of his feeble, naked fingers – *five* fingers, two missing, oh my God, I've been *mutilated*. He felt something wet dribble down his face and traced its course with a fingertip back to his eyesocket; his eyes were leaking, he'd go blind. And then he remembered that stupid human thing, tears. The shame of it, as though he'd wet himself; which, in a very real sense, he had.

He wriggled on to his side and closed his loathsome, soggy eyes, which would be useless until the Horrible Yellow Face rose and soaked the world in nasty, dazzling light.

He woke up with a start, opened his eyes and froze. Something was nibbling his foot.

He looked at it and relaxed slightly, though not much. It was probably a cow. It was cow-shaped, and it had stupid cow eyes, and it shrank back like a cow when he moved, but it was *huge*; also patchy black and white, like a runny chess-board, which was just perverse. It licked its nose with a vast pink tongue and gazed at him. "Piss off," he said. It blinked, and swished its tail.

Human or not, he told himself, I am not afraid of bloody cows. He scrambled about for a moment, spiking his putty-soft skin on the thorns, and dragged himself out of the hedge and upright. The cow bounded away a few yards, stopped and gazed at him reproachfully. He found a stone and threw it. Missed. Hand-eye co-ordination definitely on a par with all other systems.

His human neck had a crick in it, his human back ached and he'd got pins and needles in both tiny clawless feet. He looked round. The Horrible Yellow Face was high in the sky – bright and cloudless, but instead of wincing under its vicious glare he felt pleasantly warm (contradiction in terms, surely) and not at all dazzled; in fact, he could see almost as well in the light as he used to be able to in the dark. He was in a flat green field with maybe two dozen giant cows; not a building in sight. Oh, and another thing. He was hungry.

Actually, that wasn't as bad as it might have been. Hunger for a goblin is an all-consuming desire that overrides every other consideration; can't think straight, can't think of any-thing else until you feel the bones splinter between your tusks and taste the glory of the marrow. For a human, apparently, it's a gentle throat-clearing reminder that at some point it might not be such a bad idea to eat something, if it's conven-ient and not too much trouble. He considered the possibilities. There were about two dozen of them, black and white and enormous. Fine. Your cow is relatively easy prey, under normal circumstances, which these weren't. Without tusks, claws or proper legs, he wasn't entirely sure he'd be up to running one down and killing it, not even a normal-sized cow, let alone one of these monsters. Even if he could, a contest between cowhide and these silly little clawlets would be one-sided and probably quite painful, and in any event, how the hell are you supposed to eat *anything* if you have no tusks?

Ah, he remembered, but humans don't eat normal food. They eat *bread* and rubbish like that. Not they, of course. We. *We* eat rubbish like that.

He sat down on the grass and buried his head in his hands. It's no good, he said to himself. I'm done for.

Something nudged his foot. That bloody cow again – he opened one baleful eye, then did a sitting jump backwards. It was a human—

No it wasn't, or at least if it was, it was a subspecies he'd never encountered or heard about. The back of his neck tickled where his hackles should have been (phantom hackle syndrome; oh *please!)* and he growled softly in the back of his throat.

"Hello," said the human.

He gazed at it – *it*, because it was too vague and blurry to make out gender distinctions, and its voice seemed to be speaking to him from inside his own head. "You," he said. "Why are you all shiny?"

"New updates available," said the human. "Preparing to install."

"Get away from me, you—"

But the human was too quick for him. A glowing blue arm shot out and its hand enveloped his face. A blue thumb and forefinger pressed into his eyes – he saw them pass through his retinas, into his brain, while another blue finger filled his mouth until he began to choke. He tried to fight, only to find that nothing worked. He was completely paralysed. There was no pain, but he knew that was only because the bits of stuff that he felt pain with weren't working either. The blue light flooded his head, submerging, drowning—

"Configuring updates."

And then, gradually, steadily, he began to *understand*. He was – now he knew who he was, what he was, where he was; this is Lincolnshire, England, and seven miles or so down that main road over there is Gainsborough, a nice enough place if you don't mind miserable. And England is a country in Western Europe, which is the bundle of bits and pieces up in the top left-hand corner. And today is a Thursday, and a pint of milk in Tesco costs—

"Configuration complete. Closing down."

"Here, just a—" he said, and died.

Don't you hate it when that happens? Just as you reach a climax of total enlightenment, you know everything, understand everything, even all the stuff they've been keeping from you all these years, you die. The last bus leaves without you, and there you are.

Oh well, he thought. It can't have been all that important anyway. And then the human said, "Restarting," his eyes snapped open, and he looked up into the human's pale brown eyes.

She wasn't shiny and flickering any more. Instead, he was about fifty-six, with a salt-and-pepper beard and his hair drawn back tightly in a ponytail under a tall, conical hat. He was holding a mirror.

"Oh my God," he said. "What am I *wearing*?"

He took the mirror away. "Starting YouSpace," he said. "Hello."

"You what?"

"Space. I am the YouSpace orientation wizard. Beta version," he added, just a trifle self-consciously. "I'm an upgrade designed to make your YouSpace transition as easy and comfortable as possible. You may uninstall me if you wish."

"What? No, that's fine. What's—?"

The wizard smiled. "The magic that brought you here," he said. "Only here, remember, don't call it magic. No such thing in this reality."

A tiny voice in the back of his head sniggered and whispered, *That's what you think.* He stamped on it with the boot of self-control. "This isn't the Realms of—"

"No," said the wizard. "Sorry about that. By a fluke malfunction you were caught up in the nexus of another YouSpace transaction and dragged here in its slipstream. We are checking to see if anything can be done to rectify this problem. Check complete. Nothing can be done to rectify this problem. We apologise for any inconvenience."

"Hang on," he said. "You just told me, there's no magic here. But you also said you're a wizard."

The wizard nodded, with a sheepish grin. "This is a funny old place," he said. "There's no magic, and they know that, but they like to pretend that there is. They don't believe it, but they pretend. Humans," he explained.

"Ah. Did you really have to put me to death like that? I didn't like it a bit."

"We apologise for any inconvenience. What would you like to do today?"

He frowned. "Let me see if I've got this straight," he said. "I cast my spell, but someone else was casting another spell at that very same moment, and my spell sort of got sucked in to his, and now I'm stuck here, not where I wanted to be, and I can't do anything about it?"

"Checking. Confirmed. We apologise for any inconvenience. What would you like to do today?"

"Bloody hell." He closed his eyes for a moment, then opened them again. "Are you sure there's nothing I can do?"

"Checking. You can try contacting your local YouSpace users support group. Updating data. There is no YouSpace users support group in this local area. We apol—"

The wizard broke off, maybe because he'd made a grab for its windpipe. But his fingers just passed through the wizard's neck and came out the other side, feeling strangely tingly. "For any inconvenience," the wizard said reproachfully. "Attempts to kill the YouSpace orientation wizard (beta version) may invalidate your warranty and render you ineligible for further support."

"I can't kill you, you're not even real," he muttered angrily. "All right, I'm stuck here and there's no way out of it. What do I do now?"

"Sorry, that information is not available. Off the record," the wizard went on, lowering its voice, "I'd make the best of it if I were you. After all, it's not like you're the only one of your lot over here."

His eyes opened wide. "I'm not?"

"Sorry, that information is not available. Are you serious? There's dozens of you."

"Define you."

"Searching. Sorry, et cetera. People from your reality," the wizard said. "Tourists, refugees, asylum seekers, economic migrants, *gastarbeiter*, a few who got out one step ahead of their local law enforcement, the usual mix. Ever since YouSpace went online, there's been a fairly steady stream. Even a few of, you know, *your* lot." The wizard mimed tusks and claws, not very well. "Film extras, mostly. Compared with the cost of top-class CGI, it's so much cheaper to use the real thing. It only gets awkward when they start eating the cast."

"My lot. You mean gob—"

"That information," the wizard said pointedly, "is not available. Not so loud, all right? Actually, you could do worse, though it's a shame you opted for the camouflage job, they'd have to rig you up with prosthetics. Still, they do that anyway. Apparently, genuine tusks and claws don't come out right on film, they look sort of plastic. It's the grunting and the funny walk they want you for. Apparently that's really hard to do on a computer."

"Film extras." He scowled. He knew about films now, thanks to the glowing blue light in his head. It struck him as a very strange idea. "No offence, but I came here for a better life. That's not really my idea of—"

"Be like that," said the wizard. "What else are you going to do, with no skills or qualifications? Be different if you were a plumber or an electrician. As it is, your only other options are security, cleaning toilets or working in a call centre. Not that your lot seem to mind that sort of thing," the wizard added. "They see it as interesting work, free meals and a congenial atmosphere."

"Why do you think I left?"

"Ah." The wizard shrugged. "Well, that's me about done, unless you'd care to register for the premium service. Take care, be good and enjoy yourself. Actually, it may seem pretty ghastly to begin with, but there are worse realities. In an infinite multiverse. Presumably. Sayonara," the wizard added, and vanished in a haze of airborne cherry blossom.

5

Be it never so dark, damp, deep, musty and littered with yellowing bones, there's no place like home. Mordak closed the door of his private chamber, tossed his faux-Elfskin suitcase into a corner, collapsed on the bed and went to sleep.

He was woken early the next morning by the distinctive grunting, shuffling noise of a lot of goblins waiting relatively patiently. He opened his eyes and saw that his bed was surrounded by a dense cordon of his senior courtiers, all of them looking at him. He remembered just how long he'd been away. He sighed, and propped himself up on one elbow.

"Morning, Chief," said a senior councillor brightly. "Feeling rested?"

"A bit."

"Just as well. We've got a shitload of stuff to get through, and you will insist on seeing every damn thing personally."

"What time is it?"

The councillor shrugged. "We thought you'd like to make an early start. There's ever so much to do."

Mordak nodded sleepily. "Fair enough," he said, sitting up and yawning. "All right, what's first?"

Slight pause. "Well," said another councillor, "you know

when you went away, the last thing you told us was, don't bankrupt the treasury and don't start any wars?"

"Mphm."

"One out of two's not bad."

A tiny nerve at the side of Mordak's head started to throb. "Bankrupt?"

"War," said a third councillor. "With the dwarves."

"For crying out loud, I've only been away a few weeks."

"Oh, it's all right," said a fourth councillor. "We won."

"Ah."

"Sort of."

The second councillor nodded vigorously. "We really showed 'em, didn't we, boys? Down in Mineshaft Seventeen. They won't come trespassing there any more."

Mordak narrowed his eyes. "Won't they?"

"Oh no. See, it's theirs now, and properly speaking you can't trespass on your own—"

"You lost Mineshaft Seventeen."

The first councillor shrugged. "But we made 'em rue the day, didn't we, lads? Gave the bastards a bloody nose, all right. Besides," he added cheerfully, "we can always take it back again. Give the men something to look forward to."

Mordak allowed himself a moment to think. Mineshaft Seventeen; he knew it well. Horribly unstable, crawling with hidden pockets of deadly explosive gas, prone to flooding and very nearly worked out. He'd been thinking of closing it down for some time. His mind darted forward to the upcoming peace talks, and it occurred to him that if he ceded the enemy title to Seventeen and in return got exclusive rights to the unexplored bit just south of the Orcsnap Pass, which he happened to know for a fact held a particularly rich seam of high grade copper ore, that wouldn't be such a bad deal after all. And the thought of the look on King Drain's face when his surveyors reported . . . The trouble was, these fools expected him to take the useless thing back by force. "Leave it with me," he said. "What else?"

A slight awkwardness, as though he'd said something wrong. "You don't mind?"

"Probably just as well if you don't make a habit of it, but—"

"We thought you'd be livid."

Mordak's nose twitched. "But you did it anyway."

"Well." The councillors shuffled their feet. "We thought we'd win, see."

"Ah, I get you," Mordak said. "You reckoned I wouldn't mind you making an unprovoked attack on an enemy we're in the middle of complicated peace negotiations with over a fairly worthless hole in the ground while my back was turned without asking me first, provided you won."

"Right," said the first councillor brightly. "Well, you wouldn't, would you?"

It was a dreadful thing to have to admit, but there were times when he felt happier in the company of humans, or dwarves, or even Elves, than among his own kind. "Moving on," he said, "how did you get on with rolling out the new employment regulations? All went smoothly, I imagine."

"Sort of."

That tone of voice. "There were problems."

The second councillor whetted his tusks against his jaw for a moment. "The thing is," he said, "all that stuff's not very popular with the lads in the pits, you know? They don't hold with it. Goblin jobs for goblin workers is what they want. Humans and dwarves working in our mines, it just isn't right. They reckon," he added quickly.

"Tough," Mordak said. "It's fine by me. I'm the king."

"Well, there's been—"

"What?"

"Teething troubles."

"Meaning?"

"Troubles," said the councillor awkwardly, "with teeth. Like, the lads took it on the chin, they accepted they've got to have dwarves down the mine now, it's the law. But they've been sort of working to rule."

Mordak's headache got a little worse. "Have they now."

"Like," the councillor went on quickly, "it says in the law they've got to let them go down the mine, but there's nothing in the actual wording about not eating them once they're down there. But," he added quickly, "it's all sorted itself out now, because the dwarves and the humans don't want to go down the mines any more, so that's all right, isn't it? Problem solved."

Indeed. Six months of brittle, tentative negotiation with King Drain and three human princes to get the skilled workforce he so desperately needed to increase production in Shafts Nine and Thirty-seven, to extract the ore he needed to pay for the huge consignment of top-grade dwarf-made armour he'd ordered from King Dror and now had no hope in hell of being able to pay for, and a bunch of idiot miners had had his supreme diplomatic achievement for lunch. He explained this, quietly and patiently, but the councillors just looked pleased.

"That's all right, then," they said, "we were just coming to that. Dror's cancelled the order, soon as you were out of the country. He's selling all that gear to the humans instead."

Mordak was silent for a moment. Then he smiled weakly. "It just gets better and better, doesn't it?"

The councillors nodded happily. "We're glad you see it that way," said one of them. "We were afraid you might be cross."

"Mphm," Mordak said. "Get out."

His predecessor (he reflected a few minutes later, as he pulled on his trousers) would've had them all beheaded, and there'd have been a new dinner service in the royal china pantry and forty-six vacancies on the royal council; and what? Forty-six other idiots would've taken their place, and everything would have gone on the same, except that he'd have had another forty-six families plotting revenge against him. Yawn. When all was said and done, what else could he have expected? You can't stop goblins fighting dwarves, it's against nature; and eating Permitted Food Species while on mine premises wasn't even a breach of the health and safety regulations, provided they ate them raw and didn't pose a fire risk. On the other claw, if he made a fuss about it, that would give the impression that his orders had been disobeyed, and then he'd have to execute his entire council in order to save face (or at least, to keep his face from becoming a receptacle for coffee) and he didn't want to do that, it led to bad feeling and slowed everything down. No, the only sensible thing was to let them believe it didn't really matter, and work even harder to save what he could from the wreck. It was a bloody nuisance about the armour, though. And the thought of it falling into the pudgy pink paws of humans—

He stopped, one leg trousered, the other bare. Dror was selling the armour to the humans instead. Note the word *selling*. He knew (none better) the ridiculous prices Dror charged. The humans were all dirt poor, always had been, because of the idiotic way they ran their economy. Where the hell had they suddenly got that sort of money from?

One damn thing after another. If the humans had money, and were using it to buy armour, you didn't have to be a genius to figure out that bad times were on the way. He finished putting his trousers on, tightened his belt and yelled. After a long wait, a face appeared in the doorway. It had pointed ears.

"Well?" it said.

As always, Mordak had to fight back his instincts. A

goblin king having an Elf for a secretary wasn't natural, he knew that. But Tiniturel was the only personal assistant he'd ever had who actually *did* things, quite often the things she'd been told to do. It was a shame about her unfortunate manner, but never mind. "I want you to find something out for me."

"Of course you do. What?"

"The humans," Mordak said, adjusting his trollskin cape around his shoulders. "Suddenly they've got money to spend. Why is this?"

Tiniturel shrugged. "Found it in the pocket of their other trousers, probably. How do you know about this?"

He told her about Dror and the armour. She clicked her tongue and muttered something about boys and their toys which he fortunately didn't quite catch. "Granted," she said, "that's unusual. Their balance of payments is generally a mess. All right, I'll look into it. You're not going out in public wearing that, are you?"

"What's wrong—" He caught himself just in time. "Yes," he said.

"Mphm." There was a look of something like affection on her face, such as an owner might display when her dog's just learned to roll over and die for Master. *Good* goblin! "Right, I'll get started, then. It may take a while."

"No doubt."

"You do realise that while I'm swanning about the place investigating humans, there'll be nobody here with two brain cells to file the daily reports, read the incoming mail and give you a words-of-one-syllable summary, schedule your meetings, arrange your diary, tell you where you're supposed to be, when, why and what you're meant to be doing there, write your letters for you, interpret in sixteen languages, tidy your desk, keep your loyal ministers from bursting in here and interrupting you every five minutes, advise you on domestic and foreign policy, explain difficult words for you and make your coffee?"

"Yes."

"Fine." She nodded. "Just don't blame me when this whole place grinds to a juddering halt." She glanced at the water-clock dripping quietly away in the corner. "I estimate that'll be about three o'clock this afternoon. Think of me while you're struggling to cope."

"I will. Goodbye."

"*Ciao* for now. Try not to bog everything up."

Which, he reflected as her heels tapped away down the corridor, coming from an Elf, was practically flirting.

The little man almost looked right. He wore a green jerkin with a red hood and yellow stockings, black square-toed boots and a pair of round, rimless spectacles perched on the bridge of his nose. The only giveaways were the furtive way he looked round before sitting down in front of his campfire, and the fact that all his clothes were clearly brand new. The furtive look was all right, as it happened, because there was no one there to see it; and as for the clothes, the newness would wear off quickly enough, and then he'd be perfect.

Beside the campfire was a large wooden crate, festooned with delivery notes, customs declarations and other bits of paper that would have been utterly alien to a passing local. Having made another furtive check, the little man pulled a small but ergonomically designed prybar out of his sleeve and set to work demolishing the crate. The chrome molybdenum alloy steel the prybar was made of would've been worth five times its weight in gold to any smith in the kingdom, since from it he could've forged a finer, stronger sword than any to be found in the armouries of the dwarf-kings. The little man was vaguely aware of that fact, but when he'd finished opening the crate and had no further use for it, he slung the bar away into the nearby bushes. Money, after all, was the least of his concerns.

From the ruins of the crate (which the little man quickly heaped on to the fire) emerged a spinning-wheel. Like the little man's clothes, it was authentic in everything except its condition; there were no chips or dings in the varnish, and the sides of the treadle board were square and unworn. The little man sat down on a straw-bale and looked at it for a while, as if trying to decide something. Then from his other sleeve he took a small booklet, which he read twice from cover to cover before throwing it into the fire. He took a doughnut from his pocket, brushed off some fluff and ate it. His hand shook slightly as he licked the last grains of sugar off his fingertips. Then he sat down at the wheel, put his foot on the treadle and began to pump.

For the next hour or so he was pretty busy, though he didn't actually do any spinning. It was more as though he was familiarising himself thoroughly and conscientiously with the machine in front of him. Eventually he charged the bobbin with wool, pedalled the wheel up to full speed and proceeded to spin a useful quantity of first-quality yarn, which he inspected carefully, tugging at it with both hands to test for closeness and uniformity of weave, before chucking it on to the fire. Then he stood up, teased four heaped handfuls of straw out of the bale he'd been sitting on, and loaded it on to the bobbin. Just then, someone in the shadows outside the circle of firelight cleared his throat, and a voice said, "Hello?"

The little man stood up, took off his spectacles and peered in the direction of the voice. "Who's there?"

The bushes parted and a big man in a fur-trimmed cloak and hood stepped nervously into the firelight. "Hello," he repeated. "Are you him?"

The little man found that amusing. "I'd imagine so, if you're looking for me."

"Sorry," said the big man. "I don't think I quite caught your name."

"Nice try."

The big man grinned sheepishly. "So you are him, then." He came closer and sat down, without being asked, on the straw-bale. "Devil of a job finding this place," he said. "Can't say I've ever been here before."

The little man's eyes twinkled in the firelight. "Doesn't that strike you as odd?"

"No, not really."

The little man shrugged. "If I owned a piece of land, I think I'd probably find the time to go there. Still—"

"I own a lot of land. I'm a prince."

"Quite. And a busy one, I'm sure. What can I do for you?"

The prince frowned. "Well," he said, "the thing of it is, I'd quite like some gold."

"Good heavens. Would you really?"

Not a lot of call for irony in these parts, evidently. "Yes," said the prince. "And a bloke I was talking to the other day said you were the man to go to. Gold-wise, I mean."

"He was entirely right," said the little man gravely. "If you're after gold, you've come to the right place."

"Ah." The prince looked relieved. "That's what this bloke told me. First-rate chap, he said. One of the biggest names in the business." He paused. "Talking of which—"

"Go fish." The little man smiled pleasantly. "So, how much?"

"Excuse me?"

"How much do you want?"

The prince looked a bit startled by the question. He hesitated for a moment, then pointed at the bale he was sitting on. "That much?"

"No problem," the little man said. "I expect you'd like to see a sample first."

"Well, if it's no trouble."

"No trouble at all." The little man gently pushed the prince off the bale, sat on it and began to work the treadle. A minute or so later, he unwound a length of shiny yellow thread off the spool, cut it with a knife and handed it to the prince. "There you go," he said. "Have your alchemists test it, if you like. Twenty-four carat, point nine-nine-nine-nine pure or better."

The prince stared at the thread for a moment, then wrapped it into a tight bundle and tried to graze it with his fingernail. "That's—"

"Yup," said the little man, "the good stuff, guaranteed. The real thing, the genuine article."

"My God." The prince looked down at him with awe and no small degree of fear. "You really can spin straw into—"

"Yes."

"And you'll do me—" He nodded at the bale.

"Sure. For starters. Plenty more where that came from. Good harvest down your way this year?"

"Can't complain."

"Plenty of straw, then."

"Loads of it." A penny dropped inside the prince's head, and his mouth formed a perfect, silent O.

"Splendid," said the little man. "And I imagine you don't want everybody knowing about our little arrangement."

"Well," the prince said, "better not, if that's all right."

"Of course." The little man nodded. "Discretion is my middle name. Figuratively speaking," he added, with a twinkle. "Oh, and if you wouldn't mind just signing this bit of paper."

A hunted look came into the prince's eyes. "Ah," he said. "What does it say?"

"Oh, you know," said the little man. "Basic heads of agreement, standard terms and conditions, that sort of guff. You get the gold, I get the kid. All perfectly simple and straight-forward."

The prince stared at the sheet of paper in the little man's hand. "I haven't actually got a child at the moment," he said. "Does that—?"

"Oh, that's all right," the little man said. "You will have, in time. I'm patient. All the time in the world, me."

"Ah. And I don't have to, provided—"

"Provided you can guess my name, yes, that's quite right." The little man whisked away the paper, then leaned forward and tugged the gold thread from the prince's hand. "Of course, if you don't like the deal, we'll forget all about it. I mean, if you're having second thoughts or anything."

"No." The prince swallowed hard. "No, nothing like that."

"You wouldn't like to go away and, oh, I don't know, maybe talk it over with your wife or anything?"

"No, that's fine."

The little man gave him a look you could've cut diamonds with. "Jolly good," he said. "Right, let's have your John Ha—your signature on that contract, and I can get started."

"Um."

The little man looked puzzled for a moment, then he grinned. "X will do just fine," he said. He held out a quill to the prince, who scrawled a wobbly cross at the foot of the page, squashing the nib. "And I'll just sign too," the little man added. "No peeking." He smiled. "Not that I'm worried, in your case. That's the joy of doing business with the aristocracy. Unimpeachable sense of fair play, and they can't read what they're not supposed to, even if they wanted to."

"Who's John Ha?"

The little man ignored him. "All done," he said, folding the paper and thrusting it down the front of his jerkin. "How is your good lady, by the way? In the pink? Drinking plenty of milk?"

The prince shuddered. "Right," he said. "When can I expect delivery?"

"You bring me the straw, I'll spin it. Get your men to stack it up there, under those trees. And tell 'em to sling a tarpaulin over it, I hate spinning soggy straw. Everything you thought you knew about blisters is suddenly obsolete." He dragged a handful of straw out of the bale. "Well, this is nice but I'm sure you've got ever such a lot of things you should be doing. Give my best to the missus."

The prince stood for a moment as if unable to move. Then he said quietly, "What do you do with them?"

"Excuse me?"

"The children."

The little man clicked his tongue. "We don't ask that question."

"Why not?"

"If I tell you the truth you won't believe me. If I lie to you, you will believe me." He sighed, drew the paper out from his shirt-front and held it over the fire. "I don't have to make this offer," he said, "because you signed, and that makes it legally binding. But if you like—" He opened his fingers, so that the paper was retained by forefinger and thumb alone. "Say the word. Up to you. You've got five seconds. This does not affect your statutory rights."

"No." The prince was sweating, though he wasn't very close to the fire. "No, that's fine. You're sure that if I guess your name—"

The little man smiled. "Then you keep the gold and the kid. Three, two, one. There, now." He put the paper back inside his jerkin. "That was your last chance. But I'm sure you know what you're doing. Been married long, have you?"

"About six months. Why?"

"As long as that." The little man shook his head. "Goodbye."

The prince turned, walked away, stopped, hesitated, then pushed his way through the bushes and disappeared into the darkness. The little man watched him go, shrugged and went back to his spinning. He was counting under his breath; twenty-nine, twenty-eight, twenty-seven. He'd got down to three when the bushes parted and the prince reappeared. His eyes were wild and there was a ferocious scowl on his face. The little man didn't look up.

"John Ha," he said. "Your name is John Ha."

"Two guesses left."

"Oh *God*."

The little man twirled a length of gold thread round his finger and reached for his knife. The prince opened and closed his hands helplessly.

"My wife's going to kill me when I get home."

"Mphm," said the little man.

"You never told me I only had three guesses."

"Should've read the small print, then, shouldn't you?"

"I can't—" The prince took a deep breath. "You haven't heard the last of this."

"So sue me."

"I might just do that."

"Fine. Oh, sorry, you can't, you'd need to know my name first."

I shouldn't tease, the little man said to himself, as the crash of splintering branches tracked the prince's retreat through the woods. They can't help it. By their own lights, they're behaving perfectly reasonably. It's just that— He shrugged. People who live in glass houses, he thought.

Human nature, he said to himself. Stupid, complicated human nature. Why are people so easy to cheat, and why's it so damned hard to give them money?

6

"So," said the assistant director, "what do you think of New Zealand?"

It was one of those long, inexplicable delays. This time it was something to do with the lighting. The stars had withdrawn to their trailers, the director was huddled over his laptop with his phone tucked under his chin and a handkerchief pressed to his nose because of his hay fever, the noonday sun was beating down on six men playing cards in full goblin prosthetics and steel plate armour, while a frowning young man in jeans wandered to and fro across the set, backwards and forwards, carrying an aluminium ladder. In the background, the snow-capped mountains soared up unnoticed into a pale blue sky.

"It's all right, I suppose."

"Reminds you of home, I guess."

"Not really."

The assistant director had never met a real goblin before. He'd known for some time that there were a few of them working in the biz, but although he'd been on four out of the seven films in the franchise so far, circumstances had conspired to prevent him from crossing paths with one, until now. He wasn't sure if he was excited or disappointed.

"So," he said, glancing down at the screen of his LoganBerry, "you're Archie."

"Mphm."

"But that's not your real name. Your goblin name, I mean."

"Mphm."

"Fine," the assistant director said, determined to stay relaxed and friendly if it killed him. "You don't want to tell me your goblin name because of deeply and sincerely held cultural imperatives, that's cool, sorry if I said the wrong thing. So, what's it like being a goblin?"

The entity called Archie looked up at him sourly. "Fantastic," he said. "In fact, it's so fantastic I ran away from Goblinland and came here. A decision," he added, "that I'm beginning to regret, but there you go."

Usually extras didn't talk to assistant directors like that, but presumably that too was a cultural thing. He decided to move on to safer topics for a while. "So," he said, "what's it like working with Kurt?"

"Who?"

The assistant director blinked. "Kurt," he repeated. "The star." A blank look. "The guy playing the lead."

Archie shrugged. "I don't know, I've only seen him once, in the distance. He was throwing a hissy fit about something, but I wasn't close enough to hear. If he's playing the lead, my guess would be the lead is winning. I gather," Archie went on, frowning slightly, "that he gets paid a lot of money for doing that stuff."

"Well, yes."

"That's just silly. Never mind. I'd like to have a go at it."

"What, you mean acting?"

"If that's what it's called. Actually, it strikes me it's pretty much the same sort of thing as I'm doing now, except you've got to say things. I can say things." He paused, apparently aware that his offer hadn't immediately been accepted. "I don't need as much money as he does. Tell you what, whatever you're paying him, I'll take ten per cent less. Well?"

The assistant director breathed in and out slowly before answering. "Don't you have films in Goblinland?"

"Oh yes." Archie suddenly grinned. "But not like this. You wouldn't like what we've got."

"Wouldn't I?" The leer on Archie's face made the assistant director inclined to believe him, but he had to ask. "What've you got, then?"

Archie muttered something that sounded like—

"YouTube?" the assistant director repeated. "Oh yes, we've got that here. It's very popular."

"It is?"

"You bet."

"Oh." Archie looked impressed. "Well, hats off to you in that case, maybe you people aren't such a lot of wimps after all. Have you got Facebooks as well?"

The assistant director grinned. "That's very popular too. Nearly everybody's doing it these days."

Clearly he'd said the right thing. "Looks like I've underestimated your lot, then. I'd have thought it'd have been illegal."

"It is in China. But we're a bit more enlightened here in the West."

"Enlightened," Archie repeated. "Cool. And this is the West, right?"

"Well, yes, I guess so. Actually, we're sort of south-east of Asia, so China is actually west of here even though it's the East. But New Zealand counts as West, yes."

"Ah well," Archie said. "I might like it here after all."

Then the assistant director's phone warbled at him and he had to go; just, Archie reflected, when he was starting to get marginally less annoying. If what he'd said was true. But you could never be sure about these people, they had a tendency to say what they thought you wanted to hear, which was ridiculous. But then, nearly everything around here was like that. The only good thing about it, as far as he could see, was the money. It was almost impossible to translate human dollars into goblin *s'verk*, because the frames of reference barely overlapped at all, but at a really conservative estimate, doing this idiotic and supposedly low-paid job, he was earning more in an hour than a skilled goblin artisan – a smith, say, or a skull-polisher made in a week. Now if only there were some way he could send the money back home—

Someone was shouting at him, which meant he had to go and stand around somewhere else for a while. He sighed. He'd heard someone saying they were making an action movie, but most of the time nobody seemed to be doing anything. Still, he told himself, that's humans for you. Serves you right for coming to live with food.

He stood about in a different place for an hour, then ran from one entirely undistinguished spot to another six times along with a dozen other men supposedly dressed as goblins, and that was apparently that for the morning. He trudged away to the van to queue for lunch, and managed to find a deserted spot to eat it. Not deserted for long, though. The assistant director came bounding up to him like a happy dog, wanting to play.

"Actually, I might be able to get you in on my next job. No promises, of course, but it's looking good. They've green-lighted preproduction, so it's practically in the can."

"Another film, you mean."

"Well, yes, of course another film. Anyhow, it's something really special. It's going to break the mould."

Archie nodded sympathetically. "I used to work in a foundry," he said. "It's a bitch when that happens."

The assistant director seemed to have worked out how not to hear him when he said things he didn't understand. "It's an action historical comedy musical," he said. "It's based on a

Damon Runyon story, but they've shifted it to nineteenth-century Africa, because there's more resonances. Matt's already attached to direct, and Steve and Angie are really, really interested, so it should be really big."

"Really."

"Oh yes. Those French guys who did *Les Mis* are doing the songs and stuff, and it's so great we've got Matt, because he's so hot on battle scenes."

Archie frowned. "I thought you said it was a comedy."

"It is, yes. Action costume comedy musical. The idea is, there's this group of Zulu warriors in the 1830s who've just come back from kicking Boer ass all over the Transvaal, and then they hear about this orphanage that can't afford presents for the kids at Christmas, so they put on this big show and raise the money. It's a sure thing. They're thinking of calling it *Assegais and Dolls*. Anyhow," the assistant director went on, "plenty of openings for a guy who knows one end of a spear from another, so watch this space."

Archie thought for a moment. "It's hard to make an opening if you use the wrong end, granted," he said. "You have to push like crazy. But I'm thinking of quitting this business. It's boring."

The assistant director was staring at him as though he'd gone mad. "Boring?"

"All you do is stand about waiting, and then you do the same boring thing over and over again. And it's not like anyone ever does anything useful, even when they're not standing around. It's all *pretend*."

The assistant director had gone white as a sheet. "I'm sorry you feel that way."

"Well, it is. And it's *silly*. I mean, take this film you're making at the moment. You've got this idiot who's supposed to be a sorcerer, and he raises an army of goblins. Ridiculous. First, goblins don't work for humans, it'd be like you getting a job fetching and carrying for a plate of sandwiches. Second, any sorcerer worth a gob and a spit doesn't need an army, he just goes like *that* and suddenly you're knee deep in confused frogs. Third—" He paused, calmed down a bit. "You've got us all wrong," he said. "Goblins, I mean. We don't act like you think we do, you've got our society and culture completely cocked, and we definitely don't look like *this*." He shook himself, like a wet dog. "Any goblin that went around looking like this would be quarantined and put down, in case it was catching."

The assistant director looked genuinely distressed. "I know," he said. "It's the whole authenticity thing. They want everything a hundred per cent genuine authentic, provided it's what the audience expects to see and the colours don't clash. When I was on that big Viking flick they got all these professors in to advise, built a whole Viking city here on North Island, then found they couldn't use it because the greens came out as a sort of greeny-blue. Didn't look right, see. Not on the screen. The suits reckoned it came across like bad CGI. So they shot the whole thing on a blue screen and did it all on the computer. Won an Oscar, if you remember." Then he stopped, smiled and added, "It won't be like that on *Assegais*, though. They've got forty-six tribal chiefs signed on as special advisers, it's all going to be a hundred per cent real, the whole thing."

"With goblins to play the Zulus."

The assistant director nodded. "In motion capture suits. You ever worked in one of them? Amazing technology. They're working on the next generation right now. How it'll work is, you put on the suit and do the take, and then they feed some big star's last movie into a computer, it converts him into digital, then they input the take you just did, in the suit, and it kind of dubs the big star over you and what the audience sees is him, doing your scene. Totally amazing. It'll mean easier stunts, no expensive retakes, no scheduling conflicts, if the star drops dead one week into principal photography, so what? It'll revolutionise the business, you'll see."

Archie considered that for a moment. "We do something similar back home," he said. "When we kill a hated foe, just before we go into battle we flay his face off and plaster it over our own with fish-glue and honey."

The assistant director's eyes nearly bulged out of his head. "That's nothing like it at all," he said.

"Well, it's a bit different," Archie conceded. "We only do it to our enemies."

"Anyhow." The assistant director was hiding behind his smile. Humans did that. "I'll keep you updated regarding *Assegais*. You're going to love working with Angie and Steve, they're great. They're so genuine, you know?"

"I'm gradually getting the idea."

When the assistant director had finally drifted away, Archie ate a couple of mouthfuls of his sandwich, threw the rest away and tried to make sense of it all. Magic didn't work here, the system had said, but even so they could cast illusions that the people believed, to the point of stealing faces and wearing them with absolutely no need for fish-glue and honey. In some respects, apparently, they were almost goblinlike, whereas in others they were bewilderingly alien. Occasionally he reckoned he could see where they were coming from, but never quite fast enough to get out of the way. As for this stupid job— Still, he had to do something, and if it wasn't this . . .

Someone was standing over him. He looked up and saw a big, fat man in a leather waistcoat and sunglasses. "You Archie?"

"Yes."

The fat man nodded. "Kurt wants to see you."

Kurt? Oh yes, the actor who got paid all that money. "Why?"

"Follow me."

As good an explanation as any, Archie decided. The fat man led him to one of the shed-on-wheels things that the film people seemed to esteem so highly, knocked on the door and stood aside. A woman opened the door and looked at them both. "This him?" she said.

She had pointed ears.

Slowly and (for a goblin) carefully, the royal tattoo artist unwound what looked at first sight like a roll of tape. He put a bleached shin-bone on one end to keep it from curling up, and rolled out about a yard of the stuff; it was a very pale yellow, the colour of pancake batter, and for the record it was the dried and cured great intestine of Mordak's immediate predecessor on the goblin throne; goblins were a hundred per cent behind the idea of recycling long before it became fashionable. The artist, whose name was Girk, settled his spectacles on the bridge of his snout, opened the ivory (well, sort of) box in which he kept the tools of his trade, and said, "Ready when you are."

Goblins have quickly grown to love social media. When they aren't updating their Facebooks (having first carefully removed all traces of the fish-glue and honey), they're turning out useful and entertaining recordings, everything from destruct-testing the new Oriflamm ZZ97 E-Z-Slay to the best way to use up leftover Elf liver, via the equally popular medium of—

"Right," Mordak said. "Ready?"

"Standing by."

The manifold uses of intestine had been known to goblins

for centuries. You could make sausages. Nothing like a strip of gut, wound tight around the fracture, for mending a broken axe-handle. Thinner and more delicate than ordinary rawhide, it could be cured in such a way that it was practically transparent, which made it perfect for repairing books that had split down the spine. Or—

"Basically," Mordak went on, "I want to get across the fact that we've got this huge great army of merciless, savage goblins, and the humans don't stand a chance. So start off with a vast goblin horde marching across the plain, or something."

"With you so far, yes."

"Then they arrive at the gates of a human city, right? Do some terrified humans peering down from the battlements, women and children running screaming through the streets, that sort of thing."

Girk, who had already started work on the huge army, smiled. "I'm good at that."

"Yes, you are. Right, so then we'll have a deputation from the city going out to meet the goblin king – that's me, of course – and they've got a white flag, and they want to surrender."

"And then you kill them and eat them."

"No."

The breakthrough came when a goblin inventor discovered that if you drew a little sketch on a piece of cured translucent intestine and shone a bright light through it, you got a big, bright picture projected on the opposite wall. The uses of this discovery were obvious, and quite soon every goblin training camp had its own projector room, where guts of the correct way to throw spears and shoot arrows were exhibited to thousands of eager recruits.

"No?"

"No," Mordak repeated firmly. "The humans offer to surrender. I say yes."

"Ah." Girk grinned. "And then, as soon as we're inside the gates, we slaughter everything that moves."

"No."

Not long after that, an even greater goblin inventor found that if you drew lots and lots of little pictures on a roll of gut (ripped, of course, from the still-steaming corpse of your mortal enemy) and if each one was slightly different, and if you then pulled them quickly and smoothly past the projector lamp, you could give the impression that the picture was moving. And at that moment, YourTubes was born.

"All right, then, everything that stays still. But it won't look nearly so good on gut."

Mordak shook his head. "We don't slaughter *anything*."

It was typical of the Elves that their first reaction was to denounce goblin moving-image technology as decadent and barbaric, and their second reaction was to copy it for themselves. The goblins didn't mind about that – the sincerest form of flattery, and so forth – but they couldn't help feeling that the Elves had missed the point. For one thing, they insisted on using animal intestines, cows' mostly, which gave a much grainier effect. For another, instead of using the new medium for education, military training and propaganda, they insisted on churning out *fiction* – mostly revisionist versions of fairy-tales in which everybody's miserable all the time; a load of old tripe, in fact, and no Elvish production could hope to compete with true goblin *gut noir*. It lacked that visceral quality.

"Sorry," said Girk, laying down his needle. "You've lost me."

"The idea is," Mordak said, helping himself to chocolate-coated knuckles, "we scare them so much they don't want to fight, and then when they surrender we don't kill them, which encourages the next lot to surrender too. That way, we're spared the trouble and expense of conquering them."

Girk stared at him for a moment. "But that way we don't do any fighting."

"Got it in one," Mordak said, with his mouth full.

"But—"

"Yes, I know." Mordak frowned. "It's new, it's different, it's flying in the face of tradition. I also happen to believe there may be something in it."

"Really?"

"Mphm." Mordak knew that look. It meant; he's clearly mad, but after all, he's the king, and we've got to do what he says, at least till he gets kicked out, and all goblin kings go mad, usually within days of getting the spiky hat, and when you stop and think about it, there's worse forms of lunacy than not having wars absolutely *all* the time, or a visit to the doctor not costing you an arm and a leg (goblin doctors tended to prefer payment in kind), so maybe we'll give him the benefit of the doubt for now and then be extra-imaginative as and when there's a rebellion and he gets chucked out ... "I think it's the way forward. A dark new sunset for Goblinkind."

"Is that right?"

"For our spawn and our spawn's spawn, Girk."

"Whatever." Girk yawned. "Though if you ask me, there's more to it than that. You don't want to fight the humans because you think they'll win."

The most annoying thing about goblins, Mordak thought, is that ninety-nine per cent of the time, they're remarkably stupid. The second most annoying thing is that one per cent of the time, they're frighteningly bright. "Really? What makes you say that?"

"All this armour they've been buying lately," Girk said, as his claws traced tiny goblins on to the parchment tape. "Armour which our lads should've had and aren't getting. Put anybody off fighting, that would."

"That's just an unsubstantiated rumour put about by malicious and irresponsible troublemakers."

Girk nodded. "So it's true, then."

"Mphm."

"Well in that case—" Girk held the tape up to the light, scratched out a tiny mistake with his claw-tip and repainted. "This is quite a smart idea, really. Won't work, of course, but it's quite smart."

"Thank you so much."

"You're welcome."

The truth was (Mordak reflected later, over a rushed meal of troll spare ribs in the tunnels on the way to his next meeting) that there would be a war, no matter what he did, and that his goblins in home-produced armour, up against humans in dwarf-made kit, were in for a thrashing. They wouldn't mind that. Goblins, for all their many faults, are good losers; they have to be, since sooner or later the good guys always win, and they've never particularly resented defeat or agonised over their losses. Generally speaking, when they lose a war, they retire into their deep, dark underground lairs, which no enemy has ever penetrated (no enemy has ever wanted to), lick their wounds, regroup, execute their king and replace him with a new one, and set about gearing up for the next war. A simple and reliable approach which had always worked well; and yet, Mordak thought, one that could be improved on, particularly if you were the king. Unfortunately, until he found out where the humans were getting the money from, there wasn't a great deal he could do. His future, therefore, and that of his kingdom, rested in the bony paws of an Elf—

He emerged from the tunnels into the offices of the Goblin Arbitration & Conciliation Service, where he was due to preside over a tribunal hearing. It was called a hearing because, like most goblin judicial duels to the death, the participants and the judges were blindfolded, which was held to be fairer. Waiting for him in the main lobby was a female with pointed ears.

"I'm impressed," he said. "That was quick."

"Don't be," Tiniturel replied, "I haven't actually started yet."

"Oh," Mordak said. "Why the hell not?"

She sighed. "Well, I've had a preliminary glance at it, flicked through the back numbers of the *Face*, that sort of thing; and yes, you're quite right, several of the main human nations do appear to have come into money recently, and there's no obvious explanation for it."

"You mean, I was right."

"Well, yes."

"I knew that."

She shrugged. "Maybe you did, but naturally I had to check first. Anyway, there it is. And yes, a bunch of humans running around with money to burn is bad news for everybody. So something's got to be done about it."

"I *know*," Mordak said. "That's what I—" Pointless, he thought. Arguing with Elves is like arm-wrestling a circular saw. "So, what are you going to do?"

"Me? I'm just a lowly secretary. I do as I'm told."

"Let me rephrase that," Mordak said slowly and quietly. "If you had the misfortune to be me, what would you do now?"

She grinned at him. "Pack," she said. "Failing which, I'd send my best agents to find out where this money's coming from."

"Ah," Mordak said. "Silly me. I thought I'd already done that."

"Me? I'm just a lowly—"

"I'm promoting you."

"Sorry." Shake of the head. "I'm far too busy keeping the primordial soup you call a filing system in some vestige of order. You'll have to send someone else."

"Oh, will I?"

"Mphm. An Elf, naturally. Well, goblins are out of the question, and you can hardly expect humans to spy on other humans, and dwarves – well, quite. What you need," she said, "is a smart, resourceful Elf so desperately down on her luck she's prepared to work for you."

"I've got one."

"Another one. One you can spare. Fortunately," she went on, before Mordak could interrupt, "I've found you one. Smart kid, used to be a columnist on the *Face*."

Mordak grinned. "Ah."

"Indeed." Tiniturel gave him a cold look, which he relished. "But we haven't got time for a critique of goblin cultural vandalism. Her name's Efluviel, and she'll be in your office, half-nine sharp."

"What joy," Mordak said. "All right. But why don't you tell her what to do? You know as much about it as I do."

"More," Tiniturel said. "But I'm just a lowly secretary. You're late for your tribunal."

Which was true, as usual. As he hurried for the door, it occurred to Mordak, not for the first time, that he always ended up doing what she told him to because he never had time to remonstrate with her because he was always late for something, which might just possibly be something to do with the fact that she scheduled all his appointments.

The judicial duel turned out to be a bit of a washout. Both the prosecutor and the defendant, being duly blindfolded, spent half an hour groping about in the caverns, and never came within a hundred yards of each other. But the prosecutor blundered into a disused shaft, broke his leg and had to be hauled up on ropes, which was a bit of a laugh, and the defendant mistook the president of the tribunal for his enemy and speared him through the heart, whereupon the deputy president, instantly and automatically promoted to replace him, found in the defendant's favour on the principle that close enough is good enough. All's well that ends well, as they say in Goblinland.

"You're one of—"

"Yes. This way."

Apart from the obvious, Archie noted, she looked just like any human female; no trace of the exaggerated high cheekbones, vacant grey eyes or needle-sharp chin. He decided to chance his arm. "The spell," he said. "It doesn't work on ears."

She gave him a poisonous look, which suddenly dissipated into something approaching a smile. "Apparently not," she said.

"That must be awkward."

"You could say that." They were standing outside the door of the shed-on-wheels. "Fortuitously, in and around the movie business there are lots of weird people, some of whom wear prosthetic pointed ears as part of obscure tribal dressing-up rituals connected with religious movements called fandoms. My story is, I put the stupid things on with super-glue and they won't come off. Just so you know."

"Understood," Archie said gravely.

She put her hand on the doorhandle and turned it, but didn't open the door. "You know," she said, in a voice entirely devoid of expression, "you're quite sweet, for a goblin. In you go."

She swung the door open, shoved him through it and closed it again behind him, leaving him with no avenue of escape. Before he'd completely recovered his balance, a man's voice said, "Who the hell are you?"

"I'm Archie. Who are you?"

The speaker emerged from a sort of built-in closet, a tall, broad man wearing nothing but a towel wrapped around his head. He was dripping wet. "Sit down," he said.

Archie looked round for a seat. As he did so, he noticed something on the table so familiar that it stood out like a boil on a supermodel's chin. "Fix yourself a drink," the man said. "Pour me one, while you're at it."

Archie saw a bottle and a conventional human glass next to the familiar object. He uncorked the bottle and poured.

"Thanks." The man sat down opposite him. "Here's luck."

Archie took a drink from the glass. Then he said, "Where did you—?"

The man grinned. "Oh, it's not real," he said. "It's plastic. I had the props people make it for me. Said it'd look good in publicity shots, me in costume drinking beer from the jewelled skull of my enemy." He shrugged. "I know it's only a fake, and it makes the beer taste funny. I just wanted something from home. But there you go."

"From home."

"Yup." The big man emptied the drinking-skull and refilled it from the bottle; that strange human concoction known as *lemonade*. "You too, huh?"

"Me too," Archie said.

"Ah well." The big man raised the skull for a toast. "Here's to the old country," he said. "Call me Kurt, by the way."

"All right," Archie said. "And the Elf?"

Kurt shrugged. "We stick together over here," he said. "I think it may be something to do with that stupid skin-changing spell. I think nasty bits of human get into your head when it converts you."

"I noticed that," Archie said.

"Yes, well, it's a bugger. Anyway, whether it's that or something else, the Elf isn't so bad when you get to know her. I mean, I can talk to her for minutes at a time without wanting to break her neck."

"Just as well," Archie said. "They've got some bloody weird homicide laws over here."

"Quite. Still, as I tell the others, we're guests in this ludicrous excuse for a reality, we should do our best to abide by the local customs and superstitions. It's simple politeness, really."

Archie sipped some more lemonade, then said, "So, who are you? Really, I mean."

Kurt gave him a long, meaningful look. "A word to the wise," he said gently. "We don't ask each other that. The way we see it, what a person may or may not have got up to back home is nobody's business but their own. So, if it happened in the old country, it stays in the old country. Got that?"

"Point taken," Archie said. "Sorry."

Kurt waved his hand. "Forget about it," he said. "You weren't to know. Actually, for what it's worth, I was a sewage farmer in a remote cavern under the Beige Mountains, doing quite nicely for myself, not a care in the world, really. Then one day I met this guy in a tavern."

"Ah."

Kurt grinned. "You too, huh? What did he promise you? Excitement? Adventure?"

"A one-way trip to the Realms of Transcendent Bliss," Archie said sadly. "I think the spell may not have worked properly."

That made Kurt laugh. "Oh boy," he said. "You fell for that one. Still, I've heard dumber stories." He lowered his voice slightly. "The Elf thought she was coming here as the Otherworld correspondent of the *Face*. There's a human working on the chuck wagon, he got told he was being translated into a higher form of consciousness." Kurt grinned. "He showed up somewhere called Düsseldorf. He was not pleased." He shrugged. "They all end up here, sooner or later. It's the only place where we can last five minutes without making complete idiots of ourselves."

Archie was aware of an unpleasant feeling in the pit of his stomach, and it wasn't just the lemonade. "You make it sound like we're being—"

"Lured here?" Kurt's grin spread across his face like a desert sunrise. "It does look that way, doesn't it? Trouble is, none of us has the faintest idea who's doing it or why. Crazy," he added with a scowl. "Makes no sense. I mean, it's a hell of a lot of trouble to go to just to freak out a few poor gullible fools. There's got to be something behind it, but—" He spread his hands. "You tell me."

Archie leaned back in his seat and rested his head against the shed wall. "I thought it was just bad luck," he said.

"Me too, at first." Kurt upended the lemonade bottle over his drinking-skull and watched the last few drips fall. "Snorg, you silly sod, I said to myself, you've gone and buggered up the spell, it's your own stupid fault, no one to blame but yourself. I thought. At the time. But we can't all have got it wrong, can we? Well," he conceded, "goblins, maybe, goblins and magic don't mix. But the Elf? I don't think so. She's smart, that one."

"Yes, she is," Archie replied without thinking. "I mean, yes, they are. Bloody smartarses, the lot of them," he added dutifully, "though not bad on toast, with chutney. So," he went on, forcing his mind back on track with an effort, "you're sort of, what, the leader?"

Kurt laughed. "Not likely," he said. "You know, since I've been here, I've been thinking about the old country. Gives you a sense of perspective, if you know what I mean. And you know what, it beats me why anybody'd be stupid enough to want to be a king or anything like that. People moaning at you all the time, saying nasty things behind your back, and as soon as something goes wrong, next thing you know, some bugger's drinking cocoa out of your head. So no, I am not the leader, thank you ever so bloody much. But," he added, with a sort of a shrug, "for some reason I'm doing all right in this acting thing, so they give me lots of money, and there's nothing worth having in this shitheap reality to spend it on, so I do what I can for the rest of us. You know, see to it that everybody's okay. But that's not leadership," he added quickly, "that's just paying for things. Anybody calls me a leader to my face, I'll tear his throat out."

"Noted," Archie said. "Comrade," he added.

Kurt grinned. "That's more like it." He put his hands behind his head and yawned. "Anyway," he said. "Welcome to here, wherever the hell here is. Damn shame we can't go home again, but there it is."

Archie thought for a moment. "You're sure about that."

"What? Oh, going home. Yes, it does rather look like we're stuck here, I'm afraid. I asked, and magic doesn't work here. That's why they have movies, apparently. And if there's no magic, we can't cast the spell to take us home, even if we could do magic and the spell was a genuine one rather than a phoney we were suckered into using by the arsehole who wanted to bring us here for reasons that as yet remain obscure. Savvy?"

"Mphm."

"So in the meantime," Kurt went on, "all we can do is hang around – you pretending to be a goblin, me pretending to be a human, I don't know which is more ridiculous – until we finally find out what the arsehole wants, at which point we may or may not do it for him, he may or may not send us home when it's done, and we may or may not get to pull his liver out and eat it in front of his dying eyes. Everything's a bit up in the air, in fact, which isn't what we're used to but apparently it's how things are done here. People just drifting through their lives doing the best they can. Strikes me as a silly way to run a universe, but like I said, we're guests here, we do like they do. Any questions?"

Archie thought about it. "Nope."

"Good lad. Well, I'm going to go to sleep now, before I have to go out there and do more prancing about. You'd better leave, in case anybody wants you for anything."

"Sure," Archie said, getting up. "Oh, one thing. How many of us are there? Here, I mean."

"In New Zealand? I think about a thousand. Here on this film set, maybe three dozen."

"Got you. How do I know who's us and who's them?"

"Ah." Kurt nodded. "Sorry, should've said earlier. If you're one of us, you want to get yourself one of these little doodads, like this." He rolled up his sleeve to reveal a tattoo of a doughnut. "Only, the locals like to copy stuff, God only knows why but they do, so there's loads of them running around with those things on their arms, which is why you need to know the password."

"Password?"

"Yup. If someone comes up to you and says, 'Half a dwarf is better than no breakfast,' you say, 'I'd rather eat rats,' and then he says, 'Ah, but you can't always get 'em.' Then you know it's one of us. And the other way round, of course."

"Fine," Archie said. "Thanks."

"Not a problem. Oh, and if you need money for anything, just give me a shout. You can't imagine how much of the stuff they give me, and what the hell for? I don't know. This is a very strange place, till you get used to it."

Archie nodded. "Right," he said. "I'll let you get on."

"Cheers. One last thing."

Archie's hand was on the doorknob. "What?"

"I think the Elf fancies you. So long."

The wheel hummed.

The little man, whose left foot was sore from working the treadle, glanced down and saw to his relief that there was only a handful of straw left. He reached down for it and piled it on to the bobbin. The firelight gleamed off a six-foot-high wall of gold bales.

The things I do for other people, he thought.

Still. He ignored the pain in his foot, ankle and knee and worked the treadle a little faster, until finally the bobbin was empty and the last few strands of gold thread were curled around the spindle. The wheel came to a halt. He listened. Dead silence, apart from the hooting of a distant owl. Not to worry, he told himself. They'll come. They always do.

To occupy the time, he looped the gold thread into a skein, bundled it up and stuffed it into the last bale, which he tied firmly with twine and manhandled with terrible effort up on to the wall. Then he counted, and grinned. Something was moving about in the bushes. It could have been a deer or a warthog, but he doubted it. Deer and warthogs pay rather more attention to where they put their feet.

He whistled a tune. It was one he'd loved since he was a boy, though the locals around here probably wouldn't realise it was supposed to be music. In the bushes, a twig snapped.

Showtime.

His back hurt from crouching over the wheel; he was used to sitting all day, but in rather more ergonomically designed chairs. He winced and straightened up. Then, rather self-consciously, he began to dance.

He started with a half-hearted hop and skip, then made a brave effort at what is usually called "capering", though he wasn't sure he knew the rules. Hoppity-hoppity-hop, like someone who's trodden on a pin. Right, he thought after a dozen steps, that's quite enough of that. He cleared his throat and sang:

> Merrily the feast I'll make,
> Today I'll brew, tomorrow bake;
> Merrily I'll dance and sing,
> For next day will a stranger bring.
> Little does my lady dream
> That Rumpelstiltskin is my name.

As he sang the last line, he heard a terrific trumpeting noise in the bushes, which might have been an elephant but was more likely the sound of someone with serious pollen issues sneezing violently. He sighed. No way in hell could anyone have made out a complicated four-syllable name over that racket. So he repeated, "*Yes, Rumpelstiltskin is my name*" at the top of his voice. "With a t between the l and the s," he added. Probably at this point he was supposed to do fiendish cackling, but he really wasn't in the mood. He limped back to his stool, both hands pressed to the small of his back, and sat down carefully. Far away a fox barked.

Ten minutes or so later, he heard the unmistakable sound of a large man with big feet trying to creep stealthily through dense undergrowth. He smiled, and poured himself a cup of coffee from the magic silver flask by his feet. It was cold. Perhaps the magic wasn't working too well, or maybe some fool had dropped it.

"Well?"

Efluviel looked at him. She saw a smallish goblin with huge rose-red eyes and an almost human nose, moth-wing ears with little tufts of auburn hair growing out of them and tusks that were slightly splintered at the end, probably from crunching stale bones. His hands were on the small side too, for a goblin, and someone had made a valiant effort to manicure his claws. It was an odd feeling, finally meeting someone she'd written so much about. Her strongest impression was that he looked more comical than evil. "Pleased to meet you too," he said. "Do sit down. Oh come on," he added, as she hesitated. "I'm not going to eat you."

She frowned. "Goblin humour?"

"A light-hearted quip puts the nervous guest at her ease," Mordak replied. "It says so in my book." He held out the spine so she could see the title: *1,001 Ways To Be Liked If You're Horrible*. "It was free in a goody-bag I got given at an awards bash, so I can't ask for my money back."

Then she realised what the ghastly statuette thing on his desk was. She squinted, and read the inscription, gouged into the metal in the spiky alphabet of the Dark Script. "Most people keep them in their toilets," she said.

"Yes, well. I never won anything before. Besides, an insouciant show of disdain for something you've fought tooth and nail for is more your Elvish way of doing things. Goblins are—"

"Vulgar?"

"More straightforward. Which can seem a bit like vulgarity

at times, I grant you, but who gives a shit? Sit down, for crying out loud, before I get a crick in my neck gazing up at you."

Deciding that she'd lost that round, Efluviel sat down. "You sent for me."

"Got a job for you."

"Ah yes. I had a job once. Only some bastard took it away from me."

Mordak grinned. "So I did. And if you're really good and do what I want, I'll give it back to you. That's the deal, isn't it?"

"Apparently. Though I'm not sure I want to work for you, even if it means getting back on the *Face*."

He shrugged. "Understandable," he said. "Elves and goblins have been bitter enemies since the Seas were sundered. Nobody now remembers why, though my own theory is that it's because all Elves are arseholes. You're reluctant to work for a goblin. I have severe reservations about employing an Elf. However, with the entire future stability of the Realms at stake, I guess we'll have to sink our differences and work together. That's unless you want the humans taking over."

She repressed a shudder. "Hardly likely."

"A bloody sight likelier than you think. Listen." And he told her about the money, and the cancelled armour order. "So," he added. "What's your headline for that story?"

"Goblins thwarted in arms race bid?"

"Factually accurate," Mordak replied. "And that thing whizzing a mile over your head is the real point at issue. Make that, *Humans take lead in arms race* and think for a moment." He folded his arms and smiled at her. "Taking an overview of the last ten thousand years, what's the most significant trend in goblin military history?"

"You guys always lose?"

"Correct." His smile broadened. "Our record so far is

something like, played 26,091, lost 26,091, won 0. This," he went on, "in spite of the fact that we have the largest army and highest military budget per capita in the Realms. It's just the way things are, and that's fine."

"Unless you're the king," Efluviel pointed out tactfully.

"Unless, as you say, you're the king. But what the heck, that's the way the shin-bone crumbles. The point is, goblins taking a lead in the arms race is nothing for anyone to worry about. We've always led in the arms race, and it doesn't matter because sooner or later the race is to see who can get back down the tunnels first before the cavalry gets them. Agreed?"

Efluviel shrugged. "I've always wondered about that," she said. "Why are you people so mad keen on fighting when you're so bad at it?"

Mordak beamed at her. "Humans with superior military technology, on the other claw," he said, "is a whole different kettle of brains. Humans with superior military technology aren't going to stop with beating the crap out of us goblins. This may come as a shock to you, but humans don't really like you people very much. Can't imagine why, but there it is. They don't mind the dwarves so much, but the dwarves have got all those mines chock-full of yummy gold and iron and coal and stuff, and I've noticed how small nations with rich mineral resources have a bad habit of doing things that large well-armed nations who've used up all their minerals can never possibly forgive, such as saying *good morning*. Whichever way you dice it, it's not pretty."

Efluviel had a nasty feeling he was right; so, instinctively, she disagreed. "Rubbish," she said. "That's just goblin scare-mongering. The humans have been around for a long time, but they never achieve anything. They fall apart and start bickering among themselves."

Mordak gave her an Oh-come-on look she found hard to

meet. "Humans never do anything because they never have any money," he said, "because of the cockamamie way they run their economies. Suddenly, it appears, a load of tinpot little human princes have got gold to burn—"

"You can't burn gold, it's a metal."

"Gold to *melt*, and I want to know where it's coming from. Your mission, if you choose to accept it, is to find out the truth." He shrugged. "I know, you're a journalist, but the basic core skills are the same. Get out there, ask questions, poke your exquisitely-pointed needle nose into other people's business, it's what you're good at. Annoy them so much they tell you what you want just so you'll go away."

"I can do that, certainly," Efluviel said. "All right, but you've got to promise me, I'll get my job back on the *Face*."

Mordak looked at her for a moment. "Tell you what," he said. "If you do this for me and you succeed, I'll make you the editor."

For a moment she couldn't breathe. "You can do that?"

"Oh yes." Mordak took a clawful of sugar-coated finger-nails and popped them in his mouth. "Easy as anything. Bit of an incentive for you, I thought. I believe in motivating people."

"That's not how goblins usually go about it."

"True. But I've always taken the view that you can get more with a kind word and shameless bribery than with any number of fire-hardened pointed sticks. I guess that's why they call me unconventional. To my face, at any rate."

Her heart rate was gradually getting back to normal. "And of course it won't exactly be a disaster having an editor of the *Face* who owes you unthinking obedience and undying loyalty."

"There's that too, I guess."

She stood up. "And to think," she said, "I once called you a cunning, treacherous, manipulative, double-dealing control-freak."

Mordak grinned. "Why do you think I'm hiring you?" he said. "I love flattery."

Once upon a time, goes the old, old Elvish fairy-tale, there was a commodities broker who lived in a great city called Chicago. He was very rich and he had a great big house and many wonderful magical toys, but in spite of all that he was unhappy. One day—

At this point, the Elf-child interrupts. What's a commodities broker, Mummy?

Mummy replies that she doesn't actually know, because it's all make-believe and really there's no such thing as commodities brokers, but for the purposes of the story it's some kind of human merchant. Ah, says the Elf-child, and curls her little lip accordingly.

Anyway, Mummy goes on, one day the commodities broker, whose name was Albert (that's a funny name, Mummy. Yes, isn't it?) was sitting in his room at the top of his high tower when a strange little old man called to see him. What do you want, strange little old man? Albert said, or words to that effect. The little old man smiled. I gather you've taken a tumble on medium-term wheat futures, he said, and you stand to lose a packet. Albert pulled a sad face, because what the old man said was true. That's right, he said, and now I'm stuck with a billion tons of wheat I bought at 136, and if I'm really lucky I might be able to get rid of it on some dummy for 132. Life sucks, said Albert.

So it does, said the little man, and he made a sad face too, and what (says Mummy) are you sniggering about?

Albert said a rude word, says the Elf-child.

Yes he did, says Mummy, and that's because he was a stupid ignorant human who didn't know any better.

Meanwhile, the little man said, As well as all that wheat, I bet you're stuck with a whole lot of straw.

Straw? said Albert.

Straw, said the old man. It's kind of like a stalk thing that the wheat grows on. I never knew that, said Albert. Well, you wouldn't, said the old man, you're born and raised in the city. But I expect you'll find, if you ask, that along with the wheat you bought a whole lot of straw. Great, said Albert, is that supposed to make me feel better?

And the little man grinned at him, and said, Actually, yes, because if you'd like me to, I can turn all that straw into gold for you, using my handy-dandy magic spinning-wheel, and did you happen to notice the gold price lately, it's so high they can read it quite clearly on Mars.

And Albert looked at him and said, Get out of here, and the old man stood up and Albert explained that it was just an old commodity traders' expression. Can you really do that? Albert asked, and the little man nodded and said, Yes, I can. I can spin all your useless straw into pure gold, and all you have to give me is your first-born child.

And Albert looked at him again and said, hey, I haven't got any kids. And the little man shrugged and said, So what, you deal in futures, don't you? And Albert said, Fair enough, since you put it like that. And the old man reached in his pocket and said, it just so happens I have a watertight duly notarised contract right here, and all you have to do is sign and leave the rest to me.

So Albert signed, and the little old man thanked him and went away, and Albert called through to the front office and told them, on pain of death, not to let any more crazy people in to see him, because he had better things to do. And he forgot all about the little old man until a week later, when the little old man sent him an email, no, I don't know what an email is, probably some sort of trained pigeon, telling him he now owned a million metric tonnes of gold, copy inventory and duly notarised bill of lading herewith, and how was he getting on, had he met any nice girls lately?

So Albert made enquiries, and sure enough, the million tonnes of gold was real enough and sitting in a warehouse in a place called Zurich waiting for him to come and take it away. So Albert sold the gold for a great deal of money, and for about a quarter of an hour he was very happy indeed.

But then he remembered the contract he'd signed, promising to give the little old man his first-born child, and that made him very unhappy indeed, because he'd recently found out a really foolproof way of avoiding tax by putting money in your kids' names. And while he was sitting there fretting about it, who should turn up but the little old man?

Hi, said the little old man.

Hi, said Albert. You do realise, no court in the world is going to honour that contract.

But the little old man smiled and said, You really ought to read things carefully before you sign them. Because if you had, you'd have noticed that there's a clause stating that the contract takes effect under Fairyland law, and in Fairyland that sort of thing is entirely legal. And you may think you can hire lawyers to get you out of this, but while you have a lot of money, I have a magic spinning-wheel, so think on, fool.

Then Albert got very frightened and begged the old man to change his mind. But the old man said, You have only two options. One, you've got to guess my name. Or two, you can buy me off with ten times what you got for the gold I spun you.

Then Albert was very sad for a long time, until eventually he was talking to a clever young lady in a bar somewhere, and he told her all about the little old man and the gold, and she said, let me think about it and I'll get back to you. So she went away, and three days later she came back and said, I think I've found a way you can raise the money to buy off the little old man, but I have to warn you, it's a bit of a grey area ethically and it may make you rather unpopular. I don't mind that, Albert said, I'm a commodities broker. So the clever woman told him all about a cunning scheme she'd thought up, whereby you bundled up a load of worthless sub-prime mortgages and other toxic assets into bonds and sold them to idiots who didn't know what they were buying. And Albert said, Yes, I can see that might work, but isn't there a risk that we could trash the entire economy of the industrialised world and bring about the worst recession since the Fall of Rome, and the clever woman shrugged and said something about omelettes and eggs.

So they did that, and when the little old man came to visit him again, Albert was able to write him a cheque for the full value of the gold, in return for which the little old man handed him the contract, along with two other things and a few words of very good advice. And Albert asked the clever woman to marry him but she just laughed, and everybody lived very miserably for a very long time afterwards.

Mummy stops talking, and the Elf-child looks at her and says, That's not a true story, is it?

And Mummy says, Don't be silly, dear. Not even humans could be that stupid.

The days passed, and nothing much seemed to happen. One day he'd be told to dress up as a goblin and stand snarling. The next day, he'd be waving his shield and making grunting noises. The day after that, they'd do the snarling all over again, but from a slightly different angle. From time to time he caught sight of Kurt in the distance, but he didn't wave or anything like that. The Elf's name, he found out, was Shawna, but he didn't see anything of her either. The assistant director kept trying to talk to him, which was a pest, until he happened to be passing a dumpster one day and saw that it was full of what looked like bones. They turned out to be plastic, which was a disappointment, but he appropriated one which looked from a distance exactly like a human tibia. The next time the assistant director headed towards him he pulled it out from under his costume and started gnawing at it with a happy look on his face. That solved that problem.

Then everything was packed away in big wooden crates, as if it had never been, and they all had to crowd on to a bus and sit still for nine hours, until they arrived at a spot that looked to Archie to be identical to the one they'd just left. Everything was unpacked from the crates and set up, and the next day, Archie found himself snarling and waving his shield from yet another angle, but with the mountains to his left instead of his right.

On the fifth day after their arrival at the new location, the assistant director mustered his imitation-goblin troops and told them they wouldn't be needed for a bit and they could have a day off. Before the echo of his words had died away, the army had scrambled aboard the bus, which lurched dangerously off down the local excuse for a road. Archie asked where they were going. The man he asked just shrugged.

Seven hours later, they arrived. The town didn't seem to have a name. There were five wooden shacks, with pine-shingle roofs, standing beside the dusty ribbon of the road. One of the shacks was their immediate destination. It had the words HOTEL & BAR over the door in flaking paint, which sort of explained things.

After a brief consultation, a duly delegated officer approached the bar, where a small, round woman was dusting a bowl of peanuts. "Two beers," he said, "and thirty-seven lemonades."

The woman looked at him. "Say again."

"Two beers. Thirty-seven lemonades. Please."

The woman nodded and went away. Archie thought about the order for a while, then went up to the duly delegated officer. "Who ordered the beers?" he said.

"Those two." He jerked his head toward the corner without looking round.

"Humans?"

"Mphm. Not locals, though, so that's all right."

Archie went and sat down, as far away from the others as he could get. That explains that, then, he thought.

As it happened, he'd tried the this-reality beer once; just a mouthful, so he didn't have to be rushed to hospital to have his stomach pumped out. Kurt, he recalled, had drunk lemonade in his trailer. The two humans, if he'd understood correctly, weren't from this universe either, but apparently they could stomach the stuff. Great, he thought. All the extras on this film are Oursiders.

Kurt hadn't mentioned that, and he wondered if he even knew. He studied the others over the rim of his lemonade glass as closely as he could without being too obvious. It was hard to tell, since mostly he only saw his colleagues when they had the make-up and prosthetics on, but he was fairly sure that he didn't recognise most of them, so presumably they hadn't been at the other location, or were new recruits. Thirty-seven of us, he thought. That's a lot of goblins. Thirty-eight including Kurt. Plus two humans, and not forgetting the Elf.

Now let's suppose, he thought, trying not to let the fizz go up his nose, that someone's been to all the trouble of importing goblins and Elves and even humans from back home to this reality. Why would anyone do that? The obvious reason would be to exploit them as cheap labour; he thought about Kurt, the noughts on whose salary cheque resembled nothing so much as the string of bubbles left behind by a diving otter, and decided, no, it probably isn't that. A lot of them had ended up here in the film business, but he had no reason to suppose that there weren't pockets of them somewhere else as well, in some other industry where weird people who come and go on a casual basis aren't noticed particularly much. The word 'infiltration' drifted into his mind and stuck there, like a fly in a cobweb.

"What're you having?"

He looked up. The duly appointed delegate was looking down at him. "Another lemonade, please."

"Fine. It's your shout, by the way."

On the long ride back to the set, he thought, so let's suppose someone's infiltrating this reality with goblins. Why would anyone do that? If the idea is to use us as an army (and let's face it, what else are we good for?) you'd have thought he might have seen fit to mention it, rather than simply turning us loose. Also, now we're here we aren't actually goblins any more, physically we're human, so goblin strength, endurance, redundant systems and big sharp teeth aren't what he's after. In which case, what's so special about us that makes it worth his while going to all this bother, rather than just hiring the local thugs?

Over the next few days he tried sounding out his fellow goblins, in case they knew anything. Either they stared at him as though he were mad, or else they just shrugged and walked away. He found this hard to account for, since goblins are naturally sociable, liking nothing better than to gather in groups of five or six, sharing a beer and a joke before eating the smallest goblin present. But he shrugged it off as a side-effect of the shape-shifting, and noted that he'd been quite happy to spend most of his time on his own since he'd got here. As for the grand conspiracy, he still believed in it, sort of; but since as far as he was aware nothing was actually happening, he couldn't see any point in worrying himself sick about it. Then, in a eureka moment that smacked him between the eyes like a slingshot as he stood in line for the only chemical toilet on the set, the answer came to him. Yes, there was (or had been) a nefarious plan. Yes, there was or had been a sinister mastermind who'd lured them all here for a purpose. But, before the sinister mastermind could set the nefarious plan in motion, something had happened – he'd been arrested, killed by a passing hero, trampled by stampeding elephants, or maybe he'd just changed his mind, or the backers had pulled out – and the whole venture had been quietly cancelled, and that was that. Tough luck on the purpose-imported goblins, of course, but that's how it goes. And, since magic didn't work here, there was no way to send them back, even if anyone else knew about them and wanted to, so there they all were, left to fend for themselves in a strange and not particularly hostile environment. A bummer, to be sure; still, when you're cast ashore on a desert island, you can either starve to death brooding on your sad fate, or you can devote your energies to coming up with 1,001 delicious new ways with coconuts. In the final analysis, it's a lifestyle choice.

After a very long day doing nothing in full makeup under an unseasonably hot Horrible Yellow Face, he was trudging off the set when he heard someone call out his name. He turned to see Kurt's Elf hurrying toward him, with a large buff envelope in her hand. She slowed down, caught her breath, smiled and said, "Hi."

Once upon a time he'd had proper bristles on the back of his neck, not just the soft rabbit-fur fluff that grew there now. Nature had put them there for a very good reason, and at times like this he missed them sorely. His skin twitched, but it wasn't the same. "Hello," he said.

Her smile faded. "Don't look at me like that, it's nothing nasty. Kurt would like to see you, that's all."

"Why?"

"I don't know, do I? Maybe he wants to buy you a yacht. Or maybe he's sick of corned beef."

Only an Elf could've said that. A goblin who's tired of corned beef is tired of life. "You sure he meant me?"

"That gormless idiot Archie, to quote his exact words."

True, the cap fitted. "Now?"

"Oh for crying out loud. Why are you so suspicious all the damn time?"

"Why would he want to buy me a yacht? All goblins hate water."

The obvious comment, he noted, went unmade, which was so not like an Elf. "Come on," she said. "He's waiting."

"Yes, but—"

"*Now.*"

Kurt wasn't in his trailer; he was sitting outside it in a deck-chair, with white goo all over his face and slices of cucumber on his eyes. "My God, he's dead."

"No he isn't," the Elf said. "It's to make him look beautiful."

With cream cheese and salad? "Thanks, I already ate."

"You." Kurt was frowning under the goo. "Go away. No, not you. Her." He sat up a little. A circle of cucumber slipped, and he pawed it back into place with his knuckles. "Archie?"

"You sent for me."

"Sit down. They make me do this muck," he explained sadly, "it's in my contract." He lowered his voice. "You remember the Chasm of Pirith Undrod back home?"

Archie shuddered as he nodded. "Where the nameless watcher lurks."

"And eats the souls of the unwary, yes. Kids' stuff. Compared to a Hollywood lawyer, the nameless watcher's a total pussycat. A while back, I think it was just before you got here, they caught me eating a chocolate bar. You can't do that, they said; watch me, I said, so they flew in a lawyer from LA. Ten minutes I was in there with him, and when I came out I was shaking like a leaf. Haven't even looked at chocolate since." He yawned, reached for a glass of lemonade and glugged it down, leaving a white creamy semicircle on the rim. "After this it's four hours in the gym. I told them, it's pointless, I'm already so strong I could tow a truck uphill with the tow-rope round my little finger. Yes, they said, but you don't *look* strong." He sighed. "Next Tuesday they pull out all my teeth."

"My God. What did you do wrong?"

"Nothing. It's in the contract. They pull them out and put in plastic ones. Shinier."

Archie felt a cold chill run down his spine. A goblin's teeth are his soul. "You wanted to see me," he prompted.

"What? Oh, yes. Listen, I hear you've been going round asking a lot of weird questions."

Two seconds passed before Archie replied. "And if I have?"

"If you get any answers, tell me. But you won't. I've tried, God knows." He hesitated, just for a moment. "You haven't got anything, have you?"

"No."

"Thought not. It's because there's nothing to find out. Nobody knows anything. Which is dumb."

Archie outlined his theory about the cancelled plot. Kurt thought about it for a long time, then shrugged. "You know," he said, "you may be right. That'd account for it, sure. I'll give it some thought, let you know what I think. Meanwhile," he added, with a faint grin, "how are you getting on with the Elf? Any good?"

"You *what*?"

"Oh come on," Kurt replied. "She's crazy about you. Can't stop talking about you. Well, she's mentioned you twice. You should get in there quick, before she changes her mind."

"Excuse me," Archie said, "maybe we've got our wires crossed. Are we talking about non-parthenogenetic reproduction here?"

"Sure. Listen," Kurt went on, lowering his voice a little. "This isn't home, right? And we're not really goblins any more, we're humans. And humans – well, they dig that stuff. They reckon it makes the world go round."

"No they don't. They say it's the gravitational pull of the Horrible Yellow Face, acting on the—"

"We're humans," he repeated firmly, "to all intents and purposes, and you know what that means? They won't let us fight, we can't eat anybody, and because of the no-fighting thing we're probably going to live for *years*. Think about it. Years and years and years with no fun whatsoever." He breathed in deeply, then out again. "Not goblin fun, anyhow. So, I thought, why not give human fun a go?"

Archie nearly retched. "Kurt, that's *gross*."

"You say that." He had the grace to look defensive. "What I say is, these are human bodies, designed to be receptive to human pleasures. They have this saying here, when in Rome—"

"Kurt." Archie took a long step back. "You're not trying to tell me you've actually done this—"

"Non-parthenogenetic reproduction?" Kurt hesitated. "Well, no. Not yet. Which," he added, "is giving rise to a great deal of comment around here, let me tell you. Apparently a guy in my position, a big movie star, if he doesn't, that's—" He waved his arms vaguely. "They're saying things about me behind my back, I don't like it. So—"

He paused, and gave Archie what was clearly meant to be a my-best-friend-in-all-the-world look. "So you want me," Archie said, slowly and precisely, "to *research*—"

"Exactly. Got it in one. Find out, you know, what it's like. What you do. If it hurts."

"Absolutely not. No way."

"Archie—"

"We're *goblins*," Archie shouted, and a few heads turned beside the chuck wagon. "We have *tanks* for that sort of thing. We have *goo*. I don't know what's got in to you since you've been here, but—"

"Keep your voice down, for crying out loud," Kurt thundered. "Look," he went on, lowering the volume and sweetening it into syrup, "I'm not saying go *that* far, not at first, anyhow. There's this whole love rigmarole before you start getting non-parthenogenetic. The humans are nuts about the love thing. Try that, report back to me, we'll take it from there. Okay?"

Archie gave him a long look. "Have I got to?"

"Yes. Oh come on, cheer up," Kurt added, with a sudden grin. "You never know, you might even like it."

To that there could be no reply that wouldn't end up in bloodshed. Archie swallowed the lump that had formed in his throat, and nodded once. Then he said quickly, "But not the Elf, all right?"

"Why not?"

"She's an *Elf*. The ears. The attitude. Everything."

"But she likes you. And let's face it, even in an infinite multiverse—"

"Not the Elf."

"Her favourite colour," Kurt said, "is blue. Also, she likes sunsets, the smell of rain on the grass, and something called Leonard Cohen, which I gather is some sort of musical entertainment. You see? I've done all the hard work for you."

A wounded spaniel, looking at Archie at that moment, would've thought it was seeing itself in a mirror. "One question," he said. "Why me?"

"You're my friend. I like you."

"Bloody funny way of showing it."

"I like you," Kurt repeated, "but not nearly as much as I like the others. So, you're it. Sorry. Now, quit moaning and get on with it, before I have you fired from the movie and dumped beside the road somewhere two hundred miles from the nearest sandwich."

Reasoning like that Archie could relate to. "When in Rome, eh?"

"When in Rome, Archie. You're a good man."

Archie stood up slowly, leaned forward, picked one of the slices of cucumber off Kurt's face and ate it. "You owe me."

"Not yet," Kurt said. "But I will. Want the other slice?"

"No thanks. I don't like cucumber."

He turned and walked away, thinking, what kind of sentient creature actually likes smelly rain? He was all set to find out, apparently. Something occurred to him, and he turned back. Kurt was just settling a new slice over his left eye. "You again."

"Yes," said Archie. "You said, when in Rome, right?"

"I did, yes."

"You don't happen to know the rest of that one, do you?"

Kurt smiled. "As it happens, I do. It goes, when in Rome, be very careful how you cross the road." He leaned back, his hands behind his head. "Sage advice, Archie boy. Look after yourself, you hear?"

Meanwhile, in the topmost turret of the highest tower of the appalling castle of Vorgul, the mind of the Dark Lord brooded on strategy.

He had no body, no physical presence. A thousand years ago, the Last League of Elves, dwarves, centaurs, men and talking furry animals had broken his armies, thrown down his battlements and cornered him here, in the very furnace of his power. Terrible, that final battle; ten days and ten nights they strove, the princes of the West united against him alone. Finally, when the issue hung in the balance and the narrow spiral staircase leading to the Black Chamber was strewn with the broken corpses of dead chipmunks, Flinduil the Elven-Prince—

But the Dark Lord saw no need to dwell on that. It had all been monstrously unfair, in his opinion, a grossly excessive overreaction to what he still saw as a technical breach of the planning regulations (he'd neglected to file a Form EBB677/3/A2 before laying the groundworks for the Tower of Fangs), but he'd long ago conceded that the Elves had been right, on a strict interpretation of the letter of the law, and Flinduil, as hereditary Chief Planning Officer of the Blessed

Realm, had had no option but to take enforcement action. It was a shame that the dispute had cost an estimated three million lives but, as Flinduil had remarked at the time, rules is rules.

Instead, the Dark Lord preferred to learn from his mistakes and move on. And his plans were already well advanced, further than the fools could possibly know. Already, King Mordak's goblin armies were massing in the caverns of Unfoth, day and night his trolls in the forges under the Elyhn Druil were churning out weapons and armour, and only yesterday three of his most trusted servants had ridden in furious haste from the Doom Gate, bearing a properly completed and countersigned Form EBB677/3/A2, in triplicate, for filing at the Central Registry at Pom Astaroth. Meanwhile, his spies told him, his enemies were hopelessly unprepared; divided among themselves, endlessly bickering over trivial disputes, hardly bothering these days to look to the East or keep up the watch on the dismal frontier of Arys Mog. Victory, according to every projection and risk assessment his people had prepared for him, was assured . . .

Indeed. Winning is one thing, however, and staying won is another. To that end—

A small piece of paper and a stub of pencil levitated off the floor of the empty chamber. The paper stuck fast in mid-air, as though glued to an invisible wall. The pencil quivered, then began to write.

> You'd better watch out
> You'd better not cry
> You'd better not—

The pencil paused, and the shapeless, formless force of pure gravity that the Dark Lord now mostly consisted of seemed to ponder for a while. *Lout, gout, snout—*

Hearts and minds, that was the thing. Conquering the free people of the West wouldn't be a problem; like a stone through a wet paper bag, King Mordak had assured him, and though Mordak had said exactly the same thing the last time, and the time before that, the Dark Lord was nevertheless quietly confident. Keeping them firmly pressed down under his iron absence-of-heel, on the other hand, would take more than the cruel blades of goblin spears. For a thousand years he'd studied his enemies, all his mental power bent on knowing their innermost hopes, fears, dreams and nightmares. He'd enquired endlessly into their moral, ethical and political systems, perused every detail of their history, learned all their quaintly irregular languages, read the books they loved, sat through their insufferable tinkly music, grappled with the most abstruse concepts of their philosophies; and his conclusion was that it was impossible to enslave them against their will. But, if they wanted to be enslaved (only be careful to call it *politics*), no force in the Realms, the Abyss below or the Vaults above could stop them. Hence the song.

Rout, knout, about, without, *shout*. Got it.

He was quite pleased with the tune, which was just the sort of inane jingle that men and dwarves couldn't help humming along with; Elvish music was different, of course, but if he could reach a rapprochement with the other three races and the Elves alone held out and had to be ruthlessly exterminated— Ah well, omelettes and eggs, omelettes and eggs. The pencil quivered again, and wrote down the next two lines.

The Dark Lord hesitated; iron-shod boots crunching on the stone stairs. A faint ripple of air, roughly equivalent to a sigh, fluttered the dust-clogged cobwebs that dangled from the ceiling. *Mordak*, he thought, *is that you?*

"Yes, Boss."

Panting slightly, the king of the goblins hauled himself up the last few steps and leaned against the doorframe to catch his breath. "Sorry to bother you, Boss. You weren't busy, were you?"

The cobwebs twitched again. *No, not really. Hang on, though. Your opinion, please.*

"What, me? Sure. Fire away."

Mordak heard him, he knew, as a deep voice reverberating in the very depths of his consciousness. Considerately, therefore, he kept the volume down.

He sang the song all the way through three times, then paused to allow the echoes to die away inside Mordak's head. Then he said, *I'm thinking of calling it, "Vordagog Is Coming to Town".*

"Who's Vordagog?"

I am, you halfwit.

"What? Oh, right. You know, I never knew that. It's always been the Dark Lord or Guess-Who or just, you know, Him; or Boss or My Lord to your, um – when I'm talking to you, I mean. You think you know someone, and then you find out something like that. Vordagog. That's a nice name."

What do you think about the tune?

"Oh, I like it. Catchy. Tumpty-tumpty-tumpty, tum-*tum*."

And the words?

Mordak paused for thought. "Probably factually accurate," he said.

Do you like them?

"They're striking," Mordak said. "Definitely that."

Striking.

"Well," the goblin said, "it all depends on what you're trying to achieve, doesn't it? I mean, if the idea is to pierce their hearts with terror and despair so that they're bowed down by the inevitability of doom, then yes, I'd say you're bang on target."

But not cheerful.

"Not really."

Or friendly.

"No."

The Dark Lord brushed away the brief flurry of irritation. *All right, how about this bit?*

"Definitely," Mordak said. "Like, you point out that you're spying on them when they're sleeping, and when they're awake, which is pretty damn chilling if you ask me, you're compiling this hit list of everyone who's ever done anything wrong, you've been over it twice so there's no chance of anybody slipping through the net, you know the truth about who's been good and who's a sinner so there's no point even trying to argue the toss, and you're on your way right now, and when you get there – well, obviously it's not going to be pretty, is it? Bloody hell, Boss. It gives me shivers down my spine just thinking about it."

Oh.

"I mean, no offence."

None taken, thought the Dark Lord sadly. *I value your honesty.*

"Do you? Stone me. Well, always glad to help. And it's a cracking tune. You know, I never realised you were musical."

Now you mention it, neither did I. Anyway. Was there something?

"Well, actually, yes." There was a slight nervous tinge to Mordak's voice. "I'm sure it's perfectly all right and nothing to worry about, but I thought I'd probably better mention it, you know how you always say—"

Mordak.

"What? Yes, right, sorry. We've had reports, you see. Well, when I say reports—"

Mordak, you're drivelling. What's the matter?

It takes a lot to make a goblin drivel. "Well," said Mordak, "it's hard to put your claw on it exactly, but you know, straws in the wind, that sort of thing. The humans are buying armour from the dwarves."

Very sensible of them.

"Ah."

But you've put a stop to it, naturally. You've stepped in and outbid them, and the greedy dwarves, blind to their own best interests—

"No, actually. More the other way round."

Say what?

"The humans," Mordak mumbled, "outbid me. I went as high as I could, offered them top dollar, but the humans, um, had more money. So—"

Mordak felt his synapses grind together; the Dark Lord, frowning inside his head. *That's not possible. The humans haven't got any money.*

"They have now."

A surge of anger welled up in Mordak's head, pressing so hard that he could feel his eyeballs being slowly forced out from the inside. "But it's all right," he said. "I'm right on top of it."

Really.

"You bet. I've got a special agent on the case, making enquiries."

Have you indeed?

"Yes, and as soon as she's found out who's behind it, I'll be down on them like a ton of—"

She?

Mordak opened his mouth, then closed it again. It was hard to think straight when at any moment your eyes were liable to shoot out of their sockets and bounce back at you off the wall, but he realised he'd probably made a tactical error. "Um, yes. My agent is indeed female, but that's all right, you know what she-Elves are like, poking their noses in other people's bus—"

You have entrusted this vital mission to an Elf?

Mordak would've closed his eyes at this point, except he

couldn't see any point in adding tattered eyelids to the list of his forthcoming problems. "Well, yes," he said. "Like I said, when it comes to snooping around and finding stuff out, Elves are the business."

It didn't occur to you that there might be a potential conflict of interests?

Mordak explained about the editorship of the *Face*, and immediately the pressure on his retinas slackened off a little. "She'd do anything for that job," he went on, "even if it does mean selling the free peoples of the Realms down Shit Creek in a leaky canoe. Absolutely nothing to worry about on that score."

The Dark Lord's sigh made Mordak's eardrums creak in agony. *Maybe not. But I don't want this Elf prowling around unsupervised. Send someone with her. Someone we can trust.*

It was so nice now that the pain had dropped off a bit; shame to jeopardise all that just for the sake of clarity. But Mordak said, "Such as?"

Well, a goblin, naturally. One of your best.

"Um," said Mordak. "I'm not sure I've got any best, to be honest with you. Quite a few could-be-worses, but—"

Then you'll have to go, won't you?

9

The sound of his sneeze seemed to fill the valley. In the forest behind him, flights of startled birds burst from the thick canopy of leaves and rose like smoke. The mountains caught the echo and tossed it from hillside to hillside.

Gesundheit, the little man thought.

For someone with chronic pollen issues, spinning straw into gold is an unfortunate choice of occupation. The wheat straw was bad enough, but the barley – what kind of cheapskate, he asked himself, sends barley straw to be spun into gold? – was full of fine abrasive dust that got into his nose and made the base of his nostrils and his upper lip unendurably itchy. He dabbed at his eyes with his sleeve, sniffed ferociously, and carried on pedalling.

A crunching noise among the brambles to his left made him smile. Thirty seconds or so later, a young man emerged backwards from the thicket, tugging his long ermine-trimmed sleeves free of the thorns. Any minute now, he thought, he'll trip over his feet and—

"Ouch," said the young man, or words to that effect.

"Mind the brambles," the little man replied, not looking up from his work. "You can get a bit tangled if you're not careful."

A ripping noise suggested that the young man had found an effective, if not particularly cheap way out of his difficulties. "Is it ready?"

The little man jerked his head toward the stack of gold bales on the other side of the clearing. "All done."

"Oh boy." The young man was staring. "Will you look at that!"

"It's all right, I suppose, if you like gold." The little man stopped the wheel and turned round. "You're going to have ever so much fun getting a cart up here," he said. "You might do better to have it carried down the hill to the river and floated downstream on rafts."

"Whatever." The young man was counting under his breath. The little man could almost hear the creaking as he did the mental arithmetic.

"That's the lot, is it?"

"Excuse me?"

"You haven't got any more straw you want spun? No extra charge."

A sore point. Lately, the price of straw had rocketed. Worth its weight in gold, the dealers were saying. "No, that's all. We had a bad harvest this year. Not that it matters now."

"Quite," said the little man with distaste. "Except for the village people, who can't afford bread. But hey."

"Oh, that's all right," the young man said cheerfully. "With this lot I can start recruiting an army. I'll be needing every able-bodied man I can get."

For one fleeting moment, the little man was tempted to explain; supply and demand, inflation, Gresham's Law. But the prince wouldn't understand, so why bother? "Indeed," he said. "Well, pleasure doing business with you. Remember me when Old Mister Stork comes to call, won't you?"

"Ah." A big, cunning grin spread over the prince's face. "I wanted to talk to you about that."

"Really? Found Miss Right, have we? Wedding bells all set to ring out?"

"No." The grin was threatening to spread past the prince's ears and out round the back of his neck. "You said, the whole first-born child thing would all be off if I guessed your name. Yes?"

"Perfectly true."

"Well," the prince said triumphantly, taking a scrap of parchment from the purse at his belt. "I think it's time I called your bluff, Mister Rumblestitsky."

The little man sighed. "Give it here," he said, and held his hand out for the parchment. "God, who wrote this, a doctor? Look, that's a P not a B. And that's an L, and that's not a Y, it's an IN. Now," he added, handing the parchment back. "Would you care to rephrase that?"

The prince blinked at him. "Rumpleslitsni?"

The little man closed his eyes and massaged his temples with his fingertips. "What the hell?" he said. "Close enough is good enough. Curses," he added, in a weary voice, "you have guessed my secret name. Clever old you."

Pause. "Does that mean I get to keep the gold?"

"Yup."

"And no, you know, heirs or heiresses change hands?"

"The slate," the little man said solemnly, "is wiped clean. You got me, fair and square. Boy, didn't you ever screw me to the floorboards. Ah well. No hard feelings."

"Cool." The prince smiled. "So, it's all mine."

"Absolutely."

"I don't think I've ever seen that much gold before."

"Few people have. You know, I think that may have some bearing on its rarity value."

The prince sat down on a log. His eyes were shining. "I'm going straight home," he said, "and I'm going to raise a mighty army, and then I'm going to drive the Northrons into the sea."

"And why not? The seaside's nice at this time of year."

"And after that we'll deal with the goblins once and for all. And the dwarves."

The little man cleared his throat. "Just a suggestion," he said. "But since you've got so much gold now, mightn't it be a good idea if you spent *some* of it on a mighty army and *some* of it on other stuff."

"Other stuff?" The prince looked puzzled. "What, you mean expensive clothes and pedigree falcons and silk rugs for the horses?" He thought for a moment. "No, I don't think so. Not till we've wiped the goblins off the face of the earth."

"Actually," said the little man, "I was thinking, maybe you could build some roads. Repair all those bridges that are about to fall down. Maybe establish a cloth-weaving industry. Just thinking aloud, of course."

"Roads." The prince tasted the idea as if it were wine. The look on his face suggested it was corked. "No, we're fine for roads. We've got a perfectly good road that leads straight to the Northron border. Just right for soldiers to march on."

"You see," the little man went on, "if you've got roads, and bridges you feel like crossing even if you can't swim, and a really thriving cloth industry, then maybe people will come *down* the roads and *across* the bridges to buy your excellent cloth. And with taxes and customs duty and tolls and stuff, you'll have lots of money all the time, even after you've spent this lot."

The prince looked at him. "Don't be silly," he said. "Anyhow, I can't sit here all night chatting, I've got a draft to organise. Good idea of yours about the barges, by the way. I'll send some people."

"Another good thing about roads and bridges," the littler man went on, "is that you pay people to build them, so they've got money to spend, so they go away and buy stuff from other people, and then they've got money too. And so on. And then you don't have all those poor people hanging about, making the place look untidy."

"That won't be a problem when I've enlisted them all for my army, now will it?" The prince smiled patronisingly. "War is good for the country. That's what my father used to say. You see, it's not just soldiers, it's all the people who sell food and uniforms and spears and things. Universal prosperity, in fact."

The little man nodded slightly to concede the point. "Except there's nobody left at home to grow the food or make the stuff, so you end up having to buy it from somebody else at extortionate prices. But what the heck! I can spin some gold for them too, and then they'll go to war, and then your people can sell them food and weapons."

"Exactly."

"Assuming any of them survive the war. But yes, it's one way of doing it, I suppose. Better than the way you used to run things, at any rate."

"Quite. Got to let those goblins know who's boss, haven't we?"

"And if you win the war, I imagine you'll pay yourself a whopping great big bonus. Or even if you lose."

The prince scowled. "Certainly not," he said. "I'm just doing my job. I wouldn't have earned it."

Ah well, the little man thought, as the prince strode happily away, they may be idiots, but they're not as dumb as some I could name. And the military-industrial complex worked for Roosevelt, sort of, so maybe it'll be all right. Then a stray atom of pollen drifted up his nose, and he nearly sneezed a hole in the space/time continuum.

Archie closed his eyes and forced himself to speak. "I'd like a flower, please."

"Sure. Plain or self-raising?"

Bloody silly question. "Self-raising, of course. I've got better things to do with my time. Right," he went on, "chocolate."

Apparently there were all sorts of different varieties. He chose one at random, which happened to be the cheapest, so he bought six bars. Then he caught the bus to the crossroads, and walked the seven miles back to the film set. There he changed into the plain grey suit he'd borrowed from one of the cameramen, sneaked into the stores for the finishing touch, polished his shoes with axle grease till they practically glowed, and set off for the trailer the Elf shared with one of the continuity girls. He knocked on the door and waited.

"Oh," said the Elf. "It's you."

Here goes nothing, he said to himself. "I got you these." He handed her the plastic carrier bag. "Um, would you like to—?"

She peered into the bag. "Did you want me to bake you a cake?" she said. "Only if you do, we'll need some eggs."

"Cake?"

"A pound of self-raising flour and six bars of cooking chocolate. I'm quite clever, you know, I can draw inferences. Why are you dressed like that?"

"I, um, wanted to look nice."

"Really. What's that plastic thing round your neck for?"

"It's a tie."

"It's a cable tie. Hold on, though." She looked at him as though he were a thousandth of a millimetre wide and lying on a glass slide. "Are you asking me *out*?"

"Well, yes. Sort of."

"Sort of. It's not exactly a grey area."

"Yes. I'm asking you out. All right?"

"Hold on," she said. "I'll get my coat."

There are few things as disconcerting as unanticipated success. "Are you sure?"

"Yes, it might rain. Won't be a second."

He realised he was still holding the carrier bag. "Don't you want your—?" he called after her, but the question seemed fairly superfluous. He put the bag on the ground and nudged it under the trailer with his foot.

She must be a very untidy person, he thought, it's taking her a long time to find her coat. When eventually she reappeared, she'd done something to her face. In spite of himself, he was impressed. He never knew Elves did that. "Right," she said. "Where shall we go?"

He thought for a moment. "Well," he said, "round the back of the equipment store, there's a place where they've dumped a load of big galvanised iron sheets. We could try under there."

The way she looked at him suggested that maybe they were at cross purposes. "You what?"

"Rat-hunting," he said.

"Rat-hunting?"

"Well, yes. I mean, I thought—" He paused for a moment to regulate his breathing. "You've put some sort of anti-glare agent on your face," he said, "to stop your skin shining. It's what we do when we go rat-hunting, so the rats don't see us coming. Only we use brick dust. And the red stuff round the mouth is sort of symbolic of the kill. Isn't it?"

She was perfectly still and silent for a moment. Then she said, "Of course it is. Let's go hunt some rat."

A couple of hours later, Archie began to wonder if there wasn't something in this human idea of a good time after all. It soon became apparent that she hadn't done much rat-hunting before, but she was a quick learner, and her reactions were excellent. Thirty-seven rats, four mice and a hedgehog later, she looked at him with shining eyes and said, "How many do we need?"

"Excuse me?"

"For the pie, or whatever it is you've got in mind. Do we need any more, or will these do?"

He shuddered as discreetly as he could. "You want to eat them?"

"Well, no, actually. Don't you?"

"No. It sounds disgusting."

"Oh. Then why are we—?"

He blinked twice. "Rats are a pest," he said. "They spread disease, contaminate foodstuffs and gnaw the coating off the electric cables."

"Oh. Right. Silly me." She looked down at her hands, which were covered in blood and grime. "Do you think we've controlled them enough to be going on with?"

"Probably," he said. "Before now, the most I've ever caught in one day was four."

"Four?"

"That's right. I think it could be because back home we use a net, not our hands and teeth. But your way seems to work much better."

She breathed out heavily through her nose, then smiled at him. "I think I'd like to wash my face and hands," she said. "And then we could have a drink or something."

He nodded. "All that dust," he said. "Makes you thirsty."

There was a perfectly good stream nearby, where they could have washed up and drunk something without having to go any further, but for some reason she insisted on going to the canteen. "Let me guess," she said, as they sat in a corner with two glasses of lemonade, "this is your first time going out."

He nodded. "For all I know, it's the first time a goblin's gone out ever," he said. "You see, back home—"

She nodded. "Vats," she said. "Beige goo. Parthenogenesis. I've always assumed that's why goblins are so bad tempered. Because they never get any."

"Any what?"

"Quality time with a soulmate," she replied. "But that was there, and we're here. Might as well make the best of it, don't you think?"

"That's what Kurt thinks," Archie said.

"Kurt."

"This was his idea," Archie said. "Going out, I mean."

"I see. Thank you for telling me that."

"But actually," Archie said, "it wasn't as bad as I expected. In fact, it's been—" He frowned, searching for the right word.

"All right?"

He nodded. He'd heard that the humans regarded finishing each other's sentences as one of the hallmarks of true love. "Better than sitting around all afternoon with nothing to do, certainly."

"As good as that."

He considered. Another thing humans prize in their relationships, so he'd been given to believe, was perfect honesty. "Yes. Not much better, but definitely as good as."

"Mphm."

"So," said Archie. "How was it for you?"

"I think I can truthfully say it's the most fun I've ever had rat-hunting."

He smiled. "That's great," he said. "Kurt will be so pleased. We must do it again sometime."

"Tomorrow?"

"Why not?"

"All right," Archie said. "That'll be, um, fine. I'll look forward to it."

She nodded, then looked at him a bit sideways. "Did you actually want to go rat-hunting?"

"No," Archie said. "I thought you did. That's why you put the anti-glare stuff on."

He got the impression she was counting under her breath. "It's not actually anti-glare stuff."

"But you said— Oh well. No harm done. So what is it? Insect repellent?"

"Yes."

He nodded. "Well, it works. Haven't heard so much as a mosquito all evening."

She stood up. "I think I'll go back to my trailer now. Same time, tomorrow, then."

"If you like."

"Thank you for a lovely evening."

"It wasn't that good."

She smiled at him and walked away quickly. Archie finished his lemonade, then went to find Kurt. After a long search he found him in makeup. "Why are they painting your face that peculiar colour?" he asked.

"To make me look natural."

"Orange?"

"Under the lights," Kurt explained, "if I didn't have this stuff on, I'd be white as a sheet. How did it go?"

"Oh, all right," Archie said. "Actually, I think you've just solved a bit of a mystery for me. It wasn't insect repellent, or so her shiny nose wouldn't frighten the rats. It was to make her look natural."

Kurt forebore to comment, or maybe he hadn't been listening. "So what did you do?"

"Well, first we caught some rats."

"Right. And then?"

"Then we got washed and went for a lemonade in the canteen."

"Get many rats?"

"Thirty-seven."

"My God. I've never had more than three in an afternoon." Kurt shrugged. "Well, that doesn't sound so bad. Did she – I mean, she didn't mind?"

"She said she had a lovely time."

"Ah." Kurt had to hold still while they stuck on his eyebrows. They'd shaved off his real ones. The false ones looked exactly the same. "Just as well you did the recon for me. That stupid mare Jenny's been dropping so many hints, if I don't ask her out soon there's going to be trouble."

"Jenny?"

"The female lead. Tall woman, skinny arms. Barely enough on her for a good dinner. Oh well, if they like rat-hunting, that's okay."

"Oh, and don't give them flowers. Not unless you want a cake."

"Noted," Kurt said. "Actually, I don't mind cake."

"Then be sure to take some eggs."

"Will do." The makeup artist was painting broad blue rings under his eyes. "I was right, then. She does fancy you."

"I don't know." Archie picked up a stick of greasepaint, bit the end off, chewed it (too salty) and spat it out. "It's so hard to tell. Most of the time she gives me the impression she finds me really annoying, but she wants to see me again tonight. I don't know what to make of it, really."

"Oh, they're like that," Kurt said airily. "Courtship rituals. You can see why the First Goblins went over to vats. So much less aggravation for all concerned."

Like most Elves, Efluviel wasn't a morning person. She was not best pleased, therefore, when someone came hammering on her tree-house door just as the Beautiful Golden Face peeped over the horizon.

"Oh," she said. "It's you."

King Mordak took a moment to catch his breath. "Suggestion for you," he panted. "Buy a fucking ladder."

She smirked at him. "Bit of an effort, isn't it? Especially if you're not used to it. Of course, Elves learn to climb trees practically as soon as they can walk."

"Like monkeys."

"Indeed. What do you want?"

Mordak grinned at her. He was carrying, she noticed, a rucksack crammed with every sort of junk imaginable. "The good news is," he said, "I've decided to assign you a partner for your fact-finding mission."

"That's the bad news," Efluviel replied. "What's the good news?"

"Your partner is me," Mordak said. "Mind out of the way, that's a good girl. This pack is killing me."

A strange sort of numb feeling crept down Efluviel's spine. "Why are you carrying all that stuff?"

"For the journey." Mordak slid out from under the rucksack's straps and grounded it with a crash. "Bare essentials, that's all."

Efluviel could see the handle of an omelette pan sticking up from under the flap; also the eyepiece of an astrolabe and a small rosewood box of the sort that usually contains geometrical instruments. "Are you going somewhere?"

"We're going somewhere," Mordak corrected her, massaging his collar-bone. "Talking of which, why aren't you packed yet?"

"Going where?"

"To find the truth, of course."

"That's a reason, not a destination."

Mordak sighed. "Fine," he said, "little Miss Hair-splitter. Wherever the quest takes us, all right? Talking of which, you weren't thinking of wearing those shoes, were you? You'll get the most dreadful blisters."

"I'm not—" She checked herself. "I wasn't planning on going anywhere involving much walking," she said. "Down to the *Face* building, to check the archives. Maybe up as far as the University. For which," she added, "I don't suppose we'll need all that lot, unless you feel the need to stop every fifty yards and fry something."

He was grinning again. "Don't be silly," he said. "You won't find anything useful there, my people have already looked. No, I thought we might head out to Farn Snefir and check out the Unconventional Sisters."

She could feel the blood drain from her face. "Are you mad? That's miles away. It's dangerous. There's wolves and bears and—" She stopped dead.

"And goblins, yes. That," he added firmly, "is not a problem."

"There's no public transport."

"Shucks."

"There's no *road*."

"Indeed." Mordak picked up his pack and wriggled into it. "Hence my concern about your footwear. Still, you know best. I'll make a start and you can catch me up, after you've packed."

Ten minutes later she fell in beside him on the road. This time, she was the one fighting for breath.

"About time," Mordak said. "What's that you're carrying?"

"My suitcase, of course."

"Ah."

She shifted it to her other hand. "Where's the cart?"

"What cart?"

"The cart to take us as far as possible along the road."

"Oh, that cart. There isn't one. Try and keep up, there's a good girl."

"*Why* isn't there a—?"

Mordak sighed. "Oh come on," he said. "Goblins like horses but horses don't like goblins. You should know that, being a journalist."

As indeed she did, having covered the Gork Pies scandal, when Goblinland's biggest bakery chain was accused of adulterating its popular range of horse pies with cow-meat. She'd written editorials about it, now she came to think about it. "You mean we're going to have to walk the whole way?"

"Good healthy exercise," Mordak said cheerfully, as Efluviel stopped to wrap a handkerchief around her hand, where the handle of the suitcase had bitten into it. "So much better for you than being bounced around in a cart all day."

Editor of the *Face*, she told herself, what's a little stroll in the country compared to that?

"And besides," Mordak went on, striding ahead, "it'll help you get in shape for when things really start getting energetic. You know what you could do with? One of those suitcases with the built-in little wheels. Though they wouldn't be much help when we reach the Marshes."

As it happened, the suitcase came in very useful at several points over the next three days. They hid behind it from a pack of hungry wolves, sheltered under it from a rockfall in the Anguent Pass, used it as a shield in a skirmish with bandits and pushed it in front of them like a sort of float as they waded waist-deep through the cauliflower swamps of Varn Medrith. After all that, the stuff inside it wasn't good for anything much, so that when they had to dump it in order to use the case as a canoe for crossing the flood-swollen Fords of Nosen, it was no great loss. The case itself finally gave up the ghost after they slalomed down the shale-heaps of Onym Pal on it, but it held together until they were nearly at the bottom, so that was all right. It was just as well, Mordak graciously conceded, that they'd had it with them. Without it, the journey might have been a bit awkward.

On the evening of the fourth day they hobbled into the tiny fortified village of Farn Snefir, which perches on the southern escarpment of the Taupe Mountains like a small hat on a big head on a windy day. Farn Snepir had about thirty inhabitants, twenty-nine of whom fled as soon as they saw a goblin marching up the road toward them. Fortunately the one who stayed was the innkeeper, who charged them seventeen pieces of silver for a meal they'd have buried in a lead box back home, and told them the way to the Fountain.

Just before dawn on the fifth day, Mordak and Efluviel (wearing Mordak's spare boots, since her shoes were buried somewhere deep in the sand-drifts of Evlum; the boots were much too big, but she padded them out with cabbage leaves) trudged up the goat-track that led from the village to the mountain. They almost passed the cottage without seeing it, for it was set back from the track and sheltered by a screen of tall, spindly elm trees. But there was a splintered wooden board nailed to one of the trees, and if you looked closely you could just about make out

FOUNT OF ALL KNOLEDG

in faded grey lettering.

"Is this it?" Efluviel asked.

"Afraid so," Mordak replied. "Now, whatever you do, leave the talking to me. Otherwise it could get complicated."

"Suit yourself."

Mordak leaned the spear he'd been using as a staff against the cottage wall, sighed, gritted his teeth and knocked on the door.

They had to wait a long time. Eventually, though, the upstairs window directly above their heads creaked open an inch, and they saw a rusty key dangling on the end of a piece of string. Mordak took the key, turned it in the lock and took it out again; immediately it was whisked away, and he heard the window slam.

The single room that comprised the lower floor of the cottage was empty, apart from a broken milking-stool and three chickens. They looked round, and on the wall directly above the fireplace they saw, scrawled in charcoal letters

Pleas hold
Yor visit is importnt to us
A coleag will be with you shortly

"The Unconventional Sisters?" Efluviel asked.

"Weird's rude," Mordak replied. "Listen up, someone's coming."

The stairs creaked, and three women trooped into the room.

Although he'd been hearing about the Fount for years and knew plenty of people who'd gone there, it was the first time

Mordak had actually been there himself. Accordingly, he was partially but not fully prepared for what he now saw. The women: from the neck down, they were perfectly ordinary, in a genteel-shabby sort of a way; their dresses had been meticulously ironed many, many times and their shoes were so sensible they could practically speak. From the neck up—

The tallest woman, dressed in blue, said, "Who's got the eye?"

A weary sighing noise from her sister in the brown dress. Blue thought about it, opened her mouth, took out a tongue (wrinkled and sort of pinky-grey) and passed it to Brown, who popped it into her mouth and said, "She has." Blue frowned, mouthed something, snapped her fingers. Brown pulled back her hair to reveal an ear, which she pulled out with a faint plopping noise and handed over. Blue installed the ear and prodded Brown on the shoulder. "She has," Brown repeated. Then she took out the tongue and gave it to Blue, who then unplugged the ear and held it out to the third sister, in green, who took it and stuffed it in place. "Have you got the eye?" Blue said. Green nodded. "I said, have you got the eye?" Blue repeated. Green took out the ear and handed it to Blue; Blue gave her the tongue. "Yes," Green said.

"Excuse me," said Mordak.

Blue scowled, then held out her hand to Green, who passed her the tongue. "Be quiet," Blue said. "We'll be with you in a minute."

Then there was a long interval while Green and Brown gesticulated irritably, and Blue said, "It's no good you waving at me, I can't see you"; since she also had the ear, her words had no effect, and the other two carried on with their hand-signals. Then Blue gave Green the ear and said, "Give me the eye." Then Green gave her the ear, and she gave Green the tongue, and Green said, "Certainly not, it's Tuesday." Then Green gave Blue the tongue, Blue gave her the ear, and Blue said, "It's not, it's Wednesday, isn't it, dear?" Green sighed and gave Brown the ear. "It's Wednesday," Blue repeated, and gave Brown the tongue. Brown gave Blue the ear and said, "I know." Blue took back the tongue, gave Green the ear and said, "She says it's Wednesday." Then she gave Green the tongue and took back the ear, and Green said, "Dulcie always has the eye on Wednesdays."

Mordak picked a chunk of charcoal out of the grate and wrote EXCUSE ME on a scrap of paper he found lying on the floor. Then he got up, walked over to Green and held up the bit of paper so she could read it.

"Would you please not interrupt?" Green said.

Blue waved her hands angrily. "I wasn't talking to you, dear," Green said. "There's a rather tiresome young man here. He's waving a piece of paper at me, but his writing's so bad I can't read it."

Mordak nodded, went away, leaned the paper against the wall and wrote his message again, in big bold capitals. Then he showed it to Green, who said, "We're rather busy. Come back later."

Mordak sighed. I HAVEN'T GOT MUCH TIME, he wrote. I NEED TO ASK YOU SOMETHING.

"He says he hasn't got much time and he needs to ask us something," Green said. Blue shook her head vigorously. Brown opened the bag looped over her shoulder and took out some knitting. "It's not convenient right now," Green said. "Can you come back on Wednesday?"

Mordak turned the piece of paper over. IT IS WEDNES-DAY, he wrote. PLEASE?

Green sighed. "Oh, very well," she said. "What do you want?"

Mordak had run out of space on the bit of paper. So he turned to Blue and said, "Would you be kind enough to give the ear to the lady in the green dress? Thank you."

Blue shook her head. "Oh," said Mordak. "Why not?"

Blue mouthed something. Fortunately Mordak was a competent lip-reader. "No," he said, "it's Wednesday." Then he turned back to Green and said, "You couldn't possibly spare me a scrap of paper, could you?"

"No."

Efluviel's head was starting to hurt. She'd heard vague stories about the three omniscient sibyls of the north ever since she was a child, and had often wondered why the Elves went to all the trouble of reading books and building astrolabes and observatories rather than just coming here and asking. Served her right, she decided, for doubting the wisdom of her elders. Mordak meanwhile was rummaging in his right sleeve; he found what he was looking for, and turned back to Blue.

"If you give the ear to the lady in green," he said, "I'll give you a biscuit."

Blue hesitated for a moment, nodded, and unplugged the ear. Mordak handed over the biscuit (it was one of the three the innkeeper had sold them, for breakfast), as Green installed the ear. "It won't do her any good, you know," she said. "It's not her turn for the tooth till Friday."

Mordak took a deep breath. "I need to ask you a question," he said.

"We gathered that," Green said icily. "Well, don't just stand there gawping. What do you want?"

"Well," Mordak said, and launched into a full account of the human sudden-access-of-wealth crisis. He hadn't got far when Green help up her hand and said, "Just a moment."

"Yes?"

"This is all about the past, isn't it?"

"I guess so. But—"

"So sorry," Green said. "I'm the present. If it's the past you want, you need to talk to Dulcie."

Mordak closed his eyes, but only for a moment. "Which—?"

"In the brown worsted."

"Ah, right, thank you. Um, would you mind?"

Green clicked the tongue, then took it out and gave it, along with the eye and the ear, to Brown, who gave him a sad little smile and said, "How can I help you, young man?"

"Well," Mordak said, and started all over again. When he'd finished, Brown said, "Yes, I know."

"You do?"

Brown gave him a patient look. "Of course. This is the Fount of all Knowledge. I do wish people would take the trouble to read the sign."

"So you know all about the—"

"Oh yes. Now, how can I help you?"

Mordak took a deep breath. "I need you to tell me what's happening."

"What's happening?"

"Yes."

"Sorry." Brown smiled at him. "That would come under the present. You need to ask Elsie about that."

"Mphm."

"In the green tweed."

"Thank you."

Brown extracted the complete set of organs and handed them to Green, who installed them and said, "Yes?"

Mordak took a moment to phrase the question. "In the light of the sequence of unusual events which I've just described to the other lady, can you tell me what's going on?"

"Of course," Green said briskly. "It's really perfectly simple. What's happening is— *Installing wisdom updates, please wait.*"

"What?"

"*Installing upgrade 1 of 1,377. Do not discontinue enquiry until all upgrades successfully installed. Please wait.*"

The floor was quite comfortable to sit on, once you got used to it. Efluviel was just about to doze off when Green abruptly said, "*Upgrades complete*," fell over, got up again and pressed the ear, which had started to come loose, firmly back into place. "It does that sometimes," she said. "Who are you?"

"You were about to tell me about—"

"What? Oh yes." Green paused for a moment, then stood up very straight and began to recite: "There is one who is the key. He is not of this world. He that is the key has forsaken them, and hides behind the sugar-spangled hole. In his absence, the hole is open and we are not ourselves. I think that more or less covers it," she added, relaxing and massaging her neck. "So nice to have met you. Any time you're passing."

"Thank you," Mordak said. "That's quite unbelievably helpful. So, what am I supposed to do about it?"

Green's smile was almost a grin. "You seek a future course of action."

"Future." Mordak sighed. "Her in the blue?"

"Lottie."

"Thank you so much," Mordak said. Green took out the ear and the tongue and handed them to Blue, who said, "But it's Wednesday."

"Is it still? Gosh. Look—" Mordak realised what he'd said. "Listen," he amended, and he went through the whole thing all over again. And when he'd finished, he added, "So what do I do?"

Blue thought about it for a very long time. "Well," she said eventually, "it's perfectly obvious. What you need to do is, ah, a-a-a *tchoo*!" And she sneezed, and the tongue shot out of her mouth like a bullet, through the half-open door.

There was a moment of absolute silence. Then Efluviel stood up, stretched her aching back said, "It's all right, I'll go."

It took her a long time to find it, by the last rays of the setting sun, some fifteen yards from the door. She picked it up, held it pincered between forefinger and thumb, and carried it back into the cottage. "You were saying?"

"Oo *idyut*," Blue mumbled. "Ot ave oo *un* oo it?"

"Sorry," Efluviel said, "it landed in a clump of nettles."

"*Urts.*"

"That's too bad," Mordak said soothingly. "Is there anything—?"

"Ock eef."

So Efluviel went back outside again and scrabbled out in the gathering dark until she found a couple of big, juicy dockleaves. She kept one for herself and rubbed the other on the tongue with as much vigour as she could bring herself to apply. "Better?"

"A bit." Blue glowered at her through the eye, which was emerald green and slightly bloodshot. "Honestly, you two have been nothing but trouble ever since you showed up here. Now, what was it you wanted?"

"You were about to tell me," Mordak said, "what I can do, about all the weird stuff."

"Oh, that. Really, I'd have thought it was self-evident, to anyone with a bit of common sense. You must find the one who is the key before it's too late, and then you must put everything right."

Mordak waited for a moment, but there wasn't any more. "That's it?"

"Yes."

"Put everything right."

"That's what I said, wasn't it?"

"I see. And the one who is the key. Where will I find him?"

"At the place where he is."

"Of course, how silly of me. And his name?"

Blue stared at him for a moment, then giggled. "Quite," she said. "Now then, unless there's anything else—"

Mordak smiled at her. "No, thank you, that's quite enough to be going on with. Thank you so much for your time, you've been quite incredibly helpful, I shall tell all my friends to come here as often as possible. Goodbye." He walked to the door, opened it, shoved Efluviel through it and turned back. "Oh, and by the way," he said. "It's actually Monday." Then he slammed the door behind him and started to run.

With a frown that threatened to crack his newly acquired face down the middle, the Dark Lord stared at the sheet of parchment in front of him, and sighed until the Black Tower shook.

Three days now, and the new body, he had to admit to himself, wasn't turning out quite as he'd have liked. Immeasurably better than no body at all, no question about that, and after a thousand years of disembodiment there was a strong case to be made for being grateful for anything he could get. Nevertheless.

He shooed the reservations out of his conscious mind and concentrated on the pictures. They too were not quite right; nearly there, and he was as firmly convinced as ever that Evil needed a logo, a single visual image that put across the message, instantly, viscerally and at a net saving of a thousand words, the moment you saw it. Nearly there, but not quite. He'd read all about logos while he was, um, indisposed, and he could appreciate that as a weapon in the battle for hearts and minds—

Yes, fine. They needed a logo. But maybe not one of these.

A stray gust of wind, slanting in through the arrow-slit, lifted the paper a little and made it dance. The Dark Lord extended his hand and pressed it down on the table. It was nice – oh, so nice – to be able to do things like that again, instead of having to transmit a telepathic order to the Captain of the Guard to send a platoon of goblin stormtroopers up the six hundred and fifty flights of stairs that separated the guard-room from his eyrie, just to pick a stray bit of paper up off the floor. Also, it made him feel silly; and once a Dark Lord starts thinking like that, you might as well tell the lads to pack up and go home, because the end was very near. The alternative – chasing round the room as a non-dimensional force of pure energy trying to read a document as it fluttered through the air – was only marginally preferable. Yes, it was good to have hands again, even if they did come at a price.

He'd tried explaining about the need for hearts and minds to the goblins, who'd looked at him and said, yes, great for a curry; except for Mordak, of course. Ah, Mordak. Now there was a goblin who actually got it. Mordak had been a hundred and ten per cent behind the idea of a logo, except that his sug-gestions tended to be along the lines of red hands, scary staring eyes and all that sort of thing. Negativity, that was Mordak's problem. Even he, so enlightened in many ways, was still inclined to see Evil and Good purely in terms of black and white.

Mordak, he knew, wasn't going to like any of these. The rose, for instance, or the oak tree; the Dark Lord could pic-ture him now, scowling thoughtfully and carefully not saying, "What's all that supposed to be about, then?" Or the dove. Mordak would take one look at that and say, "This bloke can't draw vultures worth a toss." He'd have a point there, mind; it was a very wobbly dove, and the things sticking out of its shoulders might have been wings, or maybe the poor crea-ture was on fire; who gave a damn, really? Just rotten drawing, if you asked the Dark Lord.

He sighed again, and was just about to impale the parch-ment on the for-filing spike when he noticed a fourth image, one which he couldn't remember having seen there before. If so, it was odd, because the fourth image was far and away the most striking. He drew the parchment close to his nose and squinted at it.

The fourth image was essentially a pair of concentric circles; a fat one in the middle, and a thinner one surrounding it. What was it? Could be several things. An archery target, for not particularly ambitious goblin marksmen (plenty of those) or a partial solar eclipse. Or—

He took off his glasses and polished them on his shirt-front. A circle inside a circle; it definitely reminded him of something he'd seen recently, but what was it? It'd make a damn fine logo, he was sure of it – a wheel within a wheel, suggesting intrigue, chicanery and dark goings on; an outer circle and an inner circle, implying division, polarisation, us against them, concepts at the very heart of Evil; also, a very precise fried egg. And who in the world doesn't like fried eggs, apart from the Elves, who practically live on salad?

Where had he seen it before? Mordak might know. Mordak knew a surprisingly large amount of stuff. But (he recalled with a sigh) Mordak was off on some quest somewhere, and a long way away by now. A disembodied force of pure energy would be able to zip through the ether and into his mind in an instant, no matter where he was; the fortunate owner of a new (well, new-to-you) corporeal body couldn't face the thought of all those stairs, let alone bumping around in a badly sprung carriage on roads like potato furrows. Not that he was having regrets or anything. Perish the thought.

A circle within a circle. Definitely familiar.

There was a knock at the door – he had a door now, which was wonderful. "Come in," he said.

"Officer of the day reporting as—" The goblin soldier froze, then whipped out his sword. "Gnasz, Burgk, get up here quick. There's a sodding Elf in the chief's room."

The Dark Lord sighed. "You're new here, aren't you?"

"Shut it, Elf." The goblin had backed up against the wall,

his sword held out in front of him in trembling hands. "Soon as the lads get here, you're goulash, capisce?"

Iron boots were clumping up the stairs. The Dark Lord took off his spectacles and laid them on the table. Obviously, the changeover was going to take time, he appreciated that. Not to mention almost superhuman patience.

The arrival of two more goblin warriors seemed to put new heart into the duty officer. He took half a step forward and brandished his sword a little bit more purposefully. "Sergeant," he said. "Get that Elf."

"Um, Chief—"

"Are you disobeying a direct order? I'll have your guts for—"

"Chief."

A tiny flicker of doubt inside the duty officer's small, round head. He lowered his guard just a little, while the sergeant leaned forward and whispered something in his shoulder-length-lobed ear. "Oh," said the duty officer.

The sergeant gave the Dark Lord a sheepish grin. "Sorry about that, Boss," he said. "He's new."

"So I gathered," the Dark Lord said, as the duty officer cringed against the wall. "Also, he doesn't bother reading the memos."

"Can't read, Boss," explained the sergeant. "Wrong sort of eyes, see."

Well, of course. Goblin logic. There's a subspecies of goblins who can't see things properly if they aren't moving, so naturally it's from them you recruit your staff officers and administrative grades. "Get out," he said, not unkindly, and the soldiers withdrew. He could hear them clump-clumping down the stairs, and the duty officer's voice exclaiming, "He's a *what*?"

The Dark Lord shook his head sadly. The exceptionally difficult and dangerous piece of Dark magic that had made it possible for him to regain a physical shape had been known hitherto only to a forgotten sect of cake-worshippers far away in the jungles of the south, and where they had learned it from they had long since forgotten. There was nothing in the actual code of the spell to suggest that it had originally been Elvish magic, and it was all so long ago that the Dark Lord had clean forgotten about the Elf-sorceress Gluvior and her experiments with eternal life; rotten luck, in a way, that the cake-botherers' spell had turned out to be hers, and worse still that she'd only perfected it when she was seventy-six and nearly crippled with arthritis. Still. Even so. A body is a body is a body, and that was all there was to it.

Apart from the dreams—

A light flared inside the Dark Lord's labyrinthine brain. *That* was where he'd seen it before.

He scrabbled for the parchment and looked at it again. A circle within a circle. He closed his eyes, but the after-image remained, as though he'd been staring at the sun. A circle *surrounding* a circle. A circle encompassing a void. An abyss.

His old body, the one he'd lost after the war, when he was cast down by those annoying princes of the West, hadn't been troubled by dreams, since it never slept. It was only since he'd come to live in the reconstituted mortal shell of bloody Gluvior that he'd experienced sleep (which wasn't so bad) and dreams (which were). And it was in those dreams, those beguiling, horrible episodes, unreal and more than real, that he'd seen the void encompassed by the circle. Not just once, but every single time; no sooner had he closed his eyes and drifted away into temporary synthetic death, than there it was – a great bloated ring standing unsupported between heaven and earth, its glistening brown fabric sparkling with innumerable white crystals, its contours rounded, its scent strangely mouthwatering, and in the centre ... In the centre, the void, the abyss, empty yet not empty, rather a window looking out on to strange, terrible, wonderful things, as a voice in his head chanted, *Look not for too long into the doughnut, lest the doughnut look into you.*

Just the thought of it made him shiver; and that said it all, really. That thing, whatever it was, that nest of concentric circles, that brown-pupilled eye, that *doughnut* – well, if that wasn't the evillest thing he'd ever come across in all his life . . . so really, no contest, if he wanted a logo for Evil, what could be better? He opened his eyes again and there it was, scowling up at him from the parchment. It took a special effort of will to stop looking at it. There you go, he thought. Better than a stupid old oak tree any day of the week.

The dreams, though; he wasn't sure he was entirely comfortable with them. It would help, of course, if he didn't forget most of them a few seconds after he woke up, because he had a nasty feeling that the stuff that happened in them was somehow important. Impossible to know for sure because he couldn't remember, but he had an impression, at the very least, that in those dreams there was a voice, a particularly irritating voice that told him to do things, and sooner or later (he had no idea what they were) he was going to have to do them, if only to make the voice shut up. That wasn't right. Nobody tells the Dark Lord what to do. It's one of the painfully few perks of an otherwise unrewarding job. In the dreams, of course, he wasn't a Dark Lord. He was just – well, a person, a small, insignificant individual with no power or personality and a voice in his ear saying, *Why haven't you done it yet, you promised faithfully you would, I ask you to do one simple thing, it's not rocket science, for crying out loud*, while in the background the great shining circle-in-a-circle glowed and throbbed, and the void peeked out at him, and just occasionally winked. It was all very trying, and he hadn't had to put up with it when he was a disembodied force of pure energy. Nor, when he didn't have a head, was he quite so prone to splitting headaches.

Even so. He yawned, settled back in his chair, stretched his arms and folded them behind his head. In a minute, he promised himself, he'd send down to the kitchens for some biscuits and a glass of warm milk. Food was definitely an advantage of being corporeal, although it was a nuisance that this body's digestion was pretty well shot, and anything fried or topped with a sauce made him feel as though he'd swallowed a volcano. Biscuits and warm milk were all right, though, in moderation. Plain biscuits, anyhow.

His eyelids were feeling heavy, and he closed them just for a moment or so. Warm milk, he thought; well, maybe not exactly what he'd had in mind when he condemned himself to a lifetime of confinement in this Elvish bucket of guts, but his researchers were working on it, and his next body would be much better, a top-of-the-range goblin or maybe a GM troll, or possibly it was time to raise two fingers to the bipedal anthropomorphs and go for something really exciting and different, such as a dragon. Now that would be something. Huge great wings to take you anywhere you wanted, and heartburn would be a positive advantage.

His breathing grew slow and regular, as his consciousness slipped away and floated helplessly, like thistledown, through vast empty space, until in the distance he saw what he knew he'd subconsciously been searching for; a great brown hoop floating in mid-air, glistening with cooking-oil, sparkling with white crystals, and far away a voice that said, *Oh there you are at last, I do wish you wouldn't keep drifting off like that, not when there's so much I want you to do for me. Now listen carefully or you'll get it all wrong, what you have to do is this—*

Hum, went the spinning-wheel, and round the red glow of the campfire, fat grey moths clustered, like commodities brokers round a famine. The little man groaned gently, because his leg was tired from pumping the treadle. All for the sake of making a little money.

"Hello?"

By now the little man could picture what they looked like just from the sound of their voices. This one, he figured, would be tall, broad-shouldered and slim, with shoulder-length golden hair and clear blue eyes. Not too difficult. They were all like that.

"This way, Your Majesty," he sang out. "Mind your sleeves on the brambles."

And guess what, he'd been right. Another day, another prince, another shedload of straw. The prince edged into the circle of firelight, sucking a pricked thumb. "Excuse me," he said, "but are you him?"

"That depends," said the little man. "Who are you looking for?"

"The straw-into-gold chappie," replied the prince, peering at the little man through the woodsmoke. "Is that you?"

"Yes."

"Mister Rum – I mean, the dwarf with no name?"

"That's me."

"Fantastic. Delighted to meet you. Everybody's talking about you, you know."

"Fancy," the little man said. "Right, then, to business. How much, and where is it?"

The prince blinked. "Excuse me?"

"The straw," said the little man. "The straw you want me to spin into—"

"Ah." A tragic look spread quickly across the prince's face. "That's the problem, actually, now you mention it. There isn't any."

"Say again?"

"No straw," the prince said with a sigh. "Not a single solitary bloody stalk."

The little man frowned. "No straw?"

"Nope."

"My God. What happened? Thunderstorms? Mice?"

The shadow of a frown flickered across the prince's handsome face. "Actually, it's all your fault. I don't mean that in a nasty way," he added quickly, "I'm sure you didn't do it on purpose or anything, you were just doing your job, you know, obeying orders, all that stuff. Only, the thing of it is, ever since you started on this straw-into-gold business, the price of straw – well, it's gone mad."

"Ah."

"Crazy." The prince shook his head in recollected disbelief. "Never known anything like it in all my life."

The little man nodded slowly. "Let me guess," he said. "The price of gold—"

"That's the other thing," the prince said mournfully. "Gone right down. Was nine hundred and seventy silver florins an ounce, now it's around four-twenty. It's making a lot of problems for people, I can tell you. The soldiers have started saying they want paying in silver."

The little man smiled sadly. "So, of course," he said, "all your fellow princes have been buying more straw to bring to me to make into more gold, to make up the shortfall."

"That's right," the prince said. "Who told you?"

"Amazingly, I guessed. And the more straw the princes buy, the more the price goes up, presumably."

"Yes, that's right," the prince said. "It's just getting silly. I tried to get a couple of dozen bales for the stables, and the chappie wanted four hundred and fifty florins an *ounce*. For straw."

The little man's eyebrow quivered just a little. Four hundred and fifty florins an ounce for straw, when the gold he'd soon be spinning that straw into was changing hands at four hundred and twenty. No doubt about it. These people had taken to free market economics with a vengeance. "I can see your problem," he said.

"Quite."

"And no fun for the horses, either."

"Oh, they're all right, we're bedding them down on dried bracken. But that's not the point. The simple fact is, I haven't got a stalk to bless myself with, and with all my neighbours raising these stonking great big armies, it seems to me I'd better get a stonking great big army too, or else things might start getting a bit unpleasant. Only – no straw."

"Indeed," the little man said gravely.

"So I was wondering," the prince said, turning on the charm-tap, "does it actually have to be straw? I mean, what about hay? We've got stacks and stacks of hay. Or nettles, possibly. Do you think you could do anything with nettles?"

"A nourishing if rather bland soup," the little man said. "Otherwise, no."

"Hay?"

The little man shook his head. "Sorry," he said, "it's got to be straw. This is a dedicated straw-matrix processing unit. If I tried to weave hay, the best you could hope for would be a very lumpy mat."

"Oh hell," the prince said, and he turned away for a moment to hide the expression on his face. "That really is confoundedly awkward. Only, you see, I've already sent out the draft notices, and there's going to be twenty thousand chaps turning up at my place in a day or so to be my army, and I imagine they're going to want paying. And with no straw—"

The little man sucked in air through his teeth. "You've got a problem, I can see that," he said. "Well, I'm very sorry for you, but I don't see what I can do."

"Oh." The prince looked very sad. "That's a nuisance. Only, I think when the chaps turn up and there's no army and no pay, and with all the neighbouring kingdoms threatening to invade on top of that, I might just be in a spot of bother. Harsh words, and all that. Not that it's your fault really," he added. "And I don't mean to burden you with all my difficulties. It's just – oh well."

The little man pursed his lips. "Of course," he said, "I could *lend* you some straw."

"Could you?"

"Oh yes." The little man nodded. "It just so happens that before the price started to rise, I bought up two hundred and ninety thousand tons of the stuff. To practise on, you know. It's in that barn over there."

"Two hundred and ninety thousand—"

"And I might be willing to lend you a bit of it," the little man went on. "Just to tide you over, you understand, until the harvest comes in."

"The harvest."

"The wheat harvest," the little man clarified. "You know, farmers and stuff."

"Oh, yes, right. We've got lots of farmers down our way."

"I'll bet."

The prince nodded. "Splendid chaps. Make excellent soldiers. That's why I've enlisted them all for my new army."

"Ah."

The prince frowned. A thought seemed to have struck him. "Which is a bit of a bugger, really," he said. "Because if they're off fighting wars and things—"

"They can't be back home sowing wheat for next year's straw harvest, quite." The little man rubbed his nose. "And no harvest, no straw. Also, for what it's worth, no corn, so no bread. But that's just a side-issue, of course. Still, it's rather inconvenient."

"I should cocoa," said the prince. "Bloody shame, if you ask me. They should be back on the land, ploughing away like mad, instead of wasting their time eating their heads off in barracks. You know what? There's thousands of acres up in the foothills country that's just right for growing wheat, only the dukes and earls will insist on pasturing their racehorses there. We could plough all that up and be absolutely rolling in straw."

"Quite," said the little man. "But instead, all your plough-men are going to be square-bashing in a barracks yard somewhere. Rather a waste, if you ask me."

"Too right," said the prince, with feeling. "But since every-body else is raising these armies, what can we do?"

The little man was quiet for a while. "You know what," he said, "it's just possible that this stuff we've just been talking about might have occurred to your neighbours as well."

"Oh. You think so?"

The little man smiled, recalling many recent conversations. "I wouldn't be at all surprised," he said. "In which case, they're going to be sending their soldiers back home to get the ploughing done and the crops sown, and nobody's going to be invading anybody, at least until the beginning of October."

"Really? Why October?"

"Think about it. Of course," he went on, "after the har-vest's in and the grain's been threshed and the straw's all safely baled, then you can recruit your army all you like."

"That's true."

The little man nodded. "It'll only take you – what, a month, six weeks at the most, to get them through basic train-ing and then you'll be ready to march."

"Absolutely." The prince's eyes lit up. "And then we can invade all our neighbours. That'll teach 'em to plan to invade us."

"Quite," the little man said. "Except that by then, it'll be mid-November, which is when you get the first heavy snow-falls around here, as I understand it, which means all the mountain passes will be blocked, and nobody's going to be able to invade anybody until March at the very earliest, probably well into April if we're going to be realistic about it."

The prince shrugged. "Ah well," he said. "Come April, we'll show the bastards—"

"At which point," the little man went on, "you will of course need every available man for the spring ploughing." He spread his hands in a vaguely consoling gesture. "But what the heck," he said. "There's always next year."

The prince, who'd been frowning, suddenly smiled. "Absolutely," he said. "Next year, we'll kick those Eastern bastards' arses out through their ears, they won't know what's hit 'em. Meanwhile—"

"Ah yes." The little man smiled. "You wanted to borrow some straw."

"Yes please, if that's all right."

"Fifty thousand tons do you?"

"Absolutely. If you could possibly manage a bit more—"

The little man pursed his lips. "We'll see how we go," he said. "Of course, I will have to charge you a teeny bit of interest on that."

"What? Oh, right. Yes. Yes, that's fine." Pause. "When you say teeny—"

"I was thinking," the little man said, "of two hundred per cent."

"Um. Is that a lot?"

"It's the going rate," the little man said. "Same for everybody, you know, no favouritism."

"Oh, of course not, absolutely." In the prince's face the little man could plainly see the agony of mental arithmetic. "Two hundred per cent, so that'd be—"

The little man smiled. "I lend you fifty thousand tons," he

said. "You give me back a hundred and fifty thousand. Perfectly simple," he added. "Nice round numbers."

"Oh, quite," said the prince. "Couldn't be rounder. Yes," he added decisively, "that'll be fine, I'm sure. Yes. As well as all the racehorse pastures, we can plough up the royal parks and all that land out on the plain we'd earmarked for the soldiers to do training manoeuvres on. Yes, that'll be just fine."

"That's a deal, then," said the little man, producing a sheet of parchment out of apparently nowhere. "So if you'd just care to sign here, and here and here and here and here, and here, oh yes, and here, please, just where my thumb is. No need to read it first," he added kindly, guessing that literacy wasn't one of the prince's greatest strengths. "Splendid," he added, folding the parchment up very small and sticking it down the front of his jerkin. "So, that's fifty thousand tons of prime straw, yours to do what you like with."

"Um," the prince said. "I think I'd like it spun into gold, please."

"I can do that for you," the little man said cheerfully. "If you're sure."

"Quite sure."

"You don't want any for the royal stables, anything like that?"

"No, just gold, if that's all right."

"Perfectly all right."

"You couldn't make that sixty thousand tons, could you? Only then we could probably afford to drain the swamps out by the Green River and plough that lot up, too."

The little man smiled. "Oh, go on, then," he said. "Since it's you."

"I say, thanks awfully." He smiled – he had a very nice smile – and turned to go. "You've been frightfully decent about all this, you know."

The little man shrugged. "I do my best."

"Shame about the nettles, though."

"Ah well." The little man sighed. "It really does have to be straw," he said. "For one thing, it's canonically correct."

"Did you ever try nettles?"

"Not as such," the little man said. "Where I come from, they did once try turning paper into gold, or at least substituting paper for gold, which is much the same thing."

"Ah. Did it work?"

The little man shook his head. "Total distaster," he said. "Absolute washout. No, you're much better off sticking with straw. You know where you are with straw. Also, it has useful by-products. This time next week suit you?"

"Sorry?"

"For the gold. Should be ready by then. Remember to bring some carts."

The prince smiled. "Will do," he said. "Lots and lots of carts." He looked round at the bramble-bushes. "In fact, if it wouldn't put you out too much, we might just build a road for them to go on. Take all the hassle out of getting stuff to and fro."

"Good idea."

"And we could probably do with a bridge over the river, come to think of it."

"Why not?"

The young man nodded briskly. "Save all that mucking about trying to swim the carthorses across the ford," he said. "Make life much easier for everybody, that would. In fact, I can't understand why nobody's ever thought of it before."

The little man grinned at him. "Clearly they weren't as smart as you are." He scratched the lobe of his ear. "It'll be something for the twenty thousand men to do, now that they're not going to be soldiers. Should keep them occupied right up to the start of ploughing season."

"That's an idea. Gosh, yes. Clever old you for thinking of it."

"Oh, just common sense, really. Mind how you go."

The usual crashing and ripping noises as the prince negotiated the bramble thicket, then nothing but the sighing of the wind in the trees, the hoot of a distant owl, the hum of the spinning-wheel. The little man was counting under his breath. Ninety-eight, ninety-nine—

"Just one last thing."

He turned and smiled. "You're back again."

"I almost forgot," the prince said. "If by some amazingly miraculous flukey chance I happen to guess what your name is, does that mean I get let off the interest on the straw?"

"No."

"Oh." The prince's face fell, then he smiled again. "Worth a try, I suppose. Never mind. Cheerio for now, then."

"Goodnight, Your Majesty."

"Goodnight, Rump – I mean, whoever you are."

Real silence this time. The little man took his foot off the treadle and let the wheel spin to a standstill. He laid his hand on the frame; it was hot. He sighed, and leaned forward, resting his head against the rim of the wheel. He'd been working flat out for – well, as long as he could remember, and he was exhausted.

Worth it, though, he told himself. Gradually, step by painful step, he was getting there. And although most of the princes and kings and dukes and earls were as dumb as he'd expected them to be, some of them showed the occasion glimmer of intelligence, and there were one or two who might eventually, with the proper guidance and coaching, one day be capable of getting it. At that point, assuming he ever got there, his work here would be done and he'd be at liberty to move on, pitch his tent and his wheel in some other ghastly, god-forsaken bramble patch, and start all over again with another consignment of deadheads.

Gosh. Put like that, it all seemed pretty bleak. On the other hand, at least he was doing *something*; and he'd known all along that if he was ever going to pay off his debt to society and make atonement for the things he'd done before he came here, it was going to be a very long road indeed, with many a sheer cliff to scale before he had any chance of reaching the moral foothills, let alone the high ground. He lifted his right foot with his hand, peeled off the shoe and the sock and examined the sole. A mass of blisters, from working the damn treadle. He pulled up a handful of grass to stuff the sock with.

I deserve it, he thought. In fact, I'm getting off lightly. When I think about what I used to be—

He shuddered, and stuffed his foot back into the sock. But I'm done with all that now, he reassured himself, I'm a reformed character, I'm the dwarf with no name – he liked the sound of that. An enigmatic stranger who blows into town, rights wrongs, succours the afflicted and then departs, as mysteriously as he'd come, to continue his mission else-where, alone, misunderstood—

Um.

Using his forefinger as a shoehorn, he eased the shoe back on to his foot, replaced it on the treadle and began to pump. The wheel whirled round, making its characteristic humming noise; not an inherently unpleasant sound, but loud enough to drown out minor background noises, such as stealthy foot-steps, the snapping of one small twig, the shallow breathing of two men trying very hard to be quiet, stuff like that. It wasn't loud enough to cover the flapping of the coarse hessian sack as it was lifted high in the air and dropped neatly over the little man's head; he heard that one loud and clear, but by then it was far too late.

"**G**osh," said the Elf, "you're all dressed up. Just a moment, I'll get my coat."

Archie shivered slightly. It can get a bit nippy after sunset in the back end of the Ashburton country, and the brightly coloured patterned shirt he'd borrowed from one of the cameramen was made of some thin material better suited to warmer climes. A goblin wouldn't have minded, of course, because goblins have thick fur, except in the early spring, when they moult. At that moment, Archie was missing the fur.

The Elf reappeared a moment later, covered from head to foot in an olive-green army surplus parka, with the fur collar up around her ears. "You'll catch your death, you know that," she said. "Still, it was a sweet thought."

"The camera guy said this is what he wears when he's out with girls."

The Elf shrugged. "Probably something to do with natural selection," she said. "It demonstrates to a potential mate that you have superior cold-resistance DNA. Come on, I'm starving."

He started in the direction of the canteen, but she said, "No, this way," and he stopped. "What's over there?" he said.

She smiled at him. "Surprise."

The other thing he missed about not having fur was the lack of hackles. Confoundedly useful things; as soon as there's danger, they puff up all round the back of your neck, providing you with a pretty reliable early-warning system and saving you the effort of having to think about things all the time. If they'd still been there, he felt sure, they'd have been doing their stuff like mad; but they weren't, so he was forced to rely on observation, experience and common sense, all of which informed him that there was nothing to worry about. You're heading into the dark unknown with a pretty girl, they said, don't be such a wuss. His residual goblin instincts got as far as *yes, but*, and then gave up.

"This way," she said. She was almost out of sight among the shadows.

"I'm not sure I like surprises."

"You're going to love this one."

Bloody Kurt and his field research. "Slow down," he said. "I can't see where I'm going."

"Nearly there."

He caught his toe on something, stumbled forward, tripped again and landed hard on the ground, with only his nose to break his fall. "Come *on*!" came a sweet voice from the darkness. He scrambled to his feet and followed, muttering under his breath.

"Surprise!"

A light flared. It proved to be a lantern, hanging inside a tent. He paused and sniffed. *Foo—*

"Is that—?"

She laughed. "Come inside," she said.

He blundered his way inside the tent, his brain reeling from the familiar smell. There was a camping stove on the floor, with a frying pan perched on top. "It can't be."

"Actually, it isn't." She was sitting on the floor, holding a white enamel plate. "For obvious reasons," she added. "But one of the props guys has a brother whose girlfriend's sister's boyfriend has a sister who works in a lab for one of the biggest processed food companies in Australia. They can synthesise any flavour you want out of chemicals. This," she lifted the lid of the frying pan, and Archie's head swam, "is *poulet à l'homme.*"

"P-poulet?"

"Chicken."

"Chicken?"

She nodded. "Sort of bird. Tastes like human."

With a soft moan he sank to his knees and waddled across the tent floor, hardly able to see for the tears in his eyes. "Oh God," he whispered. "It's been so long."

"I'm having salad."

"Are you? Rotten luck." He hesitated, torn between gratitude and longing. "Have some of mine," he mumbled. "There's enough for two. Barely."

"No, thank you," she said briskly, her mouth full of lettuce. "There's blood pudding for afters, and a bowl of crystallised teeth."

He could hold out no longer. He dug his fingers into the grey goo and pawed it into his mouth. Sensations he'd almost forgotten flooded through him, like rain on parched earth.

"Well?" she said.

"Perfect."

"Not too heavy on the cayenne pepper?"

"What's cayenne pepper?"

"That's all right, then." She ate a breadstick. "So, how was your day?"

"What?"

"Your day. How was it?"

He made an effort to remember. "Oh, we sat about waiting for eight hours, then we ran up a hill making silly noises, then we waited four hours, then we ran up the hill again. Then it rained. That was about it."

A bit of gristle had got itself lodged between his teeth. It was perfect; just the right bendy, rubbery texture. "Do you want to hear about my day?"

"Not specially." He crunched a sliver of bone. The splinters pricked the roof of his mouth, and he purred. "This is really, really good."

"Glad you like it."

"Thanks," he said. "You must've gone to a lot of trouble."

"Yes."

"Next time, though, it could do with a bit more salt."

"Thank you, I'll bear that in mind."

"It's all right, it doesn't totally spoil it."

"I'm so pleased."

"And the sauce is a bit on the runny side. But otherwise it's not bad."

She was looking at him. "More salt," she said, "sauce not so runny. Hold on, I'll write that down so I don't forget."

"Good girl."

"Thank you."

The intensity of the experience was having a powerful effect on him. He felt dizzy, his eyesight was getting blurry, he didn't seem to have much feeling in his toes or the tips of his fingers. Just goes to show, he told himself, how much I've missed proper old-fashioned home cooking. He felt his eyelids droop shut. His head slumped forward. A clattering noise told him that the plate had fallen from his hand on to the floor. Just a moment, he thought. And then he fell asleep.

If you follow the old road through the high passes of the Beige Mountains, as you reach the highest point of your ascent, you arrive at a point where the high walls of the ravine suddenly fall away, and you're greeted by a spectacular vista, looking out over the vast, flat expanse of the Wiffenmoors. Immediately, your eye cannot help but be drawn to the ancient tower that stands in the very centre of the moor.

At first, you may have difficulty figuring out what it could possibly be. None of the rules of perspective seem to apply in that place; the mountains are too high, the plain is grotesquely wide and flat, and the tower looks like a thick, two-dimensional black line, arbitrarily drawn from the earth up into the sky. If you stop and study it, and the sheer improbability of what you're looking at doesn't cloud your judgement, you may well find it impossible to believe that you're looking at a physical object. How could something so tall and narrow and straight possibly stay upright, when the bitter north-easterly winds rage across the plain? As you draw closer, the sense of utter implausibility only increases. You walk for a full day, from dawn to dusk, but the tower seems to be no nearer. The mountains behind you are smaller and further away, but the uniform black line is still just a line, created by placing a ruler against the horizon. Eventually, days later, you stand at the foot of the thing and crane your neck back in a vain attempt to see the top, you run your hand across the smooth, ice-cold masonry trying to detect a join between the massive coal-black stone blocks, you spend an hour walking round and round the base of it searching for any faint trace of a door; who built it, how, why? Men have gone mad dwelling on those questions, for this is the tower of Snorfang; it exists without the need for understanding, belief or consent. There are those who claim that it was there before the earth and the sky were split apart, that it goes down to the bottom of the earth and up through the top of the sky and far, far beyond, that it's only a tiny segment of a line drawn from one edge of infinity to the other, impaling the Middle Realms like a spit through meat; that it's the axle around which Time turns, the only fixed thing in the universe. Two thousand years ago, the first of the Wise came to this place and thought he could make out faint letters scratched on the east face (though no one has ever seen them since, and if you try and cut the stone with a diamond, the diamond crumbles in your hand like chalk). He wrote them down, and for fifteen hundred years scholars spent their lives trying to decipher the script and decode the language. Eventually, Baramond the Great succeeded, and announced to the Conclave of the Wise that the inscription spelled out *Please Use Other Door*. Since then, none of his order have come here, saying that even to the Wise there are some things better not known.

Until now. Efluviel and Mordak stood at the base of the tower and leaned their heads back until Mordak's hat fell off; immediately, the wind caught it and whisked it away, like a bad dog with a stick. He shivered. The sun was high in a sea of unblemished blue, but his hands and face were almost numb with cold.

"Is this it?"

Mordak sighed. "Well," he said, "it's either this one or one of those ones over there. Oh look, there's nothing over there except a whole lot of sand. Yup, I'm guessing this is it."

"Snarky," Efluviel said, not without a hint of admiration.

Three hundred years ago, a star had fallen from the sky just outside the northern suburbs of the Golden City. When the dust-cloud had settled and the survivors crept down into the huge crater, they found that the burnt-out star had split open like a walnut. Inside it was a single slab of crystal, on which was written a prophecy: *When the dark times come and all is doubt and confusion, Porridge-for-brains and Stupid will go to the tower of Snorfang, and their question will be answered.* Oddly enough, none of the Wise had ever put themselves forward as the foretold ones, even though all had been doubt and confusion on a number of occasions. The terms of the prophecy, it was generally felt, had never quite been fulfilled.

Mordak crossed his arms over his chest and folded his aching hands under his armpits. The way he saw it was, only Porridge-for-brains would be stupid enough to come here. I've come here. Therefore—

Above the howling of the wind he heard a faint pecking sound. It reminded him of chicks hatching from eggs. He looked up, and saw a thin but unmistakable horizontal line slowly forming in the black stone, as though drawn by an invisible pencil. Not daring to breathe, he watched as the line extended itself, three feet, three feet six inches, then two vertical lines dropping at right angles from each end, until a rectangle more or less the size of a small door was clearly etched on the tower wall. He took a step back. There was a loud click, and the door swung open.

"Did you do that?"

"No," Mordak replied. "Did you?"

"No."

"Oh."

Ninety years after the star fell, a three-headed goat was born in the Arcantha valley. It died the next day, and when the local priests examined its entrails, they cut through the liver and found that in cross-section the blood vessels spelled out the words, *A perfect fool will go inside the tower of Snorfang.* Or rather, that was one interpretation. Owing to the obscure dialect used and some sloppy knifework by the priests, the text was marginally ambiguous. It could also have been, *Only a complete idiot would go inside the tower of Snorfang.* You paid your money and you took your choice.

It was pitch dark inside the tower, and they'd only gone a couple of steps when the door swung shut behind them with a horrible clang. It must've been the wind, Mordak told himself, although he couldn't help remembering that the door opened inwards.

He stood quite still for a moment, completely at a loss as to what to do. Then, out of the darkness, a voice spoke to him. It was rather a nice voice, female, but entirely devoid of expression.

"Thank you," it said, "for using the Snorfang automated facility. Please note that anything you say or do may be recorded for training purposes and as an awful warning to others. You will now hear a list of options. When you reach the option of your choice, please say stop."

Then dead silence, for what seemed like for ever. Efluviel took a book from the side pocket of her rucksack and started to read.

"Enquiries about the meaning of the universe," said the voice. "Enquiries regarding personal destinies. Enquiries regarding forthcoming lottery draws. Enquiries regarding the current state of doubt and confusion."

"Stop," Mordak said.

"Thank you for choosing option four," resumed the voice, a semitone lower. "Your enquiry is important to us. Please hold until an adviser is available."

Strange music began to play; soft, ethereal and somehow intensely annoying. When the same fifteen-bar sequence had repeated for the ninety-third time, the voice said, "Please access the tower using the third door on the right."

Forty years after the birth of the three-headed goat, a poor fisherman living on the desolate northern coast of Sherm caught an enormous sea-bass. He took it as a gift to the king, and when it was cut open, in its stomach was found a gold coin, on which was written; *Should anyone ever be stupid enough to enter the tower of Snorfang, let him remember to take a lantern.* Damn, thought Mordak. I knew I'd forgotten something.

Twenty minutes of methodical wall-groping later, he

turned an unseen doorknob and fell through into a wide, spacious chamber, dimly lit by an amber glow whose source he couldn't identify. On the wall was a gold plaque. It read:

GROUND FLOOR: RECEPTION
FLOOR 215: ENQUIRIES

"Are you sure we're in the right place?" Efluviel said behind him. "This looks more like a post office or something."

Mordak closed his eyes for a moment, then looked round. There was a small door in the opposite corner of the room. It opened on to a staircase. "Come on," he said. He started to climb.

There was, of course, no light whatsoever in the stairwell, but he could tell by the feel of them under the thin soles of his boots that the steps were shallow, smooth to the point of being slippery, and dished in the middle by centuries of constant use – what could have worn the treads away like that he really didn't want to think, particularly since no member of any species known to the Wise had been inside the tower since records began. He counted as he climbed, and soon found out that after every seventy steps he came to a landing. He'd just passed the one hundred and ninety-ninth landing when he remembered that forty years ago, in the far-distant northern city of Grembold, the temple of the Moon had been struck by lightning and the ensuing fire had melted the inch-thick gold in which the entire outer surface of the temple's great dome was encased. Droplets of molten gold had fallen into the deeply packed snowdrifts below, and when the spring thaw came and the snow melted away, they were discovered to have formed runes, which when duly translated spelled out: *The fifth door on the left is the elevator.* Ah well, Mordak told himself, another mystery cleared up.

The two hundred and fifteenth landing was illuminated by the same unearthly amber glow he'd seen at the bottom of the stairs. By its light he saw an ancient oak door, with six hinges, twelve massive locks and no doorknob, and a notice which read:

NO ADMISSION TO ENQUIRIES
WITHOUT A VALID VISITOR'S PASS.

VISITOR'S PASS AVAILABLE FROM RECEPTION.

Well, of course, he said to himself. He turned round and started down the stairs.

"Where are you going?"

"Reception. Where do you think?"

Efluviel yawned. "Get one for me while you're down there, will you? I think I'll just wait here and read my book."

She, he couldn't help noticing, seemed completely fresh and unwearied by the climb. "Sure," he panted. "You rest there a minute, catch your breath."

In Reception, in the far right-hand corner of the room, he found a small rosewood and ivory box. Inside it were two little enamel badges marked *Visitor*. One he pocketed, the other he pinned to the lapel of his coat. Then, remembering the runes in the snow at Grembold, he went out and groped around until he found the fifth door on the left. It opened easily, and revealed another door, to which was pinned a note reading *Out of order, use stairs*. He smiled and tipped an imaginary hat, then went back the way he'd come and started to climb.

This time, when he stood in front of the oak door, there was a doorknob. "Thank you so much," he said politely, and turned it.

The room they found themselves in was long and narrow,

and lit by a single high window, which was strange, since there were no windows visible from the outside of the tower. Mordak craned his neck and peered through it. He saw a lush green river-valley, with rolling wooded hills far away in the distance, and far away on the left, the mountain that over-shadowed the mineshaft where he'd been born, nine hundred miles away on the Southern Continent. "Ah," he said, "that sort of window."

"Mphm." Effluviel turned down a corner to mark her place and closed her book. "I wouldn't take any notice if I were you. There's one that does that in the Central Planning Archive back home. If you look into it for too long, it shows you the most embarrassing thing you've ever done in public."

He turned so his back was to it, and saw a doorway.

Fine, he thought. Through the doorway, more stairs. They climbed a flight, and came to a landing, with a notice that read:

WE'RE HERE TO HELP YOU.

Up another flight to another landing. This one had a sign saying:

PROUDLY SERVING THE
LOCAL COMMUNITY SINCE 00000001.

Up a third flight; this time they found themselves facing another door; white, with a brass knob.

Mordak frowned at it. "Your turn," he said.

"Ever the gentleman." Effluviel turned it and went in. He took a deep breath and followed.

He saw a desk, and behind it, a man. He was elegantly dressed in a dark scholar's gown. His silver hair was neatly parted and he had a handsome, distinguished-looking face and immaculate fingernails. He was maybe just a whisker under two feet tall.

"Hello," said the man, with a charming smile. "Do sit down."

There was, of course, no chair. "Is this Enquiries?" Efluviel asked.

"Yes."

"Really?"

"Really and truly."

"Good heavens. Um, can we ask you a question?"

"That's what I'm here for."

Mordak shouldered past her. "What the hell is going on?"

"Ah." The man smiled, steepled his fingers and leaned back a little in his chair. "I'm glad you asked me that, it's a very good question. The answer is actually perfectly simple. It's going round and round."

Mordak waited for a moment. Then he said, "Excuse me, I don't think I quite grasped that. Could you run it by me again?"

"Certainly." The man leaned forward a little and said, very loud and clear, "It's going round and round." He paused, looked at them both and added, "It's going round, and stuff goes in, and other stuff comes out. That's what's happening right now."

Mordak counted to five under his breath, then said, "Who and what stuff, and what's it got to do with humans being able to afford armour?"

Immediately the man picked up a sheaf of papers and started looking at them. "Sorry," he said. "This is Enquiries. What you need is Supplementary Information. Different department," he explained, glancing up briefly. "So glad to have been able to help. Goodbye."

A blood vessel was pounding like a drop-hammer on the left side of Mordak's forehead. "Where do I go for Supplementary Information?"

"Sorry, I can't answer that, it's not a new enquiry, you need Supp— *Put me down.*"

He looked rather comical dangling by one ankle from Mordak's right hand. Effluviel had taken a nail file from her pocket and was seeing to a slightly jagged forefinger. "Where do I go," Mordak repeated politely, "for Supplementary Information?"

"Mountains," gasped the man, struggling for breath. "Please, put me down, I'm feeling all dizzy."

"Mountains?"

"*Mountains.* You know. Tall things with snow on top. That's all I can tell you. Really."

"Mountains," Mordak said wearily. "Thank you so very much." He lowered the man gently until his hands touched the desktop, then let go. "Are you sure you can't give me just a tiny hint?"

The man scrambled onto all fours, scattering papers everywhere, and glowered at him. "No."

"Why not?"

"Because I don't know, do I? I'm Enquiries, not Supplementary, it says so on the board downstairs, can't you *read*? Now please go. I really don't feel at all well."

Some time later, as Mordak took one last look at the tower before turning his back on it and starting the long trudge to the mountains, he called to mind the incident, thirty years before, when the High Priest of Haslet the crocodile god in far-distant Aphir had dreamed a dream, after a heavy meal of lobster in cheese sauce, in which the god came to him and, standing over his bed suffused in an unearthly green light, had uttered the cryptic words, *He who eventually succeeds in penetrating the mysteries of the tower of Snorfang will wish he hadn't bothered.*

Effluviel, who'd been unusually quiet for some time, cleared her throat. "So," she said. "Mountains."

Mordak sighed. "Which could mean anything."

"Mphm." She uncorked her water bottle, took a sip and replaced the cork without offering him any. "But I'm guessing he means the old hermit who lives in a cave at the summit of the Golden Crag in the very centre of the Taupe Mountains. Stands to reason," she added. "Very famous hermit. He knows everything, apparently."

He turned slowly and looked at her. "The old hermit," he said.

"In the Taupe Mountains, that's right. Actually," she went on, "if I'd been leading this expedition, I'd have gone straight there and not bothered with all this. But I'm not, so—" She shrugged. "No skin off my nose. And it's nice to be out in the fresh air."

"You knew."

She nodded. "I know lots of things."

"And you let me—"

"You were having so much fun," she said. "Leading. Being heroic. After all, why be right when you can be happy instead?"

Mordak unslung his pack, dropped it on the ground, sat down and took his boots off. "Tell you what," he said, "and this is just a suggestion. Why don't you lead the way from now on?"

"All right."

"Thank you."

"That'd make much more sense."

"Of course it would."

"Me being an Elf," she added, "and you being a goblin."

"Quite."

"Put your boots back on," Efluviel said, "we'd better be making a move. We need to be the other side of those dunes by sunset."

"Of course we do."

"You've got a hole in your sock."

"So I have."

Efluviel smiled at him. "I think we're getting along splen-didly together," she said. "Don't you?"

"**E**xcuse me," the little man said to the darkness, "but would you mind taking the bag off now, please?"

Various grunts, followed by a sudden flood of orange light. The little man blinked and looked round.

He was in a cave, or a tunnel, or just possibly a mineshaft. The roof, he noted, was low, so that he doubted he'd be able to stand fully upright without banging his head. It was rough-hewn grey rock, like the walls, and shored up at intervals with massive wooden beams. The light, which came from a single lantern hanging from one of the beams, showed him a dozen very short, very hairy men with beards, who were glaring down at him where he lay. Behind them, he could just make out his spinning-wheel.

"Bastard," said a short, hairy man.

The little man smiled weakly. "Let me guess," he said. "You're Drain."

He got a boot in the ribs for that. "King Drain," snarled the short man. "Son of Drag, son of Driri, King under the Mountains." The king sneezed, and wiped his moustache with the back of his hand. "So show a bit of respect, all right?"

"You're dwarves."

"So? What about it?"

The little man would have spread his hands in an appeasing gesture, only they turned out to be tied behind his back. "Nothing. I mean, that's good. The dwarves are an ancient and honourable people, famous for their industry, craftsmanship and integrity. It's a real pleasure to meet you."

The dwarves huddled together and whispered, and the little man thought he could make out, "What's integrity?", at which the king trod on the enquirer's foot. "Yeah," Drain growled. "Says you."

"And an audience with the king in person," the little man went on. "What an opportunity. It's the sort of chance you'd give your right arm for."

"That can be arranged."

The little man shuffled forward on his bottom and sat up as best he could. "And you brought my wheel," he said. "How thoughtful. I'd hate for it to get stolen while I was away."

"That thing," Drain growled angrily. "We're going to smash it," he added. "Then we're going to smash you."

"Oh?" The little man looked politely surprised. "Why would you want to do that?"

"Because." The king clenched his massive fists, then unclenched them again. "Because you're ruining us, that's why. Putting us out of business. Screwing us over. So we're going to smash you, see."

"Ah." The little man looked thoughtful, though not unduly concerned. "I believe there may have been a slight misunderstanding."

King Drain grinned unpleasantly. "I don't think so."

But the little man shook his head and smiled. "Let me explain," he said. "For generations, the dwarvish nation have been gold-miners. Yes?"

"Man and boy," grunted the king. "Man and boy."

"Quite. You've worked really hard at it, you've hacked miles and miles of these quite splendid mineshafts out of the living rock, you've fought off hordes of savage goblins who wanted to take the mines away from you. Gold-mining makes up a substantial proportion of your economy; more than that, it's part of your cultural identity, it's made you what you are." He paused, then went on, "And now, because of me, the gold price is tumbling and you're staring ruin in the face. Does that more or less cover it?"

The king had taken a short-handled axe from his belt and was tapping the blade with his fingertips. "More or less."

"Mphm. Yes, I can see how this misunderstanding has arisen."

"I think we all understand just fine."

"Ah." The little man beamed at him. "All due respect, but I'd venture to disagree. What you're actually looking at," he went on, "is the biggest and best opportunity you've ever had in the entire history of dwarfkind."

There was a deep silence. Then a short, hairy man off to the left said, "Just bash him, all right? He's making my head hurt."

But Drain was frowning thoughtfully. "Shut it," he said. "You," he went on, "Explain."

"Well." The little man wriggled a little to make himself slightly more comfortable. "As well as mining gold," he said, "you also manufacture high-class metalwork. Luxury goods. Tableware. Armour." He paused. "Weapons."

"The best there is," Drain said; not a boast, a statement of fact. "So?"

"And," the little man went on, "ever since the human princes have been awash with gold, you've been selling them lots and lots of luxury goods, gold and silver dinner services, armour and especially weapons."

"Don't tell me about it," Drain groaned. "We just can't keep up. The lads are working flat out, and still the orders keep coming in. They're not happy, the lads aren't. Nothing but work, work, work, all the damn time."

"Mphm." The little man nodded. "Of course, you could try raising your prices."

"Oh, we did that. Got to, with the gold price going down the toilet. Doesn't make any odds. They still keep ordering, the bastards."

"Quite," said the little man. "So on the one hand, there's all your metalworkers with too much work, and your gold-miners at risk of being out of a job."

"Yeah. And it's all your fault."

The little man nodded. "Of course, if your gold-miners were to give up mining and learn to be metalworkers, that might—"

He got no further, because the short, hairy men all started shouting at once. But the king was frowning again. He held up his hand for silence. "Say what?"

"Turn your miners into metalworkers. Solves both problems. Actually, I'm sure you'd already thought of that, a highly intelligent man like yourself, King under the Mountains and so forth. You were just waiting till you'd ironed out all the minor details before you made your announcement."

There was another long silence. Then all the short, hairy men started yelling again. Half of them yelled that they were miners, not bloody smiths; the other half howled about bloody miners, coming in their workshops, stealing their jobs. The king closed his eyes, counted to three under his breath and shouted, "Quiet!" Then he turned back to the little man and said, "Yeah. That's just what I was doing. I'm smart, me."

"Very smart," the little man said. "Which means you don't need me to tell you about how you can use this situation to become very rich indeed."

The king's tiny eyes widened. "You lot," he said without looking round. "Piss off. You," he added, "with me."

"I rather think my feet are tied. I can't imagine how it happened and I do apologise for any inconvenience."

The king rolled his eyes, looked round for someone to give an order to, realised they'd all gone, sighed, stooped down and cut the ropes with a small knife. "This way," he grunted.

The little man stood up, wincing as his pins-and-needles-ridden feet took his weight. "My pleasure," he said. "Thank you so much."

The king led him down two miles of tunnel, taking a left here, a right there, until they emerged into a vast cavern, hewn from a vein of sparkling pink quartz. To match the walls, everything in it was pink – the long tables and benches, the sumptuous wall-hangings, the massive carved throne, even the bear-pelts and wolfhides strewn on the polished pink floor. "Nice place you've got here," the little man said.

"Sit."

The little man looked round and noticed a sort of footstool thing at the foot of the steps leading up to the throne. Pink, naturally. He perched on it and waited as the king clambered awkwardly up into the throne, which the little man guessed had originally been built for a human (and then painted pink) "So," said the little man. "Where were we?"

"Very rich indeed."

"Oh yes, so we were. Or rather, so you will be. But you know all about that, so I won't bore you with the details."

The king looked at him. "Bore me," he said. "If you know what's good for you."

"Delighted," the little man said.

"But it won't do you any good," the king said, and his tiny eyes flashed with triumph. "Because there's something wrong with your clever idea, see, and I know what it is."

"Goodness," said the little man. "Tell me, please."

"All right." The king settled himself in the throne. It was far too tall for him and not nearly wide enough. "You figure," he went on, "that we'll sell weapons and stuff to the idiot humans and get all their gold, and then we'll be on top and they'll be fingernail dirt. Right?"

"Broadly speaking, yes."

"Ah." The king wagged a carrot-like forefinger. "But you missed something, you prune. Thing is, we don't do food. We don't grow stuff or keep animals or any of that crap, we get it all from the idiot humans. So if they got pissed with us, like maybe because we've got all their gold, we'll starve, see? And that's no bloody good, is it?"

The little man nodded sagely. "I can see you're a dwarf of unusual intelligence and perspicacity," he said. "In a few crisp words, you've gone right to the heart of the matter, like a perfectly aimed arrow."

The king frowned. "No shit?"

"No shit. You clearly have an intuitive grasp of supply-side economics. Which means," he went on, "that you know perfectly well why that isn't really a problem, and you're testing me to see if I'm as bright as you. Having a bit of fun with a silly old man. And why not? It's a poor heart that never rejoices."

The king was gazing at him with a mixture of loathing and deep curiosity. "I know that, do I?"

"Of course you do. But you need me to spell it out, so I can prove I'm your intellectual equal. Well, here we go." The little man folded his hands in his lap and beamed. "You're perfectly well aware that gold is no longer the real currency around here, straw is. It can't have escaped your attention that the princes of the West are locked in a desperate bidding war with each other to get every last stalk of straw they can lay their hands on. Which means," he continued, "that even as we speak, human ploughmen are ploughing up every last headland, roadside verge, mountain ledge, sand dune and window box with a view to sowing wheat, which will in due course produce straw, which I will then turn into gold. What you've realised, the true essence of the situation, which you've grasped like an eagle swooping on a dove, is that gold and straw are now essentially the same thing; which is to say, gold is now basically a finished form of straw, the end of an industrial-economic process that starts with a grain of seed and ends with a coin. Isn't that right?"

"Well, yeah. Stands to reason."

"Indeed. And furthermore, you've zeroed in on the most important fact of all, namely that straw has a by-product, namely wheat. As in grains of. As in the stuff you make bread out of and feed to livestock. Of which, come harvest, there's going to be an awful lot. Mountains of it."

The king frowned. "You mean food."

The little man snapped his fingers and pointed at the king, who was too preoccupied to be affronted by the gesture. "Precisely," the little man said. "Far more food than the humans will be able to consume themselves, though if I know them they'll have a damn good try. But even so, there'll be masses of it left over, which nobody will want. They'll be practically giving it away. So when you come along and make them an offer for it, they'll be all over you. Result; they get some of their worthless gold back, you get all the food you want cheap, and everybody's happy."

There was a long silence, as the merits of this argument soaked into the king's brain like puppy-wee into an expensive carpet. "Yeah, but there's another thing," the king said.

"Of course there is."

The king looked at him, then went on, "If the idiot humans keep buying weapons and armour and stuff off us, quite soon they'll have loads of weapons and masses of armour and there'll be the most god-awful war, and they'll wipe each other out, and then there won't be anybody left to grow our food. And that'd be really bad."

The little man pursed his lips, and for a moment the king felt something akin to panic, in case he'd missed something obvious and was about to prove he wasn't as smart as the little man thought he was. "Not bad?" he queried.

"Not bad," the little man said.

"Right." The king thought for a moment, and the effort was like carrying an anvil in each arm and another one on his head. "Because the princes don't want to go to war, because they want all their men out in the fields, growing wheat to turn into straw."

The little man smiled kindly. "Of course," he said. "You knew that. And you know precisely why, when the harvest's in and the princes don't need the men for farm work any more, they won't then proceed to enlist all those men into the army and start a war." He paused. "You do know that, don't you?"

"Course I do," the king said, and then his face went blank. "Perfectly obvious."

"Quite," the little man said. "It's perfectly obvious that as soon as the princes realise that they've got masses and masses of the latest deadly weapons and so have all their neighbours, it'll occur to them that the only possible outcome of a war would be that they'd exterminate each other, and nobody would win."

"I knew that."

"I know you did. You also know that they'll realise that the only way anybody could hope to win a war would be if one side got hold of even newer, better, deadlier weapons. So they'll keep on buying new ones, just to make sure the others don't get ahead of them in the arms race—"

"The what?"

The little man paused for a moment. "It's an expression," he said, "which I've only just thought of. It means you see that the prince next door has just bought ten thousand new improved crossbows with horn-and-sinew bows and improved lock mechanisms, so you go right out and buy fifteen thousand crossbows with steel bows and even better lock mechanisms, whereupon your neighbour—"

"I get the idea," said the king. "I mean, I'd already got it, but you just said what I thought of ages ago."

"Of course. Anyway, all the princes will keep on buying more and more stuff, which means your people will be kept busy for ever and ever."

"Exactly. You took the words right out of my mouth there."

"And they'll tell themselves," the little man went on, "and anybody else who'll listen, that they're not buying all this stuff for fighting humans with anyway, it's all just to scare the goblins so they won't dare to attack – which is true, because the goblins will be terrified, understandably enough; at which point—" The little man paused. "But that's enough from me," he said. "Why don't you tell me what happens after that?"

That's the thing about thinking. It's like falling out of a window. Once you start, it's actually quite hard to stop. The king furrowed his brow, crumpling it the way tectonic shift once created mountains. After a long, long time, he suddenly smiled. "At which point," he repeated.

"Yes?"

"You start spinning straw for the goblins."

Archie's head hurt, and a drowsy numbness pained his sense, as though of bourbon he had drunk, or emptied some dull opiate to the dregs. Also his tongue felt like sandpaper, his mouth was full of foul-tasting glue and his right arm had gone to sleep where he'd been lying on it. His mind was a total blank. Make it stop, he thought, make it stop. What it was in this context he wasn't sure, though if pressed on the point he'd probably have said life.

"How are you feeling?" someone asked.

He opened his eyes. "Ouch," he said, and closed them again.

The voice, which was male, deep and friendly, laughed. "Sorry about that," it said. "I expect you're feeling rotten. It's that damn sedative. We had to give you rather a lot, because of you being a goblin. And it's your poor frail human body that has to carry the can. Life can be so unfair."

The hell with the pain, and the murderous brightness of light. Archie opened his eyes again, and saw a lot of people. Men mostly; they were the ones with the guns. The women were nearly all in white coats. Talking of which, why did the room have to be so very glaringly white and so very, very brightly lit?

"I know," said the voice. "Bloody, isn't it?"

The voice turned out to belong to a short, round bald man, sitting in a chair directly in front of him. Everybody else was standing, which was probably highly significant. "I'd offer you an aspirin," the bald man went on, "but you should see what that stuff does to goblin intestinal tracts. Of course, your insides are probably human, but we can't be sure without taking them out and looking at them under a microscope, and I told them, you can't do that, he hasn't finished with them yet." He smiled pleasantly. "Sometimes they just don't think things through."

At last Archie's survival instincts started to kick in. "Who are you? Where is this? What have you done to me? I was on a *date*."

"Alas." The bald man looked very sad. "I have to tell you, the course of true love isn't running as smooth as it could be in your case." He leaned forward a little and lowered his voice. "She doesn't actually fancy you at all," he said. "Sorry about that."

Archie looked up and saw that the men with guns were

trying to look properly sympathetic. "That's all right," he said, "I didn't like her much either. I was only—"

"Researching non-parthenogenetic reproduction for a friend, I know." The bald man grinned. "Good old Kurt. I'm amazed anyone ever falls for that, but they do, all the time."

One of the gunmen shook his head sadly. A woman in a white coat sniggered, then looked embarrassed. "Who are you?" Archie said.

The bald man sat back in his chair and folded his hands in his lap. "Now that," he said, "is a very good question."

Efluviel smiled and pointed.

The broad sweep of her outstretched arm encompassed a panorama practically unmatched in the whole of the Middle Realms. Directly ahead loomed the three peaks that mark the highest point of the mighty Taupe range; Clordarf, Simithoel and Old Big Pointy. Around their summits mist swirled like a bridal veil, although the midday sun was searingly bright. "Mountains," she said.

Mordak dragged himself the last few yards and dropped at her feet. "You what?"

"Mountains."

"Really. So what were those things we just came up?"

"Foothills."

"Oh *God*." Mordak struggled out of the rucksack straps, stretched out on his back and shaded his eyes with his forearm. "It's not fair," he said. "I'm the king. I shouldn't have to do this."

"Don't whine," Efluviel said without looking round. "And we're not stopping. We need to be right down in the valley by nightfall."

"Oh shut up." Mordak closed his eyes. "My feet," he said, "are killing me."

"You're such a slob," Efluviel said, her eyes still fixed on the horizon. "A gentle stroll in the country—"

"Three days," Mordak groaned. "Like the side of a house. I hate uphill. We goblins have a saying, *down with up*."

"Rubbish. Mountains are your natural habitat."

Mordak scowled at her without opening his eyes. "The *insides* of mountains are our natural habitat," he pointed out. "Caves, caverns, mines, all that stuff. Nice level tunnels. Our legs aren't designed for all this horrible *climbing*."

"Do you good." Efluviel took a biscuit from her pocket and nibbled it. "Get some of the fat off you."

"I am not fat."

"Over there," Efluviel went on, indicating some arbitrary location in the mist. "That's where we need to get to."

Mordak risked opening one eye. "We can't go there. There's nothing to stand on. We'll slide off."

"Don't be feeble. And stop squinting."

"I'm nocturnal," Mordak growled. "Bright light doesn't agree with me."

She gave him a typical Elf smile. "Ninety-nine per cent of the time, neither do I. But I put up with you, because I have a beautiful nature. Come on, porkchop, on your feet."

"I am *not*—"

Efluviel was already twenty yards down the track. Mordak scrambled to his feet, snatched up the rucksack and hobbled after her. "Wait for me."

"Why should I?"

Another thing Mordak regarded as unfair, though he hadn't mentioned it because he suspected she'd only make fun of him, was that there should be such a colossal disparity between the proportions of up and down. It was hard to account for, if you believed at all in geometry, but he could attest to it from bitter experience. Three days to climb up the hill, one afternoon to climb down again. So where had all the rest of the down got to?

That night, as scheduled, they rested in the valley. Horribly bright and early they set off to follow the winding zigzag path that led all the way up to the snow-capped top of Clordarf, where the hermit lived. It was a very long way, and very, very steep. "Why aren't you tired?" Mordak kept asking. "You ought to be worn out by now, I'm worn out, I'm a battle-hardened goblin warrior and you're just an effete, decadent bloody Elf. I demand that you be tired immediately."

"Wuss."

"I am not a wuss. Can we stop now? Just for a bit?"

"If you talked a bit less, maybe you wouldn't be out of breath all the time."

The last two hours were probably the worst. Goblins, whose natural habitat is underground caverns, where the temperature is always just on the warm side of pleasantly mild, don't do well in snow up to their knees. True, losing all feeling in his feet stopped them hurting, but the glare of the sun on the white, white snow seemed to bleach every last trace of intelligence out of his brain, and the cold-induced numbness still had a long way to go before it reached his knees, thighs and back. The worst thing of all, however, was Efluviel's cheerful whistling.

"We're here."

"Wassa?"

"We're here," Efluviel repeated. "Look, you can just make out the mouth of his cave in the rock-face over there."

"Ung."

"There now." Efluviel took a moment to pat a few stray strands of hair back into perfect place. "That wasn't so bad, was it?"

"Uck oo."

She turned and looked at him. "Oh for pity's sake," she said, "look at you, you're a mess. How can you expect the hermit to take you seriously in that state? And stop wheezing, for crying out loud. It's embarrassing."

"*Tired.*"

"Nonsense."

Ahead of them was a level plateau, about fifty yards across, before you reached the sheer face of the mountainside. Mordak's woefully light-abused eyes could just make out a darker patch, about the size you'd expect a cave mouth to be. "I don't know," he said. "I don't like this."

"You seem not to like a great many things. Hence the whining."

"I know caves," Mordak said stubbornly. "I have instincts. That's not a good place."

"Chicken."

"I am not—"

"You're afraid. Admit it."

She took a few steps toward the cliff. Mordak stayed resolutely where he was. She paused and looked back at him. "Oh come *on*," she said. "You're a goblin. Goblins don't know the meaning of fear."

"I don't know the meaning of half the words in the dictionary. That doesn't make me a bad person."

"Don't be silly. Look, there's nothing to be afraid of. It's just a cave, right?"

Mordak folded his arms. "We goblins have another saying," he said. "We have nothing to fear but fear itself and scary things. That," he added firmly, "is a scary thing. You go."

Efluviel hesitated. On the one hand, Mordak had a point – two, if you counted the top of his head. Goblins knew caves, that was undeniable, and if Mordak reckoned there was something wrong, there was a good chance he knew what he was talking about. On the other hand – that would be the hand she'd cheerfully bite off at the wrist rather than squander such an opportunity as this for putting the loathsome little upstart in his place. "With pleasure," she said. "You go and hide somewhere, if you can find a biggish crevice you can squeeze into—"

"I am not f—"

"And when you get bored of cowering you can come in and join me. So long."

She walked away, her heels crunching in the snow. Mordak looked round and found a deep fissure in the rock, just wide enough for a goblin – a thin one, like himself – to hunker down in. He crawled into it and hunkered. Efluviel had reached the cave mouth; she went in and disappeared. Silly cow, Mordak thought. Some people just don't listen.

He hunkered a bit more. The wind was getting up, and iron-grey clouds were sailing in from the far side of the mountains. Obviously what they should have done, what they would have done if she hadn't insisted on flouncing off like that, was work their way cautiously round the side of the plateau so as to approach the cave from its blind side; then, waiting till nightfall, edge their way even more cautiously to the cave mouth and wait there for an hour or so in case they saw or heard anything, before creeping inside a few yards at a time while maintaining a clear escape route. But no. Charge in where goblins fear to tread. And he wasn't fat.

Time passed, and the hunkering started to tell on Mordak's knees. Big chunky gobbets of snow drifted down and covered his shoulders like dandruff. He was shivering, and it wasn't fear. She'd been gone over an hour, probably closer to two. He didn't know what to make of that. She might be dead, or dying, or dangling captive in the web of a giant spider. Or she could be sitting by the hermit's fire drinking tea and toasting crumpets. If she'd got herself into trouble, she'd have screamed – a screamer if ever he saw one, first sign of danger and she'd be yelling the place down. Assuming, of course, that she'd seen the danger coming which, being an Elf rather than a goblin, she almost certainly wouldn't have. So, Mordak thought, either she's in there in the warm and dry or she's in desperate peril and I suppose I've got to go and save her.

He blinked.

I suppose I've got to go and save her. That was hero stuff; where in the Dark Lord's name had that come from, all of a sudden? That was what you got for associating with Elves and freezing your claws off on mountain-tops; eventually the brain goes, the instincts decay, the moral fibre turns to mush, the categorical imperatives gurgle away down the U-bend and you might as well be dead. Worse still, you might as well be human. The hell with all this, Mordak told himself. I'm going to go in there and bite something. It's my only hope.

Feeling incredibly stupid, he got up and walked across the plateau. The cave mouth – he could see why they called them that, it did look just like a big, wide-open mouth, just waiting to gobble him up. Inside it was pitch dark, even for goblin eyes. Oh poo, he thought, and plunged in.

He couldn't see a damn thing, but he could smell – what? Definitely a food sort of smell, which served to remind him that he hadn't eaten anything but dry biscuits for a week, thank you so much, but with overtones of mildew, sweat and some strong, volatile chemical. Wonderful. His feet registered a smooth stone floor. Big deal, it's a cave. Onwards.

And onwards he went, until he walked into something. It was soft, and gave way. It squeaked.

"Efluviel?" he whispered. "Is that you?"

"Mmm."

Very tentatively he reached out, and his fingertip encountered something sharp, facing downwards. "Is that your ear?"

"Mmmmmm."

"What's it doing—? Yes, all right, hang on." The hell with it, he thought, we've made enough noise to tell anyone who's interested exactly where we are, so why not? From his pocket he took a tinderbox and a stub of troll-tallow candle. "Won't be a jiffy. Oh."

Oh indeed. Efluviel was hanging by her ankle from the cavern roof. The mumbled responses were accounted for by the fact that her sensible woolly scarf had got tangled round her face, and she couldn't do anything about it because she was neatly contained in a stoutly woven net.

Mordak kept his face straight for as long as he could. It was a titanic effort, but he managed it. Worth it, he told himself; worth all the pain and exhaustion and privation, the cold and the fear. It was, he realised, the moment he'd been born for.

"Told you so," he said.

"Mmm."

"Apology accepted," Mordak said happily. "Right, hold still, we'll have you out of that in a couple of— Oh," he added, as he cut through the rope and she landed on her head. "Sorry," he said, and almost made it sound like he meant it.

Efluviel groaned, then started clawing savagely at the net. "Keep still," Mordak said, "you're only tangling it more. "There," he said, as she finally emerged. "There you are, and no harm done."

She glared balefully at him. "You're never going to let me forget this, are you?"

He shook his head. "I promise you," he said. "I'll never mention it ever again."

"Promise?"

"Promise. I'll remember it with sublime pleasure several times a day, every day until I die, but I'll never ever mention it."

She dragged the scarf off and threw it into the darkness. "Thank you."

"You're welcome." He nodded at the remains of the net. "Trap," he said.

"I'd sort of gathered that."

"Been in it long?"

"Most of my life, I'd say."

"But nobody's come along to collect you." Mordak nodded. "That's good."

"Is it?"

"I'd say so. It suggests the trap is a line of defence rather than a means of obtaining food. Or," he added, "they're not particularly hungry. You're sure we've come to the right place?"

"Yes."

"Mphm. All right, then. On we go."

She stared at him. "Are you mad?"

It just got better and better. "Not mad," he said, "just brave. You coming or what?"

Efluviel got up slowly and brushed dust off her knees. "Brave as two short planks. All right. You can go first this time."

There didn't seem to be much point in going quietly. The stop, and various other things, seemed to have lifted Mordak's spirits and put a spring in his step. It was pleasantly warm, and great to be back in a tunnel again. All in all, it was turning out to be rather a good day.

And then the ground wasn't there any more, and he was falling. And then the ground came back.

"Mordak."

He opened his eyes and looked up. About a hundred feet above him, he could see the faint glow of the candle-stub. "Ouch," he said.

"Are you all right?"

"I think so. "

"You fell down a hole."

"Apparently."

"Another trap."

"Ah," Mordak said. "That explains that, then."

Silence. Then she said, "I haven't got any rope."

"I have," Mordak said. "Loads of it, about a hundred and fifty feet's worth. Of course, it's down here with me, instead of up there with you. Pity."

"You could try throwing it up to me."

"Now there's an idea. Ow," he added, as the coil of rope fell back down again and hit him on the head. "All right, tried that."

"Try again."

"No thanks. Look," he added. "About earlier."

"What about it?"

Mordak took a deep breath. "When you got caught in the other trap and I was a bit, well, smug about it."

"Yes?"

"It was fun," Mordak said. "Now will you please stop fart-arsing about and get me out of here?"

Pause. "I don't think I can."

Mordak thought for a moment. "I don't think you can either," he said.

"The way I see it," Effluviel continued, "we have three options."

"That many? Goodness."

"I think so, yes," Effluviel said. "I can turn back, and freeze or starve to death on the mountainside. Or I can keep going, and get killed by the next trap or whoever's setting them. Or I can stay here till I starve to death. Which one would you advise?"

Mordak considered. "I don't know," he said. "Which one would you go for?"

"It's hard to say. There's not all that much to choose between them, really. It's a nuisance you've got all the food."

"And the rope, yes."

"Maybe if I'd agreed to carry more of the stuff—"

"Ah well," Mordak said generously. "You've got your own things to carry, all those books, and your extra blankets, and your special pillow. It's all right," he added. "I'm sure you'll think of something."

"You mean you'll think of something. My mind's a total blank."

There was a long silence after that, during which Mordak ate some biscuits. Then: "Mordak."

"Yes?"

Pause. "Look, I know this may sound heartless, but would you do something for me?"

"Depends what it is."

Longer pause. "Would you make me the editor of the *Face*? Only, you did say you would, if I did this job for you, and obviously that's not going to happen now, but that's hardly my fault. And I did try."

"You did. You tried a lot, including my patience."

"Please? Then when I get back I can tell them that you said, with your dying breath."

"Steady on."

"One of your dying breaths. Please?"

"Fine," Mordak said. "But somehow I don't think that's going to cut much ice with anybody. I mean, they won't believe you and you won't be able to prove it, because even if I put it in writing, you can't reach me, so that's no good. Also bear in mind that there's a deadly enemy out there who seems to want to kill us both and I've got all the food down here. I don't think you're going home, Efluviel. Sorry."

He waited. It was a while before she replied. "I know," she said. "But that's not the point. All my life I wanted that job, it's all I ever dreamed of. And if I've got to die, I want to die an editor. Please? And you're not fat. You've just got big bones."

Mordak thought for a moment. Then he said, "Efluviel, I hereby appoint you editor-in-chief of the *Horrible Yellow Face*."

"*Beautiful Golden Face*."

"Whatever."

"Thank you. Do you really mean it?"

"Yes."

"Really and truly?"

"Yes."

"You're not just saying it? You really, really do mean it?"

"Oh for crying out loud. I really, really, really mean it, all right?" He sighed. "If there's one thing I can't be doing with, it's people who won't take yes for an answer."

"Right," Efluviel said. "In that case, there's someone coming. And he's got a ladder and a coil of rope."

"What's so good about it?" Archie asked.

"Ah." The bald man smiled. Actually, he wasn't entirely bald. He had a tuft of springy white hair dead centre of the top of his head, like the grass that grows up in the middle of a country road. His cheeks were broad, flat and pink, like newly opened tins of Spam, and his eyes were small, blue and very bright. "Another good question. Tell you what. Promise me you won't do anything silly or violent, and I'll let these boys and girls get back to work and we can have a private chat and I'll tell you. How about it?"

The boys and girls, especially the boys with the Kalashnikovs, didn't look too happy about that, but the bald man didn't seem interested in what they thought. "All right," Archie said.

"Promise?"

"Word of honour."

"Thank you." The bald man turned his head slightly.

"Right then, children, thank you very much. I'll call if I need anything."

A moment or so later, they were alone. The bald man leaned forward in his chair and said, "That's better. Now, then—"

He got no further because Archie sprang off the bed, grabbed his throat and started to squeeze. It was a long time since he'd throttled anything, and all his bottled-up goblin instincts were just starting to express themselves in good, healthy violence when he found himself flying through the air. Not for terribly long, because there was a wall in the way. He slid down it like a raindrop on a windowpane and ended up slumped on the floor in a small, untidy heap.

"Now then." The bald man ran a finger round the inside of his collar. "Where were we?"

Archie opened his eyes. The room was going round and round. "You said," he mumbled, "it was a good question."

"And so it was," the bald man said. "An excellent question, very perceptive and going straight to the heart of the matter. How's your head, by the way?"

"Not wonderful."

The bald man nodded sympathetically. "Human skulls," he said. "Much thinner than the goblin sort, though they hold half a pint more beer. If you're going to do much more fighting during your stay here, you'd do well to acquaint yourself with the shortcomings of the hardware."

During your stay here. It was a pity his head was spinning, because it made it hard to think. With regret, Archie decided to postpone detailed analysis of that one until the world stopped thinking it was a centrifuge. "Sorry," he said.

The bald man shrugged. "Perfectly natural behaviour for a goblin, and you can't blame a fellow for trying. I could have warned you, I suppose, but you wouldn't have believed me. But now you know, and we don't have to go through all that again. Can you get up?"

"I think so," Archie said. "No," he amended. "I don't think I can."

"Give it five minutes and try again," the bald man said, "I don't think anything's broken. Relax, take deep breaths, you'll be fine."

Archie took his advice. It didn't help much. "How did you do that?" he asked.

"Throw you across the room? Oh, that was quite easy." The bald man smiled. "Just a gadget, that's all. To be precise, it's a miniaturised solid-state personal electromagnetic force-field projector; quite advanced stuff, though I do say so myself. Here." He reached inside his jacket and took out a little grey box. There were winking red and green lights. He pressed a button and the lights went out. "Might as well save the batteries," he said, putting the box on the floor at his feet. "They cost five million dollars each and they only run for twenty minutes."

"Is it turned off?"

"Yes. Why do you—?"

Archie hurled himself across the room, arms outstretched, fingers clawed ready to grip. He almost made it. Then he was still airborne but going the other way. He hit a different bit of wall this time, but the effect was much the same.

"It doesn't work, of course," the bald man said.

Archie spat out a tooth. "Hmm?"

"The box," the bald man said. "The solid-state personal electromagnetic force-field projector. It's really just a plastic box with some bits of wire in it, for show. I seem to remember it's a bit off an old broken washing machine."

Archie looked at him through his one remaining good eye. "You can do magic."

The bald man frowned. "Don't be silly, of course I can't. Magic doesn't work here, everybody knows that." Then his frown slipped a bit sideways, and he grinned. "Mind you," he said, "anybody who knows the first thing about science could tell you that a force-field projector small enough to fit in Asia, let alone a little grey box, is every bit as impossible as magic, and probably more so. But that's the locals for you. They're perfectly all right believing one set of impossible things, but not another. Oh, and by the way."

"Mmm?"

In the course of eavesdropping on the film crew, Archie had been introduced to the concept of frequent flyer benefits. He'd liked the sound of that, but it was proving to be illusory, like so many other things in life. All he got out of his third flight in so many minutes was another nasty bump on the head and a painfully jarred elbow.

"Hey," he groaned, "I didn't do anything."

"No." The bald man smiled. "That was by way of answering your excellent question. Who am I?" The smile broadened. "I'm the bad guy."

"I suppose you'll be wanting lunch," said the hermit.

Efluviel stared at him. From far below in the pit came the echo of a voice saying, "Yes, please."

"Fine," the hermit said sadly. "Here." He uncoiled the rope from his shoulder and dropped it on the ground. "You do it. Don't see why I should have to."

There were several things Efluviel wanted to say at that moment, but instead she went with, "All right, yes, thank you." Then she looked round for something to tie the rope to. By the time she'd done that, and Mordak had hauled himself up it out of the pit, the hermit wasn't there any more.

"You're fired," Mordak said.

"You what?"

"You're fired," Mordak repeated, carefully winding up the rope around his forearm. "Come on, we don't want to lose him. You didn't happen to notice which way he went, did you?"

"You can't do that."

"Yes I can."

"But *why*?" Efluviel wailed. "What did I do? I rescued you."

"No," Mordak said gently, "he did. You tied a bit of rope to a rock. For which," he added, "I'm very grateful. Thank you."

"You *bastard*!"

"This way, I think," Mordak said, sniffing the air. "On account of, it's the only one. Come on."

For a moment Efluviel was too shocked to move. Then she scampered after him. "Why? Why are you firing me?"

"Simple." Mordak stopped for another sniff. "Baked beans," he said. "I quite like baked beans."

"What did I *do*?"

"Nothing," Mordak said. "I'm firing you because all you've ever wanted your entire life is to be the editor of the *Face*, right? And so, until you achieve that ambition, you'll probably keep on helping me. So, you're fired. Soon as the mission's successfully accomplished, I'll reinstate you. All right?"

"That's so mean," Efluviel said. "That's just plain nasty. That's—"

"Personnel management," Mordak said. "Oops, tautology. Hurry up or he'll get away. And don't pull faces, you'll stick like it."

The scent of baked beans was getting stronger; Efluviel could smell it now, and it shows how hungry she was that she quickened her pace until she was practically treading on Mordak's heels. "That must be him," she said.

"What?"

"You know, *him*. The hermit."

Mordak held back and fell in step. "You know," he said, "just then you sounded almost like – no, it's not possible."

"Huh?"

"Respectful," he said. "Which is so not you."

"Of course I respect the hermit," Efluviel said. "He's the wisest man in the world. Why else do you think we've come here? To the Elves, he's practically a god."

"Right. A god who sets traps for visitors."

"So?"

"And who really likes baked beans. Ah, this looks promising."

In front of them they saw a rusty steel door, half ajar; by the state of the hinges, Mordak noted as they passed through, it hadn't been capable of opening and closing for many years. Beyond the door, the corridor was dimly lit with tallow candles bearded with drips, whose light revealed a large number of empty brown earthenware jars lying on the ground, their labels peeling in the damp.

"Baked beans," Efluviel said.

"So? He likes baked beans. Shows what a wise man he is."

They turned a corner and found themselves in a high-roofed vaulted cavern. A hole in the roof let in daylight, revealing small hills of empty bean jars piled against the walls. A clothes-line spanned the cavern from torch-sconce to torch-sconce; from it dangled three pairs of frayed socks. In the far corner was a pile of cushions facing a small three-legged table, on which rested a perfect sphere of milk-white crystal, about the size of a man's head. On the cushions lay the hermit, a thin man with straggly grey hair in a ponytail, wearing a brown robe. He had a bean jar in one hand and a fork in the other. He was staring at the crystal, and didn't look round as they approached.

"There's beans," he said. "In the corner, by the stove. I suppose you'd better help yourselves."

The stove was a small, spindly-legged charcoal brazier; on it was a battered copper pan, and next to it a pyramid of unopened bean jars. "Thank you," Efluviel said. She lifted the pan and peered into it. "Maybe later," she said. "But first, we have travelled far to ask you—"

"Quiet," said the hermit.

Efluviel led Mordak off to one side. "That ball thing," she said, in an awed voice, "I know what that is, they're famous, everybody knows about them back home. It's a Stone of

Seeing. They're magic, and there's only six of them in the whole world. If you look into them, you can see what's going on in distant places and—"

"Yes, I know."

"Talk to the owners of the other five Stones without – what did you say?"

"I know. The Fathers of the Wise brought them from Omeranilenarion when they came over the Sundering Seas in the Pink Ships."

"You *know*? That's impossible. They're a secret."

Mordak smiled. "That's what I like about you," he said. "Every so often you can be quite disarmingly naïve. Of course we know about them. We've got one."

"You've *got*—" Efluviel's eyes opened wide. "Oh my God. The Fifth Stone. The Fifth Stone is in the hands of *goblins*."

"Mphm." Mordak hesitated, but she did look terribly upset. "I wouldn't worry about it," he said.

"Oh really. The Fifth Stone is controlled by the enemy and he says not to worry."

"We can't get it to work," Mordak said. "It used to, about four hundred years ago. But then the picture got a bit blurry, and some fool thought he could fix that by cleaning it with nitric acid. We clean everything with nitric acid," he explained, as Efluviel stared at him, "it's the only way to get rid of those stubborn ground-in stains without the boil-wash. Anyway, since then it hasn't worked worth a damn."

"Oh." Efluviel breathed a sigh of relief. Then she frowned. "Hang on, though," she said. "If you've got the Fifth Stone, and the other five are all accounted for, what on earth is that?"

Mordak shrugged. "Why don't you ask him?"

"Oh no, I can't." Efluviel was actually blushing. "He's the *hermit*. No, no, I can't. Really."

Mordak rolled his eyes. "We've come all this way to ask him questions and now you're *shy*. I don't believe it."

"You ask him. I just can't. Sorry."

"Elves," Mordak said. Then he advanced towards the hermit and cleared his throat. "Excuse me—"

"*Quiet!*"

Behind him, Mordak could hear a little whimper, which he ignored. "I said, excuse—"

"Shut *up*," the hermit roared. His eyes were still fixed on the crystal.

Mordak could feel his hackles rising. He took a deep breath, then another. "Listen, friend," he said. "The lady and I have come a long—"

"Shut up! Go away! Oh for God's sake. Why do you people always have to show up at exactly the wrong moment? Go *away.*"

Mordak thought for a moment. Then he slipped off his tattered travelling cloak and threw it over the crystal sphere. The hermit stared for a moment, then screamed. It was possibly the shrillest noise Mordak had ever heard, and goblins have rather sensitive ears, attuned to picking out very faint noises in the dark. So he did what he had to do, whereupon Efluviel hit him with a chair. By then, however, it was too late.

"You *lunatic*," she screamed in his ear. "You've killed him."

Mordak sighed. "Don't be silly," he said. "He's just mildly stunned, that's all. He'll be fine in a minute." He picked a splinter of wood out of his collar and looked at it. "Did you just attack me?"

"Yes."

He shrugged. "Well, you're not very good at it. You can explain to him why his one and only chair is now firelighters." He leaned forward, twitched the cloak off the globe, and crouched down to listen. Very faint and far away, he heard a voice that seemed to be saying, "Dogger, Fisher, German Bight, moderate easterly, good". He shrugged. "Oh look," he said. "Your friend's waking up."

The hermit groaned, opened his eyes, saw Mordak and cringed away. "Get him off me," he shouted. "Help! Goblins!"

"Now then," Mordak said, "there's no call for that. I just—"

"*Goblins!*" The hermit scrambled to his feet, caught his bare toes in the hem of his robe, slipped, skated across the smooth floor of the cavern, banged head first into the wall and went back to sleep. "Oh come on," Mordak said. "This is silly."

Efluviel grabbed him by the sleeve and marched him over to the opposite corner of the chamber. "*Stay,*" she snapped. "I'll talk to him. You've done enough for one day."

"The silly sod tripped over his feet," Mordak protested. "How is that my fault?"

"You're a *goblin.*"

Mordak made a faint whimpering noise. "Fine," he said. "You talk to him. A moment ago you were too shy."

"That was before you started beating him to a pulp."

"I did not—"

"Goblins," Efluviel said savagely. "Bloody goblins." The hermit was stirring again. "You," she said, giving Mordak a look that would've stripped paint. "Stay there. Don't do anything. Don't say anything. Leave everything to me. Understand?"

She said the last word slowly, accentuating each syllable. It was probably the single most dangerous thing she ever did in her life, though at the time she was too preoccupied to realise. For a moment, Mordak's eyes glowed like tiny furnaces; then he suddenly smiled.

"Yes, dear."

"Clown." Efluviel turned her back on him and stalked across the chamber. By the time she reached the hermit he was sitting up, massaging his forehead with the palms of both hands. "Excuse me," she said.

"No!" yelled the hermit. "Go away! Keep back. Don't hit me."

Efluviel had a smile on her face, hard and inflexible as an axe-head. "It's all right," she said, "I'm not going to hurt you. I'm an Elf. I'm good."

"Piss off."

Efluviel dropped on one knee and leaned forward to examine the hermit's forehead. He shrank back. "Get off me."

"I just want to see if—"

"Get away from me or I'll rip your ears off."

"Mphm." Efluviel edged back a little. "You don't seem to be too badly hurt. No blurred or double vision, nausea, dizziness?"

"I've got a knife," the hermit said. "Somewhere," he added, looking round. He scrabbled on the floor beside him and his fingers closed on something. It turned out to be a fork. "Want some of this, do you, needle-ears? Come on then, if you think you're hard enough."

Efluviel's jaw dropped. "Needle-ears?"

"You heard me."

For a moment, her eyes gleamed just like Mordak's. Then she said, "It's all right, I forgive you, you've just had a very traumatic experience. Just *don't ever call me that again.* Capisce?"

There was a clatter as the fork hit the floor. "Sorry," the hermit said. "Just keep your goblin off me, all right? And don't scowl at me like that."

"I'm not scowling. This is just my face."

"Then for God's sake take it outside. It's making my teeth hurt."

Efluviel blinked twice. Then she turned round. "Mordak," she said. "Come and talk to the nice gentleman."

"Love to." Mordak got to his feet and wandered across. "Hello," he said, "let's start again. I'm Mordak, king of the goblins, though I'm sure you knew that already. Sorry if my assistant here's been bothering you. I wonder if you'd care to answer a few questions. If you do," he added quickly, before the hermit could speak, "we'll go away and never come back."

"Shoot."

Mordak smiled. "Thank you," he said, and sat down cross-legged on the floor. "First, you said something about lunch."

"Over there." The hermit waved at the bean jars.

"Thank you. My assistant will see to that. Would you like to join us?"

"I'm not eating anything she's been fiddling with."

Mordak smiled. "As you wish. Can't say I blame you. Now then, that thing over there. What is it?"

The hermit glared at him. "None of your damn business."

A crash behind him told Mordak that Efluviel was knocking the heads off baked-bean jars. "It's one of those seeing-stones, isn't it?"

"Might be. Never said it wasn't."

"But she doesn't know about it."

A broad, crafty grin spread across the hermit's face. "Loads of stuff she doesn't know about," he said. "Thinks she's so smart. Patronising cow."

"I like you," Mordak said. "In fact, I like you so much I might just decide to come and settle here permanently, and bring all my friends. Unless," he added pleasantly, "you tell me where you got that thing from and why her lot don't know about it."

The hermit's face didn't change, but his eyes grew very round. "They all came through It," he said quickly, "all the seeing-stones. All that about the Pink Ships is just bull. But that one came later than the others. Bloke who sold it to me said so. Bloke in a bar."

"Ah." Mordak gave him a reassuring grin. "And does it work?"

"Sort of."

Mordak nodded slowly. Goblins love bargains, so the properties of objects bought from men in bars were familiar to him. "It doesn't work."

"Well, no. Not for talking to the other stones, but then, who gives a damn? All the other stones belong to Elves."

"Quite."

"But it does work. Sort of."

"What does it do?"

"Ah." The hermit seemed to have forgotten that he was talking to a goblin; his voice was higher and far less whiny, and he'd stopped quivering. "That's a good question. It talks to me. I talk to it, but either it can't hear me or it isn't interested. A bit like my ex-wife."

"I see," Mordak said. "What does it say?"

"All sorts of really weird stuff," the hermit replied excitedly. "I think it must be gods or something. You get different voices at different times of day. Like, the one I was listening to a moment ago tells you what the weather's going to be, except that it's always wrong and I've never heard of any of the places. And a lot of the time it's a horrible noise like music, except it's not music. And then there's other gods telling me about stuff happening in a load of other places nobody's ever heard of, and I can understand most of the words, but none of it makes any sense."

Mordak thought for a moment. "You're sure it's real," he said, "and you haven't gone mad or anything?"

"I wondered about that," the hermit said earnestly. "I mean, at one point I was pretty sure I must be imagining the whole thing. But I asked some visitors if they could hear it too, and they could. You heard it, didn't you? Just now."

"Yes, now you mention it, I did hear something." Mordak said. "It was a little voice coming from a long way away. Dogger and Fisher and—"

"German Bight." The hermit nodded vigorously. "So if you can hear it, it must be real. But I've researched it thoroughly, I've looked in all the records of the wisdom of the ages." He nodded in the direction of the floor a few yards away; lying in the dust among the empty bean jars Mordak could see two small, rather dog-eared books, *Wisdom* and *More Wisdom*. "And there's nothing in any of them about Dogger or Fisher or German Bight, or Washington or London or Brussels or Kabul, I don't even know if they're people or places or what the hell they are. And the *stuff*. The stuff's just plain bizarre."

"The stuff."

"The stuff the gods tell me about. Crazy. Half of it's all wars and earthquakes and some really odd kind of politics, and the other half is a load of trivial nonsense about actors and musicians and people who play kids' games for money. And the god makes it sound like they're all equally important, which makes no sense at all." He sighed, and slumped against the wall. "For two pins I'd chuck the bloody thing down a volcano and be done with it, except—" He shrugged. "If it really is gods talking to me, I've got to listen, haven't I? It's my duty."

Mordak rubbed his chin thoughtfully. "You said that the ball thing came here through It."

"That's right. At least, I think so. That's what the bloke told me. Where else could it have come from?"

"What's It?"

The hermit's face suddenly went blank. "You don't know."

It occurred to Mordak that he might have made a serious tactical error. "Of course I know," he said. "I just wanted to be sure we were talking about the same It, that's all."

He'd just made things worse. "There's only one It," the hermit said. "And you don't know about it. And if you don't know, I can't tell you."

"Yes you can."

"No I *can't*. That's sacred wisdom, that is. Need to know only. Not to be shared with the likes of you."

Mordak pursed his lips. "What if I were to make a Freedom of Information request?"

"You do what you damn well like."

"All right. How about if I bite your arms off?"

The hermit's nostrils twitched. "That's different."

"Splendid," Mordak said, grinning so as to exhibit his full range of teeth. "Now then. Tell me everything."

"I'm not supposed to. I'll get into all sorts of trouble."

Mordak clicked his tongue. "No you won't," he said. "You're under the direct personal protection of the king of the goblins, who's unconditionally guaranteeing your safety. Also, if you don't, I'll hit you."

Goblin diplomacy at its finest. The hermit shuddered, then sighed. "It," he said.

"It."

"It's a thing."

"You don't say."

The hermit gave him a much-enduring look. "I don't know how you'd describe it," he said. "Basically, a few hours' march from here, there's a cliff. In the face of the cliff, about three feet off the ground, there's a hole, about six feet across. All round the hole there's this—" The strain of searching for the right word distorted his face for a moment. "Thing. It's like a big circle, it's sort of a light brown, they do say it's soft when you push against it, like a cushion, and oily and glistening, and there's sparkly things like diamonds all over it. That's it. A thing."

Mordak frowned. "A thing with a hole." He scratched his head. "Sounds like a perfectly ordinary cave to me."

The grin that covered the hermit's face had nothing o do with amusement; it was beyond pleasure or fear. "Ordinary it ain't," he said. "Anything that goes through the hole doesn't come back."

"Ah."

"Quite."

"That sort of hole."

"That sort of hole," the hermit repeated solemnly. "And if you stand next to it and keep very, very still, sometimes you can hear voices on the other side."

"I bet."

"Straight up. Distant voices, whispering. And nothing that goes in from our side ever comes back, but—" He leaned forward and lowered his voice to a murmur. "They do say, sometimes things come from the other side into our side. Things and people."

Mordak's head was starting to hurt. "Seems to me," he said, "that it wouldn't be a bad idea to get a bloody great big rock and fill it in. Just to be on the safe side."

That grin again. "Oh, they've tried that. The Wise. They've blocked it with boulders, they've built walls, they've sapped into the cliff face and brought down avalanches. Next day, the bloody thing's back again. There's absolutely nothing anyone can do to get rid of it. Believe me, they've tried. Six hundred years ago, the Jade Emperor of the East garrisoned an entire army there, six thousand men, to make sure nothing came through. When the supply wagons rolled up there two days later, they were all gone. Nothing left behind but a belt buckle and a small heap of plum stones. People try not to go near it much these days."

"For some reason."

"Indeed. Anyway," the hermit said, taking a deep breath, "that's It. And that's where the man in the bar said this stone thing came from. Through the hole. From the other side."

Cautiously, Mordak edged forward and nudged the crystal very gently with his foot. It didn't move; it was like pressing against a wall. But it was spherical. Touching it made Mordak feel sick. "Well," he said, "that's really very interesting, but it's not what I came to see you about." He picked up the cloak he'd thrown over it earlier and replaced it, taking care that his fingertips came nowhere near the crystal's surface. "All I want is to ask you a few questions."

The hermit was looking at the covered sphere. "You know what," he said, "when you do that, it's different, somehow. Like suddenly it can't see me any more." He pulled himself together with a visible effort. "Let's have some lunch," he said. "I could murder a baked-bean sandwich."

"A baked-bean sandwich wouldn't be murder," Mordak said. "It'd be self-defence."

Archie wiped blood out of his eyes and propped himself up on one elbow. His head felt like he'd been using it to drive in fence-posts, and his fingers and toes were tingling ominously. "Define bad," he said.

"Well." The bald man reached out a hand. Archie shrank away, then realised that the bald man was offering to help him up. "A bad host, for one thing. Can I get you some milk? Pineapple juice? Maybe a couple of croissants."

Archie was on his feet again. He swayed; balance sold separately. "Have I just been abducted?"

That made the bald man laugh. "If you like," he said. "Me, I'd call it relocated or maybe added to inventory, but these things are subjective. If you don't fancy croissants, I can get the lads to run you up a cheese and rocket salad." Then he frowned. "You're not going to attack me again, are you? Please don't. Human bodies can't take it like goblin bodies can."

Archie nodded. "Tell you what," he said. "Let's pretend I

have attacked you, and I've smashed you to the floor and jumped on your face a few times, and now I've terrified you into telling me exactly what's going on."

"Sure," the bald man said. "What do you want to know?"

"Who are you, where am I, what am I doing here—"

The bald man held up his hand. "That sort of thing," he said. "Yes, why not?" He sat down cross-legged on the floor, took an apple from his pocket, bit off a large chunk, pulled a face, spat it out. "Are you sitting comfortably?" he said. "Then I'll begin."

Presumably you're aware (the bald man said) of the Law of Conservation of Matter.

You aren't? Gosh. Not to worry, because I was just about to say, forget everything you've ever learned about the Law of Conservation of Matter, ignore it, expunge it from your mind entirely. But you won't have to do that, so that's all right. Actually, you're far better off than most people, because they know about the Law of Conservation of Matter, and it confuses the hell out of them when I tell them what they actually ought to know, which is the Law of Conservation of All Sorts of Things.

With me so far? Oh good.

The Law of Conservation of All Sorts of Things states that there's only a finite quantity of any amount of stuff, and that finite amount can't increase or decrease. Matter's one of them, for sure, but there are others. There's Energy, and Time, which are pretty much self-evident, and then there's other, rather more nebulous forces and agents and so on, such as Optimism—

Yes, of course, Optimism is a classic. There's only so much of it in the Multiverse, and it never dies, it just gets moved around. Give you a for-instance: for a week or so you're really optimistic that you'll get the vacant deputy assistant manager's job, but then it becomes painfully obvious that your boss wants to give it to the smarmy cow in the Harrogate office; you therefore lose optimism, and the smarmy cow acquires it. The net quantity stays constant, but it's redistributed. It's just like Happiness. In fact, unless you've got a good working knowledge of the operation of the Law of Conservation of Happiness, I really can't see how you could possibly begin to understand the first thing about sentient life. I mean, it'd make no sense at all.

But where the Laws of Conservation really matter is when you get on to Good and Evil. Yes, them too. Especially them.

All right, don't believe it if you don't want to, but it's true. There's a precisely quantified and absolutely limited quantity of both Good and Evil in every single reality in the Multiverse. It's not optional, and it's no good bringing in a note from your mother. There's x Good and y Evil, and that's that. Now in some realities, such as this one, you get what we call the Water Effect. Yes, I was just about to tell you. You've got hydrogen, and you've got oxygen; two very dissimilar substances, as I'm sure you'll agree—

Gases. They're gases. Sort of flavoured air.

All right, fine. All you need to know is that in nine realities out of ten, hydrogen and oxygen, though tending to disagree about a lot of things at a pretty fundamental level, nevertheless tend to combine to form the substance we call water; sort of like a coalition, but without all the point-scoring. Likewise, in this reality and quite a few others, low levels of Good and Evil combine to form the entity we know as human nature. In some people it's two atoms of Good to one of Evil, in others it's the other way about, but generally speaking it's a pretty even and consistent mix. Consequently, the overall reserves of Good and Evil in this reality are widely distributed at a pretty low concentration, and it means the overwhelming majority of people aren't particularly nice or conspicuously nasty. They're just ordinary folks like you and me. Well, like me.

In other realities, though, such as the one you come from, the Water Effect doesn't apply. Instead of being spread all over the place in tiny quantities, Evil and Good gather separately in massive concentrations; result, you get whole communities who are purely Good, like the Wise and the princes of the West, and entire species of rotters, such as your lot.

No offence, by the way.

Anyhow, on the whole it all sorts itself out, and so long as the balance isn't interfered with, everything chugs quietly along and nothing suddenly breaks down or goes horribly wrong. Mostly this is because each reality is a sealed, self-contained unit, in which the Law of Conservation of All Sorts of Things can cheerfully apply without fear of anything getting in or getting out. Situation normal, everything fine. Quite.

Naturally, though, you can't take all that for granted. Well, you can, but only because there are people like me. Which brings us back to your original question, who am I? Right. I am this reality's Deputy Chief Curator of the Equilibrium. My team and I fight ceaselessly to ensure that the Laws of Conservation are rigidly obeyed and enforced. My highly trained and intensely motivated Rangers are the first and last line of defence against imbalance, chaos and the abyss, and together, we hold the line against the unthinkable.

Actually, it's not a bit like that, in fact normally it's a total skive, the sort of job you get because your uncle plays golf with the chairman. Because, you see, in a closed, sealed reality – which all of them are – nothing gets in, nothing gets out. No exits or entrances, no possible risk whatever to the equilibrium. The Laws take care of everything, and we just draw our salaries and our eye-wateringly generous bonuses. Exactly how it should be in a well-ordered cosmology.

Until—

"You've gone ever such a funny colour," Archie said. "Are you feeling all right?"

The Curator nodded weakly. "Just thinking about it makes me so mad," he said. "Everything was for the most ordinary in the most ordinary of all possible worlds, and then *he* had to come along. And then everything was suddenly—"

"Yes?"

"Difficult. Complicated." The Curator practically spat the word. "We actually had to start *doing* things. It was a terrible shock to the system, believe me. Office hours. Sandwiches at my desk for lunch. For the first time in my life, I actually had to go out and buy an alarm clock." He shook his head sadly. "Where's it all going to end, that's what I want to know."

Archie waited for as long as he could bear. Then he said, "What happened?"

"*He* did," the Curator said, and if it were possible to kill someone with the letter H, there'd have been blood on the floor. "Theo Bernstein, late Principal Technical Officer with the Very Very Large Hadron Collider project, and inventor of the YouSpace device. Bastard," he paraphrased. "He ruined everything, and it's all his fault."

"Who?"

The Curator sighed. "It's a long story," he said. "All you need to know is that when you're inside the parameters of a functional coherent YouSpace field, you can move from one reality to another via a simple visual interface. And to make it even easier, you don't need special equipment or anything like that. All you need is a simple, ordinary, everyday doughnut."

Archie looked at him for a moment. "Can I go now, please?"

"Or a bagel. Basically, any kind of food that's got a hole in it. Bernstein figured that complicated electronic circuitry isn't always available in some of the more primitive realities, but nearly everywhere's got food, and practically every food-using culture has some form of deliberately perforated cereal-derivative. Therefore, wherever you go, you're never more than a few minutes away from a YouSpace interface portal that'll take you back home, or wherever you want to go next, in the blink of an eye. God, I hate that man."

In his mind's eye Archie could see a brown, glistening circle set in a cliff face, red early morning light flashing in the facets of the crystals set into the smooth curved fabric. "Really? A doughnut"

"Would I make something like that up? Oh, you can see the logic behind it. Quite well thought out, really. I mean, you can imagine some scenarios. Like, have you got a last request before we cut your heart out and offer it to the Snake-God? Yes please, I'd like a doughnut. It takes a special sort of mind to think of something like that."

"And that's how I got here," Archie said. "But I still don't get it. What does this Bernstein want me for?"

The Curator laughed. "Oh, bloody Bernstein faded out of the picture a long time ago. Waltzed off to be a god somewhere, left his nasty little invention behind. There were supposed to be safeguards, naturally. Enough said. Whether there's someone out there retro-engineering the bloody things, or whether Bernstein was just criminally careless and left a warehouse full of YouSpace generators with the key under the mat we just don't know. What we do know is, there's at least five, possibly six, fully functional YouSpace portals in operation right now, and unless we can find them and shut them down—" He stopped, fumbled in his top pocket and produced a small brown bottle of pills, one of which he swallowed with a loud gasp. "Marvellous things, those," he said. "Cure-anything tablets. Not actually from this reality, but a rotten job like mine, there's got to be a few perks. Where was I?"

"Unless you can find—"

"Oh God, yes, don't remind me." The Curator massaged his temples with his fingertips. "I haven't slept for weeks – well, not properly. Gone right off my food, can't remember the last time I was able to snatch five minutes for a round of golf. All this work," he added bitterly. "It really eats into your spare time."

He looked so sad that Archie could feel a lump in his throat. "Getting back to me," he said gently, "how do I fit in to all this? I'm nobody special, God knows."

"True," the Curator said, "very true. As an individual, you're utterly insignificant and of no account—"

"Thank you."

"You're welcome. No, it's not who you are, it's what you are." He paused, and there was a worried look on his face, as if he was trying to make a decision. "I shouldn't really tell you this. In fact, I shouldn't have told you anything. It's not like you knowing would help at all. But I guess it's all right. After all, who would ever believe you?"

"Very true. You were about to—"

"Oh yes." The Curator sat up a bit straighter. "A while back, you don't need to know when exactly, there was a massive unauthorised transfer of," he lowered his voice, "a certain commodity out of this reality into another one. Actually, the one you came from. Because this transfer was a flagrant and potentially disastrous breach of the Law of Conservation of All Sorts of Things, my colleagues and I were forced to initiate a programme of clandestine counter-transfers, of a certain commodity, from your reality into ours. And it was at the weekend, too."

Archie's head felt like it was being eaten from the inside by leeches. "A certain commodity," he said.

"Yes. A huge, enormous quantity of this commodity was smuggled out through a doughnut. The result – well, it simply doesn't bear thinking about. Fortunately, there's a time-lag before the worst of the effects take hold. That means we had a brief window for saving the universe. We had to act quickly and decisively—"

"At a weekend."

"At a weekend," agreed the Curator. "My wife had asked people over, she had to ring and cancel, God only knows what she told them. Anyway, once we'd reviewed the situation, it was obvious what we had to do. We had no choice. We had to transfer an equal quantum of this commodity from your reality over to ours. To maintain the balance, you understand. But the problem was, the sheer scale of the thing. There was absolutely no way we could make up the shortfall all in one go, so we'd have to do it a bit at a time. Ones and twos here and there, sort of thing. And that's what you are. You're a one."

"Ah."

"Which is what I meant by you not being important as *you*," the Curator went on. "All that matters is, you're a goblin. Any old goblin would've done just as well."

"That's nice to know."

"Don't mention it. Also, you're just a drop in the ocean. We actually need about four thousand of you, and so far we've only managed to scrape together about nine hundred. So," the Curator added bitterly, "I might as well sell the Miami beach house, and probably the lodge at Interlaken as well, because it doesn't look like I'll be getting any spare time at all any time soon. I wouldn't mind so much," he added bitterly, "if it was just me that was affected. But it's been sheer hell for my wife. She's hardly seen anything of me at all for months."

"Heartbreaking for her," Archie said. "Um, so what's going to happen to me? You said, a certain quantity of some commodity—"

The Curator laughed. "Oh, it's all right," he said, "there's nothing to worry about. You're not going to get boiled down or dissolved in acid or anything. We just need you over here, being a goblin."

"But I'm not a goblin," Archie pointed out. "Not a proper one, anyway."

"The monkey-suit, you mean? Oh, that doesn't matter. It's your inner essence, that's what's important. At heart, you're still goblin, no real indications of going native. We've proved that."

"Have we?"

The Curator nodded. "Thanks to Flubenoriel. That's the she-Elf, the one you've been conducting your ludicrous pseudo-romance with. Only, the human body she got issued with when she came over is seriously, seriously— But you simply didn't notice, did you? Just another self-propelled ready meal as far as you're concerned. No signs of incipient human behaviour there whatsoever."

"Ah."

"Absolutely clean bill of health," the Curator said. "Which means you're cleared for processing and onward transmission to Long-Term Storage."

"Gosh," Archie said. "That's a weight off my mind. What's Long-Term Storage?"

"Uh-huh." The Curator shook his head. "You don't need to know that."

"Don't I?"

"Security," the Curator said owlishly. "Crucially important in a sensitive operation like this."

"I suppose it would be, yes," Archie said. "But nothing horrible's going to happen to me, is it? You can tell me that, surely."

"I don't see why not," the Curator said. " Nothing horrible, you have my word."

"Really?"

"Absolutely. As far as you're concerned, it'll be just like a nice, long rest. Nothing to do all day but lie peacefully and doze."

Archie frowned. "Not in the sun, is it? I don't like bright sunlight."

"Of course you don't, you're a goblin. If you liked the sunshine, we'd know you'd gone wrong."

"Ah. Only, a lot of the humans, they like lying in the sun. It's what they do for pleasure."

"Have no fears on that score, my friend," the Curator said. "You'll be indoors. No sunlight whatsoever."

"That's a relief," Archie said.

"Below ground, in fact. In a tunnel."

"I'd like that. It'd be like home."

"Quite a lot like home," the Curator said, "only better. No work. Nobody yelling at you telling you what to do. Just perfect peace and quiet, underground, in a tunnel. Well, more of a vault, actually, but it's the same principle."

"Vaults are okay," Archie agreed. "Like treasure-vaults."

"Very similar," the Curator said reassuringly.

"And not too hot? Or too cold?"

"The temperature will be just right. We're incredibly careful about that."

Archie thought for a moment. "Well," he said, "it sounds better than New Zealand, anyway."

"Much, much better than New Zealand."

"Good. I was getting a bit fed up with all the sitting around in silly costumes."

"You won't have to wear a silly costume. Or sit."

"And the food was pretty boring, too. Same thing every day."

"You won't have to eat boring, monotonous food. Guaranteed."

Archie remembered the assistant director. "And no idiot humans asking silly questions?"

"You won't have to talk to a single human the entire time you're there."

"Cool," Archie said. "So, what do I actually have to do?"

"You don't do anything."

"Won't I get bored?"

"No chance of that. None whatsoever."

"Really?" Archie frowned. "I must say, it all sounds too good to be true."

The Curator smiled. "I promise you, you're going to love it. Are you familiar at all with the term 'cryogenic suspension'?"

"No."

"Not to worry," the Curator replied. "You'll be so happy, the time will simply fly by. And you'll have the satisfaction of knowing that you're making a tiny but significant contribution to maintaining the equilibrium."

"That's nice. Do I get paid?"

"No."

Archie shrugged. "Ah well," he said. "Can't have everything, I suppose."

"You won't be needing money. Everything's provided."

"Everything?"

"Everything you could possibly want or need, yes. The rest of your life will be one long, happy dream."

"That's all right, then." Archie smiled. "When do I start?"

Twenty minutes on his hands and knees, grubbing around in the long grass and nettles. Eventually he found it, by the effective but painful expedient of kneeling on it; one three-quarter-inch steel crank pivot retaining nut, which had skipped out of his hand as he was putting the spinning-wheel back together again after replacing a worn-out drive belt. A stupid little bit of metal, but the wheel wouldn't run without it. Two hours' production wasted, and he was already behind the clock. He sighed and rubbed his knee. The things I do for other people, he thought.

Grovelling around on the ground, he hadn't noticed that he was no longer alone, not until the newcomer cleared his throat. "Lost something?"

"Found it," the little man replied. "Oh, you're back. Sorry, it's not ready. Try again a week Thursday."

"Actually . . ."

Prince Valentine, from the fifth kingdom on the left as you come over the Apricot Mountains. Tall, blond, athletic, not even the faintest trace of a chin. Singularly gormless, even for a prince. One of his regulars. "Actually what?"

Prince Valentine sat down on the only stool available. He

simply hadn't noticed that it was the only one. Princes don't. "Actually," he said, "I was wondering ..."

"Of course you were. Anything in particular, or simply general gratuitous thought?"

To do him credit, the prince did try and translate that into something he could understand. Two seconds later, he gave up. "I was wondering," he said. "The straw into gold thing. Does it work the other way round?"

"Say what?"

"What I mean is," Valentine said, looking over the little man's shoulder, "can you sort of, well, spin gold into straw?"

The little man blinked twice. "You know, nobody's ever asked me that before."

"Really? Ah. But can you? Spin gold into straw, I mean."

"Reverse the process." The little man sat up and curled his legs round. "Interesting question. Theoretically—" He frowned. "Theoretically yes, I suppose you could. Probably just a case of realigning the drive train so the wheel runs the other way. Why?"

"Well." The prince took a moment to order his thoughts. Understandable, since there were so few of them in such a large empty space; like rounding up stray goats in the desert. "The thing of it is, lately straw's shot up. In price, I mean. It's getting ridiculous. Chappie I was talking to the other day, straw merchant, he told me straw's worth half as much again as gold. By volume, that is, not weight. But volume's what matters, isn't it? When you spin it, I mean."

"Quite."

"Well," said the prince, "there you are. Can't be a coincidence, can it? And I was thinking. Here I am with loads and loads of gold. Now, if I could get it turned back into straw, I could double my money, just like that."

The little man nodded. "Sell straw for gold, use the gold to buy straw—"

"You've got it. Quite a clever idea, I thought."

"Indeed." His eyebrows pulled together, like politicians closing ranks after a sex scandal. "You may well be on to something there."

"Absolutely. So." The prince gave the little man a hopeful look, like a dog watching his master eating. "Can you do it?"

"Gold into straw," the little man said. "Yes, I do believe I can."

"Wonderful." The prince beamed at him. "I'll get it carted up here first thing in the morning."

"Yes. You could do that, I suppose."

Quite possibly it was all the time Valentine had been spending with the little man recently that had sharpened his sensibilities. "You sound like – oh, I don't know. Like you think it's not such a good idea after all."

The little man flexed his bruised knee, which was starting to stiffen up. "I was just asking myself," he said, "if you've thought this thing through."

"Well, no," said the prince. "I got the idea and I came over straight away. No point hanging about, I always say."

"Mphm."

"There's something bothering you, isn't there?"

"Well." The little man massaged his knee. "Let's think about this, shall we? I turn your gold back into straw. You have lots of straw, which you sell for lots of gold."

"Exactly. You see, I was right."

The little man nodded. "So far so good," he said. "But then word gets about, and all the other princes bring me their gold and tell me to turn it back into straw. Before too long, everybody's got straw, nobody's got gold. Then what happens?"

"Everybody's dead rich?"

Somewhere in the distance, a dog barked. "It doesn't quite work like that," the little man said gently. "When everybody's got straw and nobody's got gold, what tends to happen is that the price of straw falls, while the price of gold goes back up."

"Oh." The prince blinked. "So we're back where we started."

"Pretty much, yes."

"A bit pointless, in fact."

"Well, yes," the little man said apologetically. "No real advantage to anybody, I'm afraid."

"Oh." The prince thought for a moment. "So basically, forget the whole thing."

"Mphm. Only—"

"What?"

"Well," the little man said, "there's a chance that you won't be the only one who comes up with the gold-back-to-straw idea. I mean, it was really clever of you, don't get me wrong, but the fact is, there's quite a few people out there, dozens of them maybe, who are almost as smart as you are. And one or two of them might think of it too, quite independently."

"Oh." Valentine frowned. "So it might happen anyway."

"That's right. Almost certain to, actually."

"So I need to turn my straw back into gold so as to get in first."

"Yes and no." The little man's toes were going to sleep. He flexed them. "Think about it. Your neighbours turn their gold into straw. Everybody's got straw. Everybody now wants gold."

"Right."

"Now just suppose," the little man said, "that you don't convert your gold. You keep your gold as gold. Then, when everybody else has got straw and wants gold—"

"I'll have it. And I can sell it."

"Yes."

"For lots and lots and lots of straw." The prince sucked his lower lip. "Or should that be gold? I'm confused."

"Or," the little man said quietly, "you might consider a third alternative."

"Really? Is there one?"

The little man nodded. Then he leaned forward slightly and lowered his voice. "Strictly between you and me," he said, "yes, there is."

"Gosh. What is it?"

The little man shook his head. "First, you've got to promise you'll keep it strictly to yourself."

"Sure."

"No telling anyone."

"Promise."

"Right, then." The little man glanced over his shoulder. "You exchange your gold," he said, "for other stuff."

The prince waited, anticipating something else. Then he said, "What other stuff?"

"Ah." The little man smiled. "This is where it gets technical."

"Oh."

"But that's all right," the little man assured him. "I understand it all, so you don't have to. If I were you, when the gold price goes right back up again, I'd exchange all my gold for land."

"*Land?*" The prince looked at the little man as though he'd just started doing chicken impressions. "What, you mean hills and woods and fields and stuff?"

"Well, maybe not hills and woods. Not to begin with, anyway."

"But I've got loads of land. Miles and miles of it."

"Quite," the little man said. "And that's a good thing. And the more of it you've got, the more straw you can grow. Then, the next time the gold price goes down and the straw price goes up—"

"I can sell my straw and buy—" The prince pulled a face. "Sorry, you've lost me again."

"More land," said the little man. "And ploughs and plough-horses and harrows and seed-drills and all that sort of thing. Farm stuff. To grow more straw."

"To buy more land?"

"To grow more straw. You've got it. We call it investing in infrastructure."

"Do we?"

"Yes. Also," the little man went on, "you can build factories for making ploughs and harrows and seed-drills, and mines for getting metal for making all that stuff. Cheaper to make them yourself than to have to buy them from the dwarves. And houses, of course. You'll need lots of houses, for all the people who do all this work to live in."

The prince rubbed his ear. "I suppose so, yes."

"Of course," the little man went on, "you'll be needing lots of people to come and work for you, so you'll have to offer them good wages, and make sure the houses you build for them are nice and clean and don't fall down. But that's all right."

"Is it?"

"Oh yes. By this stage you'll be so rich it really won't matter. You'll be able to afford it easily."

"I will?"

"Trust me. It's what we call economic growth."

"Good Lord." The prince was silent for a long time. Then he said, "But supposing the other princes see how rich I'm getting, and start copying me? Then they'll offer even higher wages, so people will go and work for them instead."

"Simple. You just pay your people even more. That'll sort that out, you'll see."

"Ah."

"And it wouldn't just be wages," the little man went on. "You could offer them other stuff as well. Like, free visits to the doctor when they're ill, schools where their kids can learn reading and writing, that sort of thing. Then everybody will want to come and work for you, and you'll have no trouble growing more straw than all the rest of the princes put together."

"And all this straw," the prince said thoughtfully. "I bring it to you and—"

"Yes. Or," the little man added, "on second thoughts, why bother? Why not just keep it as straw? Just knowing that it can be spun into gold makes it as good as gold really, doesn't it?"

There were furrows on the prince's forehead you could've planted potatoes in. "I suppose it does, now you mention it."

"It's straw *representing* gold, you see. So long as everybody knows that one bale of straw stands for a hundred thousand gold marks, it's every bit as good. Doesn't even have to be straw. Could be – oh, I don't know, little bits of paper, even. With *one straw-bale* written on them. Much more convenient, that'd be. Just so long as everyone knows that for each bit of paper, there's a straw-bale in a barn somewhere. Saves lugging the stuff about on carts. In fact," the little man went on, "you won't actually need me any more."

"Oh, but surely—"

The little man shook his head. "To all intents and purposes," he said, "straw will be gold and gold will be straw. No point having me here, turning one into the other and back again. Not when everybody understands."

"So what would you do?"

"I might retire," the little man said. "Or go somewhere else. That's not important. I'm just a simple guy with a spinning-wheel."

"I'd miss you."

The little man was suddenly aware of an unexpected constriction in his throat. "No you wouldn't," he said, a little hoarsely. "You'll be far too busy running your rich and flourishing kingdom."

"I will. I'll miss you."

"Nonsense. Anyway," the little man went on, wiping his nose on his sleeve, "that's what I suggest you do. Up to you, of course. A clever man like you, I wouldn't be surprised if you thought of something much better."

"What, me? No chance." The prince grinned. "All right," he said, "let's just run through that again, make sure I've got it straight in my mind."

"Good idea. Fire away."

"I keep my gold as gold," the prince said, counting the points off on his fingers as he made them. "I use it to buy land and ploughs and stuff, and hire a lot of men at good wages, and I grow a lot of straw. With the money I make from the straw, I buy more land and hire more men and pay higher wages. And that makes me rich." He paused. "Is that it?"

"Pretty much."

"Are you sure. It doesn't sound—"

"That's because it's technical."

"Ah, right. Of course. Right, then," the prince said, jumping up from the stool, "I'll go off and do that, right away."

"Splendid."

"Jolly decent of you to let me in on the secret."

"My pleasure."

"And of course I won't breathe a word to a soul. Promise."

"I know you won't. Mind how you—" A crash, followed by the sound of velvet tearing on brambles. "Go," the little man added. More tearing noises; then silence, broken only by the gentle sigh of the wind in the treetops.

Well now, the little man said to himself. Nearly there. Amazing, he mused, how quickly these people caught on, even the kings and the princes. With the right approach and a certain degree of patience, it was entirely possible to train them to perform simple tasks. Not as bright as dolphins or chimps, maybe, but smarter than most rats and almost on a

par with seals. And compared with the politicians and econo-
mists back home, they were a race of intellectual supermen.
Six months; as soon as the harvest's in and the wheat's been
threshed, I'll have done my job and everything will be just
fine, sure as my name is—

He laughed. Private joke.

His knee creaked as he stood up. He fished around in the
grass and found his wrench, with which he tightened the
retaining nut on the crank pivot. It slipped and took a chunk
out of the top of his thumb. He swore and bound up the cut
with a rather grubby handkerchief.

"Hello."

The little man frowned, then turned slowly. "You're back."

"Yes." Prince Valentine, his sleeves ragged and his hair
uncharacteristically scruffy, appeared from behind a tree.
"Been thinking."

"Ah."

"About what you said."

"Well, that's the trouble with thinking. Once you start, it
can be hard to stop."

"And I thought," the prince went on, "that's all well and
good, I thought, dashed clever scheme and all that, but –
please don't take this the wrong way, I wouldn't ever dream of
criticising . . ."

"But?"

"A bit complicated," the prince said. "Long-winded, don't
you know. Lots of A leading to B resulting in C, if you see
what I'm driving at."

"A slight element of complexity, certainly," the little man
conceded, "but not enough to worry about, I wouldn't have
said."

"Ah, but that's because you're smart," the prince pointed
out. "Brainy chap like you, takes all that sort of guff in his
stride. Different for us thickos, don't you know. Much better

if we can keep it simple. That way, there's less chance of me getting it wrong and ballsing it all up."

"Well—"

"And then," Valentine continued brightly, "I had an idea. Really simple and straightforward, but ends up with the same result, me getting rich and all that. Want to hear it?"

"I can hardly contain myself."

"Well." Valentine sat down on the stool again. "What I do is, I wait till all the other kings' wheat crops are nearly ready to harvest, then I send out my most trusted men, in secret and all that style of thing, and they burn it all to the ground. Well? Is that smart, or what?"

"Um."

"Because," Valentine went on enthusiastically, "if all their wheat burns down, straw'll be really, really scarce, and then I'll get you to spin my gold back into straw, like we were talking about just now, and then I'll be the only one with straw and I'll be rich." He beamed. "Great idea, isn't it? Though I do say so myself as shouldn't."

"Um."

"And the best part of it is," the prince continued happily, "if we do it that way, we'll need you more than ever to do the gold-into-straw spinning, and then you won't have to go away. Which would be nice. Because I'd miss you, like I said."

The little man opened his mouth, but nothing came out.

"Well, anyway, that was my idea," Valentine said. "I'll give it a go, see what happens. After all, if it doesn't work, we can always try it your way next year. Or the year after that. Right, then." He shuffled his feet for a moment, then said, "There wouldn't happen to be a short-cut back to the road that doesn't go through all those bloody brambles, would there? Only—"

The little man pointed. "Straight on down the hill, then left," he mumbled. "Brings you out by the Hangman's Oak."

"Got you, splendid. Well, thanks for your time. You look after yourself, all right?"

Off he went whistling, and it was a while before the little man found the strength and energy to get off the ground and back on his stool. Then he sat for a while, his foot resting on the treadle.

Burn down all the standing corn. Well, quite. Look at it one way, it's the practical, businesslike, don't-get-involved, hedge-fundy thing to do. And there was a man once, in Chicago, Illinois, who wouldn't have seen anything wrong with that. In fact, he'd have gone straight out and bought a hundred gallons of kerosene and a box of matches. And nobody would've missed him, except his enemies. And nobody liked him much, not even his mother.

He sighed. Tasked with preventing the arson and the ensuing famine, the man from Chicago would've known what to do. A discreet arrangement, just business, involving a specialist flown in from a distant city, the whole thing made to look like an accident so as not to spook the markets. Just business. Globally speaking and taking the long view, probably the right thing to do.

But instead—

"Oh hell," said the little man.

Time for Plan B.

Yes, thought the Dark Lord, *yes, I understand. I'll see to it straight away.* Then he woke up.

Wonderful thing, sleep. He yawned and stretched. This new body was really quite marvellous. True, after a week cooped up in the corporeal form of a female Elf, pretty much anything would be an improvement. But it wasn't just that. This one – he could be himself in a body like this. For the first time in ages, he could *think*.

Seven feet tall, not an ounce of fat, chest like a barrel, arms like legs. Human, most of it, but that couldn't be helped, and after the Elf body, it felt luxurious and wonderfully light and airy. He extended the arms and flexed the fingers. Fantastic. There was so much he could do with fingers like that: wield a sword, sign death warrants, crush the life out of a hated enemy, play the flute, paint watercolours, pick flowers with the morning dew still on them, anything he liked. The possibilities were endless. No limits.

Had he been dreaming? He wasn't sure. It's always disconcerting to start something new when you're no longer in the first flush of youth, and experiencing your first dreams at the age of 3,000,479 was a bit unnerving. For one thing, he wasn't sure he was doing it right. Weren't you supposed to remember what you'd been dreaming about when you woke up? He'd read about it in Wickedpedia and opinion seemed to be divided. He could only remember tiny flashes, and they faded away to nothing within thirty seconds of opening his eyes. And sometimes, in his dreams, he wasn't himself, he was someone else, which was bizarre. And was it, well, normal, for the stuff that happened in dreams to be quite so *silly*?

At his command, trembling at his frown, he had necromancers, dark wizards, masters of all the malign arts, who presumably knew all this stuff and would be able to tell him, if he asked. The trouble was, he didn't like to. It'd be embarrassing. The embodiment of evil can do a great many things, including ordering arbitrary executions and putting whole species to the sword on a whim, and nobody would think less of him for it. Quite the reverse. But blushing and shuffling his feet, he knew intuituively, were out. He'd lose respect, and without respect—

He sat up and looked out of the window. Another dark, overcast day in the Land of Shadow, with most of the useful light coming from the red glow of the molten lava dripping slowly down the slopes of Mount Snorfang. He blinked and rubbed his eyes. Sometimes, when the mountain laboured in its wrath and gushed out great torrents of blazing reflux, the glare got so bright that it was hard to sleep. What he could really do with, the Dark Lord decided, was a set of curtains for his window. Not a lot to ask, he decided, considering that without him the whole place would grind to a halt. Damn it, yes. Curtains he needed and curtains he would have.

Curtains—

He wasn't a fussy person by nature, but he did spend a lot of time in this chamber, and why the hell shouldn't he have something nice for a change? He didn't need much imagination to picture in his mind the sort of curtains he'd get if he left it to Buildings Maintenance: coarse, scratchy cloth, carelessly hemmed, and black, of course – *doesn't show the dirt*, they'd told him when he asked them the other day, and that did make a certain amount of sense; the Dark Horde's goblinpower was vast but not unlimited, and if you have thousands of goblins tied up in laundry duty, they can't be out there raiding and slaughtering. Even so. And now he came to think of it, the Captain of the Wraiths didn't have to make do with everything black, he'd just had his whole suite of offices done out in sickly livid green.

"Guards!" he yelled.

Claws and steel-soled boots skittered on the stone steps of the spiral staircase. "Boss?"

"Get me," the Dark Lord commanded, "a book of fabric samples."

"Boss?"

"You heard me. And if they're all black, you're troll-food."

It was a long time before they returned. Between them they were carrying a thin, flat cube the size of a paving-slab, completely wrapped in sheet lead.

"Sorry we took so long," panted the guard sergeant, as he

and his colleague hauled the thing up on to the dressing-table. "Only, we had to go and look in Inventory to see if we'd got one, and this is the only one we've got, and it was down in the high-security dungeon because of it being Hazardous Material. Elvish," he added, with a slight shudder. "So then of course we had to sign for it, and—"

"That's fine," the Dark Lord said. Elvish would account for the lead wrapping. "Thank you. Get out," he added quickly. The guards snapped a brisk salute. "Hold it," he added. "Get all that lead off. Right now."

"Boss? You sure? That's an Elf artefact, you just don't know with them buggers—"

"*Now.*"

They were quick about it, and his exceptional hearing meant he could hear them muttering on the stairs; they were worried about him, which was really rather sweet. But really, what possible danger to the Heart of Darkness could a collection of little squares of patterned cloth conceivably pose?

He swung open the cover of the book.

Some time later, between six and eight hours, the Officers of the Watch turned up to make their daily report. The Dark Lord didn't look up when they came in, or even register their presence. He was slumped forward on the table, his head resting on the open pages of a horrible Elf-smelling book.

"Oh shit," gasped the Castellan in horror. "He's melting."

The Captain of the Guard didn't bother to correct him, though he recognised the symptoms from his long service in the wars. Their master wasn't melting; rather worse than that. He was—

"Straight up," he told his fellow officers in a hushed voice, as they crowded round the mess-hall trestle. "I kid you not. Blubbing his eyes out, he was."

There was a shocked silence. Then someone said, "Elf book, you said?"

"Stank of the bastards. You could smell it down the corridor."

"Well, there you are, then."

The Captain nodded slowly. "Yeah, but even so," he said. "I mean to say, he's the Dark Lord. Elf magic isn't supposed to work on the Dark Lord."

"It's ever since he got that body," said another. "That *human* body. That's what's behind it, bet you a million snargs."

"He was just sort of sprawled there," the Captain said. "Just kept saying, *so beautiful, so beautiful*, over and over again. Wouldn't let go of the book. We had to prise him off it with a wrecking bar."

A brevet-major of Imperial stormtroopers looked at him sharply. "What did you do with the horrible thing?" he asked.

"Wrapped it back up in its lead sheets and locked it away in Number Six vault," the Captain replied, "pending figuring out how the hell you dispose of something like that. Can't chuck it out or bury it, there's the risk of contaminating the water supply. Can't just chuck it in the Fires," he added, "it might blow the whole place up. You just don't know, do you?"

"What sort of book was it?" asked somebody else.

"Oh come on, you don't think I *looked* at it, do you? All I saw was, the pages were like bits of old rag with patterns on."

"No words? Just pictures?"

The Captain shrugged. "Not even proper pictures," he said. "More your sort of coloured squiggles."

"Nasty."

"What the hell was he doing with something like that, anyway?" asked the brevet-major. "I mean, magical research, he's got people for that. Expendable people." He smiled at the Senior Technical Officer, who scowled back.

"Excuse me." A terrified junior officer was standing in the mess-hall doorway. "Message for the Captain of the Guard." He took a deep breath, then added, "From Him."

"Bloody hell," someone said. Even being in the same room as a message from the Dark Lord wasn't something to be taken lightly, and any show of irreverence was a mug's game (the mugs in question being neatly arranged on hooks hanging over the bar). "What's he on about now?"

"Um. He'd like his book back."

The Captain passed a scaly tongue over his suddenly-dry lips. "When you say book—"

"The one he was reading, *sir*. The one you took off him by force, *sir*."

A deathly silence fell over the assembled officers. Slowly the Captain stood up. "Well," he said quietly, "better go and see what he wants, I suppose. Cheers then, lads. Next round's in me."

The brevet-major looked at him. "You mean on."

"No," the Captain said, "I'm afraid I don't. Bye for now."

All the way down to the vaults to get the book, then all the way back up the main stair to the topmost tower. Stupid way, the Captain mused, to spend the last half hour of your life. He knocked at the door, and a rather thin, weak voice said, "Come." Oh well, the Captain thought, and opened the door.

The Dark Lord was sitting up in bed, sipping a cup (I know that face, the Captain thought, but couldn't put a name to it straight away) of what smelt alarmingly like herbal tea. "Ah," the Dark Lord said, "you've got it. Good man. Well, don't just stand there, fetch it here."

"Sir."

"Splen— Oh for heaven's sake, you silly man, you've put all that ridiculous lead sheeting round it again. Get it off, quickly."

"Um. Sir. With respect—"

"Oh, don't be such a fusspot. Give it to me, I'll do it." The Dark Lord's steely fingers ripped away the sheet as though it were tissue paper. "Ah, that's better. Now then, Captain, I'd like your opinion." The Dark Lord was leafing through the bits of ensorcelled rag. "This one? Or this?"

"Sir?"

"Curtains, man, curtains. Oh come *on*, it's not going to bite you. I quite like this one, but maybe the pattern's a bit on the busy side, especially against a darkish background."

The Captain was still struggling to come to terms with what he'd just heard. "Curtains?"

"For my window. The light from the lava flow keeps me awake." The Dark Lord frowned at him, and the Captain's knees began to shake. "You do know what a curtain is, don't you?"

"Sir, yes. But shouldn't it be—?"

The Dark Lord sighed. "I know what you're going to say," he said. "But I don't want black; it's boring and I'm sick to death of it. I've got a good mind to have the whole tower made over while I'm at it, in nice bright cheerful colours. Black is so *depressing*. Sometimes I feel, if I have to look at one more horrid old black wall, I'll scream."

The Captain was staring at the book out of the corner of his eye. Strong magic, he told himself, appallingly strong; if he'd known the Elves could do stuff like that, he'd have had trouble sleeping at night. "Well?" the Dark Lord snapped. "I asked you a question, soldier. This one? Or the dove grey and tangerine?"

A shudder ran down the Captain's spine. Death before tangerine. "The first one, sir. In my opinion."

"Yes, I think so too. And if I have the walls done in apricot, it'll go just nicely. Thank you, Captain, that was most helpful. You can run along now."

The book, the Captain thought, as he tottered slowly down

the stairs, barely aware of the slippery treads under his iron-shod feet. It's that damned Elvish book, it's poisoned, it's eating his brain. Except— The Captain paused and grabbed the iron handrail; he desperately needed something to hold on to at that moment. Except, it couldn't just be the book, because both of them had stared at it. Not just the Dark Lord, but himself as well. And *his* brain hadn't turned to mush. Well, had it?

So if it wasn't the book—

If it wasn't the book – well, maybe the brevet-major was right and it was that new human body. That or something else; it really didn't matter. What mattered was, the Dark Lord had lost it. And if it wasn't just a temporary thing, if there was any chance at all he'd stuck like it and would be that way for ever and ever—

The very fact that the Captain was still alive, of course, proved it beyond reasonable doubt. He'd done wrong, taken the Lord's book away from him, made him angry; by rights, there should be a pewter handle riveted to the back of his head for what he'd done. Instead, it had been *thank you, most helpful, run along*. And the inner sanctum of the Dark Principle, done out in apricot . . .

On the last step but one the Captain reached his decision, the only one he could possibly make. He'd served Evil for a hundred and forty-six years, and in that time he liked to think he'd come to understand the meaning of Duty. True, the decision he'd made would almost certainly mean his own death, and that of tens of thousands of his comrades, but what did that matter? The future of Evil was at stake. There comes a time when a man must stand up and do what he knows is Wrong.

"He's off his chump," the Captain muttered under his breath. "He'll have to go."

Mordak took a deep breath of clean, fresh mountain air. When he'd finished coughing, he said, "Right, now we know what we've got to—"

He stopped. Efluviel wasn't by his side. He looked back and saw her sitting on a rock, about twenty yards away. "Hey," he called out. "Come on."

No reply. She didn't seem to have heard him. He tried shouting louder, but no effect. Frowning, he trotted back up the path.

"Are you all right?"

"I'm not talking to you."

Mordak's mind was still full of revelations, theories, explanations, expediencies, and what she'd said did not compute. "You what?"

"You heard."

Elves. "All right," he said. "What did I do?"

She scowled at him. "Oh, that's typical," she said.

"What did I *do*?"

She sighed. "You there, Elf," she said, in a pretty mediocre impression of his voice. "Cook the baked beans while we *men* solve the problem."

"Don't you ever call me that again. I'm a goblin. Not what you said."

"I do apologise," Efluviel snapped. "We *males*."

"All right." Mordak spread his arms in a vague gesture of appeasement. "Like I said, I'm a goblin."

Efluviel gave him a look, but halfway through, it sort of faded into thoughtfulness. "Yes," she said. "I must've forgotten that. Goblin, as in evil."

"Yes, well," Mordak said, with a hint of discomfort. "What I mean is, we goblins have a system of robustly traditional cultural values. Also," he pointed out, "no females. I mean," he went on, "we'd definitely do chauvinistic gender stereotypes if we could, but we can't." He frowned. "What I'm trying to say is, I denigrate and belittle you because you're an Elf, not because you're a girl. All right?"

Efluviel shrugged. "If you say so. It's just—"

"What?"

"Oh, forget it," she said, and stood up. "Sorry," she said (and, five thousand miles away, the Far-Seeing Monks of Culiastre, who'd been wondering what all the comets and two-headed calves they'd seen recently had been in aid of, looked up from their crystal balls and said, Well, that explains that, then), "Just for a while there, I sort of forgot."

"What?"

"Doesn't matter," Efluviel said irritably. "Now, then. What next?"

Mordak frowned. "I was going to ask you that," he said.

For some reason, Efluviel felt absurdly pleased. "Right," she said. "Sorry, what was the question?"

Behind them, the sheer cliffs glared red in the dawn light. "What," Mordak said patiently, "do we do now?"

"Ah." Efluviel nodded. "Right. First, let's just quickly run over what we know. There's a big hole thing."

"Check."

"Anything that goes into it doesn't come back, but from time to time, truly bizarre stuff comes out of it."

"Check."

"Why do you keep saying check?"

"I'm not quite sure, now you mention it. Go on."

Efluviel sighed. "The hermit," she said, "was unwilling to commit himself on the question of where the human princes are getting all their money from." She paused to give Mordak a chance not to say *check*, then went on, "He did, however, express the opinion that anything more than ordinarily weird that shows up around here generally turns out to have come through the big strange hole. He therefore suggested that we continue our investigations there." She shrugged. "What do you reckon?"

"Go for it," Mordak said.

"Right." She nodded decisively. "Let's do that, then. Now, I wrote down the co-ordinates he gave us—"

"Clever girl."

She gave him a warning look. "So I suggest we take a look at the map and plot a course to get us there." She paused again. "The map."

"I thought you had it."

"It's sticking out of your pocket."

"Oh, that map." They spread it out on a rock. Then Efluviel said, "Right, we're here. That's the mountain range behind us there, and that's the top of the ridge running more or less north–south there, and over there we've got the— hang on. This map's not right."

"Yes it is. It's the latest edition goblin ordnance survey."

"It's *not*. It's all wrong. Look. There's all these contour lines here, where my finger is, but look, no mountain. Just a steep-sided ravine."

"That's not contour lines. That's a gravy stain."

A short pause, while Efluviel drummed her fingers on the rock. It seemed to help. Then she went on, "So if we follow the course of this river here, down the valley, circling round the base of the volcano—"

"Not a volcano."

"Not—?"

Mordak scratched the map gently with his foreclaw. The volcano disappeared. "Sorry about that. You were saying."

"Anyway," Efluviel said, grabbing the map and stuffing it back in Mordak's pocket, "it's over that way somewhere. It's probably signposted. Or we can ask someone. Well come on. Or are your feet hurting again?"

It was a long, grim march. To take their minds off the effort and discomfort, Efluviel gave Mordak the benefit of her opinions on various matters, including goblin fiscal policy, his handling of various recent diplomatic crises and his takeover and subsequent management of the *Beautiful Golden Face*; because, as she explained later, time simply whizzes by when you're furiously angry. Which proved to be perfectly true.

"And another thing—"

"We're here," Mordak said.

"Don't change the subject. Moving the opera reviews from the front page to halfway down page six was, in my opinion, one of the most appalling acts of cultural vandalism in the history of the world, and when I'm editor, the first thing I'm going to do—"

"We're here."

Efluviel blinked. "So we are," she said. She looked up at the rocky crags above them. "Where is it? It's supposed to be right here, but—"

"Efluviel," Mordak said quietly.

"What?"

"Over there."

"I can't see— Oh."

About three hundred yards away, on the skyline, two figures. "You've got better eyes than me."

"Yes," Efluviel said.

"Well?"

"Human," Efluviel said. "Coming this way."

For some reason, Mordak felt distinctly uneasy. "Coincidence," he said. "Probably just simple shepherds. I bet, soon as they see us, a goblin and an Elf, they'll run like hell."

"Oh, they've seen us all right."

"Ah. But once they get up close—"

"The short one's waving."

"Won't he be in for a nasty surprise," Mordak said nervously. "My only concern is, they'll be so scared, they'll trip on the rocks and do themselves an injury."

"Really? That's very altruistic of you."

"Maybe we should just get out of sight behind a rock or something. In the interest of public safety."

"They've definitely seen us," Efluviel said. "There's a short one and a tall one. Mordak? Oh for crying out loud. Come out of there, don't be such a *baby*."

The king of the goblins shuffled out from behind a large boulder and made an unconvincing display of doing up his fly. "Call it warrior's intuition," he said, "but I have a very bad feeling about those two."

"Interesting. Where I come from, we call it something quite other, rhymes with hit-haired." She shaded her eyes with the flat of her hand. "It's just a very old man and a skinny boy."

"Oh. Are you sure?"

"*Yes*. Yes, I'm sure. Warrior's intuition, for crying out loud."

You can't fault Elves on their eyesight. The old man was short and completely bald, with a flat cloth cap stuffed in the pocket of his brown warehouse coat and two lenses clamped to his nose in a wire frame, presumably to make his eyes look bigger. The other one was about nineteen, ridiculously tall and skinny with ears like wings, and eating a wedge of fruit cake only slightly smaller than his head. Mordak had to admit, he'd seen more dangerous-looking kittens; but somehow he couldn't get rid of that strange churning feeling in the pit of his stomach. On the other hand, that could easily be the baked beans.

"Excuse me," the old man said, addressing the space between them. "Would you be King Mordak?"

"That's him."

"Ah. So you'd be her Serenity the Lady Efluviel."

Mordak opened his mouth, but couldn't quite manage to speak. The boy finished off his fruit cake and ate three boiled eggs. "That's me," Efluviel said firmly, her face a becoming shade of boiled lobster. "Who the hell are you?"

"Technical support."

"Say what?"

"We're the guardians of the portal," the old man translated, "Art and me – he's my sister's boy, he's a good lad really, hot as mustard on the tech – the magical side of things." The boy nodded in confirmation and ate a sausage roll. "You're here for the portal, aren't you?"

"The weird hole," Mordak said. "Things go into it and don't come back, and so forth."

"That's the one," the old man said.

"Right," said Efluviel. "So, how come you know our names?"

The old man looked faintly surprised. "Oh, bless you – everybody knows King Mordak, don't they, Art? I was just saying to the lad the other day, I wouldn't be surprised if King Mordak wasn't the best-known goblin in the whole of the Realms. And if he's Mordak, miss, then you must be the Lady Efluviel, his trusty—"

Mordak grinned. "Sidekick."

"Heroine," the old man amended. "This quest of yours,

miss, it's famous, everybody's talking about it. In the *Face* and everything."

Efluviel looked up sharply. "Is it?"

"Oh yes."

"Which page?"

"Front page, miss, naturally. About how the fate of the Realms is hanging in the balance, but that's all right, because Mordak and Efluviel are on the case, all over it like flies on a – two safe pairs of hands, that's pretty much the gist of it, miss. They got confidence in you, see. Comes the hour, comes the Elf. And the goblin too, of course, sir, no disrespect."

There was a brief, stunned silence, broken only by the sound of powerful jaws crunching pastry. "Well," Mordak said, "that's another triumph for goblin security. Nobody was supposed to know."

The old man grinned. "Oh, you can't keep something like this quiet for very long, sir, not when it's a matter of life and death, so to speak. But that's all right. They're all rooting for you, behind you every inch of the way. Oh yes."

Mordak was frowning. "When you say a matter of life and death—"

"Oops." The old man clicked his tongue. "Sorry about that, sir, may have spoken a bit out of turn there. Just pretend I never said that."

"Life and death how, exactly?"

"Sorry, sir. Love to be able to tell you, but you know how it is. Rules are rules. You'll appreciate that, military man like yourself."

"I didn't think it was life and death. More of an annoying little mystery, really."

"Absolutely, sir, that's all it is. No big deal at all, sir. You hit the nail right on the head there, sir, if you'll allow me to say so."

"But you said—"

"This portal," Efluviel said firmly. "You know where it is."

"Oh yes, miss."

"Splendid. Take us there."

The old man looked very sad. "Sorry, miss. Can't do that."

Efluviel scowled at him, as if he were a compositor who'd got her name wrong on a front-page by-line. No perceptible effect. In spite of herself, she was impressed. "Yes you bloody well can. We've come a long way, you know."

"Sorry, miss. Not allowed. You know how it is."

"No I don't. What's to stop you?"

"Actually, miss, it's our job. Guardians, see, of the portal. We guard it." He lowered his voice a fraction. "Against un-authorised personnel."

Efluviel considered that for a moment. Then she said, "Mordak, hit them."

Mordak stirred, then stopped dead, as though he'd walked into a glass wall. The old man clicked his tongue. "Not mean-ing to be funny or anything, sir and miss, but I wouldn't do that if I were you. Really I wouldn't."

It was Mordak's turn to frown. "Oh? Why not?"

"You're too valuable, sir," the old man said earnestly. "You can't go getting yourself horribly injured or maybe even killed, though obviously we'd only use the bare minimum of force, sir, that's what it says in the guidelines and we're red hot on the guidelines, Art and me. Don't do it, sir. There's people depending on you. Art wouldn't be able to live with himself if you got yourself horribly injured. He's sensitive, bless him. Gets it from his mother."

Efluviel rolled her eyes. "Are you going to hit them or have I got to do it?"

"Take us to the portal," Mordak said in his best com-manding voice, which didn't seem to be working within normal parameters. "And, um, look sharp about it."

The old man looked terribly worried. The boy paused

halfway through unwrapping a cheese and onion slice and put it back in his pocket. "Really, sir, really and truly, I would not do that if I were you. It's you I'm thinking about," he added pleadingly. "You ought to know, sir, I happen to be a master adept in forty-six different secret martial arts, and the boy, well, I know he doesn't look it, but back when we was doing security, they used to call him the Destroyer. Doesn't know his own strength, sir, that's half the problem."

Whatever the boy's strength may have been, he was diligently keeping it up by eating macaroons. Even so, Mordak hadn't survived well over a century of constant warfare without developing a few instincts, all of which were telling him to listen to the old man's warning. "Look," he said, "there's no need for anyone to get hurt, just so long as we all act reasonably. Show us the way to the portal and everything's going to be just fine."

The old man sighed and took off the bag he'd got slung over his shoulder. He fiddled with the straps, stopped, fished about in his pockets, found another pair of wire-mounted lenses, took the old pair off his nose, handed them to Mordak to hold for him, put the new pair on his nose, fumbled with the straps a bit more and got them undone, opened the bag and produced what looked like a sausage, carefully wrapped in yellow dusters. It proved to be a very small club. "This'll have to go in the book, you know," he said. "Every time we draw weapons it's got to go in the book, plus a full incident report, three copies, double-spaced. I'll have my other glasses back now, if that's all right."

"He's going to beat us to a pulp," Efluviel said. "With that."

"Not to a pulp, miss, not unless it's completely unavoidable." The old man lifted the club and waggled it about. He needed both hands. "You really sure you want to do this, sir? It can only end one way."

"You know what," Efluviel said, "I think I agree with him. Oh go *on*, for crying out loud. Hit him."

Mordak frowned. "I think I'll have to," he said. "Otherwise she's going to make my life so miserable."

The young man was nibbling the chocolate off a Swiss roll. "Fair enough, sir, don't say I didn't warn you." He lowered the club to rest his arms for a second or two, then lifted it again. "Come on, then," he said, "and don't say I didn't warn you."

Mordak sighed and drew his sword; at which point, an eagle circling high overhead dropped a log on his head, and he fell over.

"Hey!" Efluviel yelled. "That's cheating."

The old man was down on his knees beside Mordak, thumbing back his eyelid. "It's all right, miss, he'll be fine, just a bit woozy. You know, he really ought to wear a helmet and appropriate safety equipment when he's on dangerous missions. It's like I keep telling Art, it's there for your protection." Mordak groaned and tried to sit up. "Now then, sir, nice and steady. How many fingers am I holding up?"

"It wasn't him," Efluviel said loudly. "It was a freak accident, a bird dropped a lump of wood on you. *He* never did a thing."

"Be quiet," Mordak said. "And you, if you carry on waving fingers under my nose, I'll bite them off. Got that?"

The old man smiled. "He's feeling better now, bless him. Art, get the gentleman a drink of water." The boy straightened up, looked round, observed that there was no water anywhere in sight, and ate a bacon sandwich. "Now then, sir, as I would've told you only you would insist on getting all aggressive, you don't really want to go to the portal."

"Yes I do."

"No sir, with respect." The old man stopped, straightened his back with an audible click, and winced. "You don't want to go to the portal, sir, nothing there for you at all. You want to know who's been going in and out of there lately, and if it's got anything to do with all the money and stuff."

Mordak lifted his head, craned his neck round and gave Efluviel a look, which she avoided. "True," he said.

"Well, then." The old man smiled. "We can tell you that, can't we, Art?"

"You can?"

"Oh yes, sir. Happy to tell you. No problem with that at all."

"Told you," Efluviel murmured. "Ask someone, I said. But you wouldn't listen."

Mordak made a faint, sad noise. "You might have mentioned that," he said, "before you started dropping trees on my head."

"Oh, that wasn't anything to do with me, sir. Freak accident, like the lady said."

"I see." Mordak carefully massaged the back of his head. "Do you get a lot of freak accidents around here?"

"Funny you should mention that, sir."

"Mphm." Mordak tried to stand up and sat down again. "You were saying," he said.

The old man was wrapping up the club in the dusters. "What you want to do," he said, "is go to the edge of the old forest at Pol Snuldor. That'd about cover it more or less, wouldn't it, Art?"

The boy looked up from his slice of Bakewell tart and nodded. "The where?" Efluviel said.

"Ah." The old man smiled. "It's dead easy to get to. All you do is, you go back down the mountain the way you just came, then you head out on the Old West Road going east until you come to a crossroads. Take the first left then the second right then the second right then the third left, keep going till you come to an old water mill. Couple of hundred yards further on, you come to a crossroads. Take the first right then the second left then the third left then the second right, should bring you out on the Old North Road heading south. Carry right on bearing left till you come to an oak tree, looks a bit like a goldfish standing on its head. Then you leave the road heading due east, two miles further on you'll come to a river, follow that due north, nine hundred yards, cross over by the bridge, not the first bridge, the second bridge, brings you out on the Old East Road headed north. Carry on, first left, seventh right, just follow your nose, you can't miss it. Okay?"

"Sorry. Say again?"

"I'll draw you a map," the old man said. "Here, Art, give us a bit of your sandwich paper." He reached behind his ear and found a stub of charcoal. "Right then, you're here." He drew something that looked like the climactic last battle of the Octopus Civil War. "And if you get lost, just ask someone, all right?"

"Yes, thank you." The old man took the paper away from him and turned it the other way up. "Right, got that," he said. "And when we get there, what will we find?"

The young man grinned with his mouth full. The old man shook his head. "Ah well, sir, that'd be telling. Anyhow, take care, mind how you go. Just follow the map, you'll be there in no time flat. It was a pleasure meeting you, sir, miss. Have a safe journey now. Come on, Art. Get a move on or we'll be late for dinner."

The boy sprang to attention like a guard-dog hearing gravel crunching, and started to walk away very fast. The old man turned to follow him. "Hold on," Mordak said. "You can't just go waltzing off. I haven't finished asking you—"

"Sorry, sir, can't stop. Oh, and make sure you look out for—" Before he could complete the warning, the boy grabbed his arm and hustled him along, so fast his feet barely touched the ground. "What will we find?" Mordak yelled after him, but a moment later they'd vanished out of sight round a bend in the road. Mordak stood and stared at where they'd been for a moment, then sat down on a rock and rested his head in his hands.

"Are you all right?" asked Efluviel.

"More or less." Something touched his hand, and he looked at it. A single snowflake. "That's all we need," he said. There was something scrunched up inside his hand. He opened it and saw the old man's map. "Well?"

"Well what?"

"Do we do like he said and go to this forest place he told us about?"

"Are you kidding?" Efluviel snatched the map from his hand and threw it away. A breeze caught it and it floated in the air, like the last leaf of autumn. "Look, if that old fool told me to breathe, I'd rather choke. He's clearly nuts. And as for you, letting him ambush you like that—"

"That wasn't an ambush, it was a freak accident. You said so."

A tiny gust of wind lifted the floating map, and it drifted gracefully down and settled in Mordak's hand. "So was that, presumably."

"If he wants us to go there, I vote we don't."

Mordak frowned. Then he carefully folded the paper into a little origami glider and launched it away. It looped the loop and came to rest in his ear. "Cute," he said. "Let's go."

It was snowing quite heavily. Efluviel pulled her coat round her ears. "You do what you like," she said. "I'm going back the way we came."

The moment she said it, there was an ominous rumbling from the cliffs above them, and the ground began to shake. She only just had enough time to grab Mordak's arm and pull him to safety before an avalanche of rocks and boulders thundered down on the place where they'd been standing, filling the air with dust. When it cleared, they saw that the path they'd come up by was completely blocked and filled in.

Mordak got to his feet and stretched his neck. "A hint, do you think?"

Efluviel looked down at the map, then sideways at the rockfall. "Guess what?" she said. "The only way out of here that isn't buried under a zillion tons of rock is the way he wanted us to go."

"Ah." Mordak nodded. "Freak accident."

"It's the only possible explanation," Efluviel said. She kicked at a small pebble to relieve her feelings. It ricocheted off a rock, Mordak's heel and the upturned root of a pine tree toppled by the earthquake, and hit her on the ankle. "One million-to-one chance after another. Have you got anything to eat?"

"No."

"Of course you don't." She sighed, and took a step along the one remaining path. "You know, sometimes I ask myself, is even being the editor of the *Face* worth all this?"

"And?"

"Don't be stupid," she replied. "And don't dawdle."

Archie woke up. He was a bit chilly. He couldn't move.

Panic attack. A human thing, presumably bundled with the hardware; he wasn't entirely sure why, because it didn't really help much, and he couldn't quite see the rationale behind it. When danger threatens and you need to be at the very top of your game, every mental and physical resource instantly available to expedite the serious business of running away, whoever designed humans thought it'd be a good idea to give 'em the shakes, the shits and the screaming heebie-jeebies. Since he couldn't move at all, not even his eyeballs, it had no real practical effect as far as the bodily side of things went; but when your mind is completely given over to the frustration of wanting to squeal, tremble like a leaf and relinquish bladder control, and then you find you can't, it's hard to think straight, or indeed at all. If one is very much and five is not at all, how do you like the human body? Six.

The fit passed, and slowly goblinness seeped back along his veins and nerves, soothing, reassuring and urging the various motor functions to pull themselves together and get a grip, until he was in a fit state to compile a detailed situation report. As follows. Eyes open, but can't see a damn thing, only white mist. Can't move anything, all systems offline. And it's cold in here. Recommended course of action? Um.

All right, then, hypothesis. I'm dead. Plausible, fits the few known facts – cold, can't move – but unsatisfactory on an intuitive level. We don't feel dead, and the consensus of opinion is that if you don't feel dead, you probably aren't. In which case, we're probably in big, big trouble. Indeed. Thank you so much for that, and keep your voice down or the human bits will hear you.

So he lay perfectly still for a while, and then he lay perfectly still some more, and some more after that. The human body didn't seem to mind all that much – restful, it called it – and Archie remembered that one of the things humans liked doing most was lying perfectly still for long periods of time, preferably adjacent to the edge of the sea, marinated in oil like a chop and exposed to the full mind-bleaching fury of the Horrible Yellow Face. He'd have shuddered like anything if he'd been able to, but he couldn't. This is no good, he thought. I don't like it at all.

Boredom isn't something that happens to goblins in the normal course of events, just as snowmen rarely catch cold; their lives are busy, violent and terrifying, and there simply isn't the time or the opportunity for tedium. Consequently, goblins don't build up an immunity to boredom the way humans do, and although the monkey-suit came hardwired with a certain level of boredom tolerance, once that was exceeded, the inner goblin was horribly vulnerable, like remote South Sea islanders exposed to European coughs and sniffles for the first time. It was a situation that called for every last scrap of Archie's resourcefulness and self-control. He tried complex mental arithmetic, counting Elves falling through a hole in the floor, imagining games of goblin hockey – not much use, because the average game lasts about two minutes before everybody's killed. He silently hummed every tune he knew, including the goblin national anthem. He made up poetry, letters to friends back home, comprehensive lists of every artefact he'd ever owned. Starting from first principles (in the Beginning was the Howl . . .) he tried to figure out what had happened to him, and where he might be, and what he could do about it. He did his best, but it wasn't long before boredom started to eat into his soul. *Get me out of here*, he longed to yell, but of course he couldn't, could he?

He thought about Elves. Elves, as everybody knows, are supreme masters of mental discipline – well, they would be, wouldn't they? Smug, condescending, insufferable prickle-eared bastards; he thought quite hard for a long time about how much he hated Elves, and that was marvellous, probably saved his sanity, for a little while – and are reputed to be able to will themselves to death, should the need arise. How they go about doing this, nobody knows, although there are theories – for example, they reflect on how unutterably superior they are to every other living thing in the cosmos, come to the conclusion that Life simply isn't worthy of them, and immediately die of natural justice. Could a goblin do that, he wondered? He tried it; no dice. So he tried not breathing instead, only to realise that he hadn't drawn a single breath since he'd woken up. Nuts, he thought.

Stuff Elves; there must be something goblins can do, equally cool but rather more productive. He set about finding out. Do they, for example, have tremendous latent powers of telekinesis? Can they communicate telepathically with other goblins over vast distances? Summoning up every scruple of inner strength, can they wiggle their big toes? Apparently not.

Ho hum. Six sixes are thirty-six. I spy with my little eye something beginning with N. Nothing, your turn. Oglak had a little troll, its coat was stiff as wire, so every time it scratched itself, it set its bum on fire. Name forty-six underground rivers in Cavern Seventeen beginning with Y. *Help!*

His thoughts returned to what the Curator had told him, just before he drank the strange-tasting blue liquid and fell asleep. *Cryogenic suspension*; whatever that was supposed to mean. The Curator had made it sound like a cross between a holiday and heaven. And it was all because of the Law of Conservation of All Sorts of Things, some incomprehensible garbage about Good and Evil—

Maybe not as incomprehensible as all that. Think about it. If what the Curator had said was true and there was only so much good and so much evil in the world, and those two so-muches balance; and then suppose something happens and a whole load of evil just disappears, then yes, you'd have an imbalance, and quite possibly that would make trouble. So, what do you do? You ship in a whole load of evil from outside, to set the balance straight again. Exactly how that worked in terms of mystic holes in cliffs and goblins and suddenly finding yourself in the wrong place and the wrong skin, he neither knew nor needed to know. The point was, he'd been brought here to make up a certain quantity (at a rough guess, somewhere in the region of a whole load) of evil, and why him? Because goblins are Dark creatures *per se*, irredeemably bad, incapable of salvation, made by the Dark Force as a cruel, mocking perversion of Elves. Cool. Having got him here, understandably enough, they'd stowed him away in some kind of permanent secure storage, like a safe or a vault. As far as they were concerned, job done, problem solved. It wouldn't, of course, occur to them to consider that he, their victim, even though he was a mere goblin, might have hopes, fears, ambitions, sensibilities, likes, dislikes, feelings, just possibly (though probably not, all things considered) maybe even one or two fundamental sentient rights, a life of his own, a place in the scheme of things; that even a mere goblin might just conceivably *matter*—

(He paused and counted to three under his breath. Ah well, he thought. Here goes nothing.)

But that's all right, he thought. I don't mind. I forgive them.

He waited. Nothing seemed to be happening. His heart fell. It had been worth a try, he supposed – convert the evil to good, thereby destroying the carefully restored balance and buggering up the whole scheme – but clearly it wasn't going to work, and it was a bit stupid, really, to have imagined that it possibly could—

Then a siren went off.

He heard it, clear as anything; like a very loud horn going honk-honk, muffled and a long way away but unmistakable. A moment later a bell started shrilling, followed by a different siren going whoop-whoop. Coincidence? He didn't think so. Just in time he caught himself thinking *Got you, bastards, serve you right* – which would, of course, have cancelled everything out and snatched defeat from the jaws of victory. So instead he thought, *I forgive you, I forgive you,* over and over again; and the more he thought it, the more sirens, alarms, buzzers and klaxons burst into song all around him. *Peace,* he thought wildly, *harmony, understanding and all that shi— all those very good things. Happiness, joy, liberty, equality, I'd like to give the world a home and furnish it with love, give peace a chance and extreme kindness to animals.* Which set off a particularly piercing tweep-tweep-tweep noise that made him want to bite his own head off just so it'd stop.

Other noises, too; running footsteps, shouting, something analogous to the lifting and banging shut of lids, getting closer. He knew he had to keep going but he was rapidly running out of stuff to think. *Make love not war, do unto others as you would have them do unto you, eat five fruit and veg a day, please dispose of can tidily.* He heard a grating sound, just possibly a crowbar being inserted into a narrow gap. *It takes seventeen muscles to smile and forty-three to frown, I have a dream, it's nice to be nice, and I says to myself, it's a wonderful—*

Light flooded down on him like an avalanche. His heart suddenly lurched into motion, his lungs filled with great solid wodges of air, he could just feel a tiny needle of pain in his big toe and a voice somewhere overhead yelled, "Over here, I've found it, it's this one."

Peace be with you, dirtbag, he thought, and passed out.

"What you should've done," Efluviel pointed out, not for the first time, "was ask that man."

Mordak sighed, sat down on the trunk of a fallen tree and let the straps of his rucksack slide off his shoulders. His feet hurt, but not nearly enough to distract him from his headache. "It's all right," he said feebly. "We're not lost. I know exactly where we are."

"So do I," Efluviel said. "In fact, I know this place like the back of my hand. I should do, we keep coming back here. In fact, ten more minutes and I'll be entitled to claim it as my domicile for tax purposes."

She had a point. With the ears, make that three. This particular conjunction of fallen tree, smelly sedge-covered pool and forked road did look painfully familiar. "Fine," he said. "This time we'll go left."

"We tried that. Time before last. And two times before that. You should've asked that man. We'd be there by now if you had."

"Asked him what? We don't know what we're supposed to be looking for. Excuse me, friend, could you tell us how to get there? Where? Sorry, we don't actually know. Yes, on mature reflection, that would've helped a *lot*."

"Goblins," Efluviel sighed, and sat down beside him on the log. "Always got to know best about everything." She glanced up at the sky. "It's getting dark."

"Yes."

"Won't be long now before the sun goes in."

"Small mercies."

"We'll just have to stay here all night and then carry on with being hopelessly lost in the morning."

"We are not hopelessly lost."

She shrugged. "All right, optimistically lost." She looked round at the gloomy eaves of the forest all around them. "We could wander round and round for days and never find the way out," she said. "It looks like it goes on for miles and miles in every direction." She sniffed. "I think it'll probably start raining soon."

"No, I don't think so."

Perfectly on cue, the first fat raindrop chose that moment to splatter on the back of his neck. "Come on," he said, "let's go and shelter under the trees. No point in getting soaked."

"We shouldn't leave the path. Trust me, I'm an Elf, we know about woods. Don't ever leave the path, not unless you know precisely where you are."

Mordak stood up. "That's all right, then," he said. "You know this place like the back of your hand, you just said so."

"If only you'd asked that man when I told you to."

Thanks to the spreading canopy of an ancient beech tree, which protected them from five out of every six raindrops, it was nearly thirty seconds before they were comprehensively drenched. "We don't even know what sort of thing we're supposed to be looking for," Mordak pointed out. "It could be a ruined tower or a charcoal-burner's hut or a forester's cottage, any damn thing. So asking would've been—"

"Oh, don't keep going on about it."

"I'm not the one who—"

"What's that? Over there."

Mordak wiped rain out of his eyes with his knuckles. "Where? I can't see anything."

"I don't suppose you can, you're a goblin. There. No, *there*. Under those trees."

In context, that was marvellously unhelpful. "Which trees?"

"Look. Where I'm pointing."

Now she came to mention it, there was something, just possibly. A structure of some kind? Or just an illusion of form created by distance, obscurity and the chance angle of a fallen branch. "You're imagining things."

"No I'm not. It's a hut or a shed or something. Go and look."

"You go and look."

"What, and get wet? You're the one who didn't ask the man, you go."

"Fine." Mordak tweaked the sodden felt of his hood a little further forward. Rain trickled up his sleeve and down his arm as far as his elbow. "Stay here and for crying out loud don't wander off."

He trudged out over the squelching wet leaf-mould,

following the line she'd pointed out. It wasn't easy, because some damn fool had left trees lying around all over the place; but as he drew closer, he realised that the vague shape in the distance was indeed a primitive sort of building. Quite a big one, in fact. Actually, it was huge.

"Hello?" he called out.

Indeed, huge was putting it mildly. It was just a single-storey shed, built of undressed logs and crudely thatched with dried bracken, but Mordak had seen smaller castles. He reached the wall and stood gratefully for a while under the shelter of the eaves. Then he started to follow the wall in search of a door. He walked for a disturbingly long time, but there wasn't one. Eventually he came to a corner, and turned it. The side of the building stretched away in front of him for as far as he could see.

"Hello?"

Something this size, he rationalised, as he walked along beside the wall, must've cost a small fortune to build. If you'd gone to all that trouble and expense, surely you wouldn't spoil it all by not having at least one door. After all, what do doors cost? Practically nothing. But a building's not much use without one.

He turned another corner. If anything, this side looked even longer than the other two, though he wasn't entirely sure that was possible. He hunched his shoulders and carried on. Eventually, just as he was about to give up, he found a door. It was solidly built out of oak planks, and wide enough for two carts. He tried the handle. It was open.

It was a barn.

Talk about your anticlimaxes. A huge great big building, hidden in the depths of the forest, and it turned out to be nothing but a stupid barn, full of straw-bales. He called out at the top of his voice, but the noise just soaked away into the sound-insulating straw. Never mind, he thought. It's dry in here, and the straw looks awfully warm and soft. He thought about Efluviel, waiting anxiously for his return out there in the driving rain. He grinned, lay down on a bale, and closed his eyes. *Must be ever such a lot of straw in here* was his last thought, and then he was asleep.

The straw was beautifully comfortable, but just occasionally when you turned over there were prickles, and one particular prickle was sharp enough to wake him up, and when he opened his eyes it wasn't a prickle at all, it was the point of a knife, scientifically pressed against his neck just below the angle of his jaw. Holding it was a little round-faced man. "Hello," the little man said.

"M," Mordak replied. It was about as much communication as he could manage without cutting his own throat.

"Are you a straw-thief? If you are, just nod."

Fortunate for Mordak that he wasn't, or his jugular vein would've been severely compromised. He kept perfectly still and mouthed No.

"That's all right, then." The little man withdrew the knife, and Mordak took a long-overdue breath of air. "Sorry about that," the little man continued. "But you know how it is. All this straw. You can't be too careful these days."

Mordak massaged his neck with his fingertips. "You stupid old fool," he said. "You could do someone an injury."

For some reason, the little man smiled at that. "You're not particularly interested in straw, are you?"

"What? God, no. Look, will you put that thing away, you're making me nervous."

"Of course." The little man slipped the knife back in its sheath. "You don't know who I am, do you?"

"Nope."

"Splendid." The little man grinned. "It's been ever such a long time since I met someone who doesn't know me. Really rather refreshing, actually. Oh, by the way, where's the Elf?"

"What? Oh, right." Mordak shrugged. "Still out in the forest, I guess."

"In the rain."

"Presumably."

"Getting wet."

"I suppose so, yes."

"It's an ill wind." The little man wandered away and came back with a bottle and two glasses. "Of course, I haven't actually met many Elves since I've been in this – in these parts."

"Lucky you."

"But I can't say I've taken to them, exactly. My fault, probably."

"No."

"Ah well. Drink? It's something I brought with me from home. It's called Scotch. You might like it."

A bit like being inside a volcano at the moment of eruption, Mordak decided, but not unpleasant. "Another?" the little man asked.

"Yes please."

"Your very good health." The little man looked at him. "You're King Mordak."

Mordak tried to say yes, but his tongue was acting all funny. He nodded.

"Splendid. You got my message, then."

"Message?"

"I asked two associates of mine to get you to come here. An elderly gentleman and—"

"Oh, them."

"I'm glad you're here. It's time for the next phase, you see, and I need you."

Mordak frowned. "What did you say your name was?"

The little man got up and wandered off again. This time he came back with a saucepan of soup. It was the colour of blood and smelt of honey. "Also from home," he said. "Heinz tomato. I brought six palletloads. God, I'm sick of it. Have some?"

Mordak peered doubtfully into the saucepan. "Is it safe to eat?"

"Opinions differ."

"Go on, then. I'm starving."

"You need to be, to eat this stuff. More Scotch?"

"Maybe later. A lot later."

"Sensible. It makes the world a better place, but wobbly. Croutons?"

"You what?"

"Little cubes of stale bread you put in the soup," the little man explained. "Why anyone should want to I have no idea, but it's traditional. Then again, in many cultures so is human sacrifice. Right, to business."

Mordak accepted a spoon. He looked at it. "You didn't tell me your name."

"No," the little man said. "You're interested in knowing," he went on, "where the humans have been getting all their gold from."

The soup tasted mostly of sugar, though with a slightly metallic taste. Maybe the spoon was dissolving in it. "Yes," Mordak said.

The little man slurped a mouthful of soup and pulled a face. "You'd better go and get the Elf before she catches pneumonia."

"After you've told me—"

But the little man shook his head. "Think how she'll moan at you."

"True." Mordak frowned. "You'll be here when I get back?"

"You have my word. As a member of my former profession."

"All right. Oh, thanks for the soup."

"Glad you enjoyed it."

"It was horrible," Mordak said. "But I was very hungry." He put the bowl down on the floor and stood up. He could hear rain pattering on the thatch, like a million mice line-dancing. "Sounds like it's really chucking it down out there," he said mournfully. "Ah well."

The little man was fishing about inside a small barrel. "Here," he said, pulling out what looked like a fancy walking-stick wrapped in a black flag. "Try this. Something else I brought with me. Look."

Mordak looked. Then he shook his head. "We had a bloke made up something like that once," he said. "They don't work. Silly sod jumped off a hundred-foot tower and broke his neck."

"It's for keeping the rain off your head."

"Oh." Mordak walked all round it, and prodded the fabric. "Like a very small tent on a stick."

"You carry it with you wherever you go. It does work, hon-estly."

Mordak shook his head. "It must be very strange where you come from."

"Yes," the little man said. "It is."

"Here, we have hats. They work more or less the same but you don't need a stick."

"**W**here the hell have you been? I've been so worried. And I'm *wet*."

Elves and goblins agree on so very little that any confluence of minds between the species is something to be celebrated. "Yes," Mordak said, "you are. But it's all right. There's a big shed over there. Oh, and I found him."

"Who?"

"Come on."

Efluviel getting to her feet was a symphony in applied hydraulics. Water cascaded from every niche and hollow of her sodden clothes, a lot of it finding its way down her neck and sleeves and the tops of her boots. "I've been here for hours and hours and hours," she said. "What were you doing all that time?"

"Sheltering from the rain."

He didn't look round but he could hear her; a three-stage squelch with every step. "Who did you find?"

"You'll see."

"Is there a fire?"

"No. It's a straw barn."

"Straw burns. It burns really well."

"*No.*" Mordak did a little hop, to avoid a puddle. "Anyway, he's got something better. It's called Scotch. Keep up, will you? You're dawdling again."

"I'm sick of all this. I want to go home."

"Don't be so feeble," Mordak replied cheerfully. "A few raindrops never killed anybody. And Elves have their faults, God knows, but I never heard they were soluble in water."

"What's that stick-with-a-flag thing you're carrying?"

"Some sort of hat, apparently. Though where your head's meant to go—"

There was a dull thud, and Mordak abruptly fell silent. Efluviel, who'd fallen some way behind on account of her boots being small portable reservoirs, stopped dead and peered into the driving rain. "Mordak?"

A shape loomed out of the darkness at her. It proved to be a young human, well over six feet tall, with pale blue eyes and long blond hair plastered to his head and shoulders. "It's all right, miss," he said breathlessly. "You're safe now. I've got him."

Efluviel took a step back. "Who the hell are you?"

The young man smiled. "Prince Florizel at your service," he said. "Now, it's perfectly all right." He had a substantial chunk of tree-branch in his right hand. "I bashed him real good, he'll be out of it for hours. There aren't any more of them, are there?"

"More of what?"

The prince frowned. "Well, goblins, of course."

It was dark, which probably explained why the prince didn't seem to have noticed the look on Efluviel's face. Or it could just be that Florizel was the sort of young man who notices young women's faces but not the look on them. "Have you just knocked out King Mordak?"

"Is that who it—? My God." Florizel grinned hugely. "Now isn't that the most amazing bit of luck?"

"Ought I to take that as a yes?"

"What? Oh, sorry. Yup, I bashed him good and hard. Broke my stick, look."

"If you've killed him—"

"Oh, no chance of that," Florizel said breezily. "Skulls like concrete, Johnny Goblin. You're right, of course, he'll be far more use to us alive than dead. You wouldn't happen to have any rope, would you? There's probably some in the barn if you *ow!*" Florizel doubled up, bringing his chin down conveniently to knee height. "For Od's sake, ot you *ooing*?"

Efluviel rubbed her knee and scowled at him. His jaw had proved to be harder than she'd anticipated. "You clown," she said.

Florizel scrambled to his feet and backed away, massaging the side of his face. "Have you gone mad? You hit me."

"Yes."

"But I rescued you, you silly girl. From the goblins."

"Goblin, singular. And he happens to be my boss."

"But that's crazy. You're an—"

"And," Efluviel heard herself say, "my friend. And if you've hurt him, I'll pull your head off and make you eat it."

"He's a *goblin*," Florizel yelled. "Goblins? You know? Implacably cruel servants of Evil? You can't be *friends* with a goblin. It's—"

"What?"

"Oh, I don't know, do I? It just *is*." He shook his head. "Sorry, I'm not much good with words, more your practical sort. But I read this thing in the paper once, it said, evil must be opposed, if we ever stop opposing it, we risk embracing the darkness, or something like that. Damn good stuff, actually. Wish I could remember—"

"About five years ago?"

"About then, yes. Why, did you see it too?"

Efluviel was suddenly very still. "I wrote it."

"What?"

"I wrote that. For the *Face*. Five years ago."

"Oh my God." Florizel's eyes lit up. "You're Efluviel," he said.

"Yes."

"This is amazing. I'm your biggest fan. I loved that thing you wrote. And the other stuff. You wrote a lot of stuff, it was dead good. I cut them out and stuck them in a book."

"Um."

"Really amazing. All about how evil is all-pervasive and insidious, and sometimes it doesn't even look like evil, but it still is really, and how it's our duty as free citizens of the Realms not to rest until the last goblin—"

"You, um, liked my stuff, then?"

"Loved it. Crazy about it. I only learned to read so I could follow your column in the paper. This is so great, they're not going to believe it back home when I tell them, I actually met *Efluviel*. You don't mind if I call you Efluviel, do you? Or Flu, for short. Listen, Flu, there's something I've always wanted to ask you. Where do you get your ideas from?"

"Oh, you know," Efluviel said helplessly. "Gosh, it's been ages since anyone said—" She hesitated. "I mean, you write the stuff, you churn it out, but you never really know if anyone actually likes it."

"Are you kidding? I used to know whole chunks of it by heart. Like that thing you did, *The Goblin Menace*. You know, the one where you said that the Realms will never know peace so long as one single goblin—"

"Um. Look, about that."

"Or there was that other one, *Goblins: Us or Them*. You remember, where you said that we were locked in a desperate tooth-and-nail battle for survival, and only by wiping goblins off the face of the—"

"I may have overstated things just a tad."

"Rubbish, you were bang on, absolutely right, every word

of it. Completely opened my eyes, you did. You made it all so clear and simple. And then there was that editorial, *No Alternative*. About how, unless we get rid of goblins once and for all—"

"Oh, that. That was when Mordak was about to take over the *Face*. I may have got a bit carried away."

"I built my entire philosophy of life round that article," Florizel said. "When I'd read it I took this solemn oath, that I'd never rest so long as one single goblin—"

"Yes. Well."

"And when I read it out at the Princes' Assembly, it was amazing, they stood up and cheered, I thought the roof was going to fall in."

"*I didn't mean it.*"

Florizel stared at her. "You what?"

"I was pissed off," Efluviel said. "Because Mordak was about to buy the *Face*, and I knew, if that happened, I'd never get to be editor. So I was pretty anti-goblin at that time. Except now, he's promised me he'll make me the editor, so really—"

"You didn't mean it?"

"Well, no. I mean, I'd hardly ever met any goblins back then. And besides, it was just journalism."

"How could you write something like that and not really mean it? I don't understand."

"Like I said, it was *journalism*." Efluviel breathed in deeply through her nose, then out again. "It's not like anybody really believes what they read in the papers."

"I did."

"Yes, well. Anyway, Mordak's my boss."

"And your friend."

"I did say that, didn't I?"

"Yes. Was that journalism too?"

"And you're not to go hitting him any more," Efluviel said firmly. "Got that?"

Florizel sighed. "I guess. Yes, you're right. It's like you said in that thing you did about ethical treatment of prisoners."

"He's not a prisoner."

"Yes he is."

"No he *isn't*. You leave him alone, all right?"

Florizel nodded slowly. "Oh I see," he said. "He's changed sides, then. Come over to us. Defected."

"No."

"Then he's got to be a prisoner, surely. He's the enemy, for heaven's sake. He's *evil*."

"No, he isn't."

"So he *has* defected, then. Only you said—"

"Oh shut up," Efluviel shouted. "And stop keeping on about stupid good and evil. Like it matters."

"What did you just—?"

"That's all just journalism too," Efluviel said. "And if you don't put that stick down right now, I'm going to take your temperature with it. Now go away, before I lose my temper."

Florizel laid the stick carefully down on the ground and backed away from it. "And anyway," he said, "you shouldn't be doing all this rough stuff. I rescued you. You're a girl. You shouldn't be threatening me, I'm *good*."

"You're an idiot," Efluviel said. "Now, I'm going to count up to seven. One."

Florizel started to back away. "Are you really going to be editing the *Face*?"

"Providing you haven't killed Mordak, yes. Two."

"Can I have your autograph? It's not for me, it's—"

"Three."

There was a crackle of crushed brambles, and Efluviel was alone once more. She found Mordak lying at the base of an oak tree, with a beautifully calm expression on his face. She kicked him in the ribs. "Hey."

"What?"

"Are you all right?"

"No. Some bloody fool just kicked me."

"Get up," Efluviel said. "I just saved your life."

Mordak hauled himself to his feet. "Did you?"

"Yes."

"Really?"

"*Yes.*"

Mordak shook his head. "You're sure you're not exaggerating? Just a bit?"

"There was a human. He bashed you on the head. He was going to kill you."

"I don't remember any human."

"Well, you wouldn't, would you? He ambushed you. You never saw him coming."

Mordak pursed his lips. "Right. So where is he now, then?"

"He just left."

"He just left. I see. Ah well, that's all right, then."

"You don't believe me, do you?"

"I didn't say that."

"You don't believe me."

Mordak shrugged. "Well," he said, "it's a bit implausible, don't you think? A single human, on his own, manages to creep up on the most fearsome goblin warrior of his generation and bash him over the head. Not that I'm saying it didn't happen, mind you," he added quickly. "And I wouldn't know, because I was asleep the whole time. But isn't it a bit more likely that I tripped over a tree-root or something, hit my head on the tree."

"Are you calling me a liar?"

"Good Lord, no. I'm just saying. It makes a good story, that's all. *Mordak Saved By Elf In Forest Drama*. Nothing wrong with that," he added kindly. "It's what I'll be paying you for, assuming we get out of all this in one piece. It's just, there's a time and a place, all right?" He straightened up and looked round. "Oh good," he said. "It's stopped raining. Well, don't just stand there. You'll catch your death. Besides, we don't want to keep him waiting."

"There's nothing for it," the Curator said sadly. "We're going to have to kill you."

One of the problems with goodness, as any saint will tell you, is that if you're not careful, you stick like it. "Oh well," Archie said. "If it'll help, I suppose that's all right."

They'd hung him by the arms from two hooks in the ceiling. It hurt quite a lot but he didn't like to complain. After all, they were busy people doing important work, and he respected that. They had enough on their plates, and he didn't want to bother them.

A siren wailed and a red light started flashing. "Stop it," the Curator snapped. "Oh God, he's doing it again. Make him *stop*."

"Sorry," Archie mumbled. "I'm being a nuisance, aren't I?"

A harassed-looking young man in a white coat handed the Curator a clipboard. He glanced at it and moaned. "Scrub that," he said, "we can't kill him. If we do, that's martyrdom. It'd be off the scale. Probably melt an ice-cap." He looked hopefully at the young man, who shrugged. "There's got to be *something* we can do," the Curator said. "Ideas, people."

Suddenly, all the young men and women in the laboratory

were busy with other things. The Curator lolled back in his chair and moaned. "Bloody goblins," he said. "Why couldn't we have stuck to trolls? Then we wouldn't have been in this mess."

Archie cleared his throat. "Actually," he said, "there's a lot of good in trolls. They're loyal, hard-working and very fond of their families. Quite sensitive and artistic, some of them. The trouble is, they're misunderstood."

Ten yards or so away, a monitor blew out in someone's face. A medical team took him away on a stretcher. "Make him shut up," the Curator yelled, "before he gets us all killed. Stick a bit of rag in his face or something."

Archie obligingly opened his mouth, but a young woman in glasses and a lab-coat said, "If we do that, he'll suffer in silence. They'd have to redraw all the maps."

The Curator leaned forward and scowled furiously. Archie smiled back. "What I want to know is," the Curator said, "how the hell did he wake up in the first place? You were supposed to have zonked him right out."

"We did," said a young man with different coloured pens in his top pocket. "And then the cryo effect should've kept his brain in neutral indefinitely. And it's not a goblin thing, because all the other goblins are still bye-byes. It's *him*. He's weird."

"We need to make him do something nasty," the young woman said.

Another young man, dark-haired, with a turkey neck and razor rash, took over the blast victim's station. "Shouldn't be too hard, surely," he said. "After all, it's their nature, isn't it?"

"For God's sake." The Curator spun round and scowled horribly at him. "Keep your voice down, can't you? If he hears you talking like that he'll forgive you, and then—" His voice was drowned out by a loud explosion, somewhere directly overhead. Plaster dust drifted down like finely sifted snow and settled on the top of the Curator's head. "Too late," he said. "I think that was probably the subsidiary reactor coil."

"Confirmed," someone said. "We're now running on back-ups of backups. Just thought you'd like to know that."

The young woman was staring fixedly at Archie, who beamed at her. "Know what I think?" she said. "I think he's perfectly well aware that the nicer and gooder he is, the more damage he's doing. Therefore, every virtuous deed and meek thought he perpetrates is actually an act of pure sublimated evil. Well? What d'you reckon?"

The Curator sighed. "I wouldn't be the least bit surprised," he said. "Pity the machine doesn't see it that way. Come on, children, *ideas*. Talk to me."

Awkward silence. Then the dark-haired man said, "Kidnap another goblin?"

"Make that two," the young woman said. "At least."

The Curator clicked his tongue. "A temporary fix at best," he said. "And has it occurred to any of you to consider what might happen if we bring over another one, and it ends up going wrong like this one has? Not pretty, boys and girls, not pretty at all."

"All right," the young woman said. "How'd it be if we just let him go?"

Dead silence, for about ninety seconds. Then Archie cleared his throat and said, "Excuse me."

The Curator glowered at him. "Well?"

"How would it be," Archie said, "if you took me back to where you got me from? Just a thought," he added quickly, "and if it's at all inconvenient, just forget I spoke, I wouldn't want to put you to any trouble, after you've all been so kind and nice."

"Ha!" The dark-haired man banged the bench with his fist. "That's not true. We haven't been kind and nice, we abducted him against his will and we've got him chained to the ceiling. Therefore he's lying, lying is evil." He folded his arms and smirked triumphantly.

The young woman leaned forward to examine her monitor. She shook her head. "No change. The discrepancy readings are still off the chart."

"He's turning the other cheek again," the Curator groaned. "I hate it when he does that."

"Well?" the young woman demanded. "What about it? Why don't we just send him back?"

"Um," Archie said meekly. "So you can do that, then."

"We've got to do *something*," the dark-haired man said. "In the next twenty-seven minutes and fourteen seconds. Otherwise, it's adios, cosmos."

"All right," the young woman said, "how about this? By continuing to be good, even though he knows perfectly well that only badness can save the world, he's deliberately trying to bring about universal armageddon, which is so Dark Lord it's not true. Therefore he's not just evil, he's the *epitome* of evil, and that bloody dial should now be reading 0.76." She looked down. "Which it isn't. Damn."

The Curator sighed. "You're not helping," he said. "Listen, people, I think the most we can hope for at this stage is some limited degree of damage control. I say we shoot the bugger."

The dark-haired man tore out a handful of his own hair. "Are you crazy?" he yelled. "You said it yourself. Kill him, he's a martyr. That'd be—"

"Offset," the Curator said firmly, "by the wickedness of gunning down an innocent, unarmed man in cold blood, which has got to count for something. With any luck, we might be able to salvage Tashkent and a fair-sized chunk of New Mexico. It'd be better than nothing."

Thoughtful silence. The young woman ran a few numbers through the computer. "He's right," she said. "Almost certainly

Albuquerque and quite possibly downtown Tucumcari. It'd be enough to ensure the survival of the human race. In some form, anyway."

The dark-haired man opened a drawer and took out a revolver. "Though I'm not sure that just shooting him would be evil enough," he said. "To be canonically correct, we ought to tie him to the railway tracks, or do something elaborate with a candle, a length of string and some dynamite."

The Curator shook his head. "We haven't got time for that."

"Oh well," sighed the young woman, "there goes Mescalero. Never mind."

The dark-haired man passed the revolver to the Curator, who cocked it and pointed it at Archie's head. "Where's the evillest place to aim for, do you think? Kneecaps first, then stomach?"

"Excuse me," Archie said.

"I wouldn't," the young woman said. "The more he suffers, the nobler it gets. Just blow his head off and have done with it."

"I said, excuse me."

"I don't want to stress you guys out or anything," the dark-haired man said, "but we are on the clock here."

"Only," Archie said, raising his voice just a little, "you aren't really going to shoot me, are you?"

The Curator clicked his tongue. "Looks like we're going to have to," he said, "if only as a pretty desperate stop-gap measure. And even then, there's absolutely no guarantees it'll work."

"But I thought—"

Suddenly they were all looking at him. "Well?" said the young woman.

"I thought you were just trying to, you know, scare me. Threats and bluster and stuff. I didn't think you really meant it."

"Twenty-four minutes and thirty seconds," the dark-haired man said. "Just so you know."

"All right, all right, I'll stop being nice," Archie said quickly. "I'll be evil. You can even put me back to sleep if you want to."

"Sorry." The Curator shook his head sadly. "I'm afraid it's all gone a bit too far for that. You see, if you renounce good and embrace evil at this late stage in the proceedings, it'd only be in order to avert catastrophe and save the universe. An act," he added bitterly, "of supreme heroism and self-sacrifice. Although it's well-nigh impossible to think of anything that could make the mess we're in even worse, that might just possibly do it." He scowled and raised the gun. "Let's not find out."

"I still want to know," the young woman said, "why he woke up. I think we're missing something. He shouldn't have been able to do that."

"I know why I woke up."

"Don't listen to him, he's playing for time," the dark-haired man said. "Talking of which, twenty-three minutes exactly."

"I'm not, I just remembered," Archie said. "There was a voice in my head, it said, *Wake up.* So I did."

"Which means nothing," the dark-haired man said. "I get voices in my head all the time. I just tell them, please hold, and hum Vivaldi at them till they go away. Meanwhile, we've just lost Farmington. Which, I have to say, under normal circumstances I wouldn't lose sleep over, except—"

But the Curator had lowered the gun. "A voice," he said, "in your head."

"That's right. And it called me by my goblin name. At least, I think it did, because I'm not entirely sure what it was any more. My name, I mean. Look, do you think you could possibly take these chains off? My arms are getting rather sore."

"This voice. Did it say anything else? Tell you to do something?"

"Drive the English out of Aquitaine, probably," the dark-haired man said. "That's what mine tell me. I try to explain, but will they listen?"

"I don't think so," Archie said. "But I can't remember."

"You can't?"

"No. The voice said, *You will not remember this message.*" He frowned. "I think. I can't really remember."

The Curator and the young woman looked at each other. "Surely not," the young woman said.

"I wouldn't put it past him," the Curator replied.

"But the sheer level of plant and equipment he'd need. Where'd he get that from? In a pre-industrial—"

"A doughnut and a crystal ball," the Curator said. "Remember, as far as we know, over there magic *works*."

"Twenty minutes and forty-five seconds," the dark-haired man said.

"And anyway," the young woman protested. "*Why?* Why would he want to sabotage everything we're trying to do?"

"Maybe he simply doesn't realise the harm he's doing," the Curator replied. "Probably he just wants to make sure we can't go over there and grab him and fetch him back. Understandable, in the circumstances."

"But he must know—"

The Curator shrugged. "Not really. Bear in mind, after everything he's been through, he probably isn't thinking straight." He thought for a moment, then nodded decisively. "All right," he said, "this is what we do. Get him down."

"What?"

"Get those chains off our friend there and make him a nice cup of tea."

"Nineteen minutes and fifty-four seconds."

"All right, forget about the tea, just give him a cake or

something." He turned to Archie and smiled. "Congratulations," he said. "You're not going to die after all."

"Really? That's nice."

"No." The Curator stood aside as the dark-haired young man brought up a stepladder. "Guess what? You're going home."

"Am I? Oh good."

"On condition," the Curator said, "that you do one simple little job for us when you get there. Right up your alley, very straightforward, and you'll save not one but two realities from total destruction. Well? Up for it?"

The dark-haired man released the chains. Archie dropped to the floor with a bump. "Yes," he said.

"Splendid. Now, we haven't got any time to lose, so Angela here will take you to the interface, just do exactly what she tells you and everything will be fine. Got that?" He turned to the young woman and said, "Plan B." She went pale, but nodded.

Archie rubbed his shin. "Sure," he said. "Really and truly back home? Exactly where I was?"

"Exactly the same place," the Curator said. "It'll be like you never left."

Archie grinned. "Cool," he said. "Oh, just one thing. This little job you want me to do."

"Well?"

"What is it?"

"Oh, just kill someone. Won't take you five minutes. Angela will give you the details on your way out." He frowned. "Oh, don't stand there pulling faces, it's not much to ask. We're sending you home. You should be pleased."

Archie hesitated. "Yes, but killing someone—"

"Don't be such a baby." The Curator straightened his spectacles on his nose and called up a long column of numbers on his computer screen. "It's all right, I understand, it's the monkey-suit. Skews your judgement. Well, you'll be rid of it soon, and you'll see things more clearly once you're a goblin again."

"Will I?"

"Guaranteed," the Curator said reassuringly. "After all, what's that old goblin proverb? A goblin who's tired of killing is tired of life? Angela, get this man his cake." He smiled. "Better make it a doughnut, don't you think?"

"Well," said the little man, tilting the kettle towards the teapot. "This is nice, isn't it?"

Efluviel and Mordak looked at him. "Is it?"

"Yes," the little man said firmly. "It's cosy and friendly. Milk and sugar?"

"No milk for me," Mordak said. "Allergic."

The little man raised his eyebrows and glanced at Efluviel, who shrugged. "And there's freshly baked scones, clotted cream and homemade strawberry jam. Homemade by people who just happen to live in a factory, but what the hell. Don't be shy, tuck in."

Efluviel picked up a scone, nibbled warily at the top edge and put it back on her plate. "The wise hermit said you could tell us the answer," she said.

"Quite likely," the little man said. "What to?"

"Where have the humans got all this money from all of a sudden?" Mordak said.

"Oh, that's easy." The little man sipped his tea. "From me."

Behind them, something small and vigorous scuttled in the straw. Efluviel shivered. "You," Mordak said.

"Me." The little man spread jam on a scone with a small blunt knife. "It's what I do."

"Give people money?"

The little man smiled. "In effect, yes," he said. "I make a wager with them. I tell them, bring me straw and I'll spin it into the purest gold, which you can keep. In return, however, you must give me your first-born child." He grinned. "Unless, of course, you can somehow guess my name. But it's a very unusual name, so that's not very likely." He turned and waved his arm at the mountains of straw that filled the barn. "Since I got here, the humans have been keeping me busy."

Efluviel frowned, as though trying to remember something. "Straw into gold," Mordak said. "That's ridiculous."

The little man smiled. "Yes."

"I mean," Mordak went on, "you can't just make up money out of thin air. It doesn't work like that. Money's got to stand for something or it's worthless."

That made the little man laugh. "You think so."

"It stands to reason. Doesn't it?"

The little man leaned back and put his hands behind his head. He gave Efluviel a bright smile. "You're looking very thoughtful," he said.

"I think I've heard of you," she replied. "Only I thought it was just a fairy story."

"It is." The little man masked a yawn with the back of his hand. "Sorry, it's been a long day. Twenty-hour shift at the spinning-wheel, and still I'm way behind schedule. You're quite right, a fairy story. Would you care to hazard a guess at my name?"

Efluviel looked at him, and for some reason felt strangely apprehensive. "Rumpelstiltskin," she said. "Rumpelstiltskin is your name."

The little man laughed. "No," he said.

Brightly shone the moon that night, though the frost was cruel, and the Dark Lord, gazing from the topmost window of his tower, could plainly see a stooped figure shuffling painfully through the snow. It was an elderly goblin, dressed in rags and bent double with rheumatism, gathering a few sticks and chunks of smashed packing-case from the dump outside the gates to build a meagre fire.

The Dark Lord frowned. Then he yelled, "Guards!"

The Captain came thundering up the stairs. "Boss?"

"Look."

The Captain stuck his head out of the window. "Right you are, Boss," he said, uncasing his bow and selecting an arrow from his quiver. "It's only about seventy yards, should be able to get him easy from here."

The Dark Lord took the arrow away from him and laid it on the floor. "We'll need some wine," he said, "and about a dozen pine logs. Oh, and some flesh."

The Captain nodded towards the distant goblin. "Will he do?"

The Dark Lord sighed. "No," he said. "Sausages."

"Sausages?"

"And veal and ham pie. *Quickly*."

"Sure thing, Boss." The Captain hesitated. "What about him? Shall I send a patrol to string him up?"

"Just get the stuff. And meet me at the guardhouse."

Shortly afterwards, a platoon of the Black Guard fell in for inspection in front of the guardhouse porch. As well as their armour and weapons they carried heavy packs, and six of them had massive sections of tree-trunk tied precariously on their shoulders with rope. "All present and correct, *sir*," the Captain said smartly. The Dark Lord nodded and pulled the collar of his coat tighter around his ears. "Right," he said. "Off we go."

"Permission to speak, sir."

"What?"

"Well, sir," the Captain said. "Just wanted to ask, sir, what the mission is. We got supplies for three days like you said, sir, sausages and pie and all, and presumably the wine's for celebrating once we've slaughtered whoever it is like sheep, and presumably we're attacking a town or something, which is why we need the collapsible battering-ram—"

"Oh shut up," the Dark Lord said. "Right, open the gate and follow me."

The Dark Lord strode ahead into the snow, and the Guard followed as best they could, though they had to struggle to keep up. The elderly goblin had made himself scarce as soon as the gates opened, but the Dark Lord tracked him easily by his footprints in the snow, which led to a ramshackle little shed, mostly composed of discarded catapult bolt boxes. At first it looked like there was no one at home, until the Captain pointed out the toe of a boot sticking out from under a pile of rags on the floor. "Get him," he ordered, and his men sprang forward. The goblin shot out from under the rags and nearly made it to the door.

"Get off me," he wailed, as the guards retrieved him. "It wasn't me, I was nowhere near the stores, I don't know how the stuff got there, it's all a plant. I done nothing."

The Dark Lord beamed at him. "Sit," he commanded. The goblin hesitated, so the guards helped him. "Sausages," the Dark Lord said. "Veal and ham pie."

"Never seen them before in my life. Must be some mistake. I found 'em, just lying there beside the road, must've fell off a cart or something."

"No," the Dark Lord said patiently. "These are for you. Because you're hungry and cold and utterly pathetic. It's called charity."

The goblin narrowed his eyes. "You what?"

"Captain, pour the wine. You two, get those logs split up

and get a fire going." He went to sit down, hesitated and stood up again. "And get this place straightened up a bit, can't you? It's like a pigsty in here."

The soldiers looked at each other and then at the Captain, who nodded, though with a certain degree of reluctance. "Sir," he said. "Permission to speak."

"Well?"

"No disrespect, sir, but do you think you should be doing this? I mean," he added desperately, "charity. That's—"

"What?"

The Captain swallowed hard. "Nothing, sir. Ignore me, sir. Just pretend you didn't hear me."

Two of the men made a start on shifting the heap of smelly rags. Under it were a couple of packing-cases, with their official lead seals still intact. One was marked *Boots*, the other *Spoons, wooden, serving*. Both were stencilled with lot numbers, and the new concentric-rings logo of the Dark Service. The Captain leaned forward, examined them and grinned. "Oh dear," he said. "Look what we've found."

The old goblin had suddenly gone still and quiet. "Well?" the Captain said.

"What?"

"Let me guess," the Captain said. "Late one night, a crack team of Special Services Elves broke in, tied you up, hid these crates under your mattress, threatened you with agonising torments if you told anyone and then left the way they came, leaving not a trace behind."

"Here," the old goblin said. "Who told you?"

"Book him," the Captain snapped, but the Dark Lord held up his hand and shook his head. "I believe him," he said.

The Captain stared. "Boss?"

"I believe him. Clearly, some passing Elves took pity on him and left him these valuable stores. Being an honest fellow and suspecting they might be stolen, he couldn't bring himself to sell them, because that would be wrong. They're far too heavy for him to lift, with his back. So he had no choice but to leave them there. I imagine he was planning to inform the proper authorities, once the weather improves." He turned to the goblin and smiled reassuringly. "Isn't that right?"

"Bang on," the goblin said quickly. "That's exactly what happened. Uncanny, the way you read my mind."

The soldiers were staring, their eyes practically popping out of their heads. "Boss," the Captain said. "You don't actually—"

"What?"

With a tremendous effort, the Captain straightened his back and removed all trace of expression from his face. "Very good, sir. Wine poured and logs split as per your orders, sir, Number Seven platoon standing by."

"Splendid," the Dark Lord said. "Well, I think that's everything, so let's clear off and leave this dear old chap to his dinner. You can send a cart to pick up those crates in the morning."

"Sir."

The Dark Lord stood up, and the Captain noticed that the box he'd been sitting on was marked *Socks, woollen, medium*. "And I think there should be some sort of finder's fee, don't you, as a reward for honesty?" The Dark Lord put his hand in his pocket, then frowned. "I seem to have come out without any money. Captain?"

Without a word, the Captain handed over seven iron coins, his last month's pay. They clinked in the Dark Lord's hand like chains as he placed them on the sock box. "There now," the Dark Lord said. "I expect we all feel a bit better now, don't we? It's so nice to be able to do something for those less fortunate than ourselves. Come on, men. I don't know about you, but I could do with a nice hot cup of tea."

As they filed out of the shed, the platoon sergeant nudged the Captain gently in the ribs. "Skip?"

"Yes." The Captain nodded. "I know."

"But what are we going to *do*, Skip? I mean . . ." He tailed off. His eyes were wide with bewilderment and terror. "He's lost it, hasn't he? The boss has gone barmy, and—"

"Quiet." The Captain looked round, but there was nobody in earshot. "Say nothing, all right? And when the time comes—"

The sergeant nodded. "Got you, Skip. Me and the lads, we'll be right behind you."

Indeed, the Captain thought; because it's so much harder to twist a prisoner's arm up behind his back when you're in front of him. But the look in the sergeant's eyes; and you couldn't keep a lid on something like this. It'd be all round the Dark Army in a day or so, and then – well. Their only chance would be to learn conversational Elvish and make themselves ear extensions out of bread paste.

"Don't worry, it'll be fine," he said, with a degree of confidence he didn't actually feel. "Just keep your mouth shut, act normal and leave everything to me."

He sat up all night thinking. He felt bad about it, very bad indeed, but what could he do? It was a terrible thing to conspire against his lord and master, but the very future of the Dark Realm was at stake. It is a far, far better thing I do now, he told himself. My only regret is that I have but one life to give for Evil.

And then he thought, there's something awfully wrong with those last two thoughts. He spent the rest of the night trying to figure out what it could possibly be, but he couldn't, so he gave up.

"**D**on't be silly," Efluviel said. "Of course it is."

The little man shook his head. "No it isn't."

"Yes it *is*. Everybody knows that. It's in the story."

"My name is Albert Winckler," the little man said, and for a moment there wasn't a sound to be heard, not even the scuttling of rats. Then the little man smiled and went on, "In the story, the evil gnome's name is indeed Rumpelstiltskin, but I'm not him."

"Great," Mordak said briskly, before another silence could form and become solid. "Glad we've cleared that up. What the hell sort of a name is Albert Winkle?"

"Winckler," the little man replied with dignity. "I come from a place called Chicago. You won't have heard of it."

"Actually—" Efluviel said, then waved her hand vaguely. "Ignore me."

Mr Winckler sipped his tea. "Chicago is a city in a country a long way from here. In fact – you wouldn't happen to be familiar with multiverse theory, would you?"

Mordak shrugged, but Efluviel said, "Oh, that."

"You know about—?"

"The idea that there's an infinite number of parallel universes existing simultaneously and occupying the same physical space in a basically helical continuum? Yup. I know loads of fairy stories. My mum gave me a book of them when I was three."

Mr Winckler took a deep breath. "The world I come from," he said, "is in just such an alternate universe. Over there, I was a very naughty boy. I did some really bad things."

Mordak looked up. "Oh yes?"

Mr Winckler nodded. "About as bad as it gets," he said. "I was a banker."

Mordak frowned. "Say again."

"A banker. With a B. I worked for a bank."

Mordak scratched his head. "That's where you look after people's money for them, and lend it to people who need it, right? What's so bad about that?"

Mr Winckler smiled. "Indeed," he said. "To be precise, I was a commodities broker. I won't bore you with the story of my life, but I got into a spot of trouble. I had to lay my hands on a huge sum of money very quickly, or else something really bad would happen to me." He turned his head and looked at Efluviel. "It involved a nasty little man whose name I think you know," he said, "but we won't go into all that now. Suffice it to say, I had to get an obscenely large sum of money very quickly. And then I met this girl, who told me how to do it. So that's what I did."

Mordak pursed his lips. "And that was the really bad thing?"

"Oh yes." Mr Winckler stopped and cleared his throat noisily. His eyes were rather red. "I took a load of useless, worthless junk and I made people believe I'd turned it into – well, not actual gold, but as good as, or better than. Pretty soon I had all the money I needed, but by then the idea had caught on, and lots of other people were doing it too. It wasn't long before practically all the money in the world – real money, not my pretend stuff – was tied up in the scam; and when the bubble burst and people started realising it was all make-believe, the consequences were— Well, let's not go into that. Like I said, I was a very naughty boy."

Efluviel clicked her tongue. "It can't all have been your fault," she said. "People shouldn't have been so stupid. They should've known better."

Mr Winckler gave her a sort of cracked grin. "They didn't see it quite that way," he said. "Where I come from, people are expected to be stupid and not take responsibility for their own actions, which is why we have governments. No, it's very sweet of you to say so, but it really was all my fault. Which is why I came here."

Mordak looked at him. "Sorry," he said. "I seem to have turned over two pages at once. Why did you come here?"

"Ah." Mr Winckler grinned. "Partly, I guess, because once I realised what I'd set in motion, I thought it'd probably be a good idea to get as far away as I could, before all the people I'd screwed realised it was me who screwed them. But mostly," he went on, his face straightening, "to make amends."

"Really," Efluviel said.

"Yes. Well," Mr Winckler conceded, "actually, no. When I escaped, I was feeling really, really guilty. And then I came here, and I hadn't been here long when I realised that this place wasn't so very different from where I'd just come from. I mean yes, there are differences; like, magic works here, and back home it doesn't. But basically, a lot of the setups and infrastructures are pretty much the same as they used to be at home, a long time ago. Which meant, of course, that what had happened where I came from could happen here one day. All it would take, I realised, would be for some evil bastard like me to come along, and you'd end up in the same horrible mess as we're in, because of me. And I couldn't bear the thought of that."

Mr Winckler stopped talking and looked down at his hands for a while. Eventually, Efluviel said, "So you decided—"

"I'd make sure it would never happen," Mr Winckler said, and his eyes were bright with anger and tears. "I'd fix things so you'd never have to go through what we went through. I reckoned it was the least I could do. My way of putting things right."

"Fair enough," Mordak said. "But what's all that got to do with the humans suddenly getting rich?"

"I'm coming to that," Mr Winckler said. "Once I'd discovered that magic works here – to a very limited extent and within strictly defined parameters, which is cool – I knew exactly what I had to do. I borrowed an idea from the Old Country. We used to call it *quantitative easing*."

Efluviel blinked. "Say what?"

Mr Winckler smiled. "I know," he said. "It's meant to be confusing and meaningless, that's so people won't understand what you're proposing to do until it's too late. What it means is, you make up vast amounts of pretend money that doesn't actually exist, and then you give it to people to spend." He shook his head. "It never worked worth a damn back home, naturally, because magic doesn't work there, and without magic it's just a really, really stupid idea. Here, though—" He leaned back and pointed at the spinning-wheel. "A different story entirely. "Here, you genuinely can turn straw into gold, instead of just pretending to the voters that that's what you're doing. And then I found out that everybody over here knows the Rumpelstiltskin story too. Perfect, just what I needed. The point being, everybody knows the horrid little gnome's true name. If I just went around handing out fistfuls of gold at random, people would be suspicious, they'd assume I was up to something. But if they truly thought they were getting the better of me – well, no problem. It's all about perceptions, you see, and what people can be suckered into believing."

Mr Winckler poured himself some more tea. Efluviel said, "Just a minute, though. I don't see the point."

"Excuse me?"

"Of giving the humans loads and loads of make-believe money. How's that going to make them happier, or stop this disaster of yours from ever happening?"

Mr Winckler shook his head. "That was just the first step," he said. "We've gone way beyond all that. Essentially, while you've been away, traipsing up and down mountains enjoying yourselves, I've taken the humans in this reality through a controlled and greatly accelerated version of what we went through back home. The difference being, I knew what I was doing, and where to press the buttons and levers. What we stumbled blindly through over hundreds of years, I've guided your humans through in a matter of months." He yawned, and stretched. "It's been a long, hard slog, but I think I can safely say my work here's nearly done. Very soon now, I'll be able to pack up and slip quietly away, and everything will be for the best in the best of all possible worlds."

There was a long silence. Then Mordak said, "All right, let's assume you're right and you've made things all nice for the humans. Maybe it's escaped your attention, but there's other species besides them – goblins, dwarves—" He paused for a moment. "Elves. And if you've made the humans happy and rich, the first thing they're going to do is come down on my lot like a ton of bricks. And stop shaking your head like that, it's incredibly annoying."

"All taken care of," Mr Winckler said. "The humans will be too busy creating and fairly distributing wealth to have the time or the energy for making war. And if they don't start anything, you won't have to fight back. Same for the Elves. With the humans off your backs, you can get on with whatever it is you do. To be honest," he added, "I haven't quite managed to figure out what that is yet, but so long as you know, that's all that matters."

"Easy," Efluviel said. "We're better than everyone else. And we tell them so. It's a full-time job, believe me."

"Whatever," Mr Winckler said. "The point is, take the humans out of the equation as a nuisance-creating agent, and the rest of you can live in peace and plenty."

But Mordak was scowling. "You've missed the point," he said. "Maybe not about her lot, but you're definitely wrong about the goblins. We don't want to live in peace and harmony, we want to fight and break things and grind the other races under our iron heel. Yes we *do*," he added, as Efluviel looked at him oddly. "It's what we do, it's what we're for. We're *evil*."

Mr Winckler just smiled at him. "Not for much longer," he said.

Mordak's jaw dropped. "You what?"

"Oh, let's not spoil the surprise," Mr Winckler said. "But next time you run into your Dark Lord, you may notice a few changes, that's all I'm saying. I think you goblins are standing on the threshold of a bright new tomorrow, as we say where I come from. Whether you like it or not."

"You've convinced the Dark Lord to give up Evil? That's just so—"

Mr Winckler shrugged. "Evil," he said, "what good does it do? Better off without it, in my opinion. I talk to him in his dreams, which he can't remember when he wakes up. But the subconscious effect remains, which is what matters. I think you'll be pleasantly surprised next time you speak to him. And once you don't have to do Evil any more, you goblins can settle down, act normally and turn into regular folks, just in time to share in the general prosperity." He shrugged. "Compared to sorting out the humans, your Dark Lord was a slice of seed cake. Which only goes to show the advantage of dealing with a strong centralised authority. Only one idiot to bamboozle, rather than dozens."

Mordak jumped up. He was quivering all over. "You can't do things like that," he said, "it's not *right*. You can't just decide to abolish Evil and say, okay, from now on all you goblins are going to be nice. It's unethical. It's a violation of our fundamental goblin rights. It's *wrong*."

Mr Winckler grinned. "Pretty bad, huh?"

"Very bad. Very bad indeed."

"Wicked?"

"To put it mildly."

"You might almost go so far as to say—"

"No!" Mordak shouted. Then he seemed to deflate. "Well, actually, yes, evil is a good way of describing it. Evil, as in imposing your ideas of what's good for people on them against their will, and the hell with what they want."

"So, if I succeed, evil will have triumphed."

"Yes. No. Sort of."

Mr Winckler clapped his hands together. "Evil, as personified by me. Meet the new Dark Lord. But you can call me Albert."

Mordak walked round and round in circles for a bit, then sat down again. "That's just so—"

"Yes," said Mr Winckler happily, "isn't it? That's the thing about good and evil," he added pleasantly. "It's just like the gold-into-straw thing, it's all simply what people believe. And meanwhile, you've got a kingdom to run and everyday problems to solve and people to feed and bills to pay. I think you'll find it easier my way. At least give it a chance." He turned to Efluviel. "He's not really evil, is he? Be honest."

Efluviel thought for a moment. "Inconsiderate, devious, chauvinist and a pain in the bum, yes. Evil?" She shrugged. "Not really, no."

Mordak glowered at her. "I'm not speaking to you. Ever again."

"And you're no better than he is," Mr Winckler said cheerfully, "and you're one of the Children of Light, God help us all. In fact, there's so little to choose between you, I really can't be bothered to try. The point is, when the chips were down, both of you—" He shrugged. "To paraphrase one of your greatest goblin philosophers, the things we do because we care are beyond naughty and nice. And you can tell your friend, if he carries on scowling at me like that, the wind'll change and he'll stick like it."

"I think that already happened," Efluviel said, "some time ago. Oh, and I'm not talking to you either. Mordak, tell him."

Mr Winckler sighed happily. "There you are, you see. Goblin and Elf united in harmony against the common enemy. And I did all that," he added happily, "with my little hatchet."

Mordak shot him a poisonous look, realised that it had no effect whatsoever, and gave up. "Fine," he said. "I can sort of see what you're getting at, and I suppose – well, it's nasty and mean and totally out of order, but it *might* just make things better for everyone. *Assuming,*" he added quickly, "that you really have thought it all through, and you haven't overlooked anything that'll screw it all up, and there won't be any horrible side-effects that you aren't telling us about. Assuming."

"Oh, there'll be side-effects all right," Mr Winckler said, looking away. "Nasty ones and plenty of them. But not here. Here, nothing but sweetness and light. And that's all that matters, isn't it?"

Mordak and Efluviel looked at each other. "Well, no."

"Yes," Mr Winckler said firmly. "Because here – well, multiverse theory is just that, a theory. I mean, nobody's ever proved it, scientifically. So, for all we know, all the other alternate universes, including the one I originally came from, are just—" He shrugged. "Science fiction. So, if something bad has to happen to a reality far away of which we know little, which hasn't been proved to exist and probably doesn't, then so what? No skin off your noses, that's for sure."

"Hang on," Mordak said. "What does that actually mean?"

"Oh, well." Mr Winckler shrugged. "It's just possible that, by coming here and doing good, I've created a hopeless breach of the Laws of Conservation of All Sorts of Things, and my native reality could just conceivably—"

"What?"

Mr Winckler rubbed his nose with his thumb. "Blow up. But what the hell, omelettes and eggs. After all, I buggered it up so comprehensively before I left that on balance, if it does blow up it'll be doing them a favour. And if they don't even exist—"

Mordak stared at him. "You're going to blow up a whole universe?"

"It's possible," Mr Winckler said. "But there. Strictly in accordance with good banking practice. If an asset becomes worthless, you write it off. And if that means you cause endless misery and disaster to the poor devils you leave floundering in your wake, you put aside a small percentage of the profits, set up a foundation and do good works to improve the lives of a lot of other people somewhere else. That's called philanthropy. Just ask Bill Gates."

Mordak thought for a moment. "Just out of interest," he said, "is there anything we can do to stop you?"

"Not really, no." Mr Winckler sighed. "Oh come on," he said, "what's with the long faces? I told you just now, didn't I, I'm the new Dark Lord, or I will be, one day quite soon, when the present incumbent gets the boot. And it's all my fault, so nobody else has anything to feel guilty about. And besides, it's all so far away and theoretical, it hardly matters. If a star goes nova in the next galaxy but one, you don't rush about tearing your hair out and wailing, 'We should have done something'. If you think about it at all, you just say, well, it had obviously had its time, life must go on. And compared to an alternative reality, the next galaxy but one is practically on your doorstep. To put it another way, it's none of your business. Forget about it. Leave the agonies of guilt to me." He made a vague gesture with his hands. "God knows, I'm used to them."

Mordak leaned forward a little. "Old goblin proverb," he said. "Never leave a living mistake. Meaning, if you mess up, make sure everyone who knows about it is safely dead."

Mr Winckler smiled. "I rather like that," he said. "You know, when this is all over, I might settle down here and become a naturalised goblin. You people are so unfussy."

"Not as unfussy as all that," Mordak replied. "Besides, you're too tall. And your nose is the wrong shape."

"Ah well. Besides, it won't be up to you. After all, you answer to the Dark Lord, don't you? When he appoints me his new finance minister, you'll have to be polite to me then. You know what?" He beamed at Mordak, possibly the widest smile he'd ever seen. "I think I could get to like evil. This New Evil of yours, anyway. It can be whatever you want it to be. I like that."

"New Evil isn't like that," Mordak said angrily. "It's real evil, with values and stuff, but with a caring and compassionate face. It's not an excuse for not giving a damn, or covering up your mistakes by blowing up universes. That's not evil, that's—"

"Bad?" Mr Winckler sighed. "Not very nice? This is no use, we're just going round in circles. The time eventually comes when you've got to make a deal. Ask the Elf. She knows all about that."

Efluviel went bright red. "That's just so—" She hesitated. "I did not make a deal," she said firmly. "I agreed to do something

I didn't want to do in order to get something I really wanted. There's a difference, you know." She paused and frowned. "And ever since, I've been cold-bloodedly manipulating him into doing exactly what I want. That's not a deal, that's exploitation."

"No, you haven't," Mordak said.

"Yes I *have*," Efluviel snapped. "I wheedled and tricked you into making me the editor of the *Face*. Using you. Not," she added emphatically, "a deal."

"No, you haven't," Mordak repeated patiently. "You've worked really hard and had some bloody good ideas and we wouldn't have got here without you. And I'd have made you the editor anyway. You're a really good journalist."

"You—" Efluviel turned on him like a cobra, then stopped dead. "You think so?"

"Yes. Outstanding. You even check your facts and spell some of the names right. And yes, you're consistently snarky and point-scoring, but that's just being an Elf, you do it to each other all the time, it's really just a sign of acceptance, like dogs weeing down your leg. And no one could say you haven't stuck to your side of the bargain."

Efluviel turned to Mr Winckler. "Ignore him, he's delusional. It's the altitude. Goblins can't cope with more than ten feet above sea level. Elves don't do deals with goblins. Just, sometimes we deceive and betray them in a mutually beneficial way."

Mr Winckler smiled. "Bullshit," he said kindly. "There, now. See what I've achieved? The king of the goblins, and you, soon to be the most influential Elf in the Realms, best friends. I really have done an outstanding job, though I do say so myself. Now, isn't that worth a single, solitary, non-existent reality going pop, to achieve all that? Come on. It's not like there aren't an infinite number of others out there. One more or less really doesn't matter."

Mordak frowned. "You're sure killing you wouldn't put things right?"

"You haven't been listening, have you?" Mr Winckler said. "Everything would be so much easier for everyone if they just listened to what I tell them."

"How about sending you back?"

For a split second, Mr Winckler's face froze. Then he laughed. "Sure," he said. "You and whose army?"

"Well, mine, actually. A quarter of a million goblins, last time anyone counted."

"Forget it," Mr Winckler said. "Magic works here, remember? You'd only embarrass yourself. Besides, I have superior firepower." Without turning his head, he called out, "Boys."

From the shadows at the back of the barn, two figures stepped forward. One was a very old man, in a cloth cap and a battered-looking raincoat, but with very shiny shoes. The other was a tall, skinny young man, eating a muffin. "Believe me," Mr Winckler said, "you don't want to mess with them. Oh, I forgot. You met them before. As I recall, you were terrified of them."

"I wasn't," Efluviel said.

"Yes, well, you're a girl, you don't count. He's the battle-scarred veteran of a hundred bloody wars, and he nearly wet himself."

"That's a slight exaggeration," Mordak said. But he stayed exactly where he was. The young man finished his muffin, gave him a long, cold stare and started on a cherry Bakewell. "You haven't heard the last of this," Mordak said.

Mr Winckler was buttering a scone. "Oh good," he said. "It's nice when people say thank you. Well, I think that's about it for now. I've explained, so you're fully in the picture, and we've agreed that there's nothing you can do about anything, so that's fine, and we've done the exchange of veiled threats and you've admitted defeat, so I guess that just about wraps things up. You can get a lot done when you set your mind to it. Goodbye."

Mordak made a low growling noise that no human throat could ever manage. The old man shook his head sadly. Mr Winckler didn't seem to have heard. "Don't," Efluviel said softly.

Mordak turned on her. "I thought you said you weren't scared of those two."

"I'm not. But you are, and you know lots more about what's dangerous or not than I do. Let's just go."

"But—"

"Now."

"Efluviel—"

"*Outside*." She turned her head and smiled at Mr Winckler. "Thank you so much for explaining everything so clearly," she said, "it was very good of you to make time for us, specially when you're so busy. We'll be going now."

Mr Winckler raised one hand in silent dismissal. The young man took a step forward, reached inside his coat and pulled out a baguette. He held it in a faintly menacing way for about a second and a half, then bit the top off it. Mordak swallowed hard (so did the young man) and began to back slowly towards the door without breaking eye contact, until Efluviel grabbed him by the collar, said, "Come *on*!" loudly in his ear and dragged him out of the barn.

Mr Winckler looked up from spreading jam on a scone. Outside he could hear raised voices, but what they said seemed not to bother him particularly. He smiled, then handed the scone to the young man. "Dismissed," he said.

The old man saluted smartly but didn't withdraw. "Was there something?" Mr Winckler said.

"Well, sir." The old man was still at attention; an alarming sight, like a bow held at full draw, or a tree bent sideways by the wind. "Not meaning to teach you your own business or anything, perish the thought, sir, but don't you think that Mordak might be thinking of trying something?"

Mr Winckler shrugged. "So what? He's a goblin."

"Very cunning, sir, goblins. Cunning and devious. Young Art, sir, he always reckons a goblin's never more dangerous than when he appears to be retreating. Isn't that right, Art?"

"He's a goblin," Mr Winckler repeated. "He does what he's told."

"Very true, sir, very true indeed. But suppose the Dark Lord—"

"I wasn't thinking of him."

"Ah." The old man thought for a moment, then nodded. "In that case, sir, if you don't need us any more, we'll be getting along. Doesn't do for Art to miss mealtimes. He gets all faint."

"Yes, that's fine." Mr Winckler looked away; then, just as the old man was about to disappear, he called out, "Hang on a second."

The old man stopped. "Sir?"

"You do think I'm right, don't you? About those two."

"Oh, I expect so, sir. You're very confident, anyway. Essential part of leadership, sir, confidence."

Mr Winckler frowned. "She's got him on a piece of string," he said, "I'm pretty sure about that, so we don't need to worry about him. And she'll be all right. I mean, she's got what she wants, and that's all that matters. I never yet met an Elf that wasn't as self-centred as a drill-bit."

"Quite true, sir, me neither. Mind you, I only ever met three." The old man smiled. "Goodnight, sir. Mind you look after yourself. You work too hard, is your trouble."

"True." Mr Winckler hesitated, then turned his head to look at the old man. "You've been there, haven't you? Where I come from."

"Many times, sir, many times. I shall miss it."

"But you think I'm doing the right thing?"

"I don't think anything, sir, it's not my place."

Mr Winckler grinned. "Quite right, it isn't. Very well, you can go."

"Our Art, now, he thinks it's not very nice to blow up one world to help another, just so someone can kid himself he's a philanthropist. But he's young, sir, he'll learn."

"Quite," Mr Winckler said. "A sense of proportion's something that only comes with experience."

"I didn't mean that, sir. I meant, he'll learn to keep his thoughts to himself. Like me, sir. Goodnight."

"**P**refer a jaffa cake, if it's all the same to—"
… Archie broke off. He was standing on a rocky hillside. Above him towered mist-shrouded peaks. Far below, a mighty river thundered in foaming white fury along a narrow crack in the rock. He looked down. Where his feet had been he saw claws.

Oh hell, he thought. I'm home.

Which was so weird. Just a split second ago, the young woman called Angela had been offering him a doughnut, back in the Curator's lab. He remembered seeing her face through the hole in the middle. Then he'd felt a curious sensation, like being a very small sock in a very large spin-drier. And now—

Now, he wasn't Archie any more. He looked at his arms – long, hairy – and his hands, bunched up, eight-fingered, ending in the most magnificent shiny brown hooked talons. Carefully, he lifted his right hand to his face and let the pads of his fingertips trace the contours. Oh hell, he thought, oh joy. I'm back again. I'm *me*.

Then he remembered. One little thing we want you to do for us. He grinned; and, because he'd been human for so long, in doing so cut his top lip quite badly. Not that he cared. The taste of blood was like iced lemonade on a hot day. One little thing, huh? With the greatest of pleasure, he thought. Yes, no problem, no problem at all.

I'm hungry, he thought. Damn right; haven't had anything to eat except bread, vegetables and the flesh of non-sentients for ages and ages. Bloody human food; fills you up all right, but twenty minutes later you're hungry again. No wonder they're all so fat. Fat and juicy. He licked his lips. This is so great, he thought.

Behind him was the enormous golden brown circle; he vaguely remembered it, from last time. To think, once upon a time he'd been stupid and gullible enough to go through it, of his own accord. Never again. He shuffled nervously away from it, until he felt the sharp edge of the ledge under his foot. Steady on, he told himself. Probably the sensible thing to do would be to get down off the mountainside and away from the hateful glare of the Horrible Yellow Face, before it made him dizzy and sent him bumping down the rocky slope into the river. Probably not the smartest place in the world to put a magic cave, he reckoned. Or, bearing in mind the sort of thing that happened to you there, a very sensible place indeed.

It took him a long time to pick his way down through the crags and boulders; the bright light was making his head spin and he wasn't fully acclimatised to the goblin body yet, even though it was his own. But he took it slowly and steadily, one step at a time, and just as night was falling he found himself beside the banks of the river, where a well-beaten path led directly to the eastern gate of Eighty-six Mineshaft. An unbearable pang of longing and nostalgia tore at his heart. Round about now, the lads would be knocking off from the day shift, trooping back up the winding spiral stair from the ore-face towards the great hall for dinner and communal fighting, then off to the dormitories to sleep. If he ran really, really fast, he might just be in time for the main course. What would it be tonight, he wondered, and realised he didn't even know what day of the week it was. Wednesday was Giblet Stew, Thursday was Offal Club, Friday was Generic Pie; best of all was Sunday, his favourite, Leftovers. He realised he was drooling, because his chin was all wet. But not yet. Not until he'd done the one little thing. Until he'd got that out of the way and paid off his obligations, he knew he wouldn't be able to relax and settle back into real life. And in order to do the one little thing, he'd need to look at a map, which meant trudging all the way round the bottom of the mountain to the records office, which would be shut now until daybreak. Be sensible, he told himself. It's been a long day, you're tired, get some sleep and wake up refreshed and ready, and then you can do the one little thing and get your life back again. He yawned and stretched his wonderful arms, then looked at them again just to make sure they were really real. They were. Bliss.

One little thing. Find a little man with a funny name, kill him, please dispose of body tidily. One small problem, though. He hadn't got the faintest idea where to find him.

He closed his eyes, just to rest them for a minute.

A voice spoke in his head. *Listen carefully*, it said.

Dead silence.

"Well?" the Dark Lord said. "Oh come on. Surely one of you's got something to say."

The Dark Council didn't move. They'd stopped breathing some time ago. It was one of those moments when you just know that the slightest sound, the very faintest movement, will have the same effect as sticking both hands up in the air and yelling, "Me! Me!"

"Nobody?" The Dark Lord sighed. "Well, a fine lot of

advisers you are, I must say." His lidless red eyes swept around the table and lit on a certain Margrave of the Winged Death, who went very pale and tried very hard to pretend he wasn't there. "Groth," the Dark Lord said. "What do you think?"

Strictly speaking, of course, the Margrave wasn't there at all. He'd been a wraith for nine hundred years, and only the black cowl of his robe and the shiny new badge saying *Team Leader* pinned to his lapel defined his presence. That was what made it so bitterly unfair.

"I like it," he said.

His voice was faint, the hissing of a soft breeze in dead grass or the last escape of breath from a dying man. It was his sort of signature thing, and he was proud of it.

"Say what? Speak up."

"I like it," the Margrave croaked, as loud as he could manage. "It's got—"

"Mm?"

At which point the Margrave's brain froze. He knew perfectly well what the Dark Lord's new idea had, and so did everybody else. But—

"It's original," he said.

A frown creased the thin, papery skin of the Dark Lord's forehead. "You don't like it."

"I do," the Margrave said desperately. "I like it a lot. I think it's—"

"You're just saying that," the Dark Lord said. "So as not to hurt my feelings."

"No!" You can't sweat if you aren't actually there, but a drop of condensation plopped on the table out of nowhere and began to burn into the dark wood. "I wouldn't do that. Well, I would. But not this time. Unnecessary. Because I love it."

The Dark Lord pursed his thin lips. "Really?"

"Really and truly. Cross my heart and hope to live."

But the Dark Lord hadn't survived for six Ages of the world by being stupid. He stiffened slightly and looked away. "Well," he said, "thank you all for coming, I think that's about as far as we can go today. What I'd like you all to do is go back to your departments and draw up an action plan, and then we'll reconvene this time tomorrow and take it from there. All right, dismissed."

"An action plan," the Margrave hissed, as soon as he was safely out of range of the Black Ear. "What the Us is an action plan?"

A senior prince of Darkness bit his lip. "It's a plan," he said. "For action." He shrugged. "I don't know, do I? He keeps using all these strange words lately. Incentivise and pre-planning and in this space, going forward. I think he's doing it to confuse us."

"If so, he's doing a great job," growled an elderly goblin. "I blame all this New Evil stuff . Our bloke's getting just as bad. Well," he added, "maybe not. I think Mordak's only doing it to keep in with the boss," he added loyally. "Who can't," he added, after a significant pause, "last for ever."

They all looked at each other. They'd known and worked with each other a very long time, and some things are best communicated without words. Then a Dark Elf said, "Actually ..."

The goblin scowled at him. "All right," he conceded, "he's lasted for ever *so far*. Doesn't mean he's going to go on lasting for ever. Not indefinitely."

"I think you'll find that's what for ever means," said the Dark Elf helpfully. "What? I was just pointing out ... "

"We've got to do something."

They hadn't noticed the Captain of the Guard, who had no seat on the Council and hadn't been in the chamber with them. They all spun round in terror, but the Captain shook his head. "It's all right," he said. "I agree with you. He's lost it. He's completely out of his pram. If you'd seen what I've—" He broke off, his voice choked with emotion. "It's no use," he said. "He's got to go, and that's all there is to it."

The combined sigh of relief from the councillors would have powered a medium-sized sloop. "You heard the latest," whispered the Margrave.

"I wasn't at the meeting," the Captain pointed out. "What's he done this time?"

The Councillors looked at each other. "His Dark Majesty," said the old goblin, "wants us to organise a sponsored walk and Fun Day. In aid of Evil charities."

The Captain's eyebrows shot up. "What Evil—?"

"That's Phase Two," grunted the Dark Elf. "Apparently, Evil isn't doing enough to connect with local communities on a grass-roots level. So the idea is, we're going to reach out and embrace Society. Hug a human. Don't ask me," he added quickly, "I'm quoting."

There was a terrible pause. Then the Captain said, "It's the Elves, it has to be. They've got to him somehow. They've turned his brain to goo." He turned and gave the Dark Elf a nasty look. "They can do that," he said, "mess with your head, using arcane mind control techniques. Well-known fact."

The Dark Elf sniggered. "I wish," he said. "Sadly, no. You're thinking of journalism, which is slightly different. No, if someone's got inside his head, it's not my lot. In fact, I can't think of anyone who'd be capable of something like that." He grinned. "With the obvious exception of Himself, of course. I suppose he might have trained someone else how to do all that, without us knowing. But that's hardly likely, is it?"

"That's not important," the Margrave said firmly. "What matters is, he's a bloody liability and he's got to go. Are we agreed?" He waited. Five seconds, a very long time in context. "We're agreed," he said. "Fine. We do him in and get a new Dark Lord."

A senior troll-wrangler who'd been listening carefully at the back cleared his throat. "I wondered when we'd get on to that," he said. "Presumably you've got someone in mind."

The Margrave hesitated. "As it happens—"

"Thought so. Yourself, of course."

"Well, no," the Margrave said. "Actually, I was thinking of Mordak."

A stunned moment, as if someone had just exploded; followed by a gentle susurration of *Actually* ... "Mordak," the Dark Elf said. "You must be kidding. Although—"

"Quite," the Margrave said. "I mean, yes, he's a goblin. That said—"

"I'm a goblin," pointed out the goblin.

"Yes. My point in a nutshell. That said, he's bright, he's capable, energetic, knows how to get along with people, he can read a balance sheet and everybody likes him. Sort of. Anyway, who the hell else is there?"

"But he's a *goblin*," said the Dark Elf. "You can't have a goblin as Dark Lord. He's too—"

The old goblin shot out an arm and closed his talons precisely around certain strategic points on the Dark Elf's neck. "Choose your next word very carefully."

"Short," the Dark Elf said. "Well, he is. You can't have someone sitting on the Black Throne whose feet don't reach the floor. It'd be silly."

"There's that," the Margrave said. "But so what, a new throne's no big deal. Or saw a bit off the legs of the old one. You're just agin him because he's a goblin."

The troll-wrangler nodded sagely. "Prejudiced."

"Of course I'm prejudiced, you halfwit, I'm *evil*," snapped the Dark Elf, wriggling free of the goblin's claws and wiping his neck with a lace handkerchief. "Elves and goblins don't – well, they *don't*, that's all."

"Mordak does."

They all turned their heads and looked at the Captain, who shrugged. "Well, it's true," he said. "Like, right now at this very minute, Mordak's off on a special assignment for Him, and he's got an Elf with him. Boss's orders. And last I heard, they were getting along just fine."

"Wash your mouth out with soap and water," snarled the old goblin. "That can't be true."

"Straight up," insisted the Captain. "I was there, I heard everything."

"The Dark Lord told Mordak to take an Elf—"

"Yes."

"That's easily explained," the Margrave said. "I think the key words we're missing here are *packed lunch*."

"As a sidekick," the Captain said firmly. "Sure as I'm stood here."

"Well, there you go," the Dark Elf said smugly. "I withdraw my objection. Obviously Mordak's got more sense that I credited him with. So, he's it. Agreed? Show of claws?"

Voted unanimously, the Margrave abstaining (but only because he had no hand to raise) "Fine," he said. "Just one thing. How the hell are we going to do in His Majesty?"

Everyone was suddenly struck thoughtful. The torches in the courtyard flickered, casting ghastly dancing shadows. "We could—" began the goblin, then he shook his head. "No, scrub that. Ignore me."

"There are," the Margrave went on, "certain technical issues. Like, you can't kill the bugger, because he's seriously Undead. You can't imprison him in a sealed dungeon a thousand miles under the biggest mountain in the world, because that's been tried loads of times and he's always really snarky when he gets out again. Same goes for binding him on a mountain-top with adamantine chains or hurling him into the Fiery Pit. That's the thing about Himself, he's so horribly *persistent*."

"We could always—" The Dark Elf frowned. "No, he's got a point there. It can't be done. Bugger."

The old goblin shook his head. "There's bound to be a way," he said. "Got to be. It's just, we're too thick to figure it out."

"Speak for yourself," muttered the Dark Elf. "Though personally—"

"So," the goblin went on, "what we need to do is, we need to ask somebody smart. The sort of bloke who knows stuff. You know."

A pause. Then the Margrave said, "Enlighten us."

"Simple," the goblin said. "Mordak's smart. Ask him."

The *Old Giant's Head* at Blackwater is a modest, unpre-
tentious little hostelry situated beside the picturesque
Old North Road (southbound section). Serving a wide selection of local ales and a varied menu of traditional goblin, troll
and vampire transfusion cuisine, it's famous far and wide for
its friendly, no-nonsense service and its unique architecture.
It's also the only place within a hundred miles where you can
get something to eat without having to catch it yourself.

"What's this?" Efluviel demanded, pointing at her plate
with her fork.

"Ah."

They were sitting in one of the enormous bay windows on
the first floor, looking out over the Spuin valley. Far away in
the distance, Efluviel's exceptional eyes could just make out
the mist-shrouded outline of the mountains they'd come
from.

"Well? I'm waiting."

"It's a favourite of mine, actually," Mordak muttered.
"*Ghnazgk sn'arg Azkazagh*, with asparagus tips and lime
pickle. You'll like it."

Efluviel put down her fork and folded her arms. "What's in
it?"

"Oh, well . . ." Mordak made a vague gesture. "Stuff."

"What sort of—?"

Mordak looked over his shoulder, then leaned forward. "Actually, it's herring," he said. "Properly speaking it should be the wind-dried ear cartilage of your sworn enemy, but that's hardly practical in a restaurant. I mean, how's the chef supposed to know who your enemies are?"

"Herring."

"Completely swamped in herbs, spices and seasonings," Mordak pointed out, "so you could be eating any damn thing and you wouldn't know it, as is usual in goblin cookery. Look, if you don't fancy it, just eat the fries."

Efluviel thought for a moment. "No," she said, "that's fine. I like herring." She detached a tiny square of the main component with the tip of her knife, flipped it on to a corner of her bread and ate it. "Actually, that's not bad," she said. "What are these floury dumplingy things in the white sauce?"

"Oops." Mordak leaned over, impaled the four dumplingy things off the edge of her plate with the tips of his claws, and leaned back again. "You can have my bread roll to make up," he said.

She shrugged, then ate some more herring. "This is a weird place," she said.

"I'm rather fond of it. I used to come here quite a lot when I was a kid."

"I like the domed ceiling."

"Yes." Mordak nipped the dumplings off his claws and gobbled them up. "Try the beer," he said. "Worse things happen at sea, though fortunately not often."

"And that's a very oddly shaped fireplace."

"Isn't it? Well—" He picked up his goblet. "Here's to a job well done."

"What? Oh, I see." She lifted her goblet, took a sip, shuddered and put it down. "So, now what?"

"We report back – sorry, *I* report back to the Dark Lord. He says, I see, right, get out, or words to that effect, and we resume our grievously interrupted lives. I carry on ruling the goblins." He paused, and smiled. "You start editing the *Face*. You know, I'm going to have to start reading the bloody thing, now you're going to be in charge."

"Don't feel you have to," Efluviel said. "Why are the two bay windows that sort of oval shape?"

"Oh, tradition. I don't suppose it means anything coming from me, but I think you're going to be a sensational editor. I think you can bring to the job certain key qualities which—"

"And that staircase. It's such a funny shape."

"Certain key qualities," Mordak said, "which in a sense are fundamental Elf characteristics, but I think that the time we've spent together has left you uniquely qualified to approach your quintessentially Elvish worldview from at least a partially goblin-nuanced perspective—"

"But the really weird thing," Efluviel said, "is that front door. Though it's more a sort of a portcullis, really, or a draw-bridge. The way the wall sort of opens and that ramp thing drops down."

Mordak sighed. "I think you'll find the clue is in the name."

"Excuse me?"

"The *Old Giant's Head*. Well, you Elves do it, specially when you're trying to be cute. The Old Stables, the Old Mill, the Old Post Office—"

"I don't quite— Oh." Efluviel closed her mouth firmly and sort of sucked her lips in over her teeth. "And that's—"

"Cost of building materials, chiefly," Mordak said. "That's the thing about us goblins, we've always been a poor people. Lots of weapons, lots of armour, shedloads of siege engines and instruments of torture, no actual money. So we make do and mend. We find uses for stuff. So, you're walking along one day and you see a bloody great big skull just lying there, no good to anybody—"

"You turn it into a restaurant."

"Well, yes." Mordak sighed, then grinned. "Waste not, want not. It works, doesn't it?"

"In summer, maybe. In winter, I bet this place is an icebox."

"It works," Mordak repeated. "And it was useless and now it's useful, and it didn't cost anybody anything, and it means there's somewhere you can get a bite to eat and drink out in the middle of the wilderness that wouldn't otherwise be there. That's goblins for you. Straightforward. Practical. Down to earth."

Efluviel smiled. "And gross."

"And gross, certainly, but quite often in a quirky, fun way." He sipped his beer and winced. "That's what I mean," he said, "what I was talking about, just now. That's why you're going to be a great editor of the *Face*. Because you're still here, even though I told you about the—"

"The skull."

"The architecture," Mordak corrected her. "No other Elf—"

"The truly gross architecture."

"Yes, all right. No other Elf I've ever come across would still be sitting there, blithely eating *ghnazgk sn'arg Azkazagh* and not making fake retching noises—"

"Talking of which, is there any salt?"

Mordak shook his head. "No salt with *ghnazgk sn'arg Azkazagh*, not unless you want a blood feud with the chef. What you've got," he said, "is vision. You're prepared to look *through* and look *past*, to the point where you can actually *see*. That's so rare, in an Elf."

Efluviel shrugged. "I told you. I like herring."

"Mostly herring," Mordak said quickly. "No, I can honestly

say I've enjoyed us working together. I've learned a few things, and I dare say you have too. And if we can carry forward that spirit of mutual understanding and tolerance so that it's not just an emergency expedient but standard operating procedure, then I sincerely believe—"

"There's a goblin over there," Efluviel said. "Waving at you."

"What? Oh, I expect he just wants to challenge me to a duel. Like your lot collect autographs," he explained, "only with body parts. As I was saying—"

"He's coming over."

Mordak pulled a sad face and turned his head. "I don't know him," he said.

"I think he knows you."

"Entirely possible. I'm the king."

The goblin bounded over and hovered about two feet away from the edge of the table, grinning. "'Scuse me," he said. "You're him, aren't you?"

Mordak produced a very thin smile. "Yup," he said. "That's me."

"You're Mordak. King Mordak."

"Yes."

The goblin nodded eagerly. "Thought so," he said. "I saw you, and I thought, stone me, that's King Mordak over there, sitting having his tea." The goblin suddenly broke off, squinted and took a step back. "Don't know if you'd noticed, Boss, but there's an Elf—"

Mordak nodded very slowly. "I'd noticed. And it's perfectly all right."

"You sure?" The goblin stuck his face eighteen inches further inside Mordak's personal space. "Only, they could get funny about it. The management."

He was looking at something on the wall. Mordak followed his sight-line and saw a faded parchment notice: *Only food purchased on the premises to be eaten at the tables.* "Means you can't bring your own," the goblin translated thoughtfully. "So—"

"It's perfectly all right," Mordak repeated firmly. "Well, it was nice meeting you. If you haven't ordered yet, you really should try the jumbo sausage. Goodbye."

The goblin didn't move. He was grinning. Mordak closed his eyes then opened them again. "Yes?"

"You won't believe what just happened to me," the goblin said.

"Yes I will. Go away."

"You won't believe it," said the goblin, "but it's true. Mind if I join you?"

"Yes, very much."

The goblin sat down next to Efluviel, who inched away as unobtrusively as she could; she didn't get far, because the goblin was sitting on her hand. The goblin hadn't noticed. "I'll tell you all about it," the goblin said, "and then you can buy me dinner. I haven't eaten in *weeks*. Well, not proper food."

"I'll buy you anything you like if you'll only go away."

The goblin laughed. That Mordak, always kidding around. "It's like this," the goblin said.

Some time later the goblin stopped talking. Mordak, looking away, caught sight of his plate. It was empty.

"What?" Efluviel said, with her mouth full. "It was going cold. You weren't eating it. Waste not, want not, remember?"

Mordak frowned and looked back at the goblin. "That's some story," he said.

The goblin beamed. "I knew you'd want to hear it," he said. "Do I get food now?"

"Let me get this straight." Stormclouds were gathering on Mordak's face. "There's an alternate universe—"

The goblin nodded. "That's right, because of multiverse theory. Sorry, Boss, you were saying."

"An alternate universe," Mordak said, his voice dangerously soft, "where, because of something some bad person did, they've got a problem. So they come over here, they kidnap one of *my* goblins, they lock him up in a vault somewhere and throw away the key. Is that about it?"

"Yes, Boss. Well, no. It was lots of goblins, not just me, and if they didn't, their world was going to blow up. To be honest with you, I don't understand that part."

"I do," Mordak said. "It's all because of *philanthropy*. And there's more of our people over there?"

The goblin nodded. "Loads," he said. "And one of her lot, even. You know, an E-L-F." He frowned. "Actually, she was nice. Well, no, she wasn't, but—"

"*Our* people," Mordak repeated. "Goblins and Elves. So if their world blows up, our people blow up with it. Yes?"

The goblin shrugged. "I guess so. But that's not going to happen, see, because of the one simple thing I told you about."

Mordak and Efluviel looked at each other. "You tell him," Efluviel said.

"Fine." Mordak took a deep breath. "Fact is," he said, "they lied to you. Killing Rumpelstiltskin—"

The goblin was impressed. "You know his *name*."

"Actually, it's Winckler," Mordak said. "But yes, we've met. And the thing of it is, killing him won't make a blind bit of difference, even if it can be done, which I'm not entirely sure about. So either your Curator guy got his sums wrong, or he just wants revenge."

The goblin nodded. "Revenge is good."

"Well, yes," Mordak agreed. "But not when it's counter-productive. The point is, we can't do *anything*. Our claws are tied. I'm fairly sure we can't kill him or send him back. I'd just about sort of managed to reconcile myself to that, and not being able to stop a whole universe going up in smoke, when you come bouncing along and tell me there's *goblins* trapped over there. And Elves," he added, before Efluviel could add it for him. "And you know what? That really annoys me. I don't think that's right. In fact, it's not right at all."

He hadn't looked round lately, so he hadn't seen the look on Efluviel's face; probably just as well, since the situation was complicated enough already. By the time he did look round, Efluviel had got rid of it and replaced it with the usual Elf smirk. "But like you said, there's nothing you can do," she said casually. "And really, it's not our problem."

"Haven't you been listening? Goblins. An Elf. That makes it our problem."

"Fair point," Efluviel said. "But there's still nothing you can do. If Winckler dies, it won't put things right back there. It could well make real difficulties for us here, if it's true what he just said about the balance of good and evil and all those laws of conservation. I'm not sure why you've decided sending him back's not an option, though."

Mordak sighed. "Well, first off, I don't think he wants to go, so we'd have to make him, and I'm guessing he wouldn't be inclined to hold still and let us. Remember, it's not just him."

"Ah," Efluviel said. "The old man and the boy who eats. One day you've got to explain to me why you're so shit-scared of them."

"And even if we could," Mordak went on quickly, "what happens then? Does everything go back to the way it was? Only, when he left there he was evil but now he's sort of good."

"But with strong evil overtones."

"Nah, that's just the philanthropy. I think too much has

changed," Mordak said wearily. "It's a mess, that's what it is. The truth is, we have no idea what would happen. And there's no guarantee that killing Winckler or returning him would get us the goblins back. What we really need to do is get in touch with this Curator, who's the one person in all of this who might actually know what's going on—"

"That's the one who you reckon got his sums so badly wrong."

Mordak gave her his best you're-not-helping look. "Get in touch with the Curator," he said, "and see what he's got to say. You know, ask somebody, instead of trying to figure it all out for ourselves."

Effluviel opened her mouth and tried to speak, failed and tried again. "You know," she said, "that's really very good. Grown-up thinking, instead of here's-a-problem-let's-kill-someone. You have come a long way."

"Thank you," Mordak said, "I think. Anyway, I think that's got to be our next step. In which case, it's back up the mountain and see if we can get that portal thing to work. It sounds fairly simple, but I bet—"

"Your goblin."

"What?"

"He's gone."

Mordak looked round. There was no sign of the goblin. "Where did he go?"

Effluviel shrugged. "Don't ask me. I guess he just got bored and wandered off."

Mordak breathed heavily through his nose. "I don't think so," he said.

"No?"

"No." Mordak stood up. "I think he's gone to kill Mr Winckler."

"But you told him not to."

"So?"

"You're his king."

Mordak pulled a sad face. "It's possible you haven't quite grasped the finer nuances of goblin society," he said.

"You lot have nuances? Gosh."

"It'd be a matter of honour," Mordak said. "Which would tend to supervene a royal command. It's why we still have blood feuds, even though they've been illegal for a thousand years."

Efluviel nodded. "Quirky and fun," she said. "You told me."

"Yes, well." Mordak was fumbling in his pocket. "We'd better get after him and stop him. You haven't got four shillings and fourpence, have you?"

Efluviel sighed. "You've added it up wrong. It's four and twopence."

"And a tip." He scowled. "Now what?"

"It was a rubbish meal and the service was lousy, and you're leaving a tip. Mordak, what's going on? You're meant to be one of the bad guys. You don't suppose it's all part of the same—"

"Nah." Mordak shook his head firmly. "It's a *small* tip. That's bad. Come on, before the bugger gets away."

The goblin formerly known as Archie peered out from behind a fallen tree at the orange glow of firelight dead ahead, and grinned. For a while, he'd been worried. After all, he'd been human for quite some time; what if he'd lost his goblin edge, forgotten everything he knew about woodcraft and fieldcraft and sneaking up? But no. It had all come rushing back, and he knew he'd just executed a perfect stalk, silent and invisible. The little man was sitting with his back to him; one sprint, a quick swing with three feet of solid tree-branch, the human wouldn't know what hit him. Piece of—

Ironic, really, or at least a massive coincidence, because a piece of cake was the very next thing he saw. It was being fed into a slowly chewing mouth by a human left hand. The right hand, Archie guessed, was what had lifted him off the floor and was now holding him, dangling by one leg, about six feet above ground level.

"Here, Art. You got him?"

The chewing head nodded slowly.

"Good lad." A very old human hobbled into view. "Didn't give you any grief, did he, son? Only you can get a nasty nip off goblins if you're not careful."

The chewing head shook, swallowed the last of its cake and was fed a blueberry muffin. "Evil-looking little bugger," the old man said. "Come on, we'd better take him to the chief."

For the next thirty seconds, Archie had a wonderful view of the ground. Then the grip on his ankle relaxed and he landed on his head. "Sorry to bother you, sir," he heard the old man say, "but Art found this one wandering about in the woods. Probably just lost or drunk, but you never know."

Do I look like I'm lost or drunk, you fool? I'm an *assassin*! But his time spent among the moving-picture people had taught him a thing or two about acting. "Yes, that's right," he said. "I'm lost. And drunk. Hic," he added. "Oooh, everything's going round and round, I think I'm going to be sick. Oooh."

The young man took a long step backwards, but the little man laughed. "I don't think so," he said. "Goblins turn green when they're nauseous and bright red when they're drunk, and you're neither. Mordak send you, did he?"

Archie shook his head. "Nobody sent me," he said. "I'm lost. Could you possibly give me directions to the Taupe Mountains? I've always wanted to see them, I gather they're particularly tall at this time of year."

The little man grinned. "Mordak sent you," he said. "The question is, are you just a spy, or were you supposed to kill me? Don't feel you have to answer that," he added, "because I wouldn't believe you anyway. In fact, as a source of information you're not much use." He turned to the old man. "Get rid of him, will you? I can't be bothered with goblins right now."

The old man didn't look very happy about that, but he nodded to the skinny young man, who ate a Bakewell slice and picked up a lump of rock which completely filled his unusually large hand. "Careful now, Art," the old man said. "Goblin scratches can turn septic. Really, you ought to wear your gloves."

A really good time, in fact, for those dormant goblin fight-or-flight instincts to kick back in; which they did. The skinny young man took a stride forward. Archie dived at him, hit the ground all bunched up, rolled like a ball straight between his legs, scrambled to his feet and started to run. *I made it*, was his last thought before the chunk of rock hit him on the back of his head.

"You're really good at tracking," Mordak said.

"Yes," Efluviel said, her eyes fixed on the rough shale beneath her feet. "This way. He definitely came here."

"Amazing," Mordak said. "Of course, we mostly track by scent, and there's a stiff breeze, but even so. Is that how you're doing it? By scent?"

"No," Efluviel replied.

They went another hundred yards or so. Then Efluviel stopped, nodded and carried on again. Mordak had to trot to keep up with her.

"I guess it's one of those core Elvish skills," he said, "being able to follow a trail. I mean, centuries of following up leads, sniffing out conspiracies, all that sort of thing. Evolution in action. Like, presumably the ears evolved so you could over-hear scraps of conversations in crowded bars, and the thin, pointy noses are for sticking in other people's business." He paused to catch his breath, then trotted some more. "And the charm, of course. So people will like and trust you."

"Something like that," Efluviel said without turning round. She'd stopped again, and was looking right, then left. "Ah," she said. "This way."

"One damn thing after another," Mordak said, scrambling over a heap of loose shale. "I mean, I'm supposed to be the king, I really shouldn't have to do all this running around myself. I think that when I push through my next batch of sys-temic reforms, there's going to be a whole wodge of stuff about how the king shouldn't have to do his own leg work. Now what? Lost the trail?"

Efluviel had stopped dead. But suddenly she smiled. "No," she said, pointing uphill. "This way."

Over the crest of the hill, and they found themselves look-ing down into a lush wooded valley. "Where we just came from, in fact," Mordak sighed. "You knew. You figured it out. You haven't been tracking at all."

"I so have," Efluviel said. "All the way from that bizarre inn place. You'll note that we've come by a much straighter, quicker route than the last time. Of course, then, you were navigating."

Mordak sighed and sat down on a rock. "Fine," he said. "So how did you do it? Elvish magic?"

Efluviel grinned, stooped and picked something up. It was a tiny ball of screwed-up green foil. "After-dinner mint wrap-pers," she explained. "My guess is, he grabbed a handful on his way out of the inn. He's been stuffing them all the way here."

Mordak looked at her for three, maybe four seconds. "Anyway," he said, "we've got a fairly good idea of where he's headed. There's Mr Winckler's shed, look, down there in the clearing."

Efluviel nodded. "Of course, we're probably too late," she said. "I had to keep waiting for you."

"You may be right," Mordak replied. "Still, we owe it to him to try."

"I don't see why. After all, he's a rather horrible little man. And he did condemn an entire universe to death."

"It's not him I'm worried about, it's my bloody goblin. Look out," he added quickly, "someone's coming. Hide, quick."

They ducked behind a pile of rocks, as an old man, in a cloth cap and brown overalls with a very long sword hanging from his belt, and a tall, skinny boy appeared over the skyline. Between them they carried a long pole, from which a goblin dangled by his bound wrists and ankles. The disparity in their heights, and the fact that the old man was struggling a bit, made it a less than ideal arrangement; fortunately, the goblin was fast asleep, so that even when his head hit the ground he didn't wake up.

"It's them," Efluviel whispered.

"Quiet, they'll hear you."

No great danger of that. The scrunch of their boots on the shale and the occasional chunky thud of goblin forehead against stone would've masked most noises short of an earthquake. "You all right there, Art?" they heard the old man call out. "We can rest a bit in a minute if you like."

The young man mumbled something through a cake-filled mouth; it sounded vaguely negative. The goblin's head, swinging wildly from side to side, flattened a thistle.

"I say we jump them," Efluviel said. "You take the kid, leave the old fool to me."

"*Absolute silence*," Mordak hissed, so vehemently that Effluviel stayed where she was. My God, Mordak thought, she just did as she was told. And then a bit of pollen floated up his nose and he sneezed.

There was a thump as the goblin hit the ground, and a grating noise as the old man pulled a very long sword out of its scabbard. He held it with both hands, but the weight was too much for him, and he rested the point on the ground.

"Absolute silence, did you just say?" Effluviel said.

"Oh shut up."

The young man ate a nectarine. Slowly, Mordak stood up. The old man saw him and gave him a friendly smile. "Well, if it isn't King Mordak. Afternoon, Your Majesty, miss. Fancy bumping into you again. Art, take your cap off, it's the king."

"All right," Mordak said, in a voice that was slightly higher than usual. "We can do this the hard way or the easy way. Put the sword down and step away from the goblin. Now."

The old man looked puzzled. "Got you, sir, right. And what would be the easy way?"

"That's the easy way."

The old man shook his head. "Beg to differ, sir, beg to differ. That'd be a dereliction of duty, see. Very hard for us. Goes right against the grain. Physically impossible. We couldn't do it, sir. Young Art, he's so conscientious, you wouldn't credit it."

Mordak closed his eyes and opened them again. "So the easy way would be—"

"We fight, sir. To the death. *A l'outrance* is the technical term, sir, as of course you know. Last two humans standing win."

"That's the easy way."

"Comparatively easy, sir."

"Bash him," Effluviel whispered loudly in his ear. "Go on, he's an old man. Bash him."

The old man frowned. The young man took a step forward – just one – and unwrapped a sausage roll. Suddenly, Mordak realised that Efluviel had moved and was standing behind him. "On the other hand," she said.

"Not now."

"Oh be quiet." She peered out past his shoulder – she was, of course, taller than him, which helped, and said, "Hello?"

"Hello there, Miss Efluviel. Nice day."

"Yes, isn't it. Look—"

"If I can just stop you there a minute, miss, young Art was only saying earlier, after we met over at Mr Winckler's, how much he enjoyed that editorial you did back along about institutionalised sexism in the widgeonberry dye industry. Well, we both did, Art and me, bang on the nail, we thought it was."

"Really?"

"Oh yes, miss, great fans, both of us. So Art says, would it be all right if, when we fight to the death in a minute or two, would you mind terribly if he kills you and I kill King Mordak? Something to tell his grandchildren, he said. Assuming you don't mind, of course. If you'd rather it was the other way round—"

"We kill you?"

"I kill you and Art does in the king. Only, it'd mean a lot to our Art, killing you personally, and he's a good lad really, very sensitive."

Of course, that's the thing about personal combat. Nine times out of ten, when they talk like that it's all bravado and kiddology. And the tenth time, you go home in a hessian sack. "Actually," Efluviel said, "I was thinking."

"Yes. Miss?"

"What if there's three ways? The easy way, the hard way, and the, um—" Her mind had gone blank.

"Third way?"

"Yes, thank you. The thing is," she went on, "I've just been appointed editor of the *Beautiful Golden Face*, and my first priority has definitely got to be hiring a couple of top-flight defence and security correspondents to replace the brace of deadheads we've got in the post at the moment. And the thought just struck me, right out of a clear blue sky, that if you two happened to be available—"

The old man blinked. "Art and me? Write for the paper?"

"Well, you wouldn't have to do a lot of the actual writing, as such. More a consultancy and mentoring role, with the option of putting in optional input."

The old man thought for a moment. "We could do that," he said. "Young Art, now, he writes a beautiful feature. I told him, Art, you're wasted on this killing-people lark, you writing so beautiful and all."

"Quite. But if I die, of course—"

"No jobs, got you." The old man bit his lip. "Thing is," he said, "we got our duty to our employer to think of. Loyalty to the boss, that's our watchword. We live and die by that, Art and me."

"Exactly." Efluviel smiled at him. "Unswerving devotion to whoever's paying your wages. Talking of which, how much are you getting from Winckler?"

"Not really supposed to—"

"Only," Efluviel said quickly, "we'll double it. Plus a company leech plan and use of the executive hitching posts and watering trough. And then, you see, we'll be your employers and you can be unswervingly loyal to us. Well?"

The old man hesitated and looked at the boy, who was eating peanut butter out of the jar with his fingers. "Yeah, all right," he said; and then he suddenly smiled. "Well done, miss."

"Sorry, say what?"

"Well done. Took you a while," he added, not unkindly,

"but you got there in the end. Well," he added, "you were bound to, being an Elf. Ancient Elvish art of war; never send an Elf where you can send an arrow, never send an arrow where you can send thirty pieces of silver. You can get a lot of victory for thirty bob, miss, if you're waywise."

The faint sound somewhere behind her back might just have been Mordak sniggering; but she hadn't heard it, had she? "Deal," she said. "Right, your first assignment for the paper will be an in-depth analysis of the plight of goblin POWs languishing in human custody. Capisce?"

The old man nodded. "Loud and clear, miss, thank you. Art."

The boy cut the goblin's bonds with his tangerine-peeling knife, stepped back and peeled a tangerine. "All yours," the old man said.

Mordak sprang forward, grabbed the sleeping goblin by the ankle, dragged him out of the way and sat on him. Efluviel turned to the old man and smiled. "You're fired," she said.

"Thought we might be." The old man put away his sword, a process that took a long time and a cut finger. "Come on, Art," he said. "We'd better not be late for tea or your mum'll play war. Severance pay?"

"A cheque will be in the post."

"Of course it will, miss, of course it will. Cheerio, then."

They turned to go, but Mordak suddenly jumped up and ran after them. They stopped and turned back to face him.

"I want a word with you two," he said.

"Really? All right then, Chief, fire away."

Mordak glanced over his shoulder. Efluviel was approaching but not yet in earshot. "You let her win."

"That's right."

"You were waiting for her to bribe you. If she hadn't, you'd have suggested it yourselves."

The old man did something terrible and ghastly with his

face. Some time later, Mordak realised it was a wink. "Maybe," he said. "Who knows, eh?"

Mordak massaged his chin with his hand. "I don't get you two," he said. "Why did you do it?"

"Ah well, sir." The old man beamed at him. "Like we said, we're unswervingly loyal and we obey orders."

"You just sold out your employer for a bribe you knew you'd never actually get. That's just weird."

"Depends on who's really employing us, doesn't it, sir? Mind how you go, now. Have a nice day."

"Hold on," Mordak said sharply. "Just one more thing."

"Yes, sir?"

Mordak took a step forward and stopped, as though he'd just walked into an invisible wall. He looked at the old man and could tell from his face that he knew about it. "Who are you?" he said.

"Well, that's Art, and I'm—"

"I think—" Mordak leaned forward, to the point where he should've overbalanced and fallen flat on his nose. But he didn't. The invisible wall bore all his weight. "I think you're not what you look like. I think you could be spectral warriors, or daemonic forces conjured into human form, or multi-dimensional dark matter entities, or golems, or reanimated corpses, or just possibly slivers of quintessential space/time that have somehow achieved consciousness, or—"

"Young Art's a Sagittarius, if that's what you mean, sir. Me, I'm West Ham, have been since I was a nipper."

"Just tell me," Mordak said. "I'm a skilled, experienced, lucky and tolerably brave fighter. Why the hell am I so scared of you two?"

The young man ate a blueberry Danish. The old man's beam widened. "Because you're sensible, sir," he said. "Very intelligent and perceptive." He turned, paused, turned back, as if undergoing a moral struggle of epic proportions. Then he poked around in the frayed cuff of his brown coat and produced a slip of bent cardboard. "Our card, sir," he said quietly. "Just in case you ever need us. Not that that's likely, but just in case. Good luck," he added, and the next moment there was no trace that either of them had been there, except for a few wisps of cellophane floating on the evening breeze.

"They're weird," Efluviel said.

Mordak was looking at the card. It was, of course, completely blank. Which was comforting, in a way, because it implied he didn't need them yet. "Yes," he said. "Way past thirty-ferrets-in-a-cider-press weird and groping their way towards profoundly strange."

"And scary."

"Oh, I don't know," Mordak said, putting the card away before Efluviel could see it. "Depends whose side they're on."

"No, they're scary," Efluviel said. "Still, we've rescued your stupid goblin. We can go home now."

"Guess so." She'd never seen Mordak look so exhausted. His shoulders had slumped, and his chins were on his chest. "You know what? I've had about enough of this. It's just not me."

"You're a goblin king. Surely—"

"I'm an administrator." Mordak looked up at her sharply, and there was a trace of the old fire in his small red eyes. "I run things. Over budget, behind schedule, under target, but I get things done, just about, more or less, close enough for jazz. Mostly I just sort of bash my way through, but sometimes I try and be clever, in the hope that rather fewer goblins will get hurt that way. The thing is—"

"Um."

"No, let me finish. The thing is, goblin society and civilisation just don't *work*, not if you just leave them to get on with it. We're a nation of ignorant, bloody-minded fighters with no aptitude whatsoever for agriculture and a cuisine largely based on eating each other. In the normal course of events, when we're left to our own devices, sixty-two per cent of our food supply and thirty-seven per cent of all our manufactured goods are made out of goblin. The only reason we've survived this long is because the Dark Lord needs us for arrow-fodder, so he won't let us wipe ourselves out, like it would seem we want to. Well, I don't know about you, but I think that's *silly*. So I do my best. It's nothing special, but I do it twenty-four-seven-three-sixty-five. Only, I can't do very much, because if my goblins thought for one minute that I was interfering with their ancestral cultural traditions of bloodletting and mayhem, they'd have my head up on a pike so fast it'd just be a blur. They think I'm a dangerous idealist with a neo-Elvish liberal agenda, your lot write snarky bits about me in the papers saying I'm playing a crafty long game with a view to eventual world domination, the humans are buying weapons by the cartload to use against my goblins, and now I've got multiverse theory, magic portals, terrifyingly weird polite old men, Laws of Conservation and the equilibrium of an alternate universe that's going to go kerboom, and which has somehow managed to transform itself, through some form of mysterious ethical alchemy, into *my fault*. And you know what? I think I may have reached the point where I no longer—"

"Mordak."

"Where I no longer give a damn," Mordak concluded with a rush. "There, hissy fit over. Wanted to get it off my chest before I exploded. Sorry, what were you saying?"

"Your goblin." Efluviel pointed at an empty space. "It looks like he's gone off again."

21

M r Winckler unstoppered a big jar of turpentine, splashed it liberally all over his spinning-wheel, took a long step backwards and smiled. Then he looked round for his tinder-box, which wasn't where he thought he'd left it. A pity, he thought, that they hadn't got around to inventing insurance in this reality yet, because he could really have cleaned up; it had been on his list of things to do, but you know how it is. He found the tinderbox by treading on it, picked it up and cranked the little handle. A thin plume of smoke rose straight upwards from the bone-dry moss. He lowered his face over it and blew gently. A tiny orange rose glowed into life. He counted to five, then blew it again.

Job done, he said to himself, mission accomplished. He'd run the projections, done the math, and as far as he could tell, nothing that could happen at this stage in the proceedings could possibly derail the sequence of events he'd set in motion. Whether they liked it or not, the people of this reality were ineluctably on course for a fully functional and guaranteed bulletproof economy whose workings would bring about social justice, fairness and a living wage for all, together with peace in their time and mutual respect and understanding between the fascinatingly diverse communities who inhabited this shitheap. And, most of all, there would be no over-mighty banks, no greedy, effete bankers, no credit derivative swaps, therefore no financial train wreck. A pre-emptive Never Again.

In the back of his mind, he could hear the Dark Lord's thoughts, buzzing away like a bee in a bottle. They made his head hurt, a bit, though it wasn't so bad when you got used to it – tiny, peevish, stupid thoughts, as you'd expect from a tiny little mind (but that had been no bad thing; the smaller the mind, the easier it is to control) and he'd be heartily glad to be rid of them, quite soon now, when the *coup d'état* came. He'd been especially proud of that part of the overall plan. It had been alarming at first to find himself in a universe where all the evil was concentrated in one place, instead of being a universal trace element, like radon; once he'd got his head around it, though, he'd seen the wonderful opportunity that circumstance offered. If Evil is basically just one guy, and you can get to him, worm in through his ears while he's asleep, subvert and compromise him to the point where his subordinates can't stick him a moment longer and then leave it to them to get rid of him – well, then, a world without evil, or at least a world where evil's so divided and weak that it won't be bothering anyone for a long, long time. He smiled to himself. The things I do for other people, he thought.

The moss in the tinderbox was glowing nicely now. He gave it one last puff, then emptied it on to the spinning-wheel seat and jumped smartly back out of the way. A brisk *whoosh*, and suddenly the whole machine was on fire, flames bursting and blooming out of the component parts like leaves and flowers. Goodbye, straw-into-gold. He felt a brief stabbing pain in his chest and left arm, which he rationalised as the magic leaving him, and then he was fine again and the wheel was a charcoal fossil. He hefted the big bucket of water he'd filled earlier and let fly. There was an angry hiss and a puffball of steam, followed by the rich smell of evaporation. He made sure the fire was properly out, just in case. The last thing he wanted was for his precious barnful of straw (twice its weight in gold at close of trading) to pick up a stray spark and burst into flames. One thing he didn't have right now was money to burn.

I'm rich, he realised. Not just rich, but stupidly, toxically, violently rich, the way nobody would ever be rich again back where he'd come from. He did some more mental arithmetic and came to the conclusion that, if only there were some way he could move all that wealth across the interdimensional portal, he could actually pay back every cent he'd cost the combined economies of his homeworld and still have enough left over for a caramel latte and a small slice of baklava. But he couldn't do that – what a shame, there it is, never mind – so he'd just have to move on and live with it, opulently ever after; which would be that much easier to do once Back Home exploded in a blaze of violated Laws of Conservation and ceased to exist, to the extent that it would be a moot point, philosophically and mathematically speaking, whether it had ever been there in the first place. And nobody, no matter how liberal, can really be expected to feel guilty about something that almost certainly never happened, now could they?

A slight movement registered at the farthest extent of his peripheral vision, and he swung round to see what it was. Then he frowned. "For crying out loud," he said. "I thought I told those two clowns to get rid of you."

The goblin grinned at him. He was holding a pitchfork he'd acquired from somewhere, most likely left lying around by one of the carters who'd delivered the straw. In one of those sudden lightning flashes of insight that almost always come just a tad too late, Mr Winckler realised what a superbly efficient weapon the humble pitchfork can be in the right hands, or the wrong ones.

Damn, he thought, I'm going to die now. And me with all this money. Hardly seems fair.

The goblin, who once in a universe long ago and far away had been called Archie and had worn a suit to impress a girl, advanced on him snarling, with the feline grace of the truly efficient predator. "Oh come on," Mr Winckler heard himself say, "this is ridiculous. What the hell did I ever do to you?"

The goblin's eyes flashed. He took one hand off the pitchfork and traced a pair of concentric circles in the air. Kind of like a doughnut.

"Oh," Mr Winckler said. "You're one of those goblins."

The goblin nodded, resumed his grip on the fork handle, and closed the distance to just over a fully extended lunge.

"Sorry about that," said Mr Winckler. "Actually, I'm surprised. How did you get back?"

But the goblin was either too stupid or too smart for diversionary conversation. Mr Winckler noticed that he'd positioned himself just right so as to cut off any attempt at sneaking past him and making a run for the door. Bloody creature's smarter than me, he realised, and the realisation irritated him profoundly – outthought and outclassed by a semi-human, what the hell kind of epitaph is that for the brightest spark on Wall Street? "Here's the deal," he said. "This straw is actually worth approximately seven and a half trillion dollars. It's all yours. Just put the fork down."

Either the goblin hadn't heard him, or didn't understand, or didn't give a damn; or maybe he'd figured out (in his simple-minded, subhuman way) that killing Mr Winckler and having all the straw for himself weren't nearly as mutually exclusive as the offer was intended to make him think. He took another long, tactically perfect stride forward; not rushing, because he didn't need to, but not hanging about either. One more such stride and he'd be in optimum striking range, and there was nothing at all Mr Winckler (for all his wealth and his cleverness and his philanthropy unparallelled in the whole wide multiverse) could do about it

"Mr Winckler," Mordak called out, as he tore open the barn door and dashed inside. "Mr Winckler, are you—? Oh nuts."

The little man had his back to the barn wall, with nowhere left to go. Mordak could only see the goblin's back, but the set of the shoulders told him all he needed to know. "Nuts," he repeated loudly, and jumped. A double back somersault over the straw-bales brought him up just short, and not quite in time. The goblin was lifting the fork for a short, lethal thrust. "Hey, you!" he yelled. "Pack it in!"

The goblin hesitated and glanced over his shoulder, and his eyes were full of regret; sorry, Boss. Then, before Mr Winckler could move, he turned back again. The points of the fork were level with the little man's heart. Mordak reached for his sword, then remembered that he'd left it at the inn. Meaning he was unarmed, and unarmed combat is a skill goblins don't practise, for the same reason they don't go in much for jumping off very tall buildings. There was only one thing to do; and I'm damned, Mordak thought, in mid-air, if I'm going to do *that*—

But he did it anyway. He jumped, and landed directly between the goblin and Mr Winckler. The prongs were about four inches from his chest. "If you don't put that fork down right now, I'm going to be seriously annoyed."

An agonised look passed over the goblin's face. "Chief," he said, "just bugger off, can't you? I got to do this. I promised a bloke."

"I'm giving you a direct—"

The goblin shrugged, and stabbed. He felt the fork-tines penetrate and go in deep. And then they stopped.

"Just a—" he said, but got no further. There was a deep, chunky thud. The goblin rolled his eyes, folded at the knees and fell over. Behind him stood Efluviel, holding a drastically bent length of lead pipe.

A bit late, that was the only thing. Mordak reached up and slowly pulled the fork out of himself; got it free, threw it aside, and frowned. Then a thought struck him. He reached inside his coat and, from an inside pocket, drew out a rolled-up newspaper. Closer examination showed two deep puncture-marks, going almost but not quite all the way through.

"Well," Efluviel said, "there's Monday's headline. *It Was The* Face *Wot Displaced It.*"

Mr Winckler was staring at him. "You let him stab you."

"What? Well, yes."

"You were prepared to give your *life*—"

"Particularly stupid thing to do," Efluviel pointed out, "since one of the salient features of pitchforks is that they're reusable. Still," she added, "it was kind of sweet. In a singularly thick-headed sort of a way. Oh don't look at me like that," she added irritably. "Also, while we're at it, you might like to ask yourself who single-handedly subdued the crazed lone forkman, thereby saving both your idiotic lives."

But Mordak was gazing at Mr Winckler. Then he shook his head. "I must've been out of my tiny mind," he said.

Mr Winckler pulled a wry face. "Behold the eternal paradox of self-sacrifice," he said. "The life lost, being that of a sublimely good hero, must always be of lesser value than the life saved. In strictly economic terms, it's a dead loss."

"Shut your face, you."

"Shutting it right now."

Mordak looked round for something to sit on, but the straw-bales were too high. He sat on the goblin instead. "So," he sighed. "What the hell are we going to do with you?"

Efluviel came up and sat down beside him, having first

covered a length of goblin flank with her handkerchief. "Well," she said. "The old man and the boy who eats are on our side now."

Mr Winckler looked up sharply. "Hey."

"So," Efluviel went on, "we aren't scared of this toad any more, are we?"

"That's a point," Mordak said.

"So," Efluviel said, "I assume from the fact you took a fork for him that you aren't minded to kill the little creep, but I can't see there's anything stopping you from sending him back where he came from."

Mr Winckler jumped back, as though he'd trodden in something. "No way," he said. "That's powerful, complicated magic. You have no idea of the damage you could do."

"He's right," Mordak sighed. "We don't know how this portal thing works. And if all that stuff about Laws of Conservation was true, if we just frogmarched him to the portal and stuck him in it, we could end up blowing up whole universes."

"He's quite right, you know," Mr Winckler said. "Pretty smart, for a goblin."

Efluviel was studying him, in a way he didn't quite like. "He knows," she said.

"What?"

"Presumably," she said, "he used that thing to get here, so I'm guessing he knows how it works. I say we hit him with bits of wood until he sets up the portal to send himself safely back where he came from. Well?"

Mordak stared at her. "You know," he said, "you've been hanging around with me far too long. Whatever happened to the Elf who wrote that passionate diatribe about abusive treatment of asylum seekers?"

"I met one."

"Mphm. Well, he's not exactly typical." Mordak wiped a

bit of straw dust out of his eye. "I don't know," he said. "I really don't."

Efluviel nodded. "It's one of those ethical dilemma moments, isn't it? Where there's no guaranteed way of figuring out what's the right thing to do."

"Indeed. Or, in my case, the wrong one. I mean, beating him to death with a pick-handle would be evil, but not if he's done all the bad stuff he says he's done, in which case letting him go would be even eviller. Except that ever since he got here, he says, he's been doing good stuff, which really confuses the issue. Sending him back to face the music where he came from would be good, and if sending him back means their universe doesn't explode, that's very good, so really I shouldn't do it, but arguably he's redeemed himself by all the good stuff he says he's done over here, and if I sent him back they'd probably tear him limb from limb, which would be pretty bad, so really I ought to do it. Assuming," he added, with a sudden frown, "I really am Evil, and not just a goblin. I'm not sure I even know that any more. God, I hate moral philosophy. It's like doing a crossword puzzle in hieroglyphics."

Efluviel laughed. "You should do what everybody else does," she said, "and read the newspapers. Then you wouldn't have to think about anything. That's the point. We do it for you."

"Yes, and look what happens. You get Elves." He shrugged. "All right, what about this? We assume he's innocent until proven guilty, lock him up on remand in a disused mineshaft and put the whole question of right and wrong to a committee." He grinned. "And if that's not evil," he said, "I don't know what is."

All the while they were talking, Mr Winckler's hand had been creeping, glacier-slow and glacier-steady, towards the secret pocket sewn into the lining of his cape. It was, he'd told himself over and over again, the very last resort, because he didn't properly understand this technology, anything could happen, he didn't know the rules and there was absolutely no way of being sure where or even as what he'd end up. On the other hand, he was descended from a subsection of humanity who'd learned the hard way that once those around you start discussing what to do with the prisoners, any way out has got to be better than staying put. His fingers, fingertiptoeing along like little mice, found the hem of the pocket. He reached inside and grabbed.

"Excuse me," he said.

Mordak and the Elf looked up at him. They saw him holding— Well, they probably didn't recognise it for what it was; a very old, stale doughnut he'd bought from a stall at Grand Central just before his first Great Escape, but they were bright enough to realise that it was important. Mr Winckler positioned the doughnut so that it was pressed flat against his forehead; just a tiny movement needed to deploy it to maximum effect.

"A few home truths," he said. "First, you're a joke, both of you. Don't think for a moment that the Elf's changed, she hasn't. Given half a chance, she'll wheedle you, manipulate you, wind you round her little finger. As for you, Your Majesty, you're about as evil as my old mother's cat. In fact, considerably less. It's not just that you've let her corrupt you, you were as wet as a watercress farm long before you even met her. Face it, you're just not cut out for it; though," he added with a grin, "that might well change once your goblins lose patience with you." He paused briefly for breath, then went on, "One thing I've learned, one simple fact. There's no capital-E Evil and no capital-G Good, there's just a load of confused and misguided intentions and a load of consequences, mostly unintended, a lot of them pretty bad. Everything else—" He grinned. "You know what everything else is? It's *fashion*. Like hemlines. Last year, homosexuality was out and racism was in, this year it's the other way around. Next year it'll probably be wide ties, flares and platform heels, even though we all made a solemn vow before everything we hold sacred, *never again*." He did a wide, melodramatic shrug, just in case God up in the peanut gallery might have difficulty seeing. "There is no evil," he said, "there is no good. There's just the best you can, and pray like crazy not too many people get hurt. Right, then. I go I know not where. So long, idiots."

Mordak tried a frantic lunge, but he was too late. With a tiny adjustment of his fingers, Mr Winckler let the doughnut slip a little until it was over his left eye. Then he vanished.

There was a long silence. Then Efluviel said, "Was that some sort of cake?"

"I don't know. I think so."

"I'm starving. Let's go eat."

"You just ate."

"That was goblin food," Efluviel pointed out. "What's called for right now is extreme patisserie."

Mordak thought – about that, and other things – for about four seconds. Then he nodded. "Is there anywhere round here?"

"There's a little treetop café I know the other side of the big wood that does really wicked cupcakes."

"Wicked," Mordak repeated gravely. "A meaningless term, as we now know. Just cupcakes, or other things as well?"

She frowned at him. "About this food business," she said.

"Now, you know me, I do my very best not to be judgemental—"

"How true."

"But this whole goblin eating-people thing. I have to say, I've got very serious reservations about that. Why are you smirking?"

Mordak looked round, then underneath, to make sure the goblin was still fast asleep. Then he beckoned her to come closer. "You've got to promise," he said. "Not one word, all right?"

It was a struggle, but Efluviel nodded.

"If this was to get out, there'd be so much trouble—"

"I promise."

"Your word of honour as a journalist?"

"You think that's one of those oxywhatsit things, don't you?"

"Moron," he said kindly. "Oxymoron. And yes, I do. But it's all right, I know I can trust you, because I've never told anyone else about this, so if word ever does get out, I shall know precisely who to kill. Goblin food," he said.

"Yes?"

"Well." He took a deep breath. "In theory, we eat only what we kill. The flesh of our enemies makes us stronger, their hearts make us braver, their brains make us wiser and so on."

"Got you. And what do their arms and legs make you?"

"Sausages. Anyway, that's the theory. Nothing goes into goblin cuisine other than freshly sourced, inhumanely slaughtered, traceable organic prime cuts of enemy." He paused. "In theory."

"Right. And in practice?"

He sighed. "Mostly it's horse," he said. "And cow and pig, and occasionally a bit of bird. Well, it's the cost," he said, "not to mention continuity of supply and transport issues. And if you bung in enough colourings and flavourings and riboflavin and monosodium glutamate, nobody's ever going to know the difference, so what the hell?"

Efluviel was actually shocked. "And they all think—"

"It says on the label, *made with real Elf*, but that's a whatsit, a term of art. Why do you think Goblin Foods Inc. buys up the clippings from every hairdressing salon in Elfhome? Perfectly legitimate and a hundred per cent compliant, and everybody's happy." He looked round again. "Now, you did promise. Not one word, got that?"

"That's disgusting," Efluviel said. "Food with little bits of hair in it."

"Got that?"

She looked at him. It would make one hell of a story. Or, it would have made one hell of a story. "Got it," she said sadly. "So, you lot aren't really monstrous bloodthirsty cannibals at all?"

Mordak shook his head. "But we think we are," he said, "and that's what matters."

The goblin made a faint muttering noise. "He's waking up," Efluviel said. "What are we going to do with him?"

"Nothing," Mordak replied. "He acted with the best of intentions, motivated by honour and duty. Fortunately, nothing too bad happened. I suggest we walk away and leave him with his straw. I'd say he's earned it."

They tiptoed outside and closed the barn door quietly after them. It was a beautiful evening. The clearing was bathed in soft late-summer sunshine, and all around them small birds sang. "I've gone off the thought of cake," Efluviel said. "What I really need is a drink."

Mordak nodded. "Back to the *Head*?"

"Well, it's closest."

"Actually, the *Old Trolls' Arms* is closer, but I'm not sure you'd like it. Basically, the walls—"

"Back to the *Head*. Definitely."

They'd only gone a few hundred yards when Mordak stopped dead in his tracks and started sniffing.

"What are you *doing*?" Efluviel demanded. "Stop it, it's embarrassing."

"Can't you smell it too?"

"No. What?"

"You can't smell that? Oh, of course, I forgot, you're an Elf."

"You *forgot* I'm an Elf. Oh boy."

"Quiet." He looked up at the sky, and she noted that he was as tense as a fiddle-string. "We're about to have company."

"Friends of yours?"

"Business associates."

"Are they nice?"

"They're business associates."

"Ah," Efluviel said. She too was looking up, and she could just see four very fast-moving black dots rushing down at them out of the sun. "Shouldn't we be running away and hiding?"

"Don't be silly. They're business associates."

Ten seconds later, black-robed wraiths mounted on pterodactyls snatched them off their feet and swept them away.

"**S**o." The Margrave finished his long, convulsive shudder. "You see the problem."

Mordak had been sitting very still, and his face was a complete blank. "Yup."

"It's bad, isn't it?"

"Yup."

The members of the Dark Council looked at each other. "Well?" said a senior necromancer. "What do we do?"

Mordak steepled his claws. "What indeed?" he said. "Here we are, the senior representatives of Evil, forced to the inescapable conclusion that the Dark Lord, who epitomises Evil so completely that it's practically impossible to define it without reference to him, has gone potty. Someone or something—" A flicker at the corner of Mordak's mouth didn't go unnoticed. "Someone or something," he repeated, "has got to him, messed with his head, and as a result we've got to get rid of him before he utterly screws up everything we believe in or stand for. Is that about the shape of it?"

The troll-wrangler nodded. "Pretty much."

"But we can't get rid of him," Mordak went on. "Can't kill him, we all know why. Can't lock him up somewhere, because he'll only get out again, he always does. And whatever it is we do, we've got to do it very, very soon, because whatever we may think of Internal Affairs, they do a very thorough job, specially when it comes to finding out about conspiracies, so 'living on borrowed time' is a pertinent concept here." He paused, frowned, and went on. "If it's all right with you, I think I'd like to consult with my special adviser."

Sharp intakes of breath. "You mean her," said the Margrave. "That—"

"Yes," Mordak said. "Now, if you don't mind."

So they had her brought in and took the bag off her head (it had two holes pre-cut in it, for the ear-tips) and Mordak quickly summarised what he'd just been told, and immediately added, "It's not funny," before she could open her mouth, which was probably just as well. She made a very faint squeaking noise, but that was all.

"So," Mordak continued, "I was thinking. We've got an embodiment of evil to get rid of, right?"

Efluviel looked at him. "Only you can't."

"Quite so. But it's got to be done. And I was thinking—"

Suddenly she grinned. "You were thinking of a place where they're down one embodiment of evil, in consequence of which they're in grave danger of blowing up."

The Council started muttering, but Mordak silenced them with a look. "Quite," he said. "And since we can't send them back their embodiment, because we carelessly lost him—"

"Why not send them ours?" Efluviel nodded, so briskly she nearly stabbed herself to death. "Nice idea. Will it work?"

Mordak shrugged. "Search me. What do you think?"

"You need to ask someone."

"Yes."

"That Curator person."

"He'd know, if anyone would."

"Just a minute—" objected the Margrave; and then Mordak looked at him and all power of speech and thought deserted him for a moment; and when he'd recovered, he knew without having to think about it any further that the Principle of Evil had just found itself a new Dark Lord. "Sorry," he mumbled, but Mordak wasn't listening.

A few minutes later, the Dark Council shuffled quietly out, leaving the king to finalise the details of his plan of action with his senior adviser. Outside in the courtyard, the Margrave said, "So that's all right, then."

"Yes," objected the troll-wrangler, "but she's an—"

The Margrave shrugged; or at least, his empty black robe billowed in a certain sequence. "Things change," he said. "Don't be an old stick-in-the-mud. Get with the programme."

"Yes, but she's an—"

"Listen," the Margrave said; nothing so melodramatic as a hiss, he just spelled it with nine S's. "He's the boss now, and what the boss says, goes. Like I said, things change. We evolve. It's time to put the evil back into evolution. Capisce?"

"Yes," the troll-wrangler said. "But she's an—"

"Oh be quiet."

The Curator looked up from his screen and stared. "Archie?" he said.

How he knew was anyone's guess, since the last time they'd met, Archie had been human, and the creature who jumped through the doughnut portal on to the workbench was anything but. Nor was he alone. "And you've brought a friend," the Curator added. "How nice."

The sharp-faced young woman made a furious tutting noise, deleted the file she'd been working on and started again. The goblin who wasn't Archie nudged the goblin who was, and whispered, "Is that him?"

Archie nodded. The other goblin jumped down off the

table and looked round, presumably for weapons and ambushes. Most of the people working in the lab didn't appear to have noticed him.

"This is Mordak," Archie said. "King of the goblins. My boss," he explained.

"Good Lord," the Curator said. "We're honoured. Somebody get His Majesty a chair."

"He wants to ask you a question."

"Fine. Only we're a bit busy right now. We have twenty-one seconds before this universe explodes, so if you wouldn't mind taking a seat, we'll be with you shortly."

"It's about that."

The Curator raised his hand, and everything stopped dead. "Fire away," he said.

Mordak, talking fast, explained about Mr Winckler's disappearance and his planned *coup d'état* against the Dark Lord. "We can't get rid of him in our universe," he said, "so we were wondering. Do you think we could send him here?"

The Curator thought for a moment. "Is he evil?"

"He's the Dark Lord."

"Please answer the question."

So Mordak told the Curator some of the things the Dark Lord had done; the civilisations he'd overthrown, the great cities he'd laid waste, the derelict homes and abandoned farms and workshops in every region of his empire, the chaos and misery he'd inflicted on countless millions, the generations for whom there could be no hope, only despair. The Curator listened carefully. Then he said, "So basically you're suggesting we accept your Dark Lord as a replacement for our rogue investment banker."

"Yes. Will he do?"

"Well," the Curator said, "it's a start."

23

Mordak was reading the paper. He lifted his head. "Show her in," he said.

Efluviel looked tired. She sat down on the visitor's chair, carved with horribly disturbing bas-reliefs from a single block of black marble, without even dusting it first. "Well?" she said. "What do you think?"

Mordak hesitated. "Well," he said. "The cover story."

The headline, in huge letters just under the newly restored *Beautiful Golden Face* masthead, read:

EFLUVIEL TAKES OVER
(continued on pages 2–46, editorial on page 12, profile feature on page 6).

"It's a bit—"

"It's what's of most interest to our readers," Efluviel said firmly. "What?"

"Yes, all right," Mordak conceded. "And I liked some of the stuff in the editorial, about rapprochements and working more closely together and so on. Very nicely put. Even so."

"What?"

Mordak turned to page 52. On the right, near the bottom,

was a two-inch column headed *Mardik Usurps Black Throne In Blodless Coup*. "It's not the personal glory or anything," he said, "I couldn't give a stuff, naturally. But it's a legitimate news story, of considerable importance to the lives of everyone in the Realms. I think you might have found a way to squeeze it in ahead of the opera reviews."

She gave him one of her how-could-you-be-so-ignorant? looks. "I wouldn't worry about it," she said. "After all, everyone knows."

"Only if they do the crossword. Who else reads past page 50?"

"The grapevine," Efluviel said patiently. "Word of mouth, the rumour mill. Of course everyone knows you've taken over."

"Everyone knew you'd taken over," Mordak replied gently. "But you've got banner headlines."

"Well, of course. That's news. That's what people read the papers for." She tweaked the paper out of his hands, folded it and threw it on the desk. "That's enough about that," she said. "How's life in the big chair?"

"Uncomfortable. My feet don't reach the floor." He scowled at her. "Don't print that."

She narrowed her eyes. "Is that an order?" she said. "Because if it is—"

"No. It's a request. I'm asking you nicely."

"Oh, in that case, fine. Besides, who'd be interested?" She reached for the bowl of candied fingers and helped herself, then hesitated.

"Orange peel," Mordak whispered. "But for crying out loud don't tell anyone."

"All these restrictions on the freedom of the press. Though in this case, they wouldn't believe it."

"Good."

"Actually, they're quite yummy. I never knew goblins had a sweet tooth."

"Oh, we do, we do. Though really they're just sugar and condensed milk."

She laughed. "Evil's not going to be the same from now on, is it?"

He pursed his lips. "It's an approach," he said guardedly. "One that's going to work, I do believe."

"Condensed milk, sugar and orange peel?"

He shrugged. "So long as people think what we do is evil, does it really matter if it isn't? I've been thinking, about what Mr Winckler said. Suppose it really is just fashion. And suppose that the definition of evil is what the Evil One does."

She looked at him. "Go on."

"Well, it's pretty straightforward, actually. If I do it, it's evil *per se*. So, if I hatch a diabolical conspiracy to feed the poor and make sure all goblin homes have indoor toilets—"

"From the worst of all possible motives, naturally."

"Oh, of course. It's all part of a conspiracy."

"Can I quote you on that? The *Face* loves conspiracies."

Mordak grinned. "You'd be doing me a favour. From now on, I'd like to read that everything I do, no matter how reformist and progressive it may look on the surface, is part of a deep-laid plot to subvert liberal Elvish values and engulf the Realms in a Great Darkness." He looked down at his neatly manicured claws. "I don't care if the Elves believe it, so long as the goblins do."

She nodded. "The road to hell is paved with good intentions?"

"It will be from now on. Which reminds me. Number six on my list of things to do, get the roads sorted out. Good infrastructure is vital to flourishing trade and a healthy economy."

"You've been reading the business section, bless you. Oh, while I think of it. What's that hideous statuette propped up on the cabbage-leaf dispenser in your office toilet?"

"That?" He had to think for a moment. "Oh, *that*. Some award. Most Evil, or something of the sort. "

"Of course, you don't give a damn."

"No," he said. "It's just a popularity contest, after all. The hell with all that." He took a piece of candied finger from the bowl, broke it in two and handed her half. "Here's to *New* New Evil."

The Dark Lord opened his eyes.

There's not a lot to be said for having spent a hundred thousand years, on and off, as a disembodied force of pure negative energy, but it does teach you to be flexible, resourceful and not easily startled. Just as well. When he'd closed his eyes, he'd been in his purpose-built Evil Body, in his chamber at the top of the Black Tower. Now, it seemed, he was in a totally different body, in a place he didn't recognise. He frowned.

The new body wasn't a patch on the old one. It was fat, for one thing, and a bit short, and its eyesight was nothing special, and it had got cramp from falling asleep in its chair – a weird chair, weird but really cool; it swivelled and flexed when you leaned back, and it was all shiny chrome and black leather. He blinked. Dead ahead of him was a vast window, or was it a wall, made of some sort of incredibly pure crystal, so wonderfully translucent it practically wasn't there. The view from it told him that he was very high up, higher than the Black Tower, in the heart of a city the likes of which he'd never imagined possible, even in his wildest and most warped dreams. Vast glass towers reared up all around like cobras poised to strike, and as far as the eye could see was white stone, gleaming in the sunlight.

He caught sight of something on the desk in front of him.

Round, brown, with a hole in it. A memory – not one of his, presumably it came hardwired in the body – told him it was food. He was hungry. He ate it. Yum.

A door opened, and a human female in strange clothes came in. But that was all right. From experience (see above) he knew what to do. He cleared his throat and smiled.

"I just fell over and banged my head," he said. "I'm fine now, but I appear to be suffering from partial memory loss. Please tell me who I am, who you are and where this is."

The woman looked startled for a moment, but he could tell she was trained in instantaneous composure recovery. "Well, sure," she said. "You're Norman Kropatchek, CEO of Schliemann Brothers in New York." She paused, then went on, "Schliemann Brothers, the world's largest hedge fund?" She sagged slightly. "Hedge fund?"

"I seem to have temporarily forgotten what that means."

"Oh boy. Well, it's like this."

The Dark Lord listened with growing astonishment, which he had to work hard to conceal. Amazing. He'd realised quite early on that he wasn't anywhere he'd ever been or even heard of, in a world where so many of the rules were different, though by the sound of it, a lot of them were reassuringly the same. On balance, he liked what he heard. These people had good magic (though they didn't call it that), but they were strangely naïve in some respects, frighteningly sophisticated in others. He'd have to tread warily, but yes, he could do well here. And be happy.

Now there was a point. A certain amount of the recent past was filtering back in – maybe he had hit his head, after all; you never know when you might be telling the truth, as the old saying goes – and he could remember the last few weeks or months; a voice in his head, he recalled, prompting him to do all sorts of weird, crazy stuff. But the voice didn't seem to be there any more, and he wasn't sure whether that was a good thing or not. He'd hated all the unnatural things the voice had forced him to do – had he? He wasn't sure. When he tried to cast his mind back, he found he couldn't actually remember ever being happy (just angry, frustrated, terrified, exultant; plenty of joy, now he came to think of it, but no actual contentment). A phrase came into his head, presumably also pre-installed with the operating system: *the pursuit of happiness*. Hmm. Pursuit; hound it down and destroy it utterly, presumably. Or maybe not. What were you supposed to do with it once you'd caught it? Maybe that was something you only found out at the time.

"Ah yes," he said. "I remember now." He glanced at the glass-fronted box on the desk. There was clever writing on it, a bit like the seeing-stones back home, but the typeface was smaller. "So," he said. "What's this all about?"

"Oh, that," the woman said. "That's the hostile takeover of MultiSoft." She pulled a grim face. "Not going so well. Doesn't look like it's going to happen."

"Give me a minute." He read the words and figures on the glass, and found they made quite good sense. In about thirty seconds, he'd figured out what was going on. He could also see a number of tactical mistakes whoever had been doing this job before him had made, and several clever ways of getting round them. "All right," he said. "Here's what we'll do."

Later that day, as the markets buzzed and trained negotiators did their very best to talk the former board of MultiSoft down off a very high ledge on the top floor of what had that morning still been their building, the woman came back in to see him. She was smiling. "It went well," she said.

"Told you it would."

"The word on the street is, Norm Kropatchek's got his mojo back."

He frowned. "Norm Kropatchek is me?"

"Um, yes."

"What's a mojo?"

She gave him a startled look, then changed the subject. Pan-Terrestrial Foodstuffs Inc., she said, was in her opinion ripe for the picking. Would he care to look at some figures? He would.

Her voice was quite nice, when you got used to it.

Presumably I could go back, the Dark Lord thought. Something brought me here, and most processes are reversible. On the other hand, why bother? Watch out, Happiness, he said to himself. You can run, but you can't hide.

Mr Winckler opened his eyes and looked down, and saw his feet.

Well, he thought, that would explain the pain. He looked sideways, at his extended arms. Yup, he thought, check. Nails through the palms and ankles will do that to you every time.

He was not alone. On either side of him, nailed to more or less identical crosses, were two men. One of them was nearly gone, his head slumped on his chest, eyes closed, lips slowly moving. The other one caught his eye and grinned.

"Hi," he said. "I'm Mike."

"Albert," Mr Winckler replied. "How's it going?"

"Oh, hanging in there." Mike waited. Mr Winckler nodded wearily. "Great view you get from up here," Mike said.

"If you like desert."

"So," Mike went on after a pause, "what did they get you for, then?"

"You first."

"Thieving," Mike said. "Can't complain, it was a fair cop, they got me bang to rights. You?"

"I think," Mr Winckler said, "I may have invented Christianity."

"Christianity." Mike frowned. "Hey, isn't that the one where you love your neighbour as yourself and try and be nice to people?"

"That's the one."

Mike tried to shrug, but gravity wasn't having any. "Doesn't sound so bad to me," he said. "Still, the law's the law."

"It is that."

"And a lot of what you said, that was blasphemy. That was blaspheming against the Lord."

"Indeed," Mr Winckler replied. "You could say, I fought the Lord and the Lord won."

"True, my friend, very true. Even so. Ah well." Mike sighed, sucked his teeth, whistled a tune. "Hey, look, down there. Isn't that him? You know, the Roman governor. In the red cloak."

"I wouldn't know. Never met him."

"Pontius – Pontius something. On the tip of my tongue."

"Pilate?"

"That's the guy. He's all right, so they say. Good law officer. Tough on crime, tough on the causes of crime. Zero tolerance on thieving."

"So I gathered."

"He's coming this way."

Indeed he was; and behind him trotted two men, carrying a ladder. At the foot of the crosses, Pilate stopped, looked up, shaded his eyes against the vicious glare of the sun, and called out, "Hey, you. Not you," he added, as Mike looked down hopefully, "the other one. You still alive?"

"Afraid so," Mr Winckler said.

"Hold on, I'm coming up."

There was a brief flurry of activity as the two assistants propped the ladder against the arm of the cross and Pilate scrambled nervously up it. He was bright red in the face, and sweating in his heavy bronze armour.

"So let's get this straight," he said, his nose six inches from Mr Winckler's chin. "What you're basically saying is, render unto *Caesar* the things that are *Caesar's,* and render unto *God*—"

"Yup," Mr Winckler said. "That's about it."

Pilate gave him a thoughtful frown. "And all this stuff about destroying the Temple," he said. "You're going to tell me that was all whatsit, allegorical."

"Metaphorical," Mr Winckler said. "Which is roughly the same thing."

"Metaphorical schmetaphorical," said Pilate. "What I mean is, you aren't urging people to get out there with pick-axes and burning torches, and all of that crap."

"Me?" Mr Winckler said. "Advocate violence? Perish the thought."

"So really," Pilate said, "what I'm getting at is, you're not political at all, you're just some religious nut. Well?"

"I object," Mr Winckler said, "to the term 'nut'. It's pejorative."

Pilate scowled at him. "If it's politics," he said, "that's treason, I've got no choice but to string you up. If it's just religious stuff, I can't be bothered with all that. Well?"

"Religious nut," Mr Winckler said firmly. "That's me in a nutshell."

Pilate sighed wearily. "All right, boys," he called out, "get him down." He started to descend the ladder, then stopped. "A word of advice," he said. "Stay out of trouble. Lay low. Keep your nose clean. I don't ever want to hear your name again, savvy?"

(The Imitation of Christ, Mr Winckler thought to himself. Well, why not? I can do a pretty good Peter Falk.)

"What name would that be?"

"Good boy. That's the spirit."

As they were pulling out the nails, Mr Winckler recalled

some of the things he'd heard about the YouSpace device, when he'd been negotiating to obtain one. The navigation system, for one thing. Just think of a destination, and it takes you there – or somewhere close enough for jazz, which was where problems so often arose. The point being, it takes you where you really, truly want to go, in your heart of hearts.

It brought me here, Mr Winckler thought. Jeez!

They put some sort of ointment on his hands and feet. It was green, and had chives in it. It didn't help much. He told them so. They laughed. What do you expect, they said, miracles?

"Just try and keep out of trouble," Pilate told him, for the fifth time. "Have you got some place to sleep tonight?"

Mr Winckler shrugged. "Don't know."

Pilate sighed. "There's a hostel on the corner of the Via Appia and the Linen Market," he said. "Tell 'em I sent you, they'll see you right." He took a purse from the sleeve of his tunic. "Here's ten sesterces," he said. "It'll see you through while you're looking for work. Now get out of here."

What have I done, Mr Winckler thought, as he limped through the streets with the coins gripped tight in his hand. Screwed everything up again. No, because this is now a separate bifurcation of space/time comprising a brand new alternative reality, because of multiverse theory. So that's all right; except that millions of people will have to live in it, in the universe I just created. Oh, it keeps on getting better and better, doesn't it?

Eventually, after many adventures, he drifted to Rome, where he got a job cleaning out the Cloaca Maxima, the main sewer that evacuated the waste of the entire city into the Tiber. The previous record for long service in that particular job was six months. Mr Winckler kept at it for twenty years. Then, one morning as he was sploshing to work through the waist-high whatchamacallit, he saw a familiar shape floating slowly towards him. He reached out and picked it up. It was a doughnut.

The ancient Romans invented many things. Doughnuts were not among them. Mr Winckler held it between his fingertips and stared at it (sideways on) for a long, long time. Then he said, "I am not worthy", and put it back.

He started to wade on. Then his foot caught on something, and he fell forward. An instant before his face hit the meniscus, he saw—

No matter what he saw; he saw it through the hole in the middle of the doughnut. All at once he was caught up by a great rushing sensation, which swept him away through every possible permutation of reality in the smallest possible fraction of a second, and deposited him far, far away—

The YouSpace device takes you where you want to go. In your heart of hearts.

Mr Winckler opened his eyes. He looked down. He whimpered. "Oh for crying out loud," he said.

extras

orbit

meet the author

Photo Credit: Charlie Hopkinson

Tom Holt was born in London in 1961. At Oxford he studied bar billiards, ancient Greek agriculture and the care and feeding of small, temperamental Japanese motorcycle engines; interests which led him, perhaps inevitably, to qualify as a solicitor and emigrate to Somerset, where he specialized in death and taxes for seven years before going straight in 1995. He lives in Chard, Somerset, with his wife and daughter.

introducing

**If you enjoyed
THE GOOD, THE BAD AND THE SMUG,
look out for**

THE OUTSORCERER'S APPRENTICE

by Tom Holt

A happy workforce, it is said, is a productive workforce.

Mmmm.

*Try telling that to an army of belligerent goblins.
Or the Big Bad Wolf. Or a professional dragonslayer.
Who is looking after their well-being? Who gives a
damn about their intolerable working conditions,
lack of adequate health insurance, and terrible
coffee in the canteen?*

*Thankfully, with access to an astonishingly diverse
workforce and limitless natural resources, maximizing
revenue and improving operating profit has never
really been an issue for the one they call
"the Wizard." Until now.*

extras

*Because now a perfectly good business model—based on
sound fiscal planning, entrepreneurial flair,
and only one or two of the infinite parallel worlds
that make up our universe—is about to be
disrupted by a young man not entirely
aware of what's going on.*

*There's also a slight risk that the fabric of
reality will be torn to shreds. You really do
have to be awfully careful
with these things.*

Once upon a time there was a story. It was about magic
and the magical land, and the right here and the very
much now. It was about wizards and dragons, profit and loss
ratios, doughnuts, manpower coefficients, crystal portals, a
handsome prince, a poor but feisty peasant girl, Vivaldi, a uni-
corn, a LoganBerry XPXX3000, coffee stirrers, goblins and
high-speed broadband. It starts off "once upon a time".

It goes like this—

The long shadows of a summer evening were falling across the meadows as Buttercup walked from the village to the big woods. In the basket over her arm she carried her father's supper: bread and cheese, an apple and half a jar of pickled walnuts. As she approached the eaves of the wood, a rabbit poked its head out of its burrow and looked at her.

"Hello, Buttercup," it said.

She looked at it. "Get lost," she replied.

The rabbit twitched its whiskers. "It's a lovely evening," it said.

"It's always a lovely evening," Buttercup replied. "Go nibble something."

"You seem upset," the rabbit said. One of its ears was drooping adorably across its face. "Is something the matter?"

Buttercup reached into the basket, found the apple, took a quick but sure aim and threw. She hit the rabbit just above the eye, and it vanished back down its hole. Buttercup retrieved the apple, wiped the smear of rabbit blood off it with her sleeve and put it back in the basket. She felt a little better, but not much. A song thrush perched in the low branches of a sycamore tree opened its beak, thought better of it, and flew away in a flurry of wings.

Twenty yards or so inside the wood, Buttercup met an old woman sitting on the trunk of a fallen tree. She was wearing a big shawl, with a hood that covered her face. "Hello, little girl," she said, in a dry, crackly voice. "And where might you be going on such a fine evening?"

Buttercup stopped, sighed and put down her basket. "You're new here, right?"

"I come from a village twelve miles away, across the Blue Hills," the old woman replied. "I've come to visit my son. He's a woodcutter."

Buttercup slowly shook her head. "I don't think so," she replied. "Look, we both know the score, right? Now, since you're not from round here, I'm going to give you a break. I'll count to five, and if you just get the hell away from me and don't bother me again, we'll pretend none of this ever happened. If not," she added, "well."

The old woman laughed shrilly. "What a funny girl you are," she said. "Why don't you—?"

"One."

The old woman hesitated for a moment. "Why don't you come with me to my cosy little house, and I'll make you a nice cup of—"

"Two."

"Tea," the old woman said, but there was a faint feather of doubt in her voice. "And biscuits. And gingerbread. You like gingerbread."

"Three," Buttercup said. "And gingerbread sucks."

"All nice little girls like gingerbread," the old woman said. "Everybody knows that."

"Four."

"Did I mention that I'm actually your long-lost aunt from over Green Meadows way?" the old woman said, edging a little closer. "I haven't seen you since you were—"

Buttercup breathed a long, sad sigh. "Five," she said, and put her hand inside the basket, which also contained, as well as the bread, cheese, apple and pickled walnuts, the small but quite sharp hatchet her mother used for splitting kindling for the fire. "Sorry," she said as she swung the hatchet and the wolf wriggled frantically to free itself from the old woman's clothes, but it wasn't quite fast enough. The hatchet caught it right between the eyes, and that was that.

Buttercup stooped to wipe the hatchet blade on the moss growing on the side of the fallen tree. She looked at the wolf. It was lying on its side, its eyes wide open and empty, its tongue poking out between its jaws. She felt sorry for it, in a way, but what can you do?

Five minutes or so later, she found the wolf's little house. Sure enough, there was a round table covered with a chintz cloth, a rocking chair and a small upholstered stool. On the table she found a teapot, two cups, a plate of scones, ham and watercress sandwiches, jam, clotted cream and the inevitable gingerbread; also butter knives, forks, spoons (electroplate rather than actual silver, but still worth something) and, on the wall, a cuckoo clock. She emptied the teapot, the butter dish and the cream pot, then scooped everything into her basket (apart from the gingerbread, which she chucked out for the birds) then closed the door behind her and walked away, doing sums in her head. Sixpence for the tea set, maybe a shilling for the cutlery; no idea what the clock was worth, but—

"Buttercup?" She looked up and saw a tall, fair-haired young man standing in the path looking at her. He had a big axe over his shoulder. He'd been running. "Are you all right?"

She shrugged. "Hi, John," she said. "Why wouldn't I be?"

John was peering at her, as though something wasn't quite right but he couldn't quite figure out what it might be. "Oh, I don't know," he said. "Though they're saying there's been wolves seen in these parts, so I thought—"

"John, there's always wolves in these parts," she said wearily. "Also bears, trolls, lions and at least six gryphons. Which is odd," she added, frowning. "Makes you wonder what they live on."

A shadow fell across John's face. "Children, mostly," he said. "Which is why—"

"Yes, but they don't," Buttercup pointed out. "Think about it. When was the last time a child got eaten this side of the Blue Hills?"

John gave her a bewildered look. "Why, only last week, little Millie from the mill was nearly gobbled up by a troll at Cow Bridge. If my uncle Jim hadn't come along with his axe at just the right—"

"Exactly," Buttercup said. "Sure, there's ever such a lot of close shaves, but somehow there's always a woodcutter passing by at exactly the right moment, so no harm done. Doesn't that strike you as a bit—?"

"Lucky." John nodded. "Just as well. I've killed seventeen wolves, two trolls and a wicked witch already this week, and it's only Tuesday. Really, it's not safe for a nice girl like you alone in these woods."

"John, it's perfectly safe, that's the *point*." She sighed. "Don't worry about it," she added, as John's puzzled frown threatened to crush his face into a ball. "And thanks for being concerned about me, but I'm fine, really."

John slumped a little, then shrugged. "OK, then," he said. "I guess I'll go and chop some wood. But if you do happen to run into anything nasty, you just holler and I'll be—"

"Yes, John. Oh, one other thing," she added, as he turned to go.

"Yes?"

"Want to buy a clock?"

A little later, lighter by one clock and richer by ten shiny new pennies, Buttercup arrived at the shed in the woods, where her father and three uncles were busy at their trade.

She opened the door and walked in. "Hi, Dad."

"Hi, poppet." Her father looked up from the forty-foot plank he was planing. "Is that supper?"

"Yup."

"Just put it down on the bench," her father said. "We'll get to it as soon as we've finished these boards." He crouched down, squinted along the plank, marked a rough spot and stood up again. "Guess what," he said, "we had a visitor today."

Buttercup was unpacking the basket. "Don't tell me," she said. "The wizard, right?"

"Sure. How did you guess?"

"It's always the wizard, Dad."

With just the right degree of pressure, her father eased a wisp of wood off the plank and brushed it away with his hand. "And he had someone with him. A man."

"Yes, Dad. Hey, I got you something nice for your supper tonight. There's scones, ham and watercress sandwiches, jam—"

"Sounds great. No gingerbread?"

"Sorry, Dad."

"Never mind," her father said indulgently. "Put the kettle on and make us all a nice cup of tea."

Obediently she knelt to light the stove, which had gone out. "I met John the woodcutter's son on the way over," she said.

"He's a good boy, that John," her father said, pausing to put an edge on the blade of his plane. "You could do worse."

She knew better than to tell him what she thought about that. "Dad," she said, "I was wondering."

"Yes, poppet?"

"What do John and his dad do with all the wood they cut? Only they're always out there working, when they're not killing wolves and all, so they must cut a whole lot of wood."

"Very hard-working family," her father said with approval. "Not short of a bob, either. I heard they got a clock."

"Two now," Buttercup replied absently. "So, they cut all this wood, and then they sell it," she said. "In the market?"

"Well, yes."

She nodded. "Dad," she said, "who buys it?"

He looked at her as if she'd started talking in a language he couldn't understand. "Well, people. You know. People who need wood."

"But everybody's got plenty of wood, Dad. I mean, there's John and his dad and all his family, and there's you and Uncle Joe and Uncle Bob and Uncle George, and you've got all the off-cuts you could possibly use, and there's old Bessie in the cottage down the lane, and every time you see her she's out gathering sticks in the forest, and that's it. So, who buys all the wood?"

Her father's face froze; she could see him thinking. It was like watching a small man dragging a big log uphill. "Folks from the town, I guess. They'll buy anything, townies."

"I see," she said. "They come all the way from the town, through Silverleaf Forest and Big Oak Forest, fifteen miles on potholed roads, just to buy wood. And then they cart it all the way home again. Dad, what's wrong with this picture?"

"What picture, poppet?"

She sighed. "Forget it, Dad. Your tea's ready."

She poured tea into four tin mugs, and started dividing up the wolf-spoils between four tin plates. It'll be different, she thought, once I've saved up enough money to get the hell out of here. And, at the rate she was going, that wouldn't be too long now. Every wolf-in-granny's-clothing she ran into netted her at least a shilling – three, if they had gold earrings – and, at an average of two a week, the old sock under her mattress was starting to get encouragingly heavy. There was, of course, the small matter of who bought the stuff, but she preferred not to think about that.

"Seriously, though," her father was saying, "it's about time you were thinking about getting wed, settling down. You'll be nineteen in October."

"Sure," she replied, looking away. "And then who'll bring you your supper?"

"Well, you will, obviously. But—"

"I have no intention," she said firmly, "of getting married. Not to anybody, and especially not to any of the boys round here."

Her uncles were grinning. "Is that right," her father said.

"Yes. For a start, there's only three of them. And they're all woodcutters."

"What's wrong with that?"

"Are you serious? You know what happens to woodcutters' families while the men are out all day."

Her father shrugged. "Well, there's wolves and witches and trolls and goblins and stuff, but it's all right. The woodcutter always comes home in the nick of time and – well, it's all right. I mean, when was the last time anybody actually got eaten this side of the Blue Hills?"

She felt like she was chasing her own tail. "That's not the point," she said. "Think about it, will you? Being married to a woodcutter, I mean. Quite apart from the danger from *wildlife*, you've got an entire community whose livelihood depends on selling firewood to people who travel twenty miles over bad roads to buy something they could get just as cheap, or cheaper, a couple of hundred yards from their own front door. I mean, what sort of economic model is that?"

She stopped. Her father and uncles were staring at her, and she couldn't blame them. She had no idea what she'd just said. It was as though the words had floated into her head through her ears and drifted down into her mouth without touching her brain. Except that she knew – dimly – what they meant. "Ecowhatty what?" her father asked.

A sudden flash of inspiration. "Sorry, Dad," she said. "I was talking to the wizard earlier. That's a wizard word."

Her father scowled at her. "I told you," he said, "you're not to go talking to the wizard. Didn't I tell you?"

"I'm sorry," she said quickly.

"Things happen," her father said gravely, "to young girls who talk to wizards."

"What things?"

Her father looked blank. "I don't know, do I? Things. You're not supposed to do it. All right?"

She nodded meekly. "Yes, Dad," she said. "It won't happen again, promise. Only," she added (and if there was a hint of cunning in her voice, she masked it well), "what's wrong with talking to wizards, Dad? You do it. All the time."

"Yes, but—"

"And the wizard comes in here all the time, most days, in fact, and nothing bad ever happens. Well, does it?"

"No," her father admitted. "But that's because I talk to him. It's different."

"Sure it is, Dad." She paused, choosing the moment.

"Dad."

"Yes, poppet?"

"Why does the wizard come round here all the time?"

Her father relaxed a little. "To see how we're getting on with his job, of course."

"The planks."

"That's right."

"Remind me," she said. "What exactly does the wizard want all these planks for?"

Her father smiled. "He's building a house. You know that."

She nodded. "That's right, so he is." Another pause. "How long've you and Uncle Joe and Uncle Bob and Uncle George been making planks for him?"

Her father frowned. "You know, that's a good question. George? How long's it been?"

Uncle George counted under his breath. "I reckon it's been upwards of forty-seven years now, Bill."

"Forty-seven years," Buttercup repeated. "The wizard's been waiting to build his house for forty-seven years. Don't you think—?"

"What?"

"Well, isn't that a bit odd? I mean all that time. And there's other carpenters. Don't you wonder why he hasn't gone and got some of the planks he needs from somebody else?"

"Ah," Uncle Joe broke in. "That's because we make the best planks this side of the Blue Hills. And wizards want only the best. Isn't that right, boys?"

A chorus of agreement, against which she knew she'd make no headway; so she nodded, and said, "Right, I understand now. You can see why I was puzzled."

"Course you were, poppet. You're a girl. Girls don't understand about business."

No, she thought, but I know what an economic model is. *How* do I know that? "Dad," she said.

Her father sighed. "Yes, poppet?"

"Just one more thing, Dad."

"Well, sweetheart? What's on your mind besides your hair?"

There would never be a better time to ask. That didn't necessarily mean that this was a good time; just not as bad as all the others. "That pair of shoes Cousin Cindy sent me," she said. "For my birthday."

Her father smiled. "The red ones."

"That's right."

"They're good shoes," he said. "Really well made and stylish. And plenty of wear left in them."

"Yes, Dad."

"Hardly worn at all, in fact." Her father grinned indulgently. "Of course, now she's married to that prince, she can have all the shoes she wants. Must be great to be rich, hey, poppet?"

"Yes, Dad."

Her father sighed wistfully. "Still, it was good of her to think of you. And they fit all right, don't they?"

"Yes, Dad. They fit really well."

"Well." He shrugged. "That's all right, then. Everybody's happy."

"Yes, Dad. See you back at the house."

She walked home slowly, deep in thought. She was so pre-occupied that she didn't seem to notice the bird with the gold ring in its mouth, or the old woman gathering sticks who, if she'd stopped and offered to help her with her heavy load, would undoubtedly have granted her three wishes, at least one of which would've been worth having. Dad had been right, she decided, about two things, but not the third. The shoes from Cousin Cindy did fit, really well. And everybody was happy. But it wasn't all right. Far from it.

introducing

**If you enjoyed
THE GOOD, THE BAD AND THE SMUG,
look out for**

MONSTER

by A. Lee Martinez

*Meet Monster. Meet Judy. Two humans who don't
like each other much, but together must fight dragons,
fire-breathing felines, trolls, Inuit walrus dogs,
and a crazy cat lady—for the future of the universe.*

*Monster runs a pest control agency. He's overworked and has
domestic troubles—like having the girlfriend from hell.*

*Judy works the night shift at the local Food Plus Mart.
Not the most glamorous life, but Judy is happy. No
one bothers her and if she has to spell things out for the
night-manager every now and again, so be it.*

*But when Judy finds a Yeti in the freezer aisle eating
all the Rocky Road, her life collides with Monster's
in a rather alarming fashion. Because Monster doesn't*

catch raccoons; he catches the things that go bump in the night. Things like ogres, trolls, and dragons.

Oh, and his girlfriend from Hell? She actually is from Hell.

1

The thing was big and white and hairy, and it was eating all the ice cream in the walk-in freezer. Four dozen chewed-up empty cartons testified that it had already devoured half of the inventory and it wasn't full yet.

From the safety of the doorway, Judy watched it stuff an entire carton of Choc-O-Chiptastic Fudge into its mouth with a slurp. The creature turned its head slightly and sniffed. It had vaguely human features, except its face was blue and its nostrils and mouth impossibly huge. It fixed a cobalt eye on her and snorted.

Judy beat a hasty retreat and walked to the produce aisle, where Dave was stocking lettuce.

"I thought I asked you to stock the ice cream," he said.

"No need," she said. "Yeti is eating it all."

He raised his head. "What?"

"Maybe not all of it," she said. "Doesn't seem to like the vanilla."

"What?"

Dave wasn't the brightest of guys, and the staffing shortage at the Food Plus Mart and the extra hours he'd been putting in had taken their toll. The poor guy got maybe three hours of sleep a night, nine dollars an hour, and two days of paid vacation a year, but it was all worth it to work in the glamorous world of supermarket management, she assumed.

"It's a yeti," she said. "Big hairy thing. Belongs in the Himalayas. Except it's in your freezer, and it's eating the ice cream."

"What?"

She sighed. "Just go look for yourself, Dave. I'll handle the lettuce."

Dave trudged toward the freezer and returned.

"There's a yeti in the freezer," he observed.

"Mmm-hmm."

Dave joined her in piling on lettuce. They moved on to bananas, then grapes. He checked the freezer again.

"Is it still there?" she asked.

"Yeah. Now it's eating the frozen chicken dinners." He rubbed his fat chin. "What should we do?"

"Don't ask me," she said. "You're the manager."

Dave scratched his head. He was obviously having trouble forming a coherent thought. Judy took pity on him.

"Isn't there a book of emergency phone numbers, Dave?"

"Yeah." He yawned. "But I don't think it has anything about yetis in it."

"Have you checked?"

"Uh, no."

"It's in the office, right?" she asked.

He nodded.

"Oh, Christ, Dave. Just give me the keys to the office already."

On the way to the office, she passed the freezer. The yeti was making a mess, and she'd probably be the one who'd have to clean it up. She didn't mind. She needed the overtime.

The emergency phone number book was a spiral notebook with a picture of a happy snowman on its cover. She sat in the creaky chair, propped her feet on the desk, and thumbed through the book. It wasn't arranged in any particular order, but she wasn't in a hurry. Fifteen minutes later, she decided on the only possibly appropriate number, picked up the phone, and dialed.

The Animal Control line was automated. A pre-recorded voice informed her of the hours of normal operation, and she was unsurprised to discover that three in the morning wasn't among them. She almost hung up, but it was a choice between listening to a recording or starting on the canned goods aisle, so it really wasn't any choice at all.

After two minutes of interminable droning that Judy only half listened to, the voice instructed, "If this is an emergency, please press one now."

She did.

The phone started ringing. She counted twenty-five before she distracted herself with an impromptu drum solo using the desktop, a pen, and a pencil. She was just settling into her beat when someone answered the other line.

"Animal Control Services. Please state the nature of your emergency."

"Yeah, uh, I know this is going to sound kind of weird, but we've got, uh, like a yeti or something, I guess, in our store." She winced. She should've just said they had a big rabid dog. They might've believed her then. "I know how that sounds, but this is not a prank, I swear."

"Please hold."

Judy waited for the click and dial tone to replace the steady buzz in the earpiece. It didn't come. The clock on the wall ticked off the seconds. Maybe they were tracing the call right now and dispatching a squad car to arrest her. Or at the very least, give her a stern talking-to. Well, let them. When the cops got here, she'd just show them the yeti and it would become their problem.

"Cryptobiological Containment and Rescue Services. Can I have your name, please?" The woman sounded supremely disinterested.

Judy hesitated, but she figured it didn't make much difference at this point. "Judy Hines."

"And you believe you have a yeti in your freezer—is that correct?"

The words were beginning to lose their absurdity.

"Yes, I think so," she said, though she wasn't as certain as she had been five minutes before.

"Can you describe it?"

"It's big and white and eating all the ice cream," she said.

"What flavor?"

"What?"

"What flavor does it seem to prefer? Yetis generally go for rocky road. Now wendigos, on the other hand, prefer strawberry in my experience."

"What's a wendigo?" Judy asked.

"Like a yeti, except meaner."

Judy considered that this woman might be screwing with her. If Judy were working a lonely job in the middle of the night and got a crank caller, she'd probably do the same.

"It didn't seem to like vanilla." There was an awkward pause. "I am not making this up."

"Just stay out of its way. We've dispatched an agent. He should be there in fifteen minutes."

"I didn't tell you the address."

"We trace the emergency calls." The operator hung up.

Satisfied she'd done her job, she went to the front of the store. She shouted, "They're sending a guy, so I'll go wait for him and take a smoke break while I'm at it, Dave!" There was no indication he'd heard her, but he'd figure it out.

The night was cool, and she wished she'd thought to grab her sweater. It wasn't cold enough to bother going back. She sat on the coin-operated rocket, lit a cig, and waited.

She wondered about the yeti. It didn't make much sense for a mythical monster from the Himalayas to be in the Food Plus Mart freezer. She hoped the guy the city sent would know how to handle this. She doubted that pole with the loop of rope would be up to the task.

A white van pulled into the parking lot. The plain black stenciled letters on its side read MONSTER'S CRYPTOBIOLOGICAL RESCUE. The vehicle rolled lazily into a parking spot in the middle of the lot, though there were plenty of closer spaces available. A man in cargo pants and a T-shirt stepped out of it. The dim lot lighting kept him an indistinct blur as, whistling the theme to *Star Trek*, he went to the back of his van and retrieved something. He didn't look like much, and as he walked closer, he looked like even less. He was tall and lanky, with a narrow face. His hair and skin were blue. The hair was a tangled mess and could've passed reasonably for seaweed. He carried a baseball bat over his shoulder.

She didn't comment on his blueness. Like the inexplicable appearance of the yeti, it didn't seem odd. Like encountering an elephant at the beach or meeting an Aborigine at the mall. She wouldn't expect it, but she wouldn't classify it as bizarre as much as unexpected. Her lack of a strong reaction struck her as stranger than anything else. But Judy made an art out of indifference, so she just chalked it up to not caring.

"Are you the guy?" she asked. "The guy the city sent?"

"I'm the guy. Are you the one who called?"

She nodded.

"Let's have a look, then."

Judy stabbed out her cigarette. "I don't think that baseball bat is going to do much against this thing."

"Lady, I don't recall asking you what you thought. How about I leave the delicate art of stacking canned goods in decorative pyramids to you, and you leave the yeti wrangling to me?" He snorted. "That is, if it even is a yeti."

He gestured toward the door and smiled thinly. "After you."

Judy flicked her cig into the ash can and led him to the freezer. The yeti was still there. It'd done away with most of the inventory and was content to just sit on its big hairy ass and digest its meal.

"Yup. Yeti," said the guy.

"Told you."

"Good for you."

"How the hell did a yeti get in our freezer?" she asked.

"Tibetans make a pretty penny selling the young ones as pets. Then they grow up, and the next thing you know, some asshole drives them to a strange part of town and unloads them."

Judy frowned. "That stinks."

"What are you going to do? People are shit."

This was a philosophy that Judy shared, so she didn't argue. It did stimulate some empathy for the yeti, though, looking very much like a big fluffy teddy bear except for the claws and teeth.

"You aren't going to hurt it, are you?"

"I'm paid to bring them in alive." He pinned the bat under his arm and pulled out a small book from his back pocket. He flipped through the pages, nodded to himself, and with a marker drew a few strange marks along the bat.

"What are you doing?" she asked.

He glanced up with annoyance but didn't explain. The blue-skinned guy went into the freezer. He wasn't being sneaky.

Just walked up to the yeti and smacked it on the back of its head with the bat. It wasn't a hard blow, but it seemed to do the job. The yeti's eyes fluttered and it fell over, unconscious.

The guy kissed his bat, took out his marker, and started drawing on the freezer floor. He drew a circle around the unconscious creature, and, after consulting with his pocket guidebook again, began drawing strange letters around its edges.

"What are you doing now?" she asked.

"You wouldn't understand it."

"Try me."

"Unless you've got a certified degree in runic studies with a minor in cryptobiology from the Greater New Jersey Community Collegius Arcanus, just leave me alone and let me take care of this."

He moved around the circle, drawing strange symbols. It took three minutes, and when he finished, he stepped back as the yeti disappeared in a flash. When the spots cleared from Judy's eyes, the yeti was gone. There was a small, fluffy rock in its place. The weird writing drifted off the floor and faded like smoke.

"What did you do to it?" she asked.

"Don't worry your pretty little head." He scooped the stone up and stuck it in his pocket. "Just transmogrified it for easy transport."

"So that's it?"

"That's it. Now if you could just accompany me to my van and sign some paperwork, I'll be on my way."

They started back.

"That was easy," she said. "I thought it'd be a lot harder than that."

"That's why they pay me the big bucks."

They were halfway down the stationery aisle when a tremendous clatter and crash echoed through the store.

"Is there anyone else in the store?" he asked.

"Just Dave."

Something roared.

"Another one?" she asked.

He pulled a small square of paper from his pocket. It had a lot of those weird not-quite-letters written on it. The paper folded itself into an origami hummingbird.

"Chester, recon," commanded the blue guy.

"I'm on it," said the bird, and it soared over the aisles on paper wings before quickly returning. "We've got a yeti in the canned goods aisle."

The bang of a shelf of Chef Boyardee brand beef ravioli being tossed to the floor made Judy wince. It depressed her to realize that she'd been working at the Food Plus Mart long enough to identify the brand and product solely by the sound. Spaghetti-Os had a tinnier echo, and green beans were more muffled.

"Shit—I just stocked that aisle."

The blue guy and Judy investigated canned goods. The yeti's cheeks bulged as it stuffed pasta, cans and all, into its maw. It was a hell of a mess. This creature was bigger than the last.

"This shouldn't be a problem," said the guy. "I can handle this."

Something growled behind them. Judy whirled and came face-to-face with yet another yeti. This one bared its teeth at her and snarled. Its bloodshot eyes bore into her, freezing her in place. It knocked her aside with a glancing blow and seized the blue guy. He struggled, but the yeti lifted him to its jaws and swallowed his head. The guy flailed and twitched as the creature ambled away, sucking on him like a lollipop.

She didn't hear the man scream. Either he was dead already or his shrieks of pain were being muffled by a throat full of his own blood. The yeti stopped at the far end of the aisle and spit the man out. It hunched over him, growling and clawing.

Scraps of cloth flew in the air, but the creature's body blocked Judy's view of the carnage.

"Oh, shit. Oh, shit." Judy froze, repeating the chant over and over.

A curious grunt came from the canned goods aisle. The second yeti's claws clicked on the tile as it drew closer. It snorted and sniffed.

She bolted for the front doors. They were only a dozen or so steps away, and the lumbering yetis didn't seem very fast. A can of peas rolled underfoot, causing her to fall. She struck her head on the discarded baseball bat and it rolled noisily across the floor.

The second yeti roared as it advanced on her. "Oh, shit, oh, shit!"

She'd always known Food Plus Mart was a dead-end job. She just hadn't expected to reach the end so soon.

The paper bird, now folded into a large vulture shape, fluttered in the creature's face. "Run, miss! I can't distract it for—"

The yeti grabbed the bird and threw it to the floor. The beast stomped on the paper several times.

Judy snatched up the baseball bat and clutched it in two tight fists. The Animal Control guy had used it to knock out the other yeti. She figured she'd only get one shot so she had to make it count.

The yeti pounced.

She brought the bat up hard and smashed it across the jaw. There was an explosion of force. The yeti was blown back down the aisle. It flew fifty feet, landing with a thud beside the third yeti, the one mauling the Animal Control agent. The struck yeti stayed down, but the last one turned away from its victim and howled.

The strange writing on the bat glowed brighter. The weapon

quivered in her grip. It was only a bat and the yeti was a hulking brute, but she felt invincible with it.

"Come on," she whispered through clenched teeth. "Nobody messes with my canned goods aisle, you son of a—"

The abominable snowman charged forward. Its feral roar dissolved her sense of power. Yelping, she pitched the bat at it. The weapon sailed through the air and struck the yeti right between the eyes.

The bat exploded in a crack of thunder. Splinters of wood flew like shrapnel, slicing her face and arms. A sizable chunk collided above her right eye, knocking her to the floor. Everything went hazy as she struggled to stay conscious for a few seconds.

"Miss? Miss?" Her vision cleared enough to make out the four-foot paper man standing over her. "Are you okay, miss?"

She sat up, and the sudden rush almost made her throw up.

"Don't try to stand. That's a nasty bruise on your head."

The yeti was dead. Its head was gone, blown to oblivion. There wasn't even any blood or brains left. Just a smoking crater. She glanced down at the chunk of scorched wood that had dented her skull.

The blue guy was beside her. "Are you okay, lady?"

"She might need medical treatment," said Chester.

She struggled to speak.

"She'll be okay," the guy said. "Chester, get the healing elixir from the van. The one in the yellow bottle. That'll fix her up."

"Sure thing, boss." The paper man folded himself into his hummingbird shape and flew away.

"But...but..." Judy covered her eyes as she assembled the thought piece by piece. "But that yeti mauled you."

He helped her up, keeping her steady. Her vision cleared. The guy's clothes were ripped, but there wasn't a mark on him. Not so much as a scratch.

"Why aren't you dead?"

"I'm blue."

Judy leaned on the guy to keep from falling over. "Huh?"

"I'm invulnerable to violent harm when I'm blue."

Maybe it was her spinning head or the way that he said it so matter-of-factly, but it made sense to her.

A vaguely Dave-ish blur appeared at the end of the aisle. "What the hell happened?"

"It's okay, Dave," she said. "We took care of it. Me and this guy the city sent. Uh, what's your name?"

"Monster," said the blue guy.

"Of course it is. Well, Monster, I really have to sit down before I puke, which I really don't think you want to happen. Unless you're also immune to dry-cleaning bills while you're blue."

They went over to checkout and found a stool for her. She leaned against the counter and closed her eyes.

"Shit," said Monster. "You killed one."

She opened one eye. "It was going to eat me."

"A dead yeti is hardly worth hauling in for alchemical harvesting," he said. "Thanks a lot."

"Sorry," said Judy, but she really didn't mean it.

The paper man returned and handed Judy a plastic bottle. "Drink this, miss. It'll help you feel better."

She took the squeeze bottle and squirted some in her mouth. "Ugh. This tastes like crap."

"That's the manticore bladder," said Monster. "But without it, a healing elixir isn't much more effective than a sports drink. So deal with it."

Judy grumbled, but her head did feel better. She slurped another mouthful.

Dave's exhaustion dulled him, and so when he shook his

head and muttered to himself, Judy knew he was pissed. His store was a mess, and there was no way they'd get everything fixed before the next shift.

Monster said, "Soooo, what do we got here? Two healthy yetis…" He glared pointedly at Judy. "And one dead one."

She half scowled, half smiled. "It was going to eat me."

"Mmm-hmm."

"Screw the overtime," she said. "Dave, I'm going home."

He mumbled his approval. Or disapproval. Or indifference. Regardless of the exact sentiment, she was out of there.

Chester said, "Miss, we'll need you to sign some forms."

"Whatever. Just make it quick."

"I left the forms in the van, Chester," said Monster.

Rather than wait for Chester to go retrieve the paperwork, Judy followed him into the parking lot. While he rummaged around in the back of the van, she lit a cigarette.

"So how did that guy do that?" she asked. "Make that yeti into a stone and have the baseball bat explode?"

"I'd like to explain it to you, but I really don't understand the magic of this lower universe myself. Even if I could, you'd just forget it."

"I nearly got killed tonight. That kind of makes an impression on a girl."

"Oh, you'll sort of remember it, but you'll soon find the details a bit…fuzzy."

"Wait a minute. You're calling me a muggle, aren't you?"

Chester jumped out of the van with a clipboard. "That's not an officially recognized term."

She snatched the papers.

"I'm not a dumbass muggle."

"Whatever you say, miss. Though only muggles use the word *muggle*." His paper head had no mouth to smile with, but she sensed his condescending grin. She was tempted to flick her cigarette at him.

"There. All signed. Can I go now?"

"Certainly, miss. Have a pleasant night."

She tossed him the clipboard and headed toward her car. "And tell your boss he's lucky I don't sue his ass for giving me an exploding baseball bat."

Judy didn't see how she could ever forget this, and her contrary nature made her even more determined not to.

By the time she'd gotten home, she'd forgotten that vow.